D1261320

GROSS MISCONDUCT

The Life of Spinner Spencer

Martin O'Malley

VIKING

VIKING
Published by the Penguin Group
Penguin Books Canada Ltd, 2801 John Street, Markham, Ontario,
  Canada L3R 1B4
Penguin Books Ltd, 27 Wrights Lane, London W8 5TZ, England
Viking Penguin Inc., 40 West 23rd Street, New York, New York
  10010, USA
Penguin Books Australia Ltd, Ringwood, Victoria, Australia
Penguin Books (NZ) Ltd, 182-190 Wairau Road, Auckland 10,
  New Zealand
Penguin Books Ltd, Registered Offices: Harmondsworth, Middle-
  sex, England
First published 1988

10 9 8 7 6 5 4 3 2 1

Printed and bound in the United States of America
Canadian Cataloguing in Publication Data

O'Malley, Martin.
  Gross misconduct

ISBN 0-670-82427-5

1. Spencer, Brian, d. 1988. 2. Trials (Murder) — Florida — West
Palm Beach. 3. Murder — Florida — West Palm Beach.
4. Crime and criminals — Biography. 5. Hockey players —
Canada — Biography. I. Title.

HV6248.S68053 1988   364.1′523′0924   C88-094789-6

The book is dedicated to Irene Spencer, Brian's mother, a woman of strength, charm and dignity. She has suffered more than anyone in the story, and the telling of it will cause more pain, but I hope I have achieved a context, a perspective and a balance that approaches the truth. In his preface to *The Dog's Bark*, Truman Capote wrote, "Everything herein is factual, which doesn't mean that it is the truth, but it is nearly so as I can make it." It is difficult to recapture any life, least of all a life as large and loud as Brian's, but it was worth the try.

ACKNOWLEDGMENTS

I would like to thank Mrs. Spencer for her cooperation, for the telephone calls, the letters, and for the little things, like the drive from Fort St. James to Prince George with her husband, Bill, during a very sad time.

I would also like to thank Byron and Shelly Spencer for helping me to understand something of what it was like. And Murray and Bonnie Hill of Fort St. James for feeding me and putting me up in the tin shed again. And Leon Wright in West Palm Beach for his insight and experience.

Also Sally Gross of the Department of Sociology at the University of Calgary for sharing her remarkable thesis on professional hockey players. And Michael Radelet of the Department of Sociology at the University of Florida in Gainesville for his excellent work on innocence research. And Michael A. Smith of Eagan, Minnesota, a scholar and hockey man through and through. And Maurice Reid of Canada's Hockey Hall of Fame. And Monica Jarboe of West Palm Beach, who was always there. And Brian's friends, John and Loretta Antonacci of Toronto, and Richard and Mikey Martin and John Long of Niagara Falls, New York, without whose cooperation I would have missed so much. And the Canada Council for its generous assistance. And Peter Livingston, my agent and friend. And Jan Walter, my editor, as calm and professional as they come. And as usual, Karen O'Reilly, for her love, understanding and intelligence.

The story is over, but it will never end.

— Martin O'Malley
Aurora, July 1988

CONTENTS

CHAPTER ONE

Monday: *Florida versus Brian Spencer*

I

On Monday, October 5, 1987, Brian Spencer woke at six-thirty in the morning. It had rained during the night and the air was fresh and sweet, by Florida standards almost nippy. He could hear Monica puttering in the dining room of the modest, one-bedroom apartment. He felt cheerful, and that surprised him.

For months he had wondered how he would feel on this morning, what the fear would be like. In three and a half hours he would be in a courtroom in downtown West Palm Beach to stand trial for murder. He pulled back the sheet and slid his thickly muscled legs out of bed.

"You up, Spin?" Monica asked from down the hallway.

There was no need to reply, Brian being the sort of clamorous man who, were he to wake up in a castle, would make ripples in the moat. He was thirty-eight years old, an inch under six feet, and he weighed nearly two hundred pounds. When he had played professional hockey, he always wanted to weigh two hundred pounds; now that he did, hockey was far behind him.

There was dark stubble on his face. Brian's features once had a boyish, almost choirboy charm, but now there were ruts across the brow, tracks under the eyes, and a grim parenthesis from nose to chin. He gripped the edge of the bed with his stevedore hands — square, meaty, with patches of skin scraped away, and knuckles big as walnuts. His thick, dark-blond hair was as curly and wavy as ever, and he wore it as long as in his hockey days, but it did not look playful any more. In his late thirties, in the morning especially, the long hair made him look Neanderthal.

His body remained solid, a thick wall of white flesh — he liked Florida for the warmth, not the sun — with bits of scar tissue here and there and the zippered remnants of old locker-room sutures. Not all the scars had been won on the ice; once, in anger, he threw a hunting knife down at a swarm of red ants in a trailer home in Florida and watched in horror as the knife sliced through his foot, above the toes, and stuck in the floor. He was not as tautly muscled as in the days when it was conceded that Brian Spencer had the finest physique of any player in the National Hockey League.

He used to work at it. Starting in his junior hockey days, actually during a stint in reform school on Vancouver Island when he was fifteen, Brian set aside forty-five minutes a day for a personal fitness program, which always ended with a hundred non-stop push-ups. Friends and teammates often caught him posing, tightening his washboard abdominals, rippling his pectorals. He could not walk by a mirror without taking at least a sidelong glance. He liked the look of his body, but mostly he wanted strength. His father had reminded him repeatedly that hockey scouts lusted after players who were "tough and tireless." Brian knew he could not make it on pure talent, but if he could develop the strength, and if the fear didn't get to him, he could gain an edge.

Brian considered himself a student of fear. Not the fear of pain, though that was part of it, but more the white terror of not measuring up, of failing, losing, of cowardice, humilia-tion. When he was growing up in Fort St. James in the north central interior of British Columbia, he learned to use fear as a motivator. His father used to tell him, "Fear is a great help to an ambitious person." Brian knew how to read fear in others, how to see it in the eyes. He learned to use that, too.

A grand jury had indicted Brian in December of 1986 for murder and kidnapping, for a killing that happened five years earlier, in the early morning hours of February 4, 1982, on an isolated shell rock road off PGA Boulevard, just west of the Florida Turnpike. The victim, a thirty-two-year-old real estate salesman named Michael James Dalfo, had been pistol-whipped, shot twice in the head and left to die in a clearing of pine trees. The key witness, the only witness for the prosecution who mattered, was a former escort-service prostitute with whom Brian had shared a trailer in the early 1980s, soon after he drifted to Florida from New York, escaping another failed marriage and the detritus of a bottomed-out hockey career.

The prostitute's name was Diane Delena, but when she worked for Fantacee Island Escorts, she called herself Crystal. She was twenty-two years old in 1982. In the five years since the killing, she had rearranged her life. She had left Brian, married another man, was the mother of two baby girls, and she called herself Diane Delena-Fialco. She told her story to the police in November 1986 after being granted immunity from prosecution. The woman who used to call herself Crystal, and who earned up to $1,000 a day as a call girl, told the police Brian did it.

He was arrested on the night of January 18, 1987, a Sunday, in the parking lot of the Mount Vernon Motor Lodge, an old motel at the corner of Olive Avenue and Belvedere Road in West Palm Beach. It was a nicely choreographed police swoop, with detectives, uniformed cops, K9 dogs and a helicopter whumping overhead, aiming search lights on the scene below. That Sunday evening, Brian had been at the El Cid, a newspapermen's bar on Old Dixie Highway, around the corner from the Mount Vernon Lodge. A friend had called a taxi as Brian ordered his third Tanqueray and tonic. A few minutes later, a man entered the El Cid and shouted, "Taxi!"

"Taxi!" Brian repeated, then slid off his stool and headed for the door, still clutching his gin and tonic. The bartender told him he couldn't take the glass with him.

"Sorry," Brian said, draining the last of his drink and placing the glass on the bar.

In the taxi, Brian told the driver to stop at the Mount

Vernon Lodge because he had to pick up something from a friend who was staying there. When the taxi stopped in the motel parking lot, Brian stepped out and the rest of the team moved in. The cabbie turned out to be Detective William Springer of the Palm Beach County Sheriff's Office. It took three detectives to subdue Brian, after he had been clubbed and wrestled to the ground and after one of the uniformed policemen had twisted the barrel of his service revolver hard into Brian's face. His rights were read to him, and he was charged with kidnapping and first-degree murder.

The arrest had been planned for six weeks, but only because it took that long for the police to find Brian. He was a vagabond, a drifter. He stayed with friends, hung out at bars, washed himself in swamp ponds, relieved himself at gas-station toilets, lived in trailers and motels. The police knew Brian. He had been arrested five times for drunk driving between 1982 and 1985, and he had spent ten days in jail in 1985 for the same offence. One night in November 1984, a Florida state trooper stopped him as he was weaving up Military Trail, a major north-south route in Palm Beach County. The trooper later wrote in his report: "Subject was a combative, saying if I did not have a uniform on, he would kick my ass. Asked if I got orgasm for arresting him."

Brian knew the police were looking for him, but he thought it was for three outstanding arrest warrants, two for drunk driving, a third for driving with a suspended licence. Friends later told him that the police had arrived at a bar asking questions minutes after he left. During the Christmas holidays in 1986, Brian began to suspect it might not be simply the drunk driving charges the police were pursuing. Early in the new year, after he left a bar one night in West Palm Beach, seven detectives arrived in three cars looking for him.

On the night of his arrest, Brian was wearing running shoes, jeans and a white baseball undershirt with blue sleeves. He hadn't shaved in three days. He carried with him most of his life's possessions in a battered attaché case that had been presented to him fifteen years earlier, in the summer of 1972, when he left the Toronto Maple Leafs to play for the New York Islanders, then an NHL expansion team. There was still a New York Islanders decal on the case, just below the handle.

Inside the case were old clippings, snapshots, press kits, team programs, letters, bubblegum cards. There was a wire-service photo of Brian's first NHL goal, against the Detroit Red Wings. A Maple Leaf Hockey Club program from March 1971, with an article inside that read in part: "In this day and age where most parents are worried about how their offspring will take to the present-day society, it must be comforting to see that there are still individuals like Brian Spencer around." A glossy formal portrait of Brian and his first wife, Linda, looking down at their infant daughter, Andrea. In the picture, Brian is wearing a tweed sports jacket, his wavy blond hair is short and well groomed and he looks like a Princeton freshman. Old, curled, head-and-shoulder photos of Maple Leaf teammates: Jacques Plante, Paul Henderson, Brit Selby, George Armstrong, Denis Dupere, Mike Pelyk, Ron Ellis, Brian Glennie, Jim McKenny, Brad Selwood, Rick Ley, Darryl Sittler, Jim Harris, Guy Trottier, Jim Dorey, Bob Pulford, Norm Ullman, Bobby Baun, Johnny Bower, Dave Keon. A tattered, faded copy of the October 1971 *Globe Magazine*, with Brian's picture on the cover.

And odd things. A menu placemat from the Sweet William Restaurant in Cleveland, on the back of which is a detailed pencil sketch of a monstrous van-truck. A well-preserved red portfolio, its cover bearing the image of an eagle rampant above a swastika, and in embossed gold letters: "Adolf Hitler. Confidential. My political testament." Grisly black-and-white snapshots of women piling dead bodies on a pile of dead bodies. Written on the back of one of the snapshots: "Camp de Belsen. Some of the fat and well-fed SS women removing bodies of their victims from lorries. . . ."

After his arrest, Brian spent three months in jail, in a holding cell at the Palm Beach County Detention Center, a cream-coloured building of the Holiday Inn style down on Gun Club Road by the airport. He was released on bail in April. During the summer, he was allowed to leave Palm Beach County, once to visit his two sons in Long Island, another time to meet with old friends and hockey teammates from his days with the Buffalo Sabres at an ox-roast picnic at a farm near Niagara Falls, New York, across the Niagara River from Canada.

Following his release on bail in April, Brian took a job as a mechanic at Case Power and Equipment, working from seven in the morning until five in the afternoon, earning $9.50 an hour. There was overtime, time-and-a-half for every hour over forty hours a week, and he averaged a hundred and five hours every two weeks. Most Saturday mornings he worked for his friend Dan Martinetti, a young man who had come to West Palm Beach from Pittsburgh, where he had known of Brian Spencer as a colourful hockey player who had spent a season with the Pittsburgh Penguins. Brian did odd jobs for Martinetti at Hertz Rental Equipment. In all, he made about $600 a week.

At the height of his hockey career, in the mid-1970s when he played for the Buffalo Sabres, Brian earned nearly $100,000 a year, with his basic salary, bonuses, public appearances and playoff money. He owned a house on Long Island and a 1959 Rolls-Royce Silver Cloud. He was part-owner of a bar and restaurant. He smoked a pipe, wore leather pants, fashionable hats, and a sealskin coat. He was a celebrity, and a media darling, always available for locker-room chats with reporters. Even in the off-season summers, television crews chased him down for news features of Spinner Spencer busy at work remodelling and building motorcycles, cars and trucks.

They were good times. The best. One morning early in May 1975, he was in the Rolls, wearing his sealskin coat, smoking his pipe, driving to Buffalo Memorial Auditorium. The Buffalo Sabres had defeated the Montreal Canadiens in a playoff series, and were about to play a Stanley Cup game against the Philadelphia Flyers. Driving to the rink, Brian turned on the radio and heard Brother Shane, a popular local disc jockey, going on in his jive patter about the fantastic Sabres. At the end of his rap, Brother Shane said, "Now the Spin be on his way to the game now. Let's wish he be goin' down there to *hit it*. And I know the Spin's favourite song, by the Bellamy Brothers. So for Brian Spencer, headin' to the rink — here's to you, bud. . . ." And the big, pearl-grey Silver Cloud filled with "Let Your Love Flow."

In Florida, only Brian's closest friends knew about his hockey career. Others knew him as a good-timing, fun-loving night owl, though he had a reputation as a hard-working, skilled and inventive mechanic, with an obsessive interest in tools and machines. His moods shifted like the wind, and he could be a brooder, but he liked to tell stories, liked to laugh, and he was a good listener. He was an honest, loyal friend, but he was not comfortable with strangers. He had a way with women. They found him handsome, attentive, playful and vaguely dangerous. He could be crude, even cruel, but his manner was direct, unequivocal and unmistakably carnal. Women were curious.

At the time of his arrest he did not have a home, and he could not afford a lawyer. He was considered a legal indigent, which qualified him for a public defender lawyer. Brian blamed his poverty, and most other calamities that had befallen him, on marriage and the demands of his two ex-wives, especially his first wife, Linda, whom he supported during most of his NHL career with payments of $3,400 a month. Linda maintains that Brian did not support her, that he made only sporadic payments in the early years of the break-up and then stopped sending her money altogether. He had fathered five children: three daughters by Linda, who lived in Tulsa; two sons by his second wife, Janet, who lived on Long Island.

One of the conditions of his bail release was that he had to have a place to stay, so Monica volunteered to put him up at her apartment at Military Trail and PGA Boulevard in Palm Beach Gardens, by chance just two miles from the scene of the 1982 murder. Palm Beach Gardens is not a tourist neighbourhood, except for the golfers. Across from Monica's apartment, on the other side of Military Trail, are two large golf courses: JDM Country Club, and, immediately west of that, the PGA National. The PGA National attracts the big names of golf — Jack Nicklaus, Curtis Strange, Lee Trevino, Gary Player — who enter the sprawling complex from a major east-west thoroughfare called PGA Boulevard, then along a winding, palm-lined road called Avenue of Champions. There are expensive homes and townhouses on the golf course properties, but the rest of Palm Beach Gardens is a flat, landlocked, suburban subdivision: bungalows and apartments built in the fifties and sixties, fast-food outlets, dental offices, gas stations, churches, shopping malls. Monica's apartment is part of Tanglewood Plaza, nine miles north of downtown West Palm Beach, four miles west of Turtle Beach, the nearest shore of the Atlantic Ocean. Across the road to the south is a large open space with sandlot baseball diamonds, tennis courts and jogging paths.

While awaiting trial, Brian was supposed to divide his time between Monica's and Steve Dixon's place. Monica and Steve lived in the same Tanglewood Plaza apartment complex, across the road from one another. Brian and Steve were friends — Steve got Brian his first job when he arrived in Florida — but Brian found Steve a difficult person to live with. Steve was neat, and kept regular hours. Brian tried the arrangement for a while, but he found it bothersome moving back and forth, while Steve fussed about rings in the bathtub and crumbs in the kitchen and Brian coming in at all hours. Brian moved in with Monica full-time and soon they shared the same bed.

Monica Jarboe was thirty-five years old, with large hazel eyes and brown hair cascading in soft waves to her shoulders. She stood just over five feet five and she was full-figured, with a perpetual Florida tan, remarkably white teeth, and a spray of freckles over her nose, all projecting a healthy, outdoors look. She was friendly and outgoing, but also a bit of a worrier. She was motherly, but not in a matronly, domestic way — more a tomboy mom who'd gladly whip up flapjacks for the duck hunters. She tended to wear either long, white, cotton dresses, or a blouse and jeans. On weekends she trained horses at a small ranch out past Loxahatchee Groves, a defiantly rural and redneck community twelve miles west of West Palm Beach, in the swampy Florida interior. She spoke in a slow, pleasing drawl.

Monica was born in Washington, D.C., where she spent twelve years at all-girl, Roman Catholic schools, after which she won a scholarship to the University of Maryland. She moved to Florida in December 1979, taking a position with Fischbach & Moore, electrical contractors. She worked in payroll and as personal secretary to the project manager at a job site in Orlando. She met Brian at the job trailer in 1980, when he came up from West Palm Beach, where he worked as a mechanic for Fischbach & Moore. In April 1982, Monica moved to West Palm Beach to work at the Governmental Center as a records and information specialist for Palm Beach County. They occasionally dated in a casual, friendly fashion.

While Brian was in jail, Monica had sent him money, snacks and magazines. She consulted lawyers for him. She looked after Brian's sons, Jason and Jarret, when Janet and the boys came to West Palm Beach to attend the bail hearing. She visited Brian at the jail and talked to him on the telephone, looking through the thick glass panels in the visitors' booths. When he had a court appearance in downtown West Palm Beach, she waited on the sidewalk outside the courthouse to catch a glimpse of him being escorted out of the police van in prison blues and handcuffs and leg manacles.

Brian was older than Monica's other lovers, who were mostly younger than she was. There was something about Brian she found adventurous and exciting. He was immensely strong, and very physical. He hugged like a bear. He could get nasty — "like a fuckin' raging bull," Monica would say — but he could be playful, charming and loving. She liked his mind, how he listened. His little-boy moods, the stomping tantrums, could infuriate and frighten her one day, break her heart the next.

Brian pitched in for rent and food, for long-distance calls, for the extra costs of air-conditioning. He didn't like being tied down, but he didn't like living alone. He wanted Monica to be there for him, but he didn't want her to try to run his life. There were many nights, well after midnight, when he would call Monica and ask her to pick him up at some bar across town. He'd say, "Come and rescue me." And off Monica would go in the early morning in her white Renault. Brian called her "the beagle," a term he used with affection or derision, depending on his mood.

On the first day of his trial, while Brian showered and shaved, Monica sorted his clothes and polished his shoes. Brian hated to fuss with clothes. He did not like going to men's shops and being measured for shirts and jackets and trousers. He did not like smarmy salesmen who smiled falsities or got too close to him or patted his shoulders or slid their hands to his crotch or gave his collar a tuck and said, "Oh yes, Brian, that's you."

Janet used to drive him crazy fussing about clothes. When he was playing with the New York Islanders, he would come home from the rink, tired and aching, and strip off his clothes in the bedroom. His socks and shorts would be the last to fall, on the floor by the bed. He wanted them there when he got up. He asked Janet to leave his socks and shorts alone, but every morning they were gone, tidied up. One night he outsmarted her. When he came home he got a hammer and nails, walked to the bedroom, took off his clothes, then — Whack! Whack! Whack! — nailed his socks and shorts to the floor. Next morning, they were there.

Monica had selected Brian's dark grey suit, with a freshly laundered white shirt, and a maroon tie with light grey diagonal stripes. The problem was the pants. Brian had been out late Friday, drinking with friends at a bar called The Inlet in Riviera Beach, out on Blue Heron Road by the bridge to Singer Island. About three in the morning, he called Monica with the familiar request, "Come and rescue me." She drove to The Inlet and when she arrived, to her surprise, Brian was anxious to leave. Most nights, no matter what the hour, he'd have to be — in his words — "crowbarred" off his stool. Monica noticed rips and holes in the pants of Brian's dark grey suit and she realized he had been at it again. There were two guys, maybe three. One of them said something, and Brian said something back, and shortly thereafter they were going at it in the parking lot.

Brian was not one for fern bars and four-star restaurants. He liked the action — country-and-western bars, rock bars, motorcycle bars, bars where you can eat and drink and dance until nearly dawn. He would say that women ruined his life, shortened his hockey career, and bankrupted him, but he chased after women the way other men chased after money. In a bar with a lot of sassy women, he would say he was in "mitt city." A woman with a nicely rounded bottom had "a great shitter." Confronted with an especially attractive woman, he'd push at his nose with his thumb and finger and say, "She can sit on my beak anytime." It usually got a laugh, sometimes from the woman herself, but if she happened to be with a man who did not think it so funny, Brian might have to go out to the parking lot to settle the score. Most times he returned alone.

Monica had driven Brian home and put him to bed. Next morning, she drove to the mall to buy new pants. She wanted Brian to look his best for the first day of his murder trial, but the best match she could find off the rack were solid black pants. They would have to do.

Brian arrived at the Governmental Center shortly after eight o'clock. It is a new, nine-storey, white stucco building in downtown West Palm Beach, which tourists never visit. It is where citizens of the county go for their driver's licences, to make alimony payments, to buy marriage licences. The Governmental Center building was completed in 1984 and is the newest part of the complex, which includes the courthouse, a multi-tiered parking lot to the south and a branch of the Flagler National Bank.

Monica dropped Brian off, kissed him, wished him luck,

then walked up to the second floor of the Governmental Center building to her office in the personnel department. Today would be the opening day of the trial, but she did not take time off from her job to attend because she knew that most of the week would be devoted to jury selection. She was not even sure she would attend the following week, during the heart of the proceedings. She knew she was not popular with Brian's legal counsel, the state-appointed lawyers who worked for the Public Defenders Office for the Fifteenth Judicial Circuit, which includes Palm Beach County. Her involvement with Brian since his arrest had upset their defence strategy.

The machinations behind the scenes of a murder trial are as much show biz as law. For the bail hearing in April, the lawyers had summoned Janet and the two boys. Their presence gave the impression that here was a poor young man with his glory days behind him and a loyal ex-wife coming all the way from Long Island to be with him in his hour of need to effect a reconciliation. This was the scenario, and in the result the lawyers could not be faulted. The prosecution had wanted bail set at $1 million. The judge granted Brian his temporary freedom for a bond of only $50,000.

The lawyers intended to use the same strategy for the murder trial itself, believing it would be even more effective before a jury. They were going to bring back Janet with the boys, and every morning as the jury trekked in they could see the family together in the corridor, trying to make a go of it — Brian embracing his ex-wife, the two boys close by, hoping. Jurors are not supposed to be impressed by this sort of stage management. The judges instruct them over and over to disregard what they hear and see outside the courtroom. But lawyers know that jurors are human and impressionable and the show biz works; they can hear violins as well as anyone.

Monica's actions since the bail hearing, however well-intentioned, dashed the defence plans. How could the lawyers maintain the charade with Brian romantically and sexually involved with this loyal, sultry, freckled brunette? And there was more: the lawyers had wanted to use Monica as a defence witness because she knew the former prostitute, the woman who called herself Crystal, the prosecution's key witness. In a sworn deposition months earlier, Monica had testified that Crystal was not trustworthy. She had said, "If I asked her the time of day and watched her look at her watch and say, 'Three o'clock,' I wouldn't be sure if I could believe her."

Now she was useless to the defence. In fact, her presence in the courtroom, and anywhere around Brian, might actually be damaging. The prosecution would have a field day with her, demolishing the reconciliation scenario, hurling invective and sarcasm at the underhanded tactics of the defence. All along Monica had only wanted to help, and now she felt shunned and hurt.

Brian walked to the courthouse building in the Governmental Center complex, which surrounds a pleasant outdoor courtyard, with trees in concrete planters amid red-and-white metal umbrellas above circular concrete patio tables. It is a favourite place for office workers to enjoy coffee breaks and to brownbag it at lunch. By a reflecting pond at the south end of the courtyard is a small plaque on which is engraved Joyce Kilmer's poem "Trees."

The courtyard is known officially as Byrd Park. It is not named after any of the well-known Byrds — not Harry Flood Byrd, the famous United States senator from Virginia; or Richard Evelyn Byrd, the famous polar explorer; or William Byrd, the famous American colonial writer — but after C. Y. Byrd, who served with some local distinction as a West Palm Beach commissioner from 1933 to 1950.

Inside the courthouse, Brian headed to the takeout coffee shop where he lined up with lawyers, judges, policemen, bailiffs, court reporters and office workers for a large styrofoam cup of coffee and a pack of Marlboros. Some of the lawyers and policemen recognized him, said good morning and wished him luck. His arrest had been widely publicized, locally, nationally and internationally. *Sports Illustrated* carried a major back-of-the-book feature article on Brian in the May 1987 issue, the one with Reggie Jackson on the cover. Titled "The Case Against Brian Spencer," it went on for nine pages, with illustrations. It began:

> *Brian Spencer played in the* NHL *for four teams between 1969 and 1979. A left wing without notable talent, he was nevertheless a crowd pleaser. He was the kind of journeyman found in every sport, hustling to hold his own with more gifted athletes. He scored only 80 career goals, but did contribute four assists in the 1975 Stanley Cup playoffs for the Buffalo Sabres, who eventually lost in the finals, four games to two, to the Philadelphia Flyers. Nicknamed Spinner for his skating style, Spencer once said, "I never believed in going around somebody when I could go through them."*

In the corridor by the coffee shop, Brian deposited a quarter in the newspaper machine for a copy of *The Palm Beach Post*. Outside in the courtyard, using one of his massive hands to shield his eyes from the sun, he looked for a place to sit. Monday is the busiest day of the week because it is jury selection day and there is a spillover of potential jurors mingling with the office workers in the courtyard. Most of the tables were occupied, but Brian found an empty one by the reflecting pond.

He looked uncomfortable in his clothes. Except for his hair, a glorious mess of long dark-blond waves and curls, he could have been mistaken for an Amish farmer on an infrequent visit to the city. He placed his cup of coffee on the table and unfolded the newspaper in front of him.

All the little things he did with his hands seemed to require inordinate concentration and coordination — prying the lid off the cup of coffee, fumbling in the pocket of his white shirt to extract the pack of Marlboros, rummaging in his trousers for the tiny pink lighter, flicking and flicking the lighter, lighting the cigarette. He started by reading an article on the upper left side of the front page, above the fold. His right hand rested on the upper right side of the paper and covered it completely. The length of his hand from the base of his thumb to the tip of his middle finger measures eight and three-quarter inches. The width, with the fingers spread and measured from the tip of his baby finger across to the tip of his thumb, is nine and three-quarter inches — the width of an average-sized tennis racquet.

He sipped his coffee and read, undistracted by the breeze that intermittently swept through a fountain in the pond, spraying him with a fine, flicking mist. He had felt greater fear on other occasions, in the Spectrum perhaps, waiting to confront the orange-and-black Flyers. But now, pondering the resources of the State of Florida arrayed against him, he realized he had never before felt so pessimistic about the outcome of the contest.

II

Brian had just turned twenty-two when I first met him on a hot September afternoon in 1971. He was attending another training camp for the Toronto Maple Leafs, his third, this time as a regular member of the team. He greeted me inside the front entrance of Maple Leaf Gardens on Carlton Street in Toronto. He had just showered and dressed after a rough, two-hour workout. His hair was wet; blow-driers were not yet standard equipment in the locker rooms.

I was a staff writer for the *Globe Magazine*, which appeared every Saturday in *The Globe and Mail*. The Brian Spencer story was my idea, though I had never written a sports story for the magazine. I saw it as much more than a hockey story, though it certainly would be that as Brian represented the large mainstream of hockey players who make it on hard work and intensity. They play on the third and fourth lines; they get traded or dumped to the minors; their careers seldom last beyond four or five years. They are easily, quickly forgotten, cast adrift to pump gas or sell insurance, or give power skating lessons to peewees on Saturday mornings in the home town. I hoped the story would tell something of Canada, particularly the northern hinterland where Brian grew up. He had never seen television until he was sixteen, never eaten Chinese food until he made it to Toronto. The first National Hockey League game he ever attended, late in the 1969-70 season when the Maple Leafs called him up from Tulsa for nine games, was the one he played in.

One of my first concerns was how to make contact with one of these players. They are never listed in the telephone book, they come and they go. You hear their names, see their pictures in the newspapers, read about them now and then in magazines, watch them on television, but they never seem real. They are cogs in a dream factory, symbols of vicarious glory and what might have been. Sports writers are always asking them, in different ways, "What is it like to be you?" I called the public relations office at Maple Leaf Gardens, asked someone about Brian Spencer and within the hour my telephone rang and a boyish voice announced, "This is Spinner Spencer." Three hours later, when the taxi deposited me at the Gardens, there he was, waiting behind the glass door, grinning.

We walked west on Carlton Street, turned north up a laneway beside Maple Leaf Gardens, then headed west again until we came to the Westbury Hotel, where the players stayed, two to a room. As we entered the hotel, a young woman stood by the front door holding an assortment of pamphlets. She wore beads, a tattered blanket and what looked like army boots. She said she was from the Church of the Final Judgment. Brian bestowed a smile on the young woman, selected one of her pamphlets and took it to his room on the sixth floor. The pamphlet he selected was titled "Fear."

In his room, several books were scattered on one of the twin beds — books on war, Adolf Hitler, George Patton, psychiatry. Brian thumbed through the fear pamphlet, reaching for an orange from the night table. He broke open the top of the orange with a ballpoint pen and sucked on the orange as he talked. He was only twenty-two, but he spoke as if he had lived a lifetime. And he spoke in bursts, in gusts. "The fear of failing was the biggest fear I've ever had," he said. "Failing at school, failing in human relationships, failing on the ice. The fear of being judged incompetent within your team, and as a team." He squeezed more juice into his mouth and then, without a trace of irony, said, "I think fear is a great help to an ambitious person."

He was mercurial, full of laughter and play, then worried and downcast, or thoughtful and sensitive, then strident, angry, threatening. It was not as though he had risen on the right or wrong side of the bed that morning; his mood shifted from moment to moment. Triggered by a question, a chance remark, a random thought in his head, he could switch from Jekyll to Hyde in an instant. He was not easy to know.

After we talked for about an hour, we went down to the coffee shop on the ground floor, where Brian ordered a dish of ice cream. When he finished, he tapped a false tooth in the lower left side of his mouth and said it was the only tooth he'd ever had knocked out and it wasn't in a hockey game. "Got knocked out in a bar in Calgary," he said, and he laughed.

I kept a diary then, excerpts of which often appeared in my magazine stories. The entry for my first impression of Brian: "His face is delicately handsome, a choirboy face . . . dark blond hair, curling behind his ears . . . blue eyes cold but they can show humour. Sometimes seems shy. Vulnerable." The first day we met I noticed a resemblance to Len Cariou, an old schoolmate of mine from Winnipeg who was in the Broadway musical *Applause*, playing opposite Lauren Bacall. I had been to New York that summer to write about Cariou. Brian had rougher edges, but the energy and intensity were the same; they both seemed to inhale pure oxygen.

Not all the diary entries found their way into the final story.

The windows of the coffee shop faced Yonge Street and Brian's eyes kept being drawn to various women strolling by on the sidewalk. The hemlines never were higher than in September of 1971. The young man from Fort St. James wanted to talk about training camp, what it was like skating alongside players like Dave Keon and Ron Ellis and George Armstrong, but he clearly was distracted by what appeared as a parade of thighs outside the window. Finally, when one of the women stopped outside the window, and lifted what little there was of her dress to tug at the waistband of her pantyhose, Brian reached all the way back to the vernacular of the logging camp for the felicitous expression, "I'd roll on gravel, I'd walk on hot coals, I'd crawl through an eighteen-inch pipe, just to suck the cock of the last guy who fucked her."

Brian had shown some promise after he had been called up in December 1970 from the Tulsa Oilers. He played a rugged left wing, patrolling his position with courage and determination. He was a hustler, a hitter, fierce in the corners, and he would not back down from anyone. The fans liked him instantly. They could relate to Brian Spencer in ways they could never relate to a Bobby Orr or a Wayne Gretzky, who might as well have come from another planet. He was one of them; they could have been Brian Spencer, if they had wanted it as badly and had tried as hard. There was something fresh and crisp about him, a rough-hewn charisma that emanated from the backwoods soul of Canadian hockey. He was crackle and pop, snow and ice, blond hair flying. He played without style or pretension, crashing into players and boards with joy and abandon. You could *hear* him play. He was the sort of player coaches like to use to "shake things up" and "get things going."

When Brian joined the Maple Leafs, the team was stuck in last place. They had many experienced, skillful players, and good goaltending, but in the back alleys of hockey they were pussycats. Lesser teams pushed them around mercilessly. The day Brian arrived in Toronto from Tulsa, he played with the Maple Leafs in a game against the Montreal Canadiens at Maple Leaf Gardens. The Leafs won 4-0 and Brian won two fights, both against Terry Harper, a chippy defenceman from Saskatchewan regarded as the worst "bleeder" in the National Hockey League, meaning Harper fought often, but poorly. With Brian on the roster the Maple Leafs won ten of their next eleven games, prompting coach John McLellan to tell the sports writers, "Spencer may be just what we need to get us going. He could be one of those guys who play better in the NHL than in the minor leagues."

Soon enough, Brian met up with bigger, tougher opponents, and still he prevailed. In a game against the

Boston Bruins, Brian became involved in a standoff with big Ted Green, the veteran defenceman. Brian stood face to face with Green, exchanged a few blows, then wrapped his arms around the normally intractable two-hundred-pound defenceman and slowly squashed him to the ice. Other players watched, astounded. It was an incredible display of strength. In a game against the Philadelphia Flyers, Gary Dornhoefer, a big, lumbering rightwinger, brutally cross-checked Brian behind the Toronto net. In one sweeping motion, as instinctive as a cat twisting in the air, Spencer fell, got up, shed his gloves, chased Dornhoefer to the boards and hit him so hard on the side of the jaw that Dornhoefer collapsed. Out cold.

Brian's temper erupted off the ice, too. One night during his first winter in Toronto he parked his car at a hotel parking lot and walked with his wife and two-month-old daughter to the attendant's hut. The attendant asked for his licence number and when Brian couldn't remember it, the attendant cursed him and called him stupid. Brian grabbed the attendant by the throat, slammed him against a car and threw him to the ground. Another time, when the cashier at a hotel newsstand chastised him for reading newspapers without paying for them, he hurled a fistful of coins at her face.

He did not apologize for these acts. Being from the bush, he explained, he was not accustomed to the casual surliness of the city where people insult strangers gratuitously. "Where I come from," he said, "if anybody talks to you like that, if they swear and call you a stupid ass, it means one thing — it's a fight. These things are natural to me, instinctive." In the coffee shop that afternoon, Brian suddenly paused to reflect on the larger ramifications of this, then he said, "I just hope these things go well for me."

The conversation turned to the reason for our meeting, a bizarre and tragic incident that happened nine months earlier, before Christmas 1970. Brian was eager to talk about that, too.

The day after the Maple Leafs' 4-0 win over Montreal, a Thursday, Brian's wife gave birth to a baby girl in Tulsa.

Brian called Fort St. James on Friday to tell his family about the birth of his daughter, and to say that the Maple Leafs would be playing Chicago Saturday night. He was told the game would be televised coast to coast and he would be interviewed between periods. Brian's father, Roy Spencer, had never seen him play on television, had never seen him play professionally. On Saturday night — "Hockey Night in Canada" — the Maple Leafs won 2-1. The interview between periods had gone well and Brian had won another fight.

On the morning of Brian's game against the Chicago Black Hawks, Roy Spencer finished his chores early so he would be ready for "Hockey Night in Canada" late that afternoon. He was fifty-nine years old, and he was dying of uremic poisoning. His weight had dwindled to a scrawny one-hundred-and-forty pounds.

There is a three-hour time difference between Fort St. James and Toronto, which meant the game would be starting just before supper, as the sun was setting in the north central interior. Roy prepared himself for the game as he imagined Brian was preparing in Toronto. He ate a game-day steak, then had a light nap, thinking about the game as he had heard the players always are told to do.

Byron Spencer, Brian's twin brother, chatted with his father and mother, Irene, before leaving Fort St. James to play a hockey game himself. Byron was a speedy forward for the local Commercial League team, which was playing in Burns Lake that evening. They talked about Brian's performance in the Leafs' 4-0 win over the Canadiens the previous Wednesday night, when Brian landed in Toronto from Tulsa and arrived at Maple Leaf Gardens with barely enough time to put on his equipment and uniform. The Leaf game against the Black Hawks that Saturday night was the talk of Fort St. James and Roy basked in the reflected glory.

After Byron left, Roy heard that CKPG, the Canadian Broadcasting Corporation affiliate in Prince George, was not carrying the Toronto-Chicago game. Instead it would broadcast the game between the California Golden Seals and the Vancouver Canucks. Roy phoned CKPG and spoke with

Gerry Nairn, a newscaster. He demanded that the station carry the Toronto game. He told Nairn his son was playing for the Maple Leafs, that he was to be interviewed between periods by Ward Cornell. Nairn told him there was nothing CKPG could do about it because it was a network decision. Enraged, Roy cursed Nairn and threatened to drive down to Prince George. He said he was tired of the rest of the country "shitting on the north."

Irene Spencer had seen Roy upset before, but never this angry. She thought he seemed deranged, "as if he'd lost his mental equilibrium." She phoned several towns and cities to see if there was one within driving distance where they could watch the Toronto-Chicago broadcast. It was no use. They would have had to drive to Ontario to see the game.

When the game between California and Vancouver appeared on the television screen, Roy stomped out of the room and returned in two minutes dressed and ready for the drive to Prince George. He crashed Irene's car keys on the counter, pushed her out of the way, then stomped out to the car.

He sped off down the highway in the Ford LTD he had bought the previous summer to drive to Brian's wedding in Tulsa. He had with him a .303 rifle with twelve rounds of .303 ammunition, a 9-mm Belgium automatic pistol with fourteen rounds of 9-mm ammunition, and three hunting knives. Though Roy was not a drinking man, that night he stashed a forty-ounce bottle of muscatel under the front seat.

At the television station, Roy stopped the car on the parking lot and waited in the dark. As he looked out over the steering wheel, he saw Thomas Haerdel, a news reporter for CKPG, walking up to the rear door. Roy got out of his car, walked up to Haerdel and said, "I don't like the CBC's hockey games. Why don't you broadcast more Toronto games?"

Haerdel sensed something menacing about the man, then Roy advanced and pushed the 9-mm pistol into Haerdel's back. Haerdel heard the click of the hammer being pulled back.

Roy pushed Haerdel through the door of the television

station. Carol Russell, a receptionist for CKPG, saw what was happening and attempted to call the police. Roy tore the telephone receiver from her hand, then walked both of them to the newsroom where he ordered news director Stuart Fawcett to take the game off the air. When program director Don Prentice appeared, Roy told him, "I am very disturbed by the CBC's coverage. There is going to be a revolution unless it changes."

When Roy first entered the building, Prentice thought he looked calm and "cold sober," but soon after his voice became taut, urgent. He began to shake. Roy forced eight staff members to walk to the television studio, where he lined them up against a wall, but Prentice managed to slip away and call the RCMP. At 7:40 p.m., 10:40 p.m. Toronto time, someone pulled a master switch and CKPG-TV went off the air. Five minutes later, backing out through the front door of the television station, still holding the pistol, Roy said, "I don't want to kill anyone. I've killed many times before in the commandos."

As Roy was leaving the building, Prentice ran out the back door to the parking lot, where three RCMP officers were waiting. He told them the intruder had left by the front door. Constable David Pidruchny and Corporal Roger Post walked around the corner to the front entrance, where they were joined by Constable David Luzinski. Post decided it would be best if one of them approached unarmed, so he removed his heavy winter jacket, then his belt and holster. As he walked to the door of the station, he saw a man emerge, conspicuously carrying a newspaper in his right hand.

Post shouted, "Hold it! Drop that gun!"

The man whirled and fired two shots. One of the bullets hit the wall of the station, sending brick splinters into Luzinski's face. It ricocheted and hit Pidruchny in the foot. The other tore into Post's holster, which he was carrying in his hand. Post pulled his service revolver and returned the fire. Altogether, the Mounties fired four shots. One of them hit Roy in the left shoulder, another in the mouth, another ripped through his armpit and punctured a lung. Roy

Spencer fell to the sidewalk and rolled into a snowbank, where he died. As he fell, Brian was being interviewed between periods in Toronto.

After Roy had stormed out of the house, Irene had tried to collect her thoughts. The television was tuned to CKPG-TV and it seemed only minutes later that the station went off the air. She turned on the radio and heard a special bulletin on CKPG news that a man had entered the television station and taken the staff hostage. When a later bulletin reported that the man had been killed, she called Roy's brother who also lived in Fort St. James. Then she called Byron in Burns Lake. She was not able to reach Brian, so she called CKPG and asked them to delay reporting the news until she could reach her son in Toronto. Someone at the station said it had to go on the air immediately; it was a sensational item. Early in the morning after the Chicago game Brian woke up to a call from his mother at the family home in Fort St. James, three time zones away.

Later that Sunday, the team bus pulled up in front of Maple Leaf Gardens. Brian was one of the first to board. He took a seat near the front of the bus, where he sat alone. The Leafs were scheduled to play the Sabres in Buffalo that evening, and Brian, after talking to his mother a second time, decided to play after all. He thought his father would have wanted him to be on the ice. The players spoke in whispers on the long ride to Buffalo. That night, the Leafs won 4-0 and Brian assisted on two goals and won yet another fight. Broadcaster Foster Hewitt selected him one of the game's three stars.

When the buzzer sounded to end the game, the Leafs rushed to the ice to congratulate goaltender Bruce Gamble for his shutout. Brian remained on the bench, alone, then skated out and tapped his stick on Gamble's pads.

Maple Leaf coach John McLellan praised Brian's performance. "That was one of the gamest performances I've seen in all my years around hockey," he told reporters in the dressing room late that Sunday evening. "I knew he had the muscle and desire to play in the National Hockey League.

Now I know he has the mental toughness and heart to be a Leaf regular." Bobby Baun, the veteran Maple Leaf defence-man who once played in a Stanley Cup game with a broken leg, said, "I've bumped into a lot of sad things, but never anything to equal this. The boy has a lot of courage."

When the team emerged from the dressing-room, fans lined up to meet the players. Brian stopped to sign auto-graphs, then boarded the bus for the trip back to Toronto. When the bus arrived at Maple Leaf Gardens at one in the morning, the players said their goodbyes and dispersed. Brian stayed behind with his roommate, Doug Brindley, then followed Leaf general manager Jim Gregory into the dressing-room at the Gardens where Gregory gave Brian some sleeping pills.

The funeral for Roy Spencer was held the following Thursday at the United Church in Fort St. James. Jim Gregory and injured teammate Guy Trottier accompanied Brian on a small company jet to the west coast. An obituary in the *Caledonia Courier* mentioned that Roy Edward Spencer "was a World War II veteran, having served as an armored bulldozer in the Royal Canadian Electrical and Maintenance Engineers." The obituary said he was "an esteemed member of the community, a member of the Fort St. James Fish and Game Club and was noted not only for his good sportsman-ship but also for his award-winning marksmanship."

Brian prepared the eulogy. He began, "My father, Roy Edward Spencer, was a very kind, generous, warm-hearted man — yet sad because of the fact that the very country for which he fought and lost his good health let him down. Is there no reward? Is there no God? I ask myself...." At the end, Brian read from a crumpled telegram that his father had sent to him before the game against the Chicago Black Hawks the Saturday before. The telegram read, "Give them hell, son. We are mighty proud."

The tragedy of the episode at the television station in Prince George pushed Brian into the limelight, made him conspic-uous. The story was irresistible. He was only twenty-one, an untested rookie with limited skills, but suddenly he was getting more attention than Keon, Ellis or Ullman. The fans who had been amused by the kid from the bush with his roughneck style and whirling-dervish enthusiasm now chanted his name and hefted Brian Spencer placards at Maple Leaf Gardens. Newspaper, radio and television reporters lined up to interview him. And Brian was not a reluctant celebrity. He had always wanted to be famous. Growing up in Fort St. James, he used to tell boyhood companions he wanted to be a movie star.

It was in the months after his father had been killed that Brian's performance took fire. There was a fury to his play. He seemed possessed, driven by — what? Rage? Ambition? Guilt? He was never a finesse player, or a prolific scorer, but he played with such intensity that good things started to happen. In a game against the Pittsburgh Penguins in January, which the Maple Leafs won 5-2, Brian scored three goals. It was his first hat trick ever. Not even in peewee hockey in the bushland of northern British Columbia had he ever scored three goals in a game.

When the Maple Leafs returned from a weekend road trip, Brian and I met again in the coffee shop at the Westbury Hotel. The interview went badly. He had pulled a groin muscle and he walked about stiffly, as if he couldn't bend his knees. To make matters worse, he had heard he would be starting the 1971-72 season in Tulsa. During the night, someone had broken into his car and stolen the radio. He was angry, bitter, and his thoughts went back to that Saturday night in Prince George when his father was gunned down. He claimed he carried the names of the RCMP officers in his wallet. In my diary for September 21, I wrote, "He is a vicious young man, with the energy and frustration in his blood of a murderer. He so much as admitted he could and would kill someone if they got in his way." A private thought, after a bad day.

III

Few people in Fort St. James had known Roy Spencer well. He was moody, a loner, stubborn and unpredictable. He was honest, hard-working and respected, but people kept a polite distance from him. Sometimes, for no apparent reason, he would erupt, as he did one morning walking into town from his property on the other side of the bridge. At a crossroads, he met a man called Earl Buck walking in the opposite direction. Bruce Russell, once a neighbour of Roy, remembers it as "the goddamndest fight you ever saw in your life," both men rolling on the road and throwing haymakers. Then they got up, shook hands and continued on.

Few people in Fort St. James even knew where Roy Spencer had come from. He was born in Red Lodge, Alberta, on February 27, 1911. He had two half-brothers, Lee and Ned Cochrane. After her husband died, Mrs. Cochrane married a drifter named Spencer. They had Roy, then the drifter disappeared. Roy grew up in southern Alberta, lived for a time in Oregon and Washington working as a rancher and a cowboy, then, in the mid-1930s, headed north back to Canada and found his way up to Fort St. James.

If you look at a map of British Columbia and aim your finger at the dead centre of the province, your finger should land on Fort St. James. It is magnificent country, with mountains, streams and long, clear lakes. The winters are bleak and cruel, with howling winds and temperatures plummeting to forty and fifty degrees below freezing, but in summer and autumn the interior of British Columbia is as beautiful as any part of the world. The town of Fort St. James is surrounded by forests of black pine, fir, spruce, poplar and aspen. Logging is the primary industry, and when Roy arrived there were two sawmills operating in the middle of town, by the shore of Stuart Lake. The area used to be called New Caledonia and Fort St. James was an important fur-trading post, first for the North West Company, then for the Hudson's Bay Company. The original HBC fort is still there, renovated and staffed by youthful guides wearing early nineteenth-century garb for the few tourists who stumble by in the good weather. There is an Indian reserve in the centre of town, by Kwah Street, named after a legendary Carrier chief. The Carrier are stout, heavyset Athapaskan Indians, named after a custom whereby widows would carry the ashes of their dead husbands in a bag for a year, at which time a ceremonial distribution of goods released them of the obligation.

Roy joined the army and served in the Second World War, working with the engineers, repairing and operating military machinery, heavy equipment and armoured bulldozers. He served six years, mainly in France and Germany. He participated in the Normandy invasion, where he was hit badly by shrapnel. He had been part of an Allied clean-up team at the death camps at Belsen and Dachau. The years of riding the huge, rumbling machines in the worst of conditions over the roughest terrains jarred his body so badly he suffered permanent injury to his back, kidneys and bladder. When the war ended, he returned to Fort St. James.

Roy and Irene Spencer met and fell in love in 1947 and they married in February 1948. He was thirty-five years old, she was twenty-five. They were as different as night and day, Roy the aloof, brooding introvert, Irene the educated, well-mannered, sociable peacemaker. He was thin, dark and tightly muscled; she was pretty, blonde and vivacious. She had come from Alberta, too, from a small farm on the outskirts of Amisk, a dot on the map some hundred miles southeast of Edmonton.

On September 3, 1949, Irene gave birth to twin boys, Byron and Brian. They were born in the hospital at nearby Vanderhoof because there was no hospital in Fort St. James, which then had a population of about six hundred. For their first three years, the Spencers lived in town, where Irene taught school and later worked at the Hudson's Bay Company. Roy did some logging and odd jobs. He was a superb mechanic who could take apart and put together machines better than anyone in the community. He owned a small parcel of land on the outskirts of town, across the bridge, where he built a small dirt-floor workshop. There were many trees on the property, as well as a rock quarry, which Roy knew had great potential as a paying gravel pit.

About this time Roy learned he had a chronic bladder infection, a serious life-shortening ailment. He had always wanted to live on a farm, so to make him happy Irene agreed to leave the town and move to the property across the bridge. She worried how they would provide for the boys, but she threw herself into the new life, hoping they could fashion what Roy dreamed of as a self-sufficient "Ponderosa."

— In 1952, when Brian and Byron were three, the Spencer family moved to Roy's old workshop on the land he bought before he went to war. They covered the dirt floor with two-by-six planks, which they covered with linoleum they salvaged from staff houses at an abandoned mercury mine. There was no electricity in the province north of Vanderhoof, and they had no indoor toilet and no running water. On Saturday nights, by the light of a coal oil lamp, the Spencers listened to hockey games from Maple Leaf Gardens and the Montreal Forum. Byron cheered for the Maple Leafs because of Frank Mahovlich; Brian cheered for the Detroit Red Wings because of Gordie Howe.

In two years, Roy had transformed the workshop into a five-room house, complete with a bathroom, a water system from nearby Pitka Creek, and a diesel generator for electricity. When the generator broke down or when the creek froze solid, the family melted snow for their baths.

Over time Roy bought more property, quarter section by quarter section, until he owned nearly a thousand acres. They called the place "the farm." They kept chickens, and a goat, which gave them milk, and in the long, densely forested property that became known as Spencer's Ridge, there was a plenitude of moose, grouse, weasels, squirrels, beaver and muskrat. Roy fished and hunted and ran traplines for much of their food, which he kept in a meathouse out back. Every summer Irene planted and maintained an elaborate vegetable and flower garden.

Roy taught Byron and Brian how to camp in the woods, where to find shelter in winter, how to build a proper fire, how to hunt, what to hunt. He did not allow anyone on Spencer's Ridge to kill deer because he thought them too pretty and gentle. He taught the boys about guns. He bought them a .22-calibre repeater rifle, which Byron and Brian shared. Before they were allowed to shoot the rifle, they had to know how to take it apart and put it back together. Roy bought powder and lead and casings and taught them to make their own bullets. They had to retrieve the spent casings so they could be used again.

Roy collected guns and treated them with respect, if not reverence. When he was overseas in the army, he shipped home a German machine gun and the Belgium 9-mm Browning, a copy of the familiar automatic Luger used by German officers. He shipped the weapons in parts, which he later reassembled. The machine gun had a thirty-five-shot clip, which could be fired in three and a half seconds. Roy was a crack shot. He could bounce tin cans in the air with the Luger.

He rolled his own cigarettes and always seemed to have one in his mouth, usually unlit. He hardly drank at all. Sometimes he bought a bottle of wine so he and Irene could toast their wedding anniversary, but they seldom finished the bottle. He didn't attend church because he considered religion to be exploitive. The boys remember their father being in constant pain, with bad kidneys, a bad bladder, an aching back, diphtheria and often bronchial pneumonia, the result of working sixteen-hour days in dry, hot summers and sub-Arctic winters. The family usually drove to Vancouver three times a year so Roy could get medical attention. On these trips, Roy frequently stopped to help stranded motorists. Many photographs in the family album show Roy swallowed up under the hood of a stranger's car on the side of a highway.

Bruce Russell and Roy Spencer worked together for two years for the Department of Highways, before Roy joined the army and went to war. They worked deep in the bush, where they shared a caboose with other men. Russell remembered how Roy would be eating supper and suddenly, for no apparent reason, he would pick up his plate and throw it out the caboose door, then go out and walk off alone down the trail. At first Russell tried to intervene, tried to understand Roy, but the other workers would say, "Let 'im go, let 'im go." Another time, Roy was operating a Cat, pulling a grader, with Russell on the grader. The machine kept coughing and quitting and Roy climbed down from the controls and started kicking the machine, then beating it with his fists. When he couldn't get it going, he flailed at it with an iron bar.

"He was honest, he didn't drink, he knew guns, and he was a good shot," Russell said. "He could be good to you, and he could talk about any doggone thing when he wanted to, but he was a very moody person." Russell heard on the radio about Roy driving down to Prince George because Brian's game was not going to be on "Hockey Night in Canada." "I wasn't surprised," he said. "It was a ridiculous thing to do, going down there to take the game off the air, but if things weren't going his way he was going to change it. That was Roy's whole life, in a nutshell."

The Spencers had a summer home on the shore of Stuart Lake, with a splendid view of Mount Pope across the water. They had two hundred feet of lake frontage, with a wide, sandy beach and a small cabin. They picnicked, swam and waterskied. Byron liked to make streams in the sand. Brian collected pebbles and rocks, which Irene used to create three rock gardens. Roy built his own speedboat. They had a

Samoyed they called Ben; later, when he was playing hockey, Brian sent them a St. Bernard with the registered name of Maximilian von Beethoven.

Byron and Brian were brothers and best friends. Despite the isolation and the hardships, the farm and Fort St. James was a good place to grow up. Many of their friends in town envied them the freedom of life on Spencer's Ridge, though later Brian would say he had missed a normal adolescence, by which he meant dating girls and going to movies. The boys built tree forts and helped their father with his traplines. They were hunting grouse before they attended school. At the age of seven, Brian shot an owl perched at the top of a tall spruce behind the house. It had been pestering the chickens.

Beyond life and work at the farm, Roy's only interest was hockey, but it consumed him. He had always considered himself an athlete and many times he told Irene that his older brother had cheated him out of his chances to skate and play hockey. Irene believes he invested his own thwarted boyhood dreams in Brian and Byron. Roy bought the boys skates when they were five and took them to Stuart Lake in winter. Later, he built a rink at the farm, behind the house. He drove in the posts, nailed up the boards, and installed lights — he hooked them to a generator at the gravel pit — so the boys could practise at night. The rink measured about forty feet wide and eighty feet long. By this time they had a hot water tank and Roy punched a hole in the house so he could run a hose to the rink and flood it with warm water every night. He painted red and blue lines on the ice. He built a plywood goal, with shooting targets at the four corners.

Roy loved hockey and knew a lot about the game. He boxed and lifted weights as a soldier, but he was never a natural athlete. He could not even skate, so he marched around the ice in boots while he put the boys through their skating drills. He made them do stops and starts, and he emphasized how important it was for hockey players to be able to skate backwards. He bought a stopwatch and stood at the boards in the snow and timed them. Work was the key, he told them again and again. If they could keep improving, if they could skate faster at age six than they had at age five, and faster at seven than they had at six, they might have a chance to become professionals.

Byron was the better player in the early years, but eventually Brian showed more promise. On Saturday mornings when Byron and Brian were twelve and thirteen, Roy roused them from sleep at three in the morning and drove forty-five miles to Vanderhoof where the first hockey games started at six. The boys pulled on their equipment in the dark, clambered onto the ice of the outdoor rink an hour before the game and skated while the sun came up. Roy watched from the boards.

Brian worked harder, knew what his father wanted, and he had Roy's irascible temperament and competitiveness. In his early teens, when boys his age in the organized leagues of Ontario and Quebec were playing fifty and sixty games a winter, Brian played only eight or nine games in the north central interior, mostly on outdoor rinks where pucks sometimes got lost in the snow and ears went *ping* when they froze. On days when there was no game, Brian practised alone in the backyard rink for up to twelve hours. On one brutally cold morning when Brian was skating alone, Roy climbed over the boards, walked across the ice in his boots and planted himself at the red line. He yelled at Brian to keep skating. Brian circled the net, then came up the ice at top speed. As he approached the red line, Roy suddenly ran at him and smashed into him with a hard, cracking check, sending him sprawling into the boards unconscious.

Byron and Brian travelled occasionally to surrounding towns for games, most often to Vanderhoof, where the Fort St. James team usually won. They also played games against a Roman Catholic Indian boys school at Fraser Lake. Brian started as a defenceman, Byron as a forward, and they always played on the same team. When the team was at home the games were played on an outdoor rink, the usual makeshift affair, with boards propped up in the snow. There was a small grandstand at one side of the rink, but most spectators

watched from the boards. There were warm-up huts
scattered about, heated by wood fires in metal drums. In Fort
St. James on a cold winter afternoon the sweet smell of
burning wood was the sweet smell of hockey. Roy attended
all the games and all the practices.

The *Globe Magazine* article appeared on Saturday, October
16, 1971, nearly a year after the shooting. I remember tearing
up draft after draft, never satisfied with the results. It wasn't
just that I had never written a sports story for the magazine.
There were so many layers to Brian Spencer, like those
wooden dolls, one inside the other. He was likeable,
sometimes lovable, but ruthlessly ambitious. He was honest,
but seething with a mostly fettered rage. I had never met such
a complicated young man.

Brian's face appeared on the cover, in full colour. It was a
close-up shot that showed beads of sweat on his brow. He
looked glamorous, with his blue eyes, his wild blond hair and
that fresh, choirboy countenance he possessed as a young
man. The article was titled, "A Capacity for Anger."

Brian entered Courtroom 315 at twenty minutes after nine.
He walked in with Leon Wright, a tall black man in his late
forties who is an investigator with the Public Defenders
Office. Leon wore a dark blue blazer, light brown trousers, a
white shirt with pink stripes and a blue tie. He liked to dress
well, though he shopped carefully, buying most of his clothes
at various secondhand Thrifty shops in West Palm Beach.
His frizzled hair receded from a high, sloped brow and curled
up at the back of his neck. His moustache drooped at the
sides of his mouth and his soft, oval face was dotted with
freckles.

As they walked up the centre aisle, Leon moved ahead
of Brian and stopped at the second row from the front, left
side. He turned around and with an usher's gesture signalled
Brian to sit down. Brian stepped by, lowered himself to the
wooden pew, then slid aside to make room for Leon. Brian's
movements were stiff, formal. His body bulged under his

dark grey jacket as if it wanted out.

They were early. Only about a dozen other people occupied the courtroom: the judge, four black defendants in prison blues, the court reporter, an interpreter, three lawyers, two uniformed policemen, the bailiff. The judge — Judge Edward Fine of Florida's Fifteenth Judicial Circuit — sat in a high-backed swivel chair at an elevated desk in the right-hand corner of the room. He had a few cases to dispense with before *Florida v. Brian Spencer* could begin. Brian and Leon leaned forward in their seats, resting their forearms on the bench in front of them, each with their hands clasped. Brian looked about the plain, windowless court-room.

The room is remarkable for its lack of features — no walnut panelling, no elaborate sconces, no coat of arms. In that sense, Courtroom 315 reflects West Palm Beach itself, a mid-sized city blessed by good weather and juxtaposition to a large ocean and little else. Courtroom 315 is larger than Judge Fine's regular courtroom on the first floor — a fire department sign on the back wall says it can accommodate a hundred and thirty-seven people — but not the august surroundings to which you might feel entitled for your day in court on charges as serious as kidnapping and murder in the first degree.

The raised platform for the judge's desk is flanked by the Stars and Stripes on the right, Florida's state flag on the left. Wooden benches on either side of the centre aisle lead to the front of the courtroom, where a swinging metal gate separates the gallery from the portion reserved for the players. Low ceilings, with fluorescent lighting behind drop tiles of the sort used in offices and basement rec rooms. Speckled, off-brown carpeting. A beige, push-button tele-phone at the judge's left elbow. A schoolroom clock on the front wall. The sort of place you might expect to appear for running a red light.

Leon Wright first met Brian in January, soon after Brian's arrest, in a cell at the Palm Beach County Detention Center. Over the next nine months, they came to know each other well. They met, with Brian's lawyers, to go over tactics and strategy, first for the bail hearing in April, then for the trial. Leon worked for the Public Defenders Office in Palm Beach County, the state-funded service that provides legal aid for those not able to afford private lawyers. Specifically, he worked for the Capital Crimes Division, which confined itself to the most heinous crimes in Palm Beach County, crimes that involved the death penalty. Despite its sober public service image, there was a healthy esprit de corps in the Capital Crimes Division. Leon and the Capital Crimes lawyers liked to call themselves "Deathbusters."

Before he came to Florida, Leon had served for twenty years as a policeman in Philadelphia, the last twelve as a homicide detective. In all his years as a policeman Leon drew his gun maybe a dozen times, never fired it once.

As they watched the proceedings, now and again Leon would lean toward Brian and whisper in his ear. There was a tension between them, only part of which had to do with the approaching trial. Leon used to like Brian. He didn't any more.

When Judge Fine finished with the four black defendants — something about cocaine, an assault, a machete — one of the policemen shackled all four defendants together in handcuffs and leg-irons, then escorted them out in a clanking march. Judge Fine declared a twenty-minute recess and quickly left the courtroom. Brian got up and walked out by the rear door to have a smoke in the corridor.

Twenty minutes later, Judge Fine returned, this time in a black robe. The bailiff, a burly fellow with a handlebar moustache, wearing a bright green jacket, announced the judge's entrance and solemnly ordered everyone to please stand.

Judge Fine is a small, slight man in his early forties, with large, owlish glasses and a sparse, pointy beard. In his black robe, he looked like a magician at a children's party. He can be an irascible judge, brutal on improperly prepared or impudent lawyers, but he is well regarded by the lawyers in Palm Beach County who have appeared before him. Every year, the County Bar Association conducts a poll of lawyers in order to rate the work of the judges. In the most recent poll, ninety-five percent of the lawyers rated Fine as "highly qualified." *Florida v. Brian Spencer* was only his second murder trial since being elected a circuit judge.

In his lawyer days, Fine served as a prosecutor, assistant public defender, appellate trial attorney and for several years was a partner in the private firm of Campbell, Colbath, Kapner and Fine. He wrote a small book titled *Your Public Defender*, which is given to all prisoners to explain the criminal justice system. Born in Pontiac, Michigan, Fine grew up in Florida and studied law at the University of Florida Law School. He served a term as president of the local B'nai B'rith. His wife, Marcy, works as a critical care nurse.

Fine first ran for a County Court judgeship in 1978 on a platform of keeping the courts open to the public. Convinced that secrecy breeds suspicion, he championed the use of television cameras in court. During the final weeks of the campaign, he received death threats against his wife and their six-year-old son, Andrew. After two sinister calls to Fine's home, someone called Andrew's school and warned the principal, "Better watch out for the Fine kid." That's when he hired two off-duty sheriff's deputies as bodyguards. He did not mention the threats until after the election, which he won easily.

The preliminary skirmishing started when Richard Greene, an assistant public defender, made a motion that Brian's arrest record was "irrelevant" and should not be mentioned during the trial. This was quickly but quietly countered by Charles Burton, the state attorney, who argued he intended to mention Brian's arrest on an assault charge back in 1975, when he played for the Buffalo Sabres. He also mentioned "a lot of hearsay evidence from the people" that Brian was always armed — rifles, pistols, knives.

Greene is tall and slender, with short, glistening blond hair, wisps of which tend to slide over his forehead as he gesticulates with copies of precedents to support his motions. Greene came to Florida from his native Texas. Though only in his early thirties, he is an authority on appellate law and consults regularly on appeals throughout Florida, well beyond the jurisdiction of the Fifteenth Circuit. Friends call him "a walking encyclopedia," not only on law, but also on the arcane trivia of baseball, football and basketball. A scholarly, gentle man.

Burton — everyone calls him Chuck — speaks in rolling cadences, smiles easily, strides about the courtroom with an athletic gait. He is personable, gregarious, handsome — the prototypical frat man. He is also the third lawyer to appear for the state in *Florida v. Brian Spencer*. The first was Lynne Baldwin, who knew that the state's case rested entirely on the credibility of the former prostitute. Early on, Baldwin refused to release the woman's name, which was Diane Delena — Delena-Fialco since she had married. Baldwin identified her only as "Crystal," the name she had used when she worked for the escort service. Even in copies of official statements passed on to the defence lawyers, in the legal process known as "discovery," the name Diane Delena had been deliberately whited out on every page. Baldwin stressed how Crystal had "turned her life around," abandoned prostitution, got married, given birth to two children. She had no hesitation in speaking her mind to the press. Less than a month after Brian's arrest, Baldwin told *The Palm Beach Post*: "Crystal was not your nickel and dime hooker. She's a very beautiful young girl and even though she worked for an escort service, there's something about her that makes her seem vulnerable, sort of like Marilyn Monroe."

In subsequent interviews, Baldwin became even more freewheeling. Speaking to Ed Bouchette, a sportswriter with the Pittsburgh *Post-Gazette*, she again compared Diane Delena to Marilyn Monroe ("a very fragile innocence about her") and then, with astonishing candour, spun out a personal theory on what made Brian Spencer kill.

She told Bouchette, "Here he is on top of the world, doing so well financially, making $60,000 ten years ago, and it's not peanuts now. Then, wham, he's out of the business, he's down here working as a mechanic. He's not making much money at it. He's got to have some resentment. . . . It's like when people are angry they may kick the dog. They vent their anger on something else and I think Dalfo happened to be in the wrong place at the wrong time."

The *Sports Illustrated* story that appeared in May deftly ridiculed Baldwin's handling of the case. Writer Pete Dexter observed, "Lynne Baldwin is the last person you want to see talking about you to a jury. Or the newspapers." Soon after, Baldwin was taken off the case, and replaced by state attorney Fred Susaneck. Before the case came to trial, Susaneck was gone, replaced by the affable Chuck Burton.

Greene stood to make more motions before Judge Fine. He moved to prohibit any reference to Brian being represented by public defender lawyers, to prohibit mention of the grand jury indictment, to prohibit mention of polygraphs. Watching these pre-trial skirmishes from the defence table was Barry Weinstein, the chief assistant public defender. He would be Brian's primary lawyer over the next two weeks.

Weinstein is short, nearly elfin, with tiny feet, thinning hair and a bushy brown beard. He speaks in a raspy twang, sometimes tugging at the underside of his nose with thumb and index finger, pausing now and then to inspect what nasal detritus has emerged. When he smiles, his lips smack apart, as if someone had yanked a string. Something about Barry Weinstein evokes Toulouse-Lautrec.

For a public service lawyer, however, Weinstein has impressive credentials. By the time of the trial, at age thirty-eight, he had earned a reputation in the trenches as a brilliant litigation lawyer and superb courtroom tactician. He had graduated cum laude from Nova University Law Center in Fort Lauderdale — eleventh in a class of a hundred and fifty-six. He had been president of the student bar association, founder and executive editor of the Nova Law Center newspaper and was named "outstanding graduating senior." From July 1983 to September 1985 he taught at

Philadelphia's Temple University School of Law as a Freedman Fellow. Two years earlier he had made the short list for a vacant judgeship in Palm Beach County.

All along, Weinstein had insisted on a course entirely different from that taken by the state, especially when the state was represented by Lynne Baldwin. Weinstein eschewed publicity, refusing to be interviewed by local reporters or the reporters who called from cities where Brian had played hockey. He would not discuss the case with *Sports Illustrated*. All along, his standard response was, "This is a person's life. I take this seriously." Others on his staff were only slightly more forthcoming, as Leon Wright was when he said, "You've got to understand, they like to fry people down here."

When the pre-trial motions had all been adjudicated, Judge Fine announced court would resume at one o'clock, when jury selection would begin.

At the appointed hour the bailiff escorted thirty-six prospective jurors into Courtroom 315. He motioned them to sit in the wooden benches on the righthand side of the courtroom. Men and women, all ages, shapes and colours. Sitting at the defence table beside Weinstein and Greene, Brian turned in his chair and stared at the jurors. This is what he had been told to do. Also, don't smile (so as not to appear cocky); engage the eyes of the jurors (nothing to hide); don't cross your legs (too complacent). Unfortunately, because he was nervous, Brian looked stolid, stone-faced. Even with his blond curly locks, he looked unmistakably hard, even mean, not the sort of person any of the jurors would want to hear asking, "What the hell's your problem?"

Judge Fine explained to the jurors the process of *voir dire* by which each one is interviewed by lawyers for both sides, one by one, in the anteroom behind the courtroom. They are asked about their work and hobbies, their families. They are asked what newspapers and magazines they read, what television programs they watch. They are asked if they could sentence someone to death in the electric chair.

One by one, they were called, by number. The first juror

was a woman in her forties with streaked blonde hair. She was interviewed for twenty minutes, then the next number was called.

In the jurors' room, Judge Fine sat at the end of a rectangular table, greeting each juror. Barry Weinstein sat at one side of the table, beside Brian, to Judge Fine's right. Greene sat behind them, peering over Brian's shoulders. Chuck Burton sat across from Weinstein at the other side of the table with Robert Zaun, a young paralegal from the state attorney's office. The room was small and cramped. The court reporter had to squeeze herself and her dictating machine into a corner beside Judge Fine. Three reporters sat with notebooks in their laps in chairs along the wall to Judge Fine's left.

The door opened and the bailiff motioned into the room a middle-aged man wearing beige pants and a short-sleeved shirt. He wore a copper bracelet on his right wrist. He sat at the opposite end of the table from Judge Fine, who said, "Hi! You're Fred Adams? I'm Judge Fine."

Burton started by asking the man his views on capital punishment.

"I'm a born-again Christian," he answered. "I believe in forgiveness. It would be against my beliefs to put another human to death."

Burton then asked if he ever read *Sports Illustrated*.

"Not regularly. Sometimes I pick it up in the dentist's office."

When it was Weinstein's turn, he asked right away, "Could you vote for the death penalty?"

The man steepled his fingers at his chin, looked down and after a moment replied, "That's tough." Then he fell silent.

Weinstein waited.

"If you chose me, I guess I could apply the death penalty," the juror said. "Under the judge's instructions."

Judge Fine told him if he was chosen he would be obliged to follow the law.

"Oh, I'd follow the law," the juror said.

Burton asked him if it would make any difference if it was "a gruesome, awful, terrible case."

"I imagine it is a man," the juror mused, not knowing that Brian, only a few feet away, staring into his eyes, was the defendant.

After ten minutes, the man was excused and the bailiff appeared with another juror.

"Hello," Judge Fine greeted him briskly. "Are you Gerald White?"

"Yes."

"Pleased to meet you. I'm Judge Fine."

On the way back to Monica's, Brian stopped at the Palm Beach Mall. Leon had instructed him to meet him at a hair salon called the Cut 'n' Dry. Leon did not like Brian's long, unkempt hair. He thought it made him look like a caveman. He also did not like Brian's dark grey jacket and black pants, thought they made him look heavy, somber — "too poly-estered." He wanted something lighter. "Elegantly casual," maybe a lightweight sports jacket. He wanted Brian to look like a successful former athlete, like someone "with his shit together."

At Monica's place, as soon as he stepped in the door, Brian stood in the hallway and pulled off his jacket, his tie and his white shirt, throwing them where they landed.

"What's up, hon?" Monica asked.

He stood at a chair in the dining-room, his body stiff with rage. He tried to scream.

"Clothes! Hair!"

And then, the singsong voice, "Go get your hair cut, Brian. Get some nice clothes, Brian. This goes nice with this. And, oh — Jesus fucking!" He was near to tears. Monica watched from the couch by the window.

And then, the rage was gone. He started making a joke of it. "In hockey, you just had to get your uniform, no matter what city you were in. You got your skates. You got your pads. You put 'em on and you played."

He walked over to the couch and pulled Monica to him

and wrapped his arms around her, engulfing her. They stood together for about a minute and then Brian said, "Let's go to a movie tonight. I don't care what. Jesus, even 'Mary Poppins'."

Late that night, Leon arrived at his two-storey townhouse in Lake Worth, far to the west of downtown West Palm Beach in a suburban community. He plunked a plastic Wynn-Dixie shopping-bag on the kitchen counter, then pulled out a bag of pasta, frozen vegetables and a thick steak.

He went upstairs to change, came down in faded denims. As he prepared dinner, the stereo in the living-room played trumpet solos by Chris Brown, one of Leon's favorite jazz artists. The music curled around the apartment, clear and haunting. Leon ate his steak at the kitchen counter.

He thought the day had gone well. There had been some testiness from Brian — Leon's antenna detected some of it was racial — but Brian looked much better with his new haircut, certainly less guilty. Leon was growing weary of Brian's childishness, and worried that he was beginning to enjoy the attention. It was what Leon did not like about professional athletes, their barn-door egos. As for Brian's future, if the jury acquitted him, Leon hoped he would leave West Palm Beach the day after the trial ended.

CHAPTER TWO

Tuesday: *The Letter from the Gardens*

I

Early in the morning, Brian was back in the courtyard at the Governmental Center, all smiles. He wore a lightweight brown sports jacket, beige trousers and, with his hair trimmed, he looked like a successful former athlete.

He headed to the takeout coffee shop in the courthouse building. Minutes later, he emerged with a styrofoam cup of coffee and *The Palm Beach Post*. There was a story about him on the front page of the local section, with a photograph. He spread the paper on the table and eagerly read the article by reporter Christine Van Meter, which began, "None of 23 potential jurors had heard of former professional hockey player Brian Spencer when his murder trial began Monday, but three recognized the 1982 shooting that led to his trial."

The jurors were being interviewed individually because Barry Weinstein assumed that most of them would recognize Brian, that his celebrity might influence them in a collective group-think — pro or con. Weinstein had presented to Judge Fine a stack of news clippings, including the nine-page article in *Sports Illustrated*. As it turned out, none of the jurors knew anything about Brian, even when his name was mentioned in the small room behind the courtroom where the interviews were conducted. And whenever it was brought to a juror's attention that the young man in the dark grey jacket was the defendant, invariably the juror was surprised. Most of them assumed Brian was one of the lawyers. Chuck Burton, having come from Boston where he

49

once followed the Bruins, knew more than his colleagues on the defence side about the evanescent fame of professional hockey players. "I figured if six people knew who Brian was he'd be lucky," he said.

The *Post* article described Brian as "a journeyman player who never distinguished himself in a ten-year career with four National Hockey League teams." It quoted an editor for *Hockey News*, a Toronto weekly, who said, "He was never a superstar by any standard. He was known for his hitting game . . . he was never a good hockey player."

It was an assessment Brian often heard throughout his hockey career. He was not a Gordie Howe, not a Bobby Orr, not a Wayne Gretzky; ergo, he was not a good hockey player. Brian had come to accept that it did not matter that he managed to stay in the major leagues of hockey for ten years when players who had barely survived a season, sometimes only four or five games, lived on the experience for the rest of their lives.

"Never a good hockey player," he muttered, staring at the newspaper at the table in the courtyard. He looked more bewildered than hurt.

II

When they were fourteen, Brian and Byron had attended a summer hockey school in Nelson, a town of 10,000 in lower British Columbia, across the border from Washington. It was the only summer Byron attended the school. Brian kept returning, saving his money from odd jobs during the winter and spring in Fort St. James.

When they finished elementary school, Brian and Byron had to travel to Vanderhoof, forty-five miles away, for high school. Brian enjoyed high school and did well in the sciences and geography, but when the boys were fifteen, they were both expelled from high school, and on the same day. Brian and Byron were in different classrooms because Byron had failed a year. On that day, Brian got in trouble, something about a beer bottle in the classroom, and the teacher told him to leave the school. He left and wandered the streets of Vanderhoof. Meanwhile, in Byron's classroom, there was an unholy uproar, kids yelling and tossing books around. When the teacher walked in, he decided Byron had been the instigator. Byron complained he had nothing to do with it, but the teacher wouldn't believe him, so Byron picked up his books and threw them at the teacher, telling him to "Stick 'em where the sun don't shine." He left the classroom, walked out of the school and later met Brian on the street. They compared notes, concluded their school days were over, then hitchhiked back to Fort St. James. They worked for a time in the sawmills, then returned to Vanderhoof, where they spent most of the winter bumming around and scrounging for food and warmth.

⟋ Early the next summer, after a wild party at Stone's Bay on the shore of Stuart Lake, Brian and Byron were in trouble again. They were hanging out with a boisterous gang of teenagers and one evening they found themselves at the cottage of a wealthy doctor from Prince George. They were drinking beer and wine and some of the gang started playing badminton on the lawn in front of the cottage. Someone set fire to one of the shuttlecocks, then the racquets. They started a bonfire by the lake; the door of the cottage was knocked down and thrown on the fire.

It became a frenzy of vandalism. One of the boys jumped up and down in a boat at the dock until he broke through the bottom. Byron drank wine and watched. Brian wasn't even there. He and an Indian girl had wandered down the road to a parked car where they were amusing themselves. A neighbour called the RCMP and when they arrived one of the girls at the party told them the Spencer brothers started it. The Mounties arrested Brian and Byron the next morning. They had been in trouble that winter in Vanderhoof — Brian spent a night in jail for stealing eighty dollars in quarters from a laundromat — and both of them were on probation when they returned to Fort St. James. They were sent to reform school at Brannon Lake, an institution just north of Nanaimo on Vancouver Island, where they celebrated their sixteenth birthdays.

At Brannon Lake, Byron worked in the kitchen, learned how to cook and became friends with the chef, who taught him how to play chess. Brian worked in the shops, enjoying the tools and machinery. In the evenings, Brian concentrated on bodybuilding, rigidly adhering to a regimen of weights and calisthenics, doing pushups, chinups and situps. Seven nights a week, he worked himself to exhaustion, his muscles fibrillating and red with strain. He liked the discipline. He felt a sense of purpose. And he packed on hard weight, bringing himself to a hundred and eighty-five pounds. Brian and Byron have mostly pleasant memories of Brannon Lake.

One of the conditions of Brian's parole from Brannon Lake was that he could not return to Fort St. James, so Roy and Irene sent him to stay with Ed and Greta Godfrey, friends of the family in Kitimat, a company town south of the Alaska Panhandle. He stayed with the Godfreys only a few weeks, then moved in with Rick Kennedy, a friend he met at the hockey school in Nelson. Brian became part of the Kennedy family. He applied himself to his school work, finished grade eleven, and worked at several part-time jobs to pay for his room and board and save for the summer hockey school. It was in Kitimat that Brian switched from defence to forward. He played on three local teams — juvenile, senior and an industrial-league team.

In the summer of 1967, Brian met Red Berenson, who then played for the St. Louis Blues, at the hockey camp in Nelson. Berenson — he was called "the Red Baron" in St. Louis — was a shifty, effective centre and one of the most highly educated players in the National Hockey League. He was born in Regina, but had come up through the ranks of college hockey in the United States. He earned a BA and an MA from the University of Michigan and later became president of the NHL Players Association.

Berenson liked Brian's evident desire and rough style. He arranged for him to play with the Regina Pats, a western Canadian junior team. Brian boarded a plane for Regina in September 1967, just before his eighteenth birthday. When he arrived, Berenson's parents met him at the airport and drove him to their home, where he stayed. On the drive into the city, Brian stared out the window of the car, mesmerized by the lights, the traffic and the buildings. "This is amazing!" he told the Berensons. "What's the population?"

"A hundred and ten thousand," Mrs. Berenson answered.

Brian said nothing, but at the Berenson residence, before he unpacked his bags, he called home to say he had arrived safely and that there were a hundred and ten thousand people in Regina, "all in one city."

Regina is the national training centre for the Royal

Canadian Mounted Police. Brian visited the RCMP barracks, which was not far from the Berenson's home. He addressed postcards to Fort St. James showing the Mounties in their full scarlet regalia, on their black horses, lances at the ready. Fort St. James is policed by the RCMP, but in their day-to-day duties they do not look nearly so glamorous. Brian had never seen real Mounties in full dress uniform.

Brian had finished grade eleven in Kitimat, but because Saskatchewan's curriculum was more advanced, he had to start grade eleven over again in Regina. Most of the players on the Pats attended high school. Brian did not stay long in Regina, however. He hated the coach, and he did not get along with the players. He considered them mostly city kids, boys who once belonged to the Boy Scouts and who made model airplanes. They talked a different language. When he tried to express his alienation, he would say he felt like an "out-of-culture person."

Early in the 1967-68 season, the Pats traded Brian to the Calgary Centennials, a new junior team in Alberta. In Calgary, adjusting again to a different school system, Brian advanced to grade twelve. He loved Calgary, but did not enjoy playing for a losing expansion team. He liked the coach of the Centennials, Cec Papke, but despised the owner, Scotty Munro. When Brian returned to the Centennials for training camp at the start of the 1968-69 season, Munro berated him in the dressing-room in front of the entire team. As Brian remembers it, Munro stood in the middle of the dressing-room and said, "In thirty years in the game I've never seen a dumber hockey player."

"Meaning me," Brian said, shouting and close to tears as he recalled the incident. "You don't come up to me, coming out of the bush, working like a man since I was thirteen, in the logging camps and lumber mills. You don't talk to me like I'm a little city boy who didn't bring the paper home."

It struck him as ludicrous that a soft, balding, middle-aged team owner would do something so outrageous. "I'm amazed how someone like that can stand there and say these things to a hockey player, even a junior hockey player, who is almost genetically violent, playing a violent sport, sitting on a powder keg all the time."

Brian played in fifty-six games for the Calgary Centennials, the most games he had ever played in a season. In the 1967-68 season he scored 14 goals, with 12 assists and a gentlemanly 24 penalty minutes. Not statistics to make a hockey scout swoon.

Next season, Brian returned to Saskatchewan, this time to the Estevan Bruins, the team which promised to be the class of the junior league in 1968-69. He had to start grade eleven over again.

He was skating better, controlling the puck with greater ease. He still was not a polished goal scorer, but he was bigger, tougher, more confident. Then came an ugly skirmish with a teammate, Greg Polis, one of only a few junior players from the western Canadian league that season who eventually made it to the NHL. One day Brian was lifting weights and Polis started needling him about trying to make himself a he-man. Brian dismissed it at first, but when Polis persisted, Brian walked up to him, lifted him over his shoulders and dropped him on his head on the floor. Polis was in such agony Brian thought he might have broken his neck. The coach tried to get the two players to cool it and shake hands, but Brian refused. Later, in a show of hands in the dressing-room, the players decided they didn't want Brian on the team, so he was traded to the Swift Current Broncos, the league's last place team. He played better that season, scoring 19 goals, with 29 assists — and 120 penalty minutes.

Brian earned a reputation in Swift Current as a player not to be trifled with, and not just on the ice. He was so strong that once, in the off-season, he broke a man's arm, just below the elbow, in an arm-wrestling match. Brian was not surprised he could do this; what surprised him was the sound the bone made — "like a two-by-four cracking," he said.

In the summer of 1969, when he was nineteen, Brian worked in a logging camp in the north central interior of British Columbia. One day in July, he received a letter with the Maple Leaf Gardens logo in the top lefthand corner. He tore it open, eager as any student waiting for his final marks. The letter was from R. E. Davidson, chief scout for the Toronto Maple Leafs. It began: "During the recent amateur draft meeting in Montreal, we acquired the exclusive rights to put you on our negotiating list and we are prepared to negotiate a contract with you personally for your professional services for the 1969-70 season and thereafter. . . ."

Brian had been selected fifth by the Maple Leafs in the 1969 amateur draft, fifty-fifth overall among NHL teams. For Roy Spencer, it was a vindication of the work he had done on the backyard rink, the cold mornings on the road to Vanderhoof, and the hours he spent planted in the snow by the boards with his stopwatch. He was proud of Brian. He could not have been happier if the letter had been a scholarship to Harvard. Brian read the letter over and over, studying the logo on the envelope, pausing at the words "professional services" and "thereafter." He refolded the letter and put it back in its envelope, and he carried it with him wherever he went. He had it with him in the New York Islanders attaché case when he was arrested eighteen years later in the motel parking lot in West Palm Beach.

Early in September, when he turned twenty, Brian flew to Toronto on a ticket paid for by the Maple Leafs. After he arrived in Toronto, he boarded a shuttle flight for Peterborough, where the Maple Leafs held their training camp. He took a taxi to the hotel where the team stayed. The first Maple Leaf he saw in the flesh was George Armstrong. Armstrong, an Indian from Skead, Ontario, was the captain of the Maple Leafs, preparing for his nineteenth and penultimate season in the NHL. He was standing in the lobby. "I recognized him immediately," Brian said. "They didn't wear helmets in those days."

Early the next morning, Brian stood outside the hotel, waiting to go to the rink for his first workout. Armstrong walked out of the hotel and said good morning as he passed. Then Johnny Bower, the old warhorse goalie playing his last season, walked out of the hotel and he too said good morning. Brian watched Armstrong and Bower clowning in the parking lot. Armstrong was in his car and just as Bower started to open the door, Armstrong gunned the engine and spurted ahead. Bower walked up to the car and tried to open the door a second time and again Armstrong gunned the engine and spurted further ahead. Brian laughed out loud. It was the most hilarious thing he had ever seen.

There were ninety-three players in training camp that September, with the regulars and players from the farm system. Brian played on lines with Dave Keon and Norm Ullman and Paul Henderson. What impressed him wasn't the speed — he did not find it much faster than junior hockey — but the experience and know-how, and the specialty work. He watched how the regulars ate and dressed, how they assembled their equipment, sharpened their skates, what cars they drove, what pranks they played. He wrote home about the daily "George and Johnny Show" — George Armstrong nailing Johnny Bower's shoes to the floor, Armstrong pouring ice water into Bower's pants, Armstrong giving Bower the wrong set of teeth before a television interview. And if Dave Keon sliced bananas into his corn flakes at breakfast, that too might be something they would want to know about in Fort St. James. It mattered not a whit when one of the sports writers referred to him in print as "Ted" Spencer. When Brian was issued a regulation Maple Leaf jersey, he thought he had never seen a more dazzling white or a truer blue; even the polyester and cotton fibres seemed to have a big-league intensity.

Training camp moved to Maple Leaf Gardens in late September. Brian's earliest memories of Toronto are of the unseasonably warm autumn temperatures and of eating Chinese food for the first time. "Vietnam was still going on and there were about sixty thousand American draft dodgers in the city. And the miniskirts! The open, raw sex! It was a wild city. Wild!"

The number of players dwindled, but Brian stuck it out, thumping in the corners, all elbows and knees. As impressed as he was, it never bothered him to take one of his boyhood heroes hard into the boards. "Oh no," he said, "not when the puck drops. You're driven to excellence *because* they're on the ice."

Brian was one of three rookies in camp to be awarded major-league contracts. The others were Ernie Moser and Bobby Liddington, both from western Canada. Brian had played junior hockey with Moser in Estevan and with Liddington in Calgary. They signed what were called two-way contracts; Brian received a major-league salary of $12,500 if he played with the Maple Leafs, and a minor-league salary of $6,500 if he played with the farm team in Tulsa. And he got a $4,000 signing bonus.

Brian started the 1969-70 season with the Tulsa Oilers in Oklahoma. After staying two weeks in a hotel, paid for by the Maple Leafs, Brian and Bobby Liddington found an apartment in downtown Tulsa for $240 a month. Soon after they arrived, they met two young women and on a Saturday afternoon they visited them at their apartment. Before they left the room to change, one of the women prepared a pitcher of iced tea for the young hockey players. Brian had never tasted iced tea before. He poured himself a glass, took a swallow and grimaced. When Liddington poured himself a glass, Brian leaned forward to warn him, "Jesus, Bobby, don't try that water. It's gone bad."

Brian played 66 games for Tulsa, scoring 13 goals, with 19 assists and 186 penalty minutes. His rugged play was attracting attention. There was a rough new style developing in the NHL. It would get rougher over the next few seasons, with expansion teams trying to capture an American audience. A scrapper from the backwoods like Brian would be a valuable commodity. The Maple Leafs were not known as a team of heavy hitters.

III

Jury selection continued when court resumed at ten o'clock.

The first prospective juror was a woman in her sixties, dressed in a pink pantsuit, her hair freshly styled. She took her seat at the end of the table in the jury room and Burton started by asking how she felt about the death penalty. She said she once strongly favoured it, but her views had since been "tempered."

"What about an awful, gruesome, terrible homicide?" Burton asked.

She replied, "If it was that, yes. I could vote for it."

Then, in a soft voice, she said she had something to say before they asked any more questions. Despite Judge Fine's remarks the day before that jurors must not read newspaper reports on the case, she confessed she read the article in the *Post* at breakfast and recognized one of the names. The name she recognized was Diane Delena.

She used to be in a car pool with Diane's mother, in a neighbourhood in North Palm Beach. She knew one of Diane's boyfriends, someone called Douglas, who was always in trouble with the law. She remembered that Diane had an "unsavoury" reputation.

"I think it's fortunate I did read the paper," the woman said.

"Why?" Weinstein asked.

"I don't think I could believe whatever she said."

The paragraph in the *Post* article that mentioned Diane Delena was merely a rehash of the basics of the case, one of those background paragraphs reporters keep in front of them during a running story to insert where appropriate in subsequent articles. It read: "In January, Spencer was charged with first-degree murder and kidnaping in the 1982 shooting death of Michael Dalfo. Spencer's ex-girlfriend, former call girl Diane Delena, gave investigators a statement in November 1986 claiming that Spencer shot Dalfo twice and left him for dead on Feb. 4, 1982."

What was curious, however, was the elapsed time — February 1982 to November 1986 — nearly five years. It raised all sorts of questions. What had happened during the nearly five-year interval? What finally prompted Diane to tell her story to the investigators? Why did it take so long? The investigators were on to Diane Delena the day after Dalfo was found in a pool of water off a dirt road in Palm Beach Gardens.

In Dalfo's condominium apartment, about a mile from where he was discovered by a passing truck driver, the investigators found matchbooks on which had been scribbled the names and numbers of several escort agencies. One of them was Fantacee Island Escorts, the one Diane worked for under the name Crystal. They also found a cheque made out to cash, for seventy-five dollars. The phone number for Fantacee Island Escorts was written on the cheque. It did not take much sleuthing to establish that Diane had been sent to Dalfo's apartment late on the evening of February 3, 1982.

Three days after they found the matchbooks, the investigators obtained a warrant to search the trailer Diane Delena shared with Brian Spencer on Skees Road, a scratchy neighbourhood carved out of the bush on the western edge of West Palm Beach. When they finished rummaging through the trailer, the investigators left with two pairs of women's high-heeled shoes, one black and one brown. The shoes were wrapped in plastic baggies, along with twenty soil samples taken from the scene of the crime in twenty little plastic film containers, and the package was sent off to a Federal Bureau

of Investigation laboratory in Washington, D.C. When the FBI
report arrived in West Palm Beach, it said: "Soil found on the
black pair of high-heeled shoes owned by Diane Delena
could have originated from the source of soil taken from the
area where the body of Michael Dalfo was found."

Diane Delena and Michael Dalfo were there on the shell
rock road on the night of February 3, 1982 — that much is
known. But was Brian Spencer there? If he wasn't, did Diane
do the killing herself? And if she didn't, who did? And why?
All sorts of questions.

Detectives at the Palm Beach County Sheriff's Office
suspected Brian from the beginning. The day they searched
the trailer on Skees Road, they took Diane to the station with
them for questioning. Brian followed them, right into the
interrogation room, then pulled her from the office. He
grabbed her by the arm so forcefully he lifted her off the
floor.

The detectives did manage to interview Diane in 1982.
She told them enough to fill two reels of tape, but, incredibly
for a first-degree murder case, someone in the sheriff's
department borrowed the tapes and recorded over them,
erasing what Diane had said. Over the next few months, the
detectives kept track of Diane. Early one morning in May
1982, in rush-hour traffic, Detective Robert Halstedt stopped
Diane when she was driving on Military Trail, north of
Okeechobee Boulevard. He spoke to her for several minutes
in his car, accusing her of knowing more than she was saying
about the killing of Michael Dalfo. When Diane got out of
Halstedt's car, she walked back to her car on the shoulder of
Military Trail and sat motionless behind the wheel for a short
time. Halstedt thought she was "very emotional." When
Diane drove away, she headed in the opposite direction to
where she had been going when Halstedt stopped her.
Halstedt followed her all the way to Dyer Boulevard and the
gates of Fischbach & Moore, electrical contractors, where
Brian worked as a mechanic.

It was not until November 1986 that Diane finally, and
permanently, put her story on the record for the detectives. In

the course of a routine review of unsolved cases undertaken every five years, the sheriff's office resumed its investigations. Diane had long since left Brian and the trailer on Skees Road. She had married Leslie Raymond Fialco in a civil ceremony in November 1984. They had started a family, two baby girls. She worked as a receptionist at Good Samaritan Hospital, which is where she was when two detectives served her with a subpoena. At first Diane did not know what it was for. It all seemed so long ago.

On the afternoon of November 6, 1986, Diane walked into the Law Building on 3rd Street in downtown West Palm Beach, which is directly across from the Palm Beach County Courthouse. She headed for a room on the third floor, where she was greeted by state attorneys David Bludworth and Paul Moyle and Detective Springer. When Diane recognized them, she started to cry.

"I thought this was over," she said.

Springer began the questioning.

"Ma'am, I want you to think back to the evening of February 3, 1982. Did you have occasion to go over to Michael Dalfo's townhouse?"

"Yes," Diane answered.

"Approximately what time did you arrive?"

"I don't remember, somewhere just before midnight, I guess."

"Tell me what happened when you arrived at his place. Take your time."

"I can't do this. I can't." Diane broke down in tears again.

"Ma'am," Springer said, sharply, "I have subpoenaed you with a state attorney's investigative subpoena. I've also explained to you prior to going on the record, and you've had a chance to speak with attorneys, that I'm granting you use-immunity under Florida State statute and I am now compelling your testimony." Springer paused a moment, then continued, "Tell me what happened there, in the apartment, the best you can recall."

Weakly, Diane began to tell her story. "When I got there, he was doing all that coke."

"Who was doing all that coke?" Springer asked.

"I don't remember his name."

" 'Michael Dalfo' ring a bell with you?"

"Yes."

"And describe that man to me, please."

"Why do I have to do this? Why? You know —"

Early on the evening of February 3, 1982, a Wednesday, Michael Dalfo had dinner at the home of his father, who lived a short distance from Michael's golf-course condominium townhouse. Michael shared the townhouse with his brother, Christopher, who happened to be away that week visiting in North Carolina. Michael's father, also called Michael, was a wealthy and prominent land developer in south Florida. Michael worked for him at Michael Dalfo and Associates, the family real estate firm on U.S. Highway 1 in North Palm Beach. His parents were divorced.

In the late 1970s, Michael and Christopher and their mother, Tina Dalfo, owned a restaurant on Okeechobee Boulevard called Christopher Michael's Ristorante. Michael liked to cook and was regarded as an excellent chef. The restaurant closed in 1980, reopened a year later as Don Luigi's, then burned to the ground in a fire that investigators described as arson.

Michael was thirty-two years old, with Italian charm and good looks — dark skin, deep brown eyes, black hair, a black and brown flecked moustache. He was five feet, eight inches tall and weighed a hundred and fifty pounds. He looked after his body, but he liked the good life and spent his money freely on women, liquor and drugs. Only three days earlier, he had told his girlfriend, Paula Saccomanno, that he soon expected to make between $10,000 and $15,000 in a cocaine deal.

At about ten o'clock that Wednesday evening, Michael walked home from his father's place. It was warm and languid with the smell of sand and grass in the night air. Crickets chattered. It was the height of the season. The denizens and dowagers of Palm Beach, that fourteen-mile sandspit of old money — Pucci, Lauder, Carnegie, Pulitzer, Rockefeller — had long since arrived by private jet and stretch limo and were comfortably barricaded in their winter palaces by the Atlantic Ocean. Soon the baseball teams would arrive for the *clink-boink-clank* liturgy of spring training.

When he got to his apartment, Michael put on some music, poured himself a liqueur and sniffed a line of cocaine from a small mirror on the coffee table. Then another, and another. He took off his clothes until he was wearing only his black bikini briefs and a gold chain around his neck with a small horn-of-plenty pendant. When he felt like sharing his good time, he reached for the Palm Beach County telephone book, cracked it open at the yellow pages and ran his finger down the listings of the escort services: Young Sophisticates, 24K Escorts, World Dating, Rainbow Escorts, Southern Ladies, Fantacee Island Escorts. The agencies were listed separately, but many had the same number.

Michael wrote down the number for Fantacee Island Escorts on a matchbook. He had called the number before. The escort-service people knew him as a regular customer, and not a welcome one. At about ten-thirty, he called and spoke to a friendly woman who identified herself as Liz. Her real name was June Langley. An attractive blonde in her late thirties, Langley had been working the telephones for Fantacee Island Escorts for fifteen months. It was the perfect job because she could work from her home. She was paralyzed and confined to a wheelchair.

Originally, Langley thought it was merely a dating service, "arranging lovely ladies for inquiring gentlemen." If any of the gentlemen asked about sex, Langley would tell them politely they had the wrong agency and she would hang up. She never met any of the lovely ladies but on several occasions she met her boss, a man called William Workman, and his wife Elaine. It was Workman who told Langley it would be best if she used a nickname, so she chose Liz. She did not think there was anything unusual about that. She thought Workman and his wife were "lovely people, really sweet." Workman had told her that if she ever suspected trouble, if she ever thought one of the gentlemen might be causing problems, she was to notify him immediately.

When Michael Dalfo called the number for Fantacee Island Escorts, Langley answered, took down the information — his address, the type of woman he wanted — and told him a lovely lady would be calling him shortly. She checked through her list to see who was available. All the escorts were listed on small cards, with pertinent details on their height, weight and predilections. Some customers wanted women who looked like little girls. Some wanted older, motherly women. Some wanted big, fat women. Some wanted women who could boss them around. Most of the cards were accompanied by two polaroid photographs, one showing the women dressed, the other showing them undressed. It was a precaution to prevent policewomen from infiltrating the agency. The escort agency owners knew that policewomen on undercover assignments could not be made to pose in the nude.

Three months earlier, right after Thanksgiving weekend, Diane Delena noticed an ad for a "hostess job" in the classified section of *The Palm Beach Post*. She visited an office on Northlake Boulevard and filled out a job application, but she did not pose in the nude. Instead, she wore a softball uniform, with "Wolf's Gang" across the front of her jersey. She was twenty-two years old, five feet, two inches, with good legs, a trim waist and large breasts. Her hair was long, dark and wavy, falling in tangles past her shoulders.

Diane had read an article in *Cosmopolitan* magazine about escort agencies, but she found nothing in it that said anything about prostitution. Once, soon after she started working for Fantacee Island Escorts, a customer complained and Bill Workman warned her that if she did not have sex with customers he would fire her. He said she was stupid and naïve. She decided to stay on. The pay was good, one hundred dollars an hour, which she split, fifty-fifty, with the agency. She usually turned over the money to Workman, who met her at night at a 7-Eleven store. She thought she could save enough in four months to invest in a small restaurant on Okeechobee Boulevard.

Langley called Diane at the trailer on Skees Road, gave her Dalfo's address and reminded her to check in when she arrived and after she was finished — another of the precautions the agency requested in order to protect the escorts. Diane left the trailer wearing a blue and white dress, a dark blue blazer and high-heeled shoes. She drove to Dalfo's townhouse in her Fiat, arriving shortly after eleven. At the entrance to the condominium complex, she encountered a security guard in a small booth. Diane told him she was there to see Michael Dalfo. The guard called Dalfo's townhouse, then waved Diane through.

"Do you say he was doing cocaine?" Detective Springer asked.

"Yes," Diane said.

"What happened? Did he become upset with you?"

"Yes."

"Tell me about that."

"He wanted me to stay longer than I was supposed to. He wanted to give me a cheque. I said no, I can't take a cheque. So I left."

"How did you leave?"

"I just left."

"What kind of vehicle were you driving?"

"Oh, a blue Fiat. I don't remember what year it was."

"Was he still upset when you left?"

"I don't know."

"Where did you go when you left his townhouse?"

"Home."

"And where was home?"

"Skees Road, in a trailer."

"About how long were you at Michael Dalfo's?"

"A little more than an hour."

"How long were you at your trailer when you arrived there?"

"I don't know, a half hour maybe. I don't remember."

"And where did you go and what did you do from your trailer — where did you go?"

"I went over to the Banana Boat, I guess. Tried to talk to Brian and —"

"Let's back up. Let's take this slow. You went over to the Banana Boat, located where?"

"On Military and Okeechobee."

Diane had felt uncomfortable as soon as she entered Dalfo's townhouse. Her first impression was of a slight, nearly naked man, wearing only black bikini underwear. She found him "wired" on cocaine, ready for anything. He wanted a blow job, but he couldn't get an erection. He wanted Diane to take a shower with him. She refused.

Diane stayed until just past midnight. Dalfo was becoming increasingly frustrated, hyperactive, hostile. He liked Diane. Her small, voluptuous body pleased him, he wanted to get it on with her, but he couldn't. He asked her to stay longer. She wanted to leave. He wrote out a cheque for $75, payable to cash, but Diane said she could not accept it. Diane called Liz to report that she was finished and ready to leave. While she was talking to Liz on the telephone, Liz could hear Dalfo shouting in the background. He sounded crazy. Liz thought she might have to ask Bill Workman to go there to protect Diane. When Diane hung up, Dalfo grabbed the phone and called Fantacee Island Escorts to order another woman.

When Diane started to leave, Dalfo took her by the arm and pleaded with her to stay. She hurried out the door and Dalfo followed her outside. She got into her Fiat and drove home to the trailer on Skees Road. Exhausted and frightened, she kicked off her shoes and turned on the television. After half an hour, the telephone rang. It was Liz, asking her to go on another date, this time across town to the Hyatt Hotel. Diane told Liz about her session with Dalfo and asked her not to send any more women there because he was "a creep."

On her way to the Hyatt Hotel, Diane drove by the Banana Boat, a popular drinking and eating spot at

Okeechobee Boulevard and Military Trail, one of the busiest intersections in all of Palm Beach County. Statistically, based on the number of motor vehicle accidents — grinding head-ons, pedestrians smashed into eternity, fender-benders — it is also the most dangerous intersection in all of Palm Beach County. It is the gaudy Mecca of an otherwise flat and dreary neon wasteland: used-car lots, fast-food joints, gas stations. The Banana Boat attracted a young, good-timing crowd, many of them tourists. The music was loud and brassy, the oysters delicious. Brian Spencer was one of the regulars. He knew the bartender, Martin Malveso, and after an evening of drinking and eating and talking he usually left a ten-dollar tip on the counter. The Banana Boat stayed open until nearly dawn.

Diane noticed Brian's truck in the parking lot at the Banana Boat. It was hard not to notice Brian's truck. It was an enormous, monstrous vehicle, painted a dull camouflage. Brian had started building it in 1974, when he played for the Buffalo Sabres. It weighed sixteen tons. Brian called it the Hulk.

Diane found Brian at the bar, talking to friends. She told him what had happened at Dalfo's and said she was afraid to go home because he might have followed her. Brian did not like to be interrupted by her. They had an arrangement whereby they lived together and shared expenses, but each was supposed to be free to entertain themselves as they wanted. Nevertheless Diane could be jealous and possessive. One night she dropped by the Banana Boat, saw Brian with another woman and became so enraged that she ripped his shirt open.

Brian said it was none of his business. Diane left the Banana Boat and drove to her appointment at the Hyatt Hotel. She had a date with a middle-aged married man who worked as district sales manager for a television station in Fort Myers. She had sex with him, but stayed only half an hour.

"And where did you go from the Hyatt?" Detective Springer

asked.

"I think I went back home," Diane answered.

"To the trailer?"

"Yes."

"And what happened when you went back to the trailer?"

"He called me."

"Who?"

"Brian."

"Called you on the telephone?"

"Yes, I think so. And then he came home."

"Brian Spencer came home?"

"Yes."

"What happened when he came home?"

"He was upset with me —"

"Go ahead."

"And he asked me to take him over there."

Soon after Diane left Dalfo's, two more women from Fantacee Island Escorts arrived at his townhouse. Paula Fairchild, in her early thirties, had long blonde hair and thick legs. She arrived with her roommate, Pamela Vineyard, a stout brunette. Dalfo greeted them outside, still wearing only his black bikini briefs and the gold chain around his neck. By now he was frenzied, jumping up and down, running through the sprinklers on the lawn. He nearly ran into Paula's car.

The two women followed Dalfo into the townhouse. Once inside, Paula called Liz and said she didn't feel safe there. Liz told her about Diane having been "roughed up" on her visit, then asked if she could speak to Dalfo herself, which would give Paula and Pamela time to leave. Dalfo, slurring his words, complained to Liz about the agency. He said he thought Paula and Pamela were "dogs." He wanted another woman. Liz gave him Bill Workman's number.

Dalfo waited and waited, and when nobody arrived he tried another escort agency, one listed in the yellow pages as Rainbow Escorts. It was nearly three in the morning when Sheila Andrews, slim and auburn-haired, arrived at Dalfo's townhouse. There was no guard at the booth when she drove up, so she drove through, parked her car and walked up to Dalfo's townhouse. The door was open and the television was blaring. She stood at the doorway and yelled over the din, "Mike! Mike!" Nobody came to the door.

When Sheila Andrews passed through the gate, leaving the complex, the guard was back in his booth. She told him that a friend had called and she had come to see him but nobody answered the door. She asked the guard if she could use his telephone. She called her agency, explained what had happened, and left. It was nearly three-thirty in the morning.

"So what happened when you told Brian Spencer these things at your trailer?" Detective Springer asked Diane.

"He got upset and he wanted me to take him there. And I said no. And when I started saying no, he started getting upset with me, so I thought, well, I'll just drive him by there and he'll be satisfied when I can't find the place. But like I said, when I pulled up, he was standing out there."

"Let's back up now. From your trailer, you and Brian Spencer did what?"

"We went back over there."

"What kind of vehicle?"

"My car, my Fiat."

"Who was driving?"

"I was."

"All right —"

"I think, I can't remember."

"And where did you go, you and Brian Spencer in your car?"

"I went to the PGA National and we drove — I wasn't sure if that's where he was or not — and he came outside to the car. He came right up to the car."

"Michael Dalfo did?"

"Yes. And Brian asked him to get in and he got in."

"Where did he get in the car — the front seat, the back?"

"I think in the front, probably. I don't know, it's a small car. I think Brian might have gotten in the back and he got in the front or something like that."

"And what was said?"

"What did I tell you before?"

"You tell me what you recall. Take your time."

"He told me not to say anything."

"Who told you that?"

"Brian."

"Where did you all go?"

"Drove down a street, I don't know where it was, and I got out. He made me get out of the car."

"When you say 'he', tell me who."

"Brian. And they stayed in the car and I was outside of the car, walking on the passenger side. I was leaning up against it, thinking how scared I was out there with no lights."

"Was it on a dirt road?"

"Yes. And they started talking louder, but not yelling or anything — so I ran."

Attorney Paul Moyle took over from Detective Springer and asked, "What happened when they started talking loud?"

"I covered my ears. I got scared and ran because I didn't want to hear them yelling at each other. And I just figured Brian would beat him up or something. Or hit him or something. I didn't want to hear it."

"Before that happened, before the loud talking, did you hear Michael Dalfo say anything to Brian Spencer?"

"Yeah, he said something about calling his lawyer. I don't remember exactly what the sentence was."

"Who said that?"

"He said something like, 'If you hurt me, touch me, I'll call my lawyer'."

"That's what Michael Dalfo said?"

"Yes."

"And what did Brian say?"

"He got mad. I don't remember. He got mad. I remember that much."

"Then what happened after they were talking? Real loud to each other, and you put your hands over your ears, what happened next?"

"Brian came with the car."

"Was Michael in the car?"

"No, no."

"What did he say?"

"He said what I said to you —"

"What?"

" 'Now he can't call his lawyer,' or something like that."

"Brian Spencer said, 'Now he can't call his lawyer'?"

Diane nodded her head.

"Is that yes?"

"Yes."

"Did you see him with a gun?"

"No, I didn't see a gun."

"Did you hear any shots?"

"No."

At ten o'clock on the morning of February 4, 1982, Albert Brihn was driving his truck west on PGA Boulevard, hauling a load of sludge for Seacoast Utilities. About a mile east of the Florida Turnpike, Brihn slowed to make a righthand turn at an isolated road across from one of south Florida's lush, championship golf courses. A sign by the gate at the entrance read, "PGA Wastewater Treatment Plant."

Brihn drove in and the truck rumbled up the soft, sandy road. There was nothing around but mud and puddles, phosphate pits and, in the distance, a stand of pine trees. No buildings or houses, only a small trailer about a mile north up the road from the entrance on PGA Boulevard. As he was driving, Brihn noticed something unusual lying about fifty feet off the road, in a clearing. It looked like a mannequin. He continued on up the road to the sewage treatment plant and delivered his load of sludge. On his way out a couple of hours later, driving south on the road he had come in on, Brihn looked again toward the clearing and this time noticed vultures floating in circles above the mannequin.

He stopped the truck, got out, walked across the muddy field and discovered the body of a young man in black bikini underwear, wearing a gold chain around his neck with a horn-of-plenty pendant. He noticed a small hole to the right of the man's nose, another between the nose and the mouth, another in the right temple. Even a sludge-hauler could tell that the man had been shot, probably at very close range, what police investigators call "contact range." Whoever had done it must have been strong enough to hold the man in a necklock, probably with his left arm, holding the weapon in his right hand. There were distinct powder burns at the temple and beside the nose, and dried blood caked on the man's face and hair. And then Brihn heard a sound that chilled him.

The body coughed.

Brihn ran to his truck and drove back to the treatment plant, where he called the police. Within ten minutes, paramedics from Old Dixie Fire Station arrived in an ambulance. The body was still breathing, feebly, when the ambulance reached Palm Beach Gardens Community Hospital. At three thirty-six in the afternoon, the breathing stopped and Michael James Dalfo was pronounced dead.

➤ In the room in the Law Building, Detective Springer continued questioning Diane.

"Tell me what happened right there when you got back in the car. What else was said?"

Diane answered, "I guess I said something like, 'Where is he?' He just said, 'He's back there.' And that was it. He didn't say, and I was afraid to ask. I didn't really think, like I said, that he did anything to him. I wasn't sure."

"Go ahead and tell us what happened."

"And I was still scared. I was afraid. He just, he didn't seem mad any more. And he just went home. And like I said, it was very late. I passed out. I woke up, I thought I was going to get in trouble because I thought that he would call and tell them what happened."

"That Dalfo would?"

"Yes."

"You didn't know he was dead at that point in time?"

"No."

After a few more questions, Detective Springer asked Diane about the day when the police came to search the trailer on Skees Road. Diane told him that was when she first heard that Michael Dalfo had been shot. She said she asked Brian, "How could you do something like that?"

Springer asked, "You said that to Brian Spencer?"

"Yes," Diane said.

"What did he say?"

"Something like, 'He deserved it.' "

"Michael Dalfo deserved it?"

"Yeah."

Paul Moyle, the attorney, then asked Diane, "Did you shoot Michael Dalfo yourself?"

She answered, "No."

IV

Jury selection continued in the afternoon. Much of it is routine, repetitive and even humdrum, but taken as a whole it is a remarkably effective way to form a picture of a community. The lawyers for each side probe individual beliefs, attitudes and lifestyles. They elicit from the jurors information about their favourite reading material and television programs. They uncover family rituals, methods of child-rearing, shopping habits, eating habits. Slowly patterns emerge and a microcosm of the community begins to slide into focus.

On the issue of capital punishment, for example, most jurors begin as doves. No, they couldn't sentence another human to death. It is against their principles. The Bible says, "Thou shalt not kill." But they can be highly impressionable. Often from one question to the next — What about Charles Manson? What about Adolf Hitler? What about a brutal, awful, heinous murder? — a remarkable metamorphosis occurs. *Oh, that! Yes, I could do it for something like that.* Even jurors who profess at the outset strong religious convictions against capital punishment are easily converted when the question raises the issue of "the law of the land." *If the judge asks me to follow the law of the land, yes, I could do it.*

The odd juror is stubborn, even truculent. In the morning session, a man in his mid-fifties took his seat and glared down the table at Judge Fine. "I don't want to be a juror," he declared. "I've got no time for lawyers and judges." Barry

Weinstein and Chuck Burton went through the motions of questioning him, but he proved as intractable as a fire hydrant. One of his sons was a policeman. His daughter had been beaten up. A niece had been killed in a car accident in Delray by a drunk driver. When Burton tried to continue, the man stood his ground. He said, "I'm not going to give you any answers. It's that simple."

Judge Fine excused him from jury duty.

At the start of the afternoon session, the names of twelve jurors were announced and one by one they walked to the front of the courtroom and took their places in the jury box. Twelve men and women, young and old, black and white, good and true: a real estate salesman, a retired yacht captain, a Second World War sergeant, a member of the National Rifle Association, a Harvard-educated Protestant minister, a high school teacher, the wife of a man who once played trumpet with Woody Herman, a postal clerk, a legal secretary, a social worker, a grandmother, a receptionist.

This is when the lawyers perform more like orchestra conductors. It becomes not so much jury selection as jury preparation. The lawyers are trying to assemble a jury to their liking. Each lawyer has ten "peremptories," which means they can eliminate any ten prospective jurors on a whim. Some jurors, such as the man who said he had no time for lawyers and judges, can be struck "for cause." The tendency is to silence the discordant notes in the orchestra, to achieve a harmonious blend, a sound somewhere between middle-of-the-road and Muzak. They like an occasional brassy trumpet, if it plays their tune, but in the end they want the rank and file to sound like a well-rehearsed string quartet.

At the start of the afternoon session on the second day, there were twelve randomly selected prospective jurors from the pool of thirty-six. The lawyers played with them, listened for the discordant notes, used their peremptories to drop one, add another. As the afternoon wore on the jury box always held twelve prospective jurors, but here and there would be a new face.

Chuck Burton, the prosecuting attorney, was the first to address the assembled prospective jurors. He pulled a lectern to the middle of the front of the courtroom, slowly turned through pages of notes on yellow foolscap, then looked up and faced the jurors. Now he looked less like a fraternity president, more like Chuck, the charming older brother who'd done well in the world but liked to come home and toss the football around with the kids on the block. Burton looked up from the lectern at the jurors and asked, "How are ya doin'?"

After hours waiting on the hard wooden benches, the offhand greeting made the jurors suddenly feel a little more comfortable, as if what was to follow might actually be enjoyable. Burton smiled easily. Within an hour he was addressing each of the jurors by name, without referring to his notes.

When it was Barry Weinstein's turn, he dragged the lectern aside and stood alone in all his shortness in front of the jurors. He clicked on that sheepish smile that looked as if he had just let go a slow fart. He tugged at the underside of his beard. He pinched the end of his nose. He *picked* his nose. Over at the defence table, about fifteen feet behind Weinstein, Brian lowered his head and scribbled on a sheet of paper. His face seemed to be turning grey.

Weinstein walked over to a display board on which he had written:

Burden of proof
Presumption of innocence
Reasonable doubt

Over and over, as he addressed the jurors, Weinstein would walk over to the display board and tap at each line. When he tapped on "Burden of proof," he would gesture severely to Chuck Burton sitting at the prosecution table. When he tapped on "Presumption of innocence," he would point over at Brian at the defence table. When he tapped on "Reasonable doubt," he looked directly into the eyes of the jurors, sweeping across the two rows in the jury box as if they were shelves of rare old books. By sheer repetition, like the

water-drop torture, he was attempting to overcome the easy
charm of Chuck Burton.

By the end of the afternoon, Weinstein had gained ground
on Burton by hard work and persistence. He may not have
outdistanced the prosecutor, but he was running nearly
abreast of him. When Weinstein finished questioning the
jurors he actually managed to saunter back to the defence
table.

Both lawyers solicited the jurors' views on hockey,
which, decidedly, is not a Florida game. There was a
franchise called the Miami Screaming Eagles in a league
called the World Hockey Association, but neither the
Screaming Eagles nor the WHA lasted long enough to collect
the dust of memories. Only four of the prospective jurors had
actually been to a hockey game, and only one of them could
discuss it with any familiarity. Weinstein himself kept using
the word "field" when he should have said "ice."

The juror who knew something about hockey said it was
a good substitute for football, meaning it would be nice to
have in the schools when the football season ends —
whenever that is. He called it a fast, exciting "finesse sport"
and said if the rules ever were properly applied, it could be
more like basketball. A young salesman who had come to
Florida from Long Island said he found hockey "very boring"
but enjoyed going to Islander games when they were
winning. The man from the National Rifle Association said
he only watched hockey on television but he liked it. He said
it had about the same body contact as football "except these
guys got weapons in their hands." The grandmother was
impressed by the fact that hockey was the only game she'd
ever watched that had a penalty box. The legal secretary said
all the fighting and violence in hockey was only a put-on for
the audience, like professional wrestling. At the end, a
consensus emerged that, in south Florida at least, hockey lies
in a continuum somewhere between cock fighting and jai
alai.

Later, when court adjourned and the prospective jurors
were walking out, the receptionist, an attractive blonde,

winked at Brian and wished him luck. "Isn't that something?" he asked an observer. "She's the one who said she does ten-mile runs."

He said she could sit on his face any day.

Brian and Monica went to Charley's Eating and Drinking Saloon for dinner. It is in a mall at Military Trail and PGA Boulevard, around the corner from Monica's apartment. Brian had changed into an open-necked green shirt, casual pants and running shoes. Monica ordered a screwdriver. Brian ordered two Buds. There was tension between them.

A discussion about Monica appearing in the courtroom — she had dropped by for about half an hour — soon turned into an argument. Not a loud argument, but one that could get noisy. And Brian raised something else: the time Monica brought a newspaper clipping to her office in the Governmental Center, which also houses the Public Defenders Office. It was a clipping of a front-page story in *The Buffalo News* of Brian's arrival in that city in August, the occasion of the ox roast near Niagara Falls.

Brian's lawyers didn't want him being conspicuous, didn't want him holding press conferences or giving interviews or discussing the case. The story in the newspaper was headlined, "Despite Pending Murder Case, Spencer Gets a Hero's Welcome." The story rhapsodized about how Brian's "boisterous laugh and constant effervescence made jail seem a million miles away." Monica took the clipping to her office to make copies.

Brian said, "But a lot of people saw it. And it was embarrassing to me."

Monica tried to keep the discussion under control. "I wasn't trying to embarrass you. I only brought it to the office to make copies."

Brian didn't say anything for a few seconds, then turned to Monica, who was sitting beside him, and looked down into her eyes. Very evenly, he told her, "I just want you to admit you're wrong."

"Okay!"

"Okay."

Having settled that issue, Brian's attention switched to the day in court. Some things bothered him, not least Barry Weinstein's mannerisms.

"Too jerky," Brian said, and then he imitated Weinstein tugging at his beard and pinching the end of his nose. "Chuck's smoother. He's more articulate. He's a better communicator. The jury's going to like Chuck better than Barry."

Brian did not like the juror from Long Island, the young salesman who said hockey was boring, but he liked going to the Islander games when the team was winning. "He's not a fan, not a real fan," Brian said. "He goes when they're winning. Big fucking deal. He's probably got company tickets. I know the type. They go to the games to be seen." Nor did he appreciate the young man correcting one of the lawyer's questions. "To *whom?*" he had responded. A little prissy, that.

Then he mentioned the legal secretary who said hockey fights are staged for the fans. Brian drained his first beer of the evening and said, "I can assure you, hockey fights are not a put-on."

V

Brian always talked easily about fighting. He remembered the magazine story I had written about him when he was starting out in the NHL, the one he carried with him in the attaché case when he was arrested.

The story began:

> *Some men have grown to old age without ever having been in a fist fight. Others can remember three or four. Brian Spencer is only twenty-two but he has been in so many fights he really can't remember all of them. They are a blur of hot blood and sudden rapid punches.*

"You're wearing maybe twenty-five pounds of equipment, so first you have to throw your gloves down. And you can only hit the guy in the face. You can't hit him anywhere else. I mean, what's the use? You might break your hand. You've got no footing so you try to anticipate what the other guy's going to do. Try to brace yourself and keep upright, because if he puts you on the ice he has an advantage. Try to block him, stay on your feet, maybe throw him on his back and get a few in. You use discretion, of course, but I can take all kinds of punches and I know I'm not going to get hurt. If he hits you with a stick, fine. You bleed a little, you get sewn up."

He was cocky then, ready for anything. In hockey, twenty-two is not inexperienced when it comes to hockey fights. The serious players have been in the game for more than a decade and from about the age of ten they have known the risks and challenges. Grown men like to hear about the fighting in hockey, because most of them have not been in an honest scrap since grade school. They are fascinated, intrigued. The times when they reflect on honour and courage, they wonder how they would perform if it came to fists in a bar, an alley or a parking lot. Even grown men who publicly decry the fighting often can't avert their eyes from the TV screen when two players are going at it by the boards, or when the teams spill onto the ice for a ragged Pier Six brawl.

And it sells. Hockey is the only sport outside of professional wrestling that encourages rule violations and regards penalties as valid statistics. Brian began his NHL career when the league expanded from six teams to twelve teams in two divisions, with new franchises in St. Louis, Pittsburgh, Los Angeles, Oakland, Minnesota and Philadelphia. Because Americans were not intimately acquainted with the essence of hockey, the violence and the fighting became part of an unofficial marketing strategy best captured in the remark, "I went to the fights and a hockey game broke out." There are videos produced consisting entirely of hockey fights, one flailing battle after another, often set to music. It is primitive, atavistic, a modern version of the spectacle of the gladiators.

In his first game with the Toronto Maple Leafs, when he was called up from Tulsa for the last nine games of the 1969-70 season, Brian encountered the reality of the National Hockey League. He thought he knew everything about violence on the ice and then Johnny McKenzie of the Boston Bruins crushed him from behind and tore a ligament in his shoulder. McKenzie, whose nickname was "Pie" because of his round, cherubic face, liked the rough stuff, though in the NHL he was regarded as a master of the cheap shot. In the off-season he competed as a rodeo rider in Alberta.

"He ran me from behind," Brian said. "I wasn't paying attention. I didn't know the players. Like, Phil Esposito, he's not going to run you from behind. And Bobby Orr's not going to do it. Bobby Orr's one of the nicest individuals I've ever met. I was in awe of his talent."

In Brian's mind the highest compliment he ever received came after a game in Boston against the Bruins. Brian was enjoying a beer in a bar with his Maple Leaf teammates when Orr, sitting with friends across the room, smiled at him and gave him the thumbs-up signal. On his way out, Orr stopped at Brian's table and said in admiration, "Spin, you *hurt*."

Brian's professional hockey career coincided with the worst of NHL goonery, when players like Dave Schultz of the Philadelphia Flyers became stars, their penalty minutes toted up with as much satisfaction as goals and assists. In his book *The Hammer*, Schultz confessed, "once I stepped into the rink I became a completely different person — some called me a wild animal — who succeeded in his profession because of his fists. What had once been a fast-paced, beautiful, rough but straightforward game had turned into a question of intimidation. Scaring the living wits out of the enemy was almost as important as skating, shooting, and stickhandling."

Schultz played 535 games in the NHL and accumulated 2,294 minutes in penalties. Brian played in 533 games and accumulated 634 penalty minutes, making him an angel compared to The Hammer. Brian did not like to be called a goon. He preferred the words "protect" or "counter" instead of "enforce." He knew his job was not to score goals, but to "shake things up" and "get things going" and to be a physical presence on the ice. It was never more evident than in his years with the Buffalo Sabres, when he played with high-scoring, dipsy-doodling shooters like Gilbert Perreault and Rick Martin. Brian never lost track of the ironies either. When he played for the New York Islanders, Brian once broke Perreault's leg in a game. "I hit a guy so hard in the game it actually put *me* into shock," Brian said. "The guy was Mike Robitaille. When I hit him, he flew into Perreault and Perreault went down and broke his leg. I thought they were going to murder me in Buffalo that night. As it turned out, I got traded to Buffalo and when I arrived Perreault was still out. Next season, my job was to protect Perreault. That's the way things go in the NHL."

Being a leftwinger, Brian's immediate opponent was the opposing team's rightwinger, but in games against Philadelphia, sometimes the Flyers would put a leftwinger against him, someone like Schultz, or another enforcer called Bob "Mad Dog" Kelly. With the Flyers, it was a strategy to counter an opposing enforcer, and to protect someone like Bobby Clarke, a diabetic, but the captain of the Flyers and a high-scoring centre who hid behind the brawn of his linemates.

Brian could have carved out an NHL career similar to Schultz's. He was strong enough, and willing enough, but he was not that adept at fighting on skates. He was not a slugger. His style was to use his incredible strength to wrestle opponents to the ice, then get in his licks. He did not often go looking for fights, but he never backed down, and never gave up. Opposing players did not like to go against Brian because he went wild when he was angry. They saw something snap in his eyes. There was an expression at the time and it was *Don't wake up the Spin.*

"I intimidated people too," Brian said. "I can sense if a man is afraid of me, the way a dog senses if you're afraid. I was many times afraid, but my way of being afraid was to make a stand — not retreat. Still, you shake."

He detested dirty players, those who could only intimidate, and those who used their sticks as weapons. Long after he had retired from hockey — he might be in a bar, at a dinner table — Brian's eyes would glaze over when he remembered certain players he plainly did not like. One was Ted Green, the Bruins' defenceman who once required brain surgery after a stick-swinging fight with Wayne Maki of the St. Louis Blues in a pre-season exhibition game in 1969. Two years later, in Boston, Brian ran into Green, fell to the ice and Green loomed over him and snarled, "You do that to me again, kid, and I'll kill you." Green then twisted the blade of his stick into Brian's forehead.

Another player Brian hated was Dave Hutchison of the Los Angeles Kings. In one game, Hutchison crosschecked

Brian in the side of the head with what Brian called "G-force," and then Hutchison did the unthinkable: he spat in Brian's face. "I mean, I was so violated. So now the game is absolutely not important to me any more. The next shift I didn't even know there were any people in the stands, or any game being played. I took a run at him as soon as I hit the ice. I had only one thing on my mind. I wanted to actually. . . ."

Brian stopped to edit his thoughts.

"I wanted to actually hurt this person. And I did hurt him. When I hate, I hate; when I love, I love. There's many ways of going through life real casually, but I didn't. I never have been much of a casual person. I'm pretty much of an extremist. And I hated Dave Hutchison. And I hate him today. I hate him just as violently today. I know he was just doing his job. If he didn't do some violence, he wouldn't be on the team. That was his fear."

VI

At the end of the afternoon session, Leon asked Brian to stay behind in the Public Defenders Office to listen to Diane's taped testimony to the police. Brian didn't want to stay. He was tired. He told Leon he'd heard the tape so many times he had it memorized. By six o'clock the discussion was becoming strained between Leon and Brian. Richard Greene interceded and tried to calm Brian, then he accompanied him to the elevator and down to the main floor of the Governmental Center. When the elevator doors opened, Greene was holding Brian by the elbow in a friendly, avuncular way.

"You did well today," Greene told Brian, and then they said good night.

The altercation didn't bother Leon. "I much prefer a defendant to be anxious than complacent," he said, explaining that caution is always the wisest course in any murder trial. As an investigator for the Public Defenders Office, and as a homicide detective in Philadelphia, Leon had sat through many trials, and observed many juries.

"If there's one thing I've come to believe, it's that jurors lie. They may not know they're lying, but they're lying. They say the defendant is innocent until proved guilty, but I suspect it's lip service and they really believe the defendant has to prove his innocence. They think he's guilty of something because he's there."

CHAPTER THREE

Wednesday:
Life at
the Fort

I

In the morning, Chuck Burton told the prospective jurors this story. Suppose he and his assistant over there — he pointed to Robert Zaun, the young paralegal sitting at the prosecution table — set out one evening to rob a 7-Eleven store.

"Okay? So I get out of the car and I go into the 7-Eleven. Bob over there, he's waiting outside in the getaway car. Now, after I hold up the 7-Eleven, are we both guilty of robbery?"

Some of the jurors nodded, yes.

"Right. We'd both be guilty, even though Bob's sitting out there in the car."

Burton looked down at the lectern and shuffled his papers.

"Now, what if I shot and killed the clerk? Who would be, who would you feel was more guilty?"

Some of the jurors looked confused. No doubt a few of them had learned something new about robbery and guilt, no matter who actually does the robbing, but they did not want to appear thick about murder and guilt and who actually does the murdering. Shooting the 7-Eleven clerk sounded a whole lot different, much more serious. Burton had carefully explained to them that a felony murder, a killing that happens during a felony, even if it is not planned, even if it is accidental, is first-degree murder. But, the getaway man might have had no idea the holdup man was going to shoot the clerk. If the getaway man had known the holdup man was going to kill someone he might not have agreed to be the

89

getaway man.

Burton set the scene again and took them through it slowly, juror by juror. They all came to believe that Chuck would be guiltier than Bob.

II

Brian returned to Fort St. James the summer after the 1970-71 hockey season, the summer after his father had been killed. He drove home in a gold Cadillac he had bought in Tulsa the year before, for $4,600. The car was five years old, but it was a beauty, with soft, cushioned seats and brocade trim. He bought a licence plate with the initials "BRS" and attached it below the grill at the front.

It was a good summer. In Fort St. James, with Linda, his beautiful Oklahoma wife, the new baby and the gold Cadillac, Brian returned as the boy triumphant. The town named him "Governor of New Caledonia" for a day. He was presented with a beaver skin from Ottawa. He rode in a float in a parade. Men he used to play hockey with on Stuart Lake asked him about Dave Keon and Norm Ullman. He kept in shape by loading lumber into boxcars for fifteen dollars a night.

During his hockey career, Brian liked to tell stories of growing up in the north central interior. He knew what the sports writers wanted and he dished it out, the wilder and woollier the better. The further he got from Fort St. James, in time and place, the colder it became — fifty, sixty, seventy below. The dirt-floor shack, melting snow for baths, shooting moose from the kitchen window, killing his first bear when he was in grade school. They were carefully designed "quotes," good stuff to sprinkle into the daily locker-room interviews. In the press, to his mother's chagrin, he became a hillbilly, a mountain man. Brian was the first one from Fort

91

St. James to make it to the NHL, so who was to know? And yet, the hyperbole did not go far enough. His stories were cartoons, caricatures, intended as much to appease as to exaggerate. With those he knew and trusted, and they were few, he would say, "People in the cities have no concept what it's like up there." He would tell them different stories.

The Indian reserve in Fort St. James is in the middle of town and, though there was no town ordinance governing such matters, it was understood and accepted that whites were not allowed in the reserve after nine o'clock at night. Late one evening, during the summer 1971 visit, well after nine o'clock, Brian met an old friend from his school days, a native woman, and he offered to drive her home. When they arrived at her house on the reserve, she invited him in for tea. As Brian sat in the kitchen, waiting for the kettle to boil, he heard loud, bashing noises from other rooms in the house. It sounded like a wild party. A door to the kitchen opened and an Indian man, very drunk and bleary-eyed, looked in to see a white man sitting at the table. The man banged the door shut, gunshots rang out, and Brian watched in horror as splinters cracked off the door to the kitchen. He ran from the house, jumped in the gold Cadillac and spun away. Two days later, at the pub at the Fort St. James Hotel, the man who had very nearly shot him walked over to Brian's table and said, "I'm sorry, Brian. I didn't know it was you."

To reach Fort St. James, most visitors fly into Prince George, where the air on a hot summer night smells like dirty socks. It is the smell of the pulp mills, usually one's first and last impression of the place. From Prince George, they drive or board a bus west toward Vanderhoof, then north up a winding, gravel-and-tar highway to Fort St. James. The further north one goes, the more spectacular the scenery: lakes, mountains, forests as far as the eye can see, sometimes a bear or a moose thrashing through the underbrush. Rocks spin up off the road, cracking headlights and smashing into windshields.

The people of Fort St. James call Vanderhoof "the Hoof,"

and Prince George "Prince." The official name of Roy Spencer's gravel pit was "Spencer's Aggregate Gravel," because too many people in town did not know what aggregate meant. Besides Stuart Lake, the main body of water by Fort St. James, there is a Stuart River, a Pitka Bay and Poorens Beach Provincial Park. The main industry is logging, which is interrupted twice in the year, a month at spring break-up, and a month at fall freeze-up.

Fort St. James remains proud of its fur trade origins. The traders had unloaded pelts from boats in the shallow waters by the shore of Stuart Lake, at the site of the Hudson's Bay Company fort, now the town's only tourist attraction. At the entrance to the fort, there is a plaque on which is written in English, French and Indian:

> *Simon Fraser and John Stuart established Fort St. James among the Carrier Indians in 1806. Originally a North West Company post passed to the Hudson's Bay in 1821. From the beginning it was an important centre of trade and cooperation with the Indians. It became, under the Hudson's Bay Company, the chief trading post in north central British Columbia and the administrative centre of the large and prosperous district of New Caledonia. Throughout its history Fort St. James has been an important link in communications with northern British Columbia.*

The Oblate priests established a mission at Fort St. James in 1873 and worked closely with the Indians, mainly Carrier Indians, but also Sekani, Babine and Chilcotin. The Oblates pressured the Indians to end their ceremonial potlatches, which involved days of feasting, spirit dances, theatre and gift-giving. The priests regarded potlatches as heathen rituals, though they were an important means of observing initiation rites, mourning, the investiture of chiefs, and establishing claims to names, powers and privileges. The Carrier Indians used to call Fort St. James *Nakasleh*, which meant "arrows floating by," in reference to an ancient, bloody skirmish.

During the Second World War, a big mercury mine

opened thirty miles from town. People in Fort St. James
thought it might be the first step in developing a diversified
economy, creating money and jobs, but the mine closed
down soon after the war and has been abandoned ever since.
Murray Hill's father used to haul beef and pork to the mine
camp. In those days, there were no paved roads and the few
cars and trucks travelled over "corduroy roads" made of
jackpine and gravel. If a bridge washed out in the spring
runoff, the trick was to remove the fan belt from the vehicle's
engine on one side of the creek, drive through, then put it
back on when the vehicle reached the other side. It kept
water from spraying over the sparkplugs.

Murray Hill, Brian Spencer's boyhood friend, never left
Fort St. James, or "the Fort" as it is called in the north central
interior. Many times he has driven to nearby Vanderhoof for
repairs and supplies, sometimes as far as Prince George, but
that is as much city as he can tolerate and even that much
makes him uncomfortable. He does not like city traffic,
waiting at red lights, looking for places to park. He does not
like to be surrounded by strangers. When Murray and his
wife, Bonnie, and their three children, Steven, Wesley and
Misty, went to Vancouver for a vacation in the summer of
1987 Murray did not leave the hotel for the entire week.

He is a small, compact man, about five-feet-three, with a
full beard and a mischievous, impish smile. Most days he
goes around town in jeans and moccasins, a plaid shirt
flapping open over a T-shirt. He carries a small knife in a
leather sheath on his belt. He tells a good story and likes a
good joke and his laugh is high-pitched, sometimes almost
a cackle. As he drives about town in his four-wheel-drive
truck, he shouts hellos to people, asks them how's business
and bids them okay, see ya. He has stories to tell about all of
them, young and old, men and women, whites and natives.
And he has more stories to tell about those who left and those
who died.

→ Murray used to work at the gas station next to the
two-storey white house where he grew up. It was his father's
station, but Murray took it over when he died. In the summer

of 1987, he leased the station to Chevron for $5,000 a month, which he splits with his younger brother, Kerry, who lives in a house across the way from Murray on Sowchea Road on the western edge of Fort St. James. Murray wants to clear more land, raise cows and do some serious logging.

Murray built his own house on Sowchea Road. It started as a shack, just for him, but after he married Bonnie he started adding on, using logs from the woods out back for the additions. Bonnie is about half a foot taller than Murray, but the dimensions of the house are strictly his; unwary visitors taller than five feet, five inches crack their foreheads against the door jambs going from room to room. What is now the living-room and kitchen area, the two rooms separated by a brick fireplace, used to be a pigpen. At one time Murray and Bonnie kept pigs, chickens, rabbits and ducks. They still have three cows, which they allow to roam free in the bush, and a horse.

They depend mainly on the wrought-iron stove in the kitchen for heat; when it is very cold they start a fire in the fireplace. The floors are carpeted, and there are old, comfy chairs and a chesterfield. Above the door to the side porch is a gun rack with several rifles, one of them encased in a beaded Indian sheath. On the porch is a large white freezer, which is usually stocked with fish and moose and reindeer meat. In the backyard, Bonnie grows potatoes, mushrooms, carrots, Swiss chard, peas, beets, lettuce, cauliflower, onions, beans, cucumbers, tomatoes, raspberries, strawberries, Saskatoon berries, and zucchinis the size of fire hydrants. With $2,500 a month, the huge vegetable garden, and meat and fish from the wilds, Murray and his family are well fed and healthy.

In summer, the boys sleep in a tin shed out back, by the garden. There is a bear rug over the door, a bobcat skin on one of the walls and the usual posters of rock and hockey stars and one of Miss Piggy. In a corner is a large cardboard box loaded with hockey equipment — elbow pads, tendon guards, shin pads, shoulder pads, skates. Murray floods a rink every winter in the backyard and the whole family skates on it. He works Steven and Wesley hard in hockey, trying to give them "an edge," which he says is what Roy Spencer did for Brian. Murray sees hockey as an "out," an escape from Fort St. James, which is what Brian achieved. If the boys are not good enough to make it to the National Hockey League, Murray will encourage them to play in Europe or teach in a hockey school. He does not like the "goon hockey" in the NHL and believes American college hockey is what hockey should be. The best hockey game he ever saw was a 3-3 tie between the Soviets and Canada in Montreal on New Year's Eve in the early 1970s. Murray watched it on television.

Bonnie grew up in Surrey, but because of family problems she was shipped up to Fort St. James in her teens. She moved in with Irene Spencer at the farm after Roy was killed. That was when she met Murray. She is tall and slender, with long, black, curly hair. She has a lovely, old-fashioned face. When she bakes in the kitchen the radio is always tuned to a country-and-western station. Her father didn't want her to marry Murray because he had a reputation as a wild man, which Murray doesn't deny. He is the first to admit he has a mean streak, especially when he's been drinking, which he doesn't do as much any more, though he hasn't quit altogether. "I go out maybe a couple of times a year and I like to give 'er shit — have fun like the old days. I can't see havin' two beers and sittin' around and goin' to sleep. That's no good for me. I like to get kinda wild and have fun."

He has a quick temper that has got him in trouble more than a few times, most recently at the pub at the Fort St. James Hotel, reputed to be the toughest bar in all of the north central interior, perhaps in all of Canada. He was with Kerry that night. The waitress had left ten dollars too much on the table and when she went to retrieve it, Murray refused to give it to her. The bar manager came over and, as Murray likes to say, there was a "battle." The bar manager grabbed Murray from behind and wrapped his arms around him, but Murray, wriggling and twisting like a wildcat, bit the man's finger clean off, which so startled the bar manager that he loosened his grip, allowing Murray to throw him over his shoulder. Then he spat the bloody finger on the floor. Murray and Kerry were barred from the hotel for life.

Which was just as well, he figured. He had been wasting too much time boozing anyway. His family was growing up, the boys were into hockey, and there were too many wasted Saturdays and Sundays. He was tired of feeling listless, worn out, and he was hearing about too many drinking drivers mangled in smash-ups, drowning, knifing each other, getting their heads blown off and blowing their own heads off. He heard weird reports about hallucinations. An elderly friend in the Fort told Murray he quit drinking the day he was walking along the road and watched a boy kick a stone, which shot up off the ground, circled a building and came flying around the other side at him. Another friend quit drinking the day he was driving down the main street and saw his wife and sister-in-law driving by in the opposite direction, sitting on the hood of a car. The apparition was so real the man jerked his truck to a stop in the middle of the street. He hasn't touched a drop since.

And Murray had already suffered physical injury as a result of hard drinking. One summer evening Murray was in his truck by the graveyard drinking with an Indian friend. As they talked and joked and drank, the Indian friend pulled out a small knife and for no apparent reason plunged it into the top of Murray's thigh. Murray looked down and watched the handle of the knife quiver, then felt the muscles in his leg tighten. His friend laughed and cracked open another beer. Murray pushed in the cigarette lighter, waited, and when it popped out, pushed it into his friend's cheek. The man didn't flinch, just sat there stoically as the smell of burning flesh filled the cab. When Murray removed the lighter and put it back in its socket, his friend said, "Okay, now we're even."

Murray sometimes takes his children to the Roman Catholic cemetery in Fort St. James to remind them of the evils of drink. Most of the Indians are buried in the Catholic graveyard, which is beside Our Lady of Good Hope, one of the oldest churches in British Columbia. The graveyard is enclosed by a white board fence and overlooks Stuart Lake, by the Government Pier. Murray takes them from plot to plot, from tombstone to tombstone, telling stories about the occupants.

"Here's — Drowned himself."

"This one's — Died in a car accident, drunk, thirty-three years old."

"This guy put a shotgun in his mouth, blew his head off. Said he was gonna."

"There's — Drank herself to death."

Murray walks quickly, lightly, from grave to grave, punctuating each of his pronouncements by hawking into the grass beside the graves, more from nervousness than any disrespect. Some of the graves have headstones with a carved depiction of a northern skyline or a logging truck on a highway. Some are decorated with patterns made of crushed, coloured glass. People seldom die of old age in Fort St. James. There are few graves for citizens who lived to their seventies or eighties. Most of the graves are those of young Indians. "Maybe God wants 'em quicker," Murray said. Their deaths seem to occur in clusters, as if there had been epidemics, but they were killed in car smash-ups, shootings, knifings, logging accidents, drownings, suicides. There was a cluster in 1979, another in 1982.

"This one over here — shot, murdered. He was a no good son-of-a-bitch. Somebody shoulda done it long ago."

"This guy, he was standing outside his truck, havin' a smoke, and one of the logs rolled off his load and hit him in the chest. He just went 'Ooof!' and fell down and died."

"And old — He was a good guy. Once I seen his wife chasin' him in the yard with an axe and just as she was swingin' it I yelled and he ducks and this axe goes flyin' over his head."

And there was the grave of a young Indian everyone called "Toothless." He was only nineteen, friendly and outgoing, always joking and playing pranks and grinning his toothless grin. Everyone in town liked him, Indians and whites. He had long, black hair that blew in wisps in the wind and swayed to and fro when he walked. In the pub one day, Toothless sat with a couple and, trying to be funny, joked that the man's girlfriend once gave him a dose of the clap. The remark infuriated the man. He told Toothless he was going to kill him. Toothless just laughed. The man left, fetched a gun, came back and shot Toothless dead.

Just telling the bare bones of the story makes Murray nervous. The killing of Toothless bothered him for a long time, most of a year. He would wake up in the early hours in the morning in his darkened bedroom and see Toothless's face across the room, grinning, his long black hair blowing in wisps, and then the face would slowly dissolve in the wallpaper.

Murray started grade one with Brian and Byron Spencer. Murray lived in town, in the two-storey, white house off the main drag, by the gas station. In winter there was hockey to preoccupy them, pick-up games on Stuart Lake and on frozen ponds, many of the players wearing boots instead of skates. Brian used to give Murray his old skates and hockey sticks. There was no indoor arena, not like the one today, which has grey and brown signs along one side wall advertising the New Caledonia Motel, Abe's Restaurant, Bumper to Bumper Auto Parts Professional, New Caledonia Sports and Don's Chevron. There is a grandstand on one side, with heaters suspended above it, and an electronic scoreboard. In the lobby is a concession stand and a glassed-in case for trophies and plaques. The trophies and plaques go back only to the early 1970s, so none have Brian Spencer's name on them. For a time there was a plaque in the trophy case with Roy Spencer's name on it, and the first clock at the arena was dedicated to him. After his death, the townspeople wanted to honour him this way, along with a man called Tom Velkjar, who died about the same time as Roy when his car got stuck in the snow outside of town. He died of carbon-monoxide poisoning.

The only other hockey players from the Fort who made it to the NHL are Larry and Jim Playfair, who came along a generation after Brian. Larry, who now plays for the Los Angeles Kings, won the most valuable player trophy playing bantam hockey in 1971-72 and 1972-73. His younger brother Jim was drafted by the Edmonton Oilers, then moved to the Chicago Black Hawks. Another Playfair boy, Keith, was killed one night when his car went out of control and crashed into a pole across from the graveyard where Roy Spencer is buried. Now Keith's grave is close by Roy's.

When the hockey season was over there was not much to do in town. Most days Brian and Murray would hunt squirrels, grouse, ducks and beaver on Spencer's Ridge, or slide down the hill at Roy Spencer's gravel pit. When they were older, they would take native girls to the bush and have fun with them. Some days Brian and Murray would play with stray cats. They would round them up, take them to a barn and then herd them toward a dog and watch the dog chase and kill them. Sometimes they used to go out in a boat and hook up cats with fishing tackle and drag them around the lake until they drowned. Murray cackles when he talks about the cats, says it seemed funny at the time.

One afternoon he and Brian were playing in a barn with two Indian teenagers, a boy and a girl. They made them drink wine, then they stood them on buckets and put nooses around their heads, and kicked the buckets out from under them, laughing and laughing. One of Murray's older sisters saw what they were doing and called the police and that put an end to that. There was not much to do in town. Years later, the boy ended up in a jail cell and hanged himself with his T-shirt.

During the brief summers, there were no baseball leagues with organized schedules and team uniforms. They played work-your-way-up in the scruffy field behind the school, and when Brian came to bat they could never get him out. On a summer afternoon when Brian was ten, he got in a fight with Dale Blackburn, who was three years older. They were playing work-your-way-up and Blackburn started pushing Brian around. It became a fistfight-wrestling match, with the two boys rolling in the dirt. Blackburn was bigger and stronger and he climbed on top of Brian, but the fight went on and on and Brian would not quit. Eventually Blackburn tired and Brian rolled on top of him and, as Murray remembers, he "tuned him up real good." According to Murray, that was the first time Brian realized he was tough. "He just wouldn't quit. Never! Same when he was playing hockey. It was bred right into him from his father."

Brian hated to lose, and not just at hockey or baseball or fighting. Murray is a natural artist. He can sit down with a notepad and in minutes do a beautifully detailed pencil sketch, with perspective and shading, of a moose or lynx or a skidder pulling logs out of the bush. When he was a boy, his parents and teachers encouraged him to draw and so he entered an art contest and came first, which won him a package of artist's supplies from Europe. That inspired Brian to try drawing. He was good at it, but not as good as Murray, and Brian saw this as a failure. It angered him, and for a long time he wouldn't speak to Murray.

Murray revelled in Brian's company. They grew up fast in Fort St. James, sharing good times, crazy times, their escapades involving drink and women hardly appropriate for retelling in the locker-room interviews. Of the two, Brian was the natural leader; life seemed larger to Murray when Brian was with him. Brian was courage, adventure and serendipity, Peter Pan with a five o'clock shadow. There was no telling how a day with Brian would end or what turn it might take.

Brian always worked hard during the off-season to keep himself in shape. He took the toughest jobs he could find, loading and unloading timber, and he worked out on his own. One day at the sawmill, Brian and Murray were watching logs being carried along on a conveyor belt, which was about four feet across, with a flat portion in the middle. The logs would come up fast and go flying into the reservoir. Next thing Murray knew, Brian had climbed onto the conveyor belt and was running, using it as a treadmill. He had to run flat out, too. If he didn't keep up with the speed of the belt, or if he fell, he would have been dragged along and carried over the edge into the reservoir and possibly to his death. A rowdyman literally running for his life. Murray had never seen anything like it.

Brian kept in touch with Murray only sporadically after he left Fort St. James to play hockey. He saw him in the summers when he played junior hockey, but once he made it to the NHL, except for two trips home with each of his wives, he put Fort St. James behind him. He did send Murray a letter from Florida in 1982, in which he described the Hulk and listed the weapons in and on the vehicle. The list of "armaments" included a .50-calibre demilitarized machine gun, a 1460 Weatherby, a .41 magnum pistol, two .38-calibre pistols, and a 9-mm Luger. The last item on the list was "one mean bitter dangerous ex-left-winger who is faster than speeding bullets and leaps away from alimony payments in single bounds."

He wrote Murray again early in 1987, when he was in jail. It was a long rambling letter, written on sheets of yellow paper.

> We have seen a lot of life together and no matter what the outcome of the trial you will always be a very special part of my life. There are some times when I regret leaving so young, departing my real home to land in a social atmosphere that even to this day is foreign to me. . . .
>
> Remember carrying wood after school? Remember you, Shelly (your dog) and I going up to Dickinson's Mountain? Remember fishing up the creek? Remember the tow truck trip out the North Road and the five-gallon bucket full of beer? Remember the day I was drunk on wine and stopped everyone on the road?

That was a summer afternoon after Brian's first, nine-day stint with the Maple Leafs. He and Murray spent the day with a jug of wine, prowling the roads and bushes around Fort St. James, laughing and telling stories. Late in the day, when they were stumbling back to town, they encountered some tourists gathered by their cars on the shoulder of the highway. Brian walked up to each of them, and, flushed with an inebriated bonhomie, shook their hands and introduced himself as, "Brian Spencer of the Toronto Maple Leafs." At that time, Murray thought Brian was pretty full of himself.

I'll bet you don't remember you gave me my first drink of whiskey at your house, right around Christmas. Remember the old squaw with the wooden leg?

That was another day, before Brian left Fort St. James on his hockey adventures. While their classmates were going steady, taking their girlfriends to movies at the town hall, Brian and Murray used to spend hot afternoons on Spencer's Ridge with some of the native women from town. Murray, when he lapsed into the low, monotonic patois of the natives, used to say native women "liked t'fuck d'way dey liked a gud shit." That day he and Brian were driving along one of the dusty roads near town and Brian made a bet that he would pick up the next native woman they saw and have sex with her, no matter what. Down the road they came upon a leathery old woman hobbling along the gravel shoulder ahead of them. They stopped the truck, invited her in — she was drunk, and willing, according to Murray — and drove off to an abandoned cabin where Brian had his way with her. It became a joke and Murray always referred to the old native woman as "Brian's girlfriend with the wooden leg."

I'll miss your mom and dad. They were like my parents whenever I was in town and I don't know if you knew about Nelson, down at hockey school. Every day I would drive up where they were camped and Crafty and Penny [Murray's parents] and I would build a small fire and then just sit there for hours drinking scotch. I remember your dad loved scotch. He tried like hell to get me to like the taste. After a while it got better and better. I loved that man. I only saw him mad the couple of times we fucked up, but he didn't have to say much. When Crafty was mad he wasn't smiling and telling jokes. Real simple, all you'd have to do was look at him.

I miss those times around Christmas, after school, the atmosphere of your home. A few Japanese oranges, fill the wood box. I never know why your mom's ice cream always tasted so good, from the freezer on the back porch. . . .

I'm so happy about you having a happy family and I envy your relationship with your children. I'm proud of your sons and their progress in hockey, a constitution obviously instilled in them by their old man, to never accept second in a race, to associate with kids better than you because it gives you a drive to be as good. They will be only as good as their peer group, and when they get as good as those boys older than them, move them up again. I've seen so many times in life that we get lazy when we achieve the level around us. . . .

God, I don't know where all the time is gone but when I get out of here I'm going to take this experience as a motivator to get on track again. I guess the transition from the NHL has been a shock of sorts, a post-NHL stress disorder like Vietnam. . . .

Murray there are people in New York that are going to write a book on my life so you are going to be a big part of my life in the book, especially from 0 to 17 years. You will be interviewed and asked for old pictures. Then they want to make a movie on my life story, so you will be played by some actor from Hollywood. We're going to be fucken movie stars.

Well my case goes to trial in a few months and I'm pretty sure I'll beat it. All I ever did was give that slut a place to stay, her parents didn't want her, and I couldn't get rid of the low rent. You know me, a fucken Salvation Army stupid fuck. I've got a big heart and it has been taken advantage of one last time. I'm getting bitter and Murray between you and me it might be time to come home — Fort St. James, a bush cabin and the majority of those city type fuckers better leave us alone. Now I feel like you always told

*me you felt, it's too bad progress breeds these assholes
and weak people who mooch off the hard workers.
You never know, I might just get like your cousin
Teddy's dad and live out there, because I'm tired —
divorce lawyers, women who suck my blood, people
who use me. Some days I don't care if they kill me
because it would be nothing that society already
hasn't done. . . .*

Now that he isn't working at the gas station, Murray has time
on his hands. He has a favourite spot in the woods by Lind
Lake. There is no road in. To get to it, he needs the
four-wheel-drive truck, and it is a bumpy ride. Anyone not
familiar with the bush would never find the way. Murray just
turns off a road, drives into the forest and goes on through the
trees for two or three miles, bouncing over stumps, grinding
through muck, twisting by trees as tall as ten-storey
buildings, with branches snapping and slapping at the
windshield. There does not appear to be even a trail, and on a
sunny afternoon it is dark as dusk, but Murray knows the
way. Suddenly there is a clearing, and a lake.

Here he has a cabin about the size of an ordinary
bathroom, with a long, narrow dock made of two felled trees,
and a canoe — there was supposed to be a canoe. When
Murray arrived, all he could see was an impression of the
craft in the reeds by the dock. Someone had taken the canoe,
maybe borrowed it, which is one of the courtesies of the wild,
or stolen it, which is hateful and unforgivable. Murray
walked to the end of the dock and scanned the lake and the
far shores through his binoculars. When he walked back, he
said, "I know who took it. There's a bad bugger lives on the
other side."

After the roaring, crashing drive through the forest, there
was a towering silence in the clearing, as if the world had
been turned off. You could almost hear the clouds. Murray
sat on a log in front of the cabin and in a voice barely above a
whisper he said that when they were kids, he and Brian used
to talk sometimes about killing someone, what it would feel

like. They talked about being mercenaries. But that was when they were boys, Murray said, and it was boy talk.

Murray invited Brian to live in the cabin if he ever decided to come back. He has not seen him in ten years, and maybe he doesn't know him anymore, but he told him in a letter that even if he had murdered the man in Florida it would not make a difference to their friendship. "I don't care if he popped off fifteen guys, doesn't matter to me, long as he didn't bother my family and was good to me."

On his way back to town, Murray stopped by the old Spencer farm. Irene and Byron were gone, Irene to a suburb of Victoria with her new husband Bill, Byron to a small town on Vancouver Island not far from the reform school at Brannon Lake. There were no flowers growing in the rock gardens Irene fastidiously maintained. The meathouse was still there, and the broken remains of the outdoor biffy, and in a grassy field out back the pentimento of the hockey rink Roy had built when the boys were growing up. The old five-room home was gone. It had burned to the ground in the spring.

After dinner one night in August, Murray took his dog, Puppy, for a long walk, across Sowchea Road and down a long trail through the trees to the beach at Stuart Lake. Along the way, the dog stopped and stood motionless, growling softly and staring into the trees.

"Bear," Murray said. "If it was a moose, Puppy'd be looking up. Nothin' to worry about. Puppy'd shoo it away." He walked on down the trail, less concerned about bears in the trees than about the traffic in Prince George.

The old Spencer summer home is still at the beach, with a huge driftwood stump marking the site of old bonfires and picnics. When Brian was going to school in the Fort, he carved his name on a tree behind the family cottage. Next to his name, he carved "Ingrid," the name of the prettiest girl in the school, Ingrid Hoff. Brian had a serious crush on her, but he never got anywhere with her. She works as a secretary at the school now.

In his letter to Murray from the Palm Beach County Detention Center, Brian asked about Ingrid. "Sure would love to hear from Ingrid and get a picture," he wrote. "I sure liked her, or loved or whatever. I think we all did, young and shy."

It was typical of Brian to romanticize the women who got away, the women he couldn't possess. During his first season in Tulsa, he corresponded with a woman he met when he played in Swift Current. Her name was Sharon Brown. She was a classical pianist. She moved to Toronto to study music. When Brian was playing in New York he heard that Sharon Brown once sang the national anthem at Maple Leaf Gardens. Brian thought he was in love with her.

Murray noticed changes in Brian when he returned to Fort St. James in his NHL days. "After he made it to the NHL, he got kind of a swelled head. When he brought Linda up here, he really showboated her around, this tall strawberry blonde with the big tits, from Oklahoma. But I got to know her, and she was real nice. I met both Brian's wives, and they were both nice women, but they always seemed kinda scared. The one area I disagreed with Brian was on the subject of his wives."

Murray thought Brian was cheap with them. The summer he brought Linda to Fort St. James, Brian attended the hockey school in Nelson and left her and their daughter Andrea fifty dollars to last the month. When she ran out of money, Brian was furious. She had to return pop bottles to make ends meet. In Murray's opinion, "Brian's biggest fault is the way he treats women. I think ninety percent of his problems is in his dink."

Brian met Linda in a bar after a game in Tulsa. She had been going out with Terry Clancy, the son of hockey legend Frank "King" Clancy. Toward the end of the 1969-70 season, Linda got pregnant, and they were married in July. Roy and Irene Spencer drove to Tulsa for the wedding. Brian had asked Byron to be best man, but Byron refused. He thought Brian was too young to get married.

"And he was right," Brian said years later, at a bar in Florida. "My father didn't want me to marry either. I was just so — unsocialized. I'd never dated. I'd never lived in a place where you had normal dating. Going to the movies. I don't know what to say when someone asks, 'Why did you marry her?' And I can't answer when someone says, 'How did you have three girls?' God, if only I hadn't been so susceptible to *women*."

He was shouting as he tried to explain this history. He crashed his fist on the table and the bottles and glasses rattled.

"I couldn't leave that girl! I couldn't say, 'Look, it's not my problem.' I didn't want to get married to someone I didn't love. She knew I was the type of person who would marry her, I'm honourable that way. It's a weakness. I let them get crowbarred into my life."

Brian is a romantic — tough, rough-edged, at times a loose cannon on deck, but nonetheless a romantic. When he talked of the sexual perquisites of life in the big leagues of hockey, he regretted the missed opportunity to court girls, to woo and win them. Being on the wrong side of the creek, he wasn't able to do that in Fort St. James; and when he became a professional hockey player, he found the tables were turned and the girls chased him; and before he knew it he was married, and a father.

"And then the *domestics*," Brian said, by which he meant wife and family, home and garden, cooking and shopping, the dinner parties, birthdays, Christmases, anniversaries. "These niceties, these barbecues, these rituals, these ceremonial occasions. They're not because people want to get together as much as a day that ya gotta be there!"

Even the wives' rooms at the arenas were a source of festering irritation for Brian. He did not think the wives of the players deserved a special room at the arena. He did not think they had earned it.

Brian often tells of the night he scored his first hat trick in a game at Maple Leaf Gardens. He was living with Linda in a rented house in Scarborough in the eastern suburbs of Toronto. That afternoon, Brian and Linda had an argument that became a shouting match. Furious, Brian left the house, slammed the door, drove to Maple Leaf Gardens and scored three goals against the Pittsburgh Penguins. "I always use it as a joke," Brian said. "Like, look how much better you do when you don't have to drag your wife along."

The truth was, Brian always performed better when he was emotionally charged — happy, sad, frightened, or angry. Emotion propelled him. That Sunday after his father's death, he played his best game since being called up from Tulsa. After any trade, when he had to prove himself on a new team in a new city, Brian always played with a fury. He burned like a nova. When things began to go smoothly, his game suffered, as if he were running on a lower octane.

With the marriage crumbling, Linda left Toronto late in the 1971-72 season and returned to Tulsa. Brian moved to a house in Toronto's west end, where he met the Antonaccis, a warm Italian family who virtually adopted him. Will Antonacci operated a hardware store and Brian often worked with him on weekends, loading and unloading equipment and repairing machinery. He loved being surrounded by the tools, tinkering, fixing things. The smell of oil and grease was an elixir to Brian. There was an old forklift at Will's hardware store that had not worked in years. Brian made it a special project after practices and before games, and after several weekends he got the forklift operating again.

Brian ate meals with the Antonaccis and played ball hockey with neighbourhood children in the driveway. The Antonaccis called him "Quindici," Italian for fifteen, Brian's number with the Maple Leafs. He became friends with Will's son, John, who was fourteen and an aspiring goaltender. One summer he took John with him to the hockey school in Nelson. John Antonacci later joined the RCMP. When Brian was arrested, he flew to West Palm Beach to visit him at the jail. "That's the effect he had on me," John explained. "When I read that he had been arrested, I knew I had to go and see him." He returned to Florida in October to attend Brian's trial, prepared to be a character witness.

In the summer of 1986, Brian traveled to Tulsa to visit Lee Price, an old friend he met when he played for the Tulsa Oilers. His marriage to Linda long ago ended, and Brian had not told her he was coming. Before heading back to Florida, Brian decided on a whim to drop by the high school his daughters were attending. He did not intend to meet them, he just wanted to catch a glimpse of them.

Brian entered the school and walked along the corridors until he came to the gymnasium. He knew all three of his daughters were cheerleaders. He stood at the door and looked through a window into the gym. There were about thirty girls, but he could not recognize any of his daughters. One of the mothers was standing beside him at the door and Brian told her his story. Brian thought he saw Andrea, his eldest daughter. He asked the woman, "Is that Andrea Spencer over there?" The woman said no, and she pointed to another girl in the crowd.

"I'll never forget that as long as I live," Brian said. "I had picked the wrong one."

During a break, the woman opened the door, walked into the gym and called Andrea over. She brought her out to Brian in the corridor and asked her, "Do you know him?" Andrea shook her head, and the woman said, "Well, that's your father." Andrea looked up into his eyes and said, "Brian?"

"Then the woman went back in and got Nicole and Kristen, all three of them are hugging me and they're saying, 'Don't cry, Daddy, don't cry.' Oh God, it was awful."

III

On the evening of the third day, Leon Wright arrived at his townhouse in Lake Worth at ten o'clock. He was in good spirits. After court recessed, he had been on the phone, trying to track down witnesses, some as far away as Colorado. He managed to reach a man he believed could be crucial to counter the testimony of Diane Delena. He said, "Tomorrow afternoon, when the defence and prosecution present their cases, the defence's plan will become obvious — someone else did it."

At the end of the afternoon session, the defence used one of its peremptories to strike the prospective juror who worked in real estate. The defence reasoned that because Dalfo was in real estate, the juror might sympathize with him. The prosecution struck the Harvard-educated clergyman who probably knew more about hockey than any of the other jurors. The clergyman had played hockey and was a longtime Boston Bruins fan. With considerable enthusiasm he told the court about old-timers like Milt Schmidt, who played centre for the "Kraut Line" in the 1930s. Leon knew the state didn't want too many brains on the jury.

He was still fretting about Brian's appearance. He thought it may have been a mistake insisting he appear in court in a shirt and tie. It made him look uncomfortable and hardened him. Perhaps it would be better for Brian to wear an open-necked shirt under a stylish sports jacket. That's how Gerry Hart dressed when he testified at the bail hearing in April. "He wore a polo shirt and designer jeans, and even though his nose had been broken a few times, he looked like a successful former athlete." Leon knew that Chuck Burton would be careful to make sure Diane dressed properly, projecting an image of a quiet, devoted housewife. Leon wanted Brian to look good too, because if the jury did not like the way he looked, they would not feel comfortable acquitting him, or as Leon often said, "They won't *want* to acquit him."

CHAPTER FOUR

Thursday: *The Hockey Vacuum*

I

In North America, the first week of October is a sporting extravaganza, a gridlock of jockdom. The four major professional sports jostle each other for space on the sports pages. Baseball's long, hot summer approaches the stately finale of the World Series. Pro football is in mid grunt. The basketball courts are chirping again with the squeaky sound of running shoes. It is opening week in the National Hockey League.

Brian stationed himself at his usual table in the courtyard at the Governmental Center with his coffee and newspaper. The *Post* carried a short wire service story, tucked well inside the sports section, titled, "Focus is on fighting as NHL opens season." The story explained that during the summer the NHL board of governors had ruled in favour of stiffer penalties to try to prevent bench-clearing brawls. Their decision was the result of an incident before a playoff game the previous May between the Montreal Canadiens and Philadelphia Flyers. According to the story in the *Post*, "The brawl started after Montreal winger Claude Lemieux, staging a pre-game ritual, attempted to shoot the puck into the Flyers' net. Flyers goaltender Chico Resch, since retired, was just leaving the ice when he spotted Lemieux's maneuver and threw his stick at the puck. Flyers defenceman Ed Hospodor charged Lemieux and touched off a surrealistic 15-minute brawl with some athletes in half undress at the Montreal Forum."

Brian flipped through the newspaper, looking for an account of his trial. He only scanned the sports section. He vaguely remembered Claude Lemieux from long ago; he had been a hotshot rookie at the Maple Leafs camp Brian attended in Peterborough in 1969, when they were both twenty years old. Brian had never heard of Ed Hospodor. He did not know which team had won the last Stanley Cup.

Back in May, in a lounge at the Holiday Inn on Singer Island, Brian sat at the bar with his friend Dan Martinetti. There was a television set on the bar carrying a Stanley Cup final game between the Philadelphia Flyers and the Edmonton Oilers, but the game held no interest for Brian. Instead, through the floor-to-ceiling windows of the dining room, he gazed out at the Atlantic Ocean breaking on the long, sandy beach. He once played against the Flyers in a Stanley Cup final, but it might as well have been a quiz show on the screen. He did not even bother to watch when the player he admires most in the modern game, Wayne Gretzky, stepped on the ice.

Brian was more excited about a chance encounter moments earlier, when he was standing in the lobby of the hotel. One of the elevator doors opened, two men stepped out and one of them gasped and shouted, "Spin!" It was Terry Crisp, who had played in the NHL in Boston, St. Louis, New York and Philadelphia. The man with him was Doug Risebrough, who used to play for the Montreal Canadiens. They were in Florida to attend a coaches' meeting, Crisp having been recently appointed head coach of the Calgary Flames. When Crisp played for the Boston Bruins, he was known as the other guy from Parry Sound — the main guy being Bobby Orr. Crisp and Brian were teammates on the expansion New York Islanders in the 1972-73 season. Brian was dazzled by the coincidence that they should bump into each other in the middle of May in the lobby of a resort hotel in West Palm Beach.

Dan Martinetti met Brian soon after Brian arrived in Florida from Long Island. In the office one morning at Hertz Rental Equipment in West Palm Beach, Martinetti noticed someone who looked familiar filling out an employment application —

the square shoulders and thick arms, the lumberjack face under the tangle of dark blond curls. Martinetti had come to Florida from Pittsburgh, where he was a fan of the Penguins. He thought it remarkable that one day he would be working side by side with a player he used to cheer for on the ice. Martinetti had hired Brian as a mechanic, and in April he contributed to his $50,000 bail.

Brian played a full season with the Penguins in 1977-78 — 79 games, 9 goals, 11 assists — and as usual he had established himself as a rough, flamboyant crowd-pleaser. The Penguins were a dreadful team, however, and the string was running out for Brian. His desire for hockey was waning, his second marriage was in trouble, and he hated Pittsburgh. The 1977-78 season turned out to be the last full season Brian played in the NHL. The next season, after seven games with the Penguins, he descended to the oblivion of the minors where he finished the 1978-79 season with the Binghamton Dusters, scoring five goals in thirty-nine games.

Martinetti liked to listen to Brian's hockey stories, and one of Brian's favourites concerned the evening he waited at an airport with the Binghamton Dusters for a flight home. The team was nearing the end of the season, preparing for the playoffs. Brian tried to phone his wife Janet, who had gone to stay with her mother in Long Island, but he couldn't reach her. She had left to spend a week in Manhattan.

When the flight was announced, the players picked up their bags and in a ragged line headed to the gate. Brian shuffled along with his teammates, nudging his bag ahead of him with his foot. He felt dejected, betrayed. Waiting in line, he noticed a sign far down the concourse at another wicket. The sign read "Acapulco." Brian wandered away from the line, walked to the wicket, took his American Express card from his wallet and bought a ticket to Acapulco. "I ended up drinking a Bacardi and Coke before going to bed that night," he said. He had only a woolen suit, but he stayed in Mexico for ten days.

There is something of the Old West gunfighter in the longtime professional hockey player. As one of the respected scrappers in the big leagues, Brian became a target for the shopworn never-weres and ambitious tyros anxious to build reputations. There was a player in New Haven called Frank Beaton, a tough but ragged enforcer whom the fans nick-named "Never Beaten Beaton." One night he took a run at Brian and after the fight the nickname was never used again.

Brian rode the buses from Binghamton to Hershey, New Haven and Springfield, struggling to maintain his enthu-siasm in the cold, hollow, Lady-of-Spain arenas. After the Binghamton Dusters, Brian started the 1979-80 season with the Springfield Indians, then moved to the Hershey Bears. He never had a say in any of these moves; in hockey, more than in the other professional sports, aging journeymen are so much cargo to be bartered. Brian was only in his late twenties, but the fire was dying. Ken Dryden, the Cornell-educated lawyer and former goaltender with the Montreal Canadiens, said in his elegant book, *The Game*, that it is not the legs that go first, but the enthusiasm that drives the legs. Brian never read the book, but he knew what Dryden meant.

"When the desire goes, it goes fast," Brian said. "Soon you don't even want to get up and go to the rink."

A ten-year major-league career slips by quickly, too. From the perspective of retirement, which always comes too abruptly, the teams and uniforms, the coaches and managers, the hotels and fights are a blur, life in a rearview mirror. Only the glittering memories are conspicuous, like quarters in a wishing pond. Brian could describe in eidetic detail the minutia of a third-period goal eight winters ago — who set it up, which defenceman he slipped around, what corner he shot at — but without the records in front of him he was never precisely sure when he left New York, or how he got traded to Buffalo, or how long he stayed in Pittsburgh, or where he lived in Binghamton.

When Brian started in the NHL, at the first camp in Peterborough in 1969, hockey was going through a metamor-phosis so profound it would change the game forever. There

were small things, sparks of individuality from the heyday of
the permissive sixties. The boot-camp brushcut, from time
immemorial the symbol of the jock, gave way to flowing
locks, and management clumsily issued edicts on the proper
length of hair. Jim Dorey, a young defenceman, reported to
the Maple Leafs camp with muttonchop sideburns that
measured — they were measured — five and a half inches
long. Not content with this eccentricity, Dorey took to the ice
one morning wearing skates with blue blades. That was the
year the Maple Leafs hired fitness instructors from the Royal
Military College in Kingston, and the year Harold Ballard
and Stafford Smythe, executives with the Maple Leafs, were
charged with income tax evasion.

When Brian was called up for a nine-game trial at the end
of the 1969-70 season, he played in a game against the Detroit
Red Wings and actually managed to share the rink with
Gordie Howe, who was playing his twenty-fourth season at
the age of forty-two. Howe joined the Red Wings in 1946,
three years before Brian was born. In the same nine-game
trial, Brian played against the new-breed hockey star, Derek
Sanderson, hockey's reply to Broadway Joe Namath, the
flamboyant quarterback of the New York Jets football team.
Sanderson's sideburns were longer than Jim Dorey's,
probably longer than Ringo Starr's, and in short order he
achieved a jetset celebrity, with articles about him appearing
in *Life* and *Esquire* magazines. He was as smooth and stylish
as Brian was backwoods and unsophisticated, but both had
been driven to excel by dominant, obsessive fathers.
Sanderson's father once told him, "If it's worth fighting over,
it's worth winning. So if the other fellow is bigger, use
something — a stick, a pipe, anything you want. Just make
sure you beat him." He saved Derek's first hundred sutures,
kept them in a small plastic box, including three he received
when he was hit in the head by a puck at the age of eight.

At the end of the 1971-72 season, during which Brian
played twenty games for the Tulsa Oilers and thirty-six for
the Maple Leafs while struggling with a broken kneecap, he
was sent off to the expansion New York Islanders. That was

the year the World Hockey Association was launched, when more than seventy established NHL players jumped to the new league, many for lucrative, long-term contracts to new teams in St. Paul, Edmonton, Philadelphia, Houston, San Francisco, Los Angeles, Miami and Winnipeg. Brian had been negotiating with the Winnipeg Jets, but Winnipeg eventually settled on another leftwinger: Bobby Hull, the Golden Jet from the Chicago Black Hawks. In June 1972, at an outdoor ceremony at the corner of Portage and Main, the Jets announced that Hull had signed a contract that paid him $250,000 a year for five years, with a signing bonus of $1 million.

The New York Islanders were a pitiful team in 1972-73, losing sixty games and winning only nine, but Brian enjoyed his new surroundings and the raise in pay from $12,500 to $50,000, not counting bonuses for takeouts or, as Brian called them, "hits." Brian had more hits than anyone on the team that season. He even managed to score fourteen goals, with twenty-four assists. He became an assistant captain with the Islanders, entitling him to wear an "A" on his jersey for the first time in his hockey life. At the end of the season the team's booster club selected him most popular player.

Emphasizing defence and recruiting talented young players, the Islanders improved quickly, and soon became the best team in the NHL, winning the Stanley Cup in 1980, 1981, 1982 and 1983. By that time, though, Brian was long gone from Long Island. After the 1973-74 season, the Islanders traded him to the Buffalo Sabres, where Brian stayed three full seasons, playing the best hockey of his career.

Something good happened to Brian in Buffalo. He loved the city, the team, the fans, even the surrounding countryside. He did not feel like a journeyman, a hanger-on. He made close friendships with teammates and with people outside hockey. He felt settled, almost secure, and for the first time in his hockey career he played consistently well, avoiding injuries, making life uncomfortable in the corners for opponents — and scoring goals. Brian never threatened to win the NHL scoring title, but he plugged away, scoring 12 goals in 1974-75, 13 goals in 1975-76, 14 goals in 1976-77.

The lessons Roy taught him on the backyard rink certainly helped. Being "tough and tireless" was crucial in the NHL, as much to endure the eighty-game, transcontinental schedule as any punishment on the ice. Roy's combative approach to hockey and his tutorials on fear prepared Brian for the worst of the goon era in the NHL, for those moments when he would be facing teams and players who were as intent on inflicting serious injury as scoring goals. And it was important to be able to skate backwards. Of course, there were other aspects to the modern game Roy knew nothing about. In order to play his style of hockey, bumping in the corners, making the sudden stops and starts, Brian learned how to "hollow" the blades for better side-to-side traction on the ice. "If you looked along one of my blades you'd see two sharp knife points," Brian said. He learned what to eat before a game — not steak, as Roy believed, but foods high in carbohydrate, like pasta. It was important to arrive at the rink slightly hungry.

Brian came to appreciate those brutal, full body-blocks on the backyard rink, Roy clomping over the ice in his boots, blindsiding Brian into the boards. That was what hockey was like in the NHL, getting hit when you didn't expect it, from every direction. It explains the maddening, instinctive responses, the fights and stick-swinging. No other sport is so irritating. "Hockey is a reckless-abandon game," Brian would say. "You've got to be aware of 360 degrees at all times. If you're not you're going to get hurt. Only a fighter pilot in the sky has more dimensions to worry about."

One of Brian's finest individual efforts came in a game against the touring Soviet Wings in January 1976, which the Sabres won by the startling score of 12-6. Brian scored a goal and two assists in the internationally televised game. One of the spectators at the Memorial Auditorium that day was Lefty Reid, director and curator of the Hockey Hall of Fame in Toronto. He thought Brian should have been selected one of the three stars of the game. Reid, a thoughtful man, wanted to be sure of his first impression, so he deliberately waited ten days before he wrote a letter to Brian in which he said:

> As a person who has followed your career and watched you play many times, I can truthfully say that I have never seen you play a better game. I felt there were many times when the Sabres appeared ready to sag a little but each time your gritty actions and performance seemed to give the team a lift. Keep playing like that and you'll have a long career in the NHL.

It did not turn out to be an accurate prediction. After the 1976-77 season, the Sabres traded Brian to the Pittsburgh Penguins. When he heard of the trade, Brian didn't want to go, and he considered retiring from hockey. He asked Janet about their financial situation, and she told him, "We better go to Pittsburgh."

The first season with Pittsburgh, Brian played in seventy-nine games, with nine goals and eleven assists. He was only twenty-seven, but he was beginning to feel like an old man. He didn't like the city, didn't like the team. He thought they played like cowards. Early in the 1978-79 season, Brian got off to a poor start, without a goal or assist in his first seven games. After an embarrassing 9-0 loss to the Philadelphia Flyers, who totally intimidated the Penguins, Brian did an on-air, post-game interview with Bob Prince, the longtime "Voice of the Pirates" in Pittsburgh. Brian let out all the stops, he even criticized the name of the team. "Team names should have strength and courage — like 'Colts' or 'Lions' or 'Tigers'," he told Prince. " 'Penguins' remind me of little incompetent birds that waddle around." And then Brian pushed his elbows into his sides, held up his hands like flappers and waddled around in front of an astonished Prince, singing *Squawk! Squawk! Squawk!*

The next morning, the Penguins sent Brian down to the Binghamton Dusters. His NHL career was over.

II

There is something about the end of a career in professional sports that is reminiscent of walking the plank in old pirate movies. In hockey, it matters not how many battles you fought, or how you may have distinguished yourself in some of them; when you can't do it any more, you're gone. For some there might be a brief and ceremonial drum roll, for most it's a boot in the arse and off you go.

All the clichés in the cliché-ridden world of sports apply. There is no tomorrow. When the cheering stops, the silence is deafening. You're only as good as your last game. Fame is fleeting. Fans are fickle. From the fast lane to the parking lot. From six figures to pumping gas. From public recognition, perhaps glamour, to, "Say, didn't you used to be...?"

Sociologists who have studied the matter do not refer to the transition as retirement. They refer to it as "disengagement" and "post-career trauma." The players themselves call it "the hockey vacuum." For twenty, thirty years, starting when they first take the game seriously, hockey demands everything of them. They sacrifice education, a normal childhood, family and friends, physical and mental health. The game consumes them and gives direction to their lives, but discourages them from developing and maintaining outside interests and relationships.

There was the "dream" of making it to the National Hockey League, and for those who do make it, there is a dreamlike quality to the life. The hours are good, the money is big, the acclaim is wonderful. From the time they begin to show promise as hockey players, they are pampered, scolded, disciplined, regimented, dressed and fed. Their noses are wiped, their wounds tended, their outside worries are taken away. When they become professionals, they are treated like soldiers, seminarians and convicts. Other people make their everyday decisions so that they can concentrate on the game. As in the Broadway musical "Damn Yankees," over and over they are exhorted to "think about the game . . . the game . . . the game." They develop a disdain for "civilian life," "the real world," "the nine to five." For a time — the average NHL career lasts only four and a half years — they are made to feel like special people.

When the major-league career ends, and usually it ends abruptly, the fallout can be calamitous. Without their uniforms, their numbers in the programs, their names in the newspapers, their faces on television, the "disengaged" athlete does not know who he is. What he is and always has been is a skilled labourer, no more — but no less. He is a bricklayer with a measure of fame and a six-figure income and all the pretty women he can point his trowel at, only to have them snatched from him forever at the age of thirty-two. What then?

Egos inflated by worshipful fans and a fawning press pop like soap bubbles. Marriages sustained by major-league pay cheques and major-league illusions collapse. Samson's locks have been cut, Superman's cape shredded — whatever applies. When the game is over, the sanctuary of the locker-room is reserved for the newly ordained. On a morning like any other morning, they are called to a small office where, after ten minutes and a handshake, they are banished from adolescence to middle age, kerplunk. There is bitterness, resentment and hurt. They feel cheated. They cling to the past, discussing old games like war veterans remembering Guadalcanal and Vimy Ridge. After a bumpy ride, some adjust, but nearly everyone knows one or two teammates who killed themselves instead.

Sally Gross, a sociologist at the University of Calgary,

worked for eighteen months on a study she titled, "The Retirement of Professional Hockey Players: A Process of Change in Career Identity." Gross, specializing in sports sociology, never was a team professional, but she is an athlete, having performed in rodeos in Alberta. Her specialty there was barrel-racing. She is also keenly involved in thoroughbred racing, which she calls a "developed culture," meaning a sport where one never confronts the problems of abrupt retirement — unless you are a jockey or a horse.

For her thesis, she worked closely with Alan Eagleson and the National Hockey League Players' Association. She prepared questionnaires, which she sent to every team in the National Hockey League and to a select group of former professional hockey players. For the active players, the response rate was twenty-five percent (115 of 441). For the former players, the response rate was fifty-four percent (543 of 1,043). Gross concedes that among the former players, the sample might be biased in favour of those who had less difficulty adjusting to life after hockey, much as high school reunions are more likely to attract sucessful graduates than those who have fallen on bad times. Even so, her findings are sobering.

The development of an elite athlete involves more than musculature, speed and physical skills. In her thesis, Gross says it also involves "socialization and identification processes," which, in non-sociological terms, are forms of brain-washing and indoctrination. Gross was surprised at how early it begins with hockey players, as early as age four, before they are in kindergarten.

Hockey has become a world sport, but at the professional level, Canadians do remarkably well for a sparsely-populated country, contributing eighty percent of the players in the National Hockey League. Fierce as hockey competition is, it is easier for a Canadian to make it to the top in hockey than for an American to make it to the top in basketball, baseball or football. Because hockey is the sport of choice in Canada, a major-league hockey career, with its perquisites and glamour, seems the most tantalizingly attainable.

"Formal training follows soon after he begins playing organized hockey," Gross says in her thesis. "For the majority of young players, this means involving themselves with the highly developed Canadian hockey system that will no doubt become a major factor in their lives to follow. These early roots mark the beginning of a process of identification with hockey accompanied by a process of socialization into the hockey career that clearly goes beyond occupational boundaries. For during this time, the player is not only learning hockey skills but also the values and standards of behaviour of his coaches and teammates. Because hockey has been legitimized by most Canadians as part of the Canadian way of life, these values and standards are usually readily supported by parents, friends and community, thus reinforcing the socialization and identification processes."

For players who make it to the National Hockey League, the socialization and identification processes have reached a peak. Players told Gross how the game isolates them from the outside world and sacrifices childhood and education. For most of the truly committed, and those starved for success, the demands of hockey are too voracious to permit even a sideways glance at alternative careers. There are few Ken Drydens in hockey.

"If a player is limited in his knowledge and experience of the outside world and if a strong hockey identification is carried to the extreme," Gross says, "A player's perception of his own success and failure as a person may become one and the same with the course and outcome of his hockey career. This has ominous overtones, particularly for those who are not successful. It becomes even more significant when one considers playing hockey is not a lifetime career, but instead engages only a portion of the lifespan of the individual."

She mentions one player who was told by his coach early in his amateur career that there were three important things in life — school, sports and a social life — and because there is only time to do two properly, the latter should be forsaken. She remarks, "The lack of free time indicated that much of the player's childhood was highly organized and programmed and controlled by others, thus limiting his opportunity to engage in more creative or spontaneous activities that may require him to make decisions for himself."

Michael A. Smith is another observer of retired athletes. He has coached and scouted professional hockey players and served for a time as assistant general manager of the Winnipeg Jets. He has a degree in Russian studies and has travelled extensively in the Soviet Union. In the fall of 1987, Smith wrote *Life After Hockey*, a study of retired hockey players.

He compares professional hockey players to jet pilots, who also must leave glamorous careers at a relatively young age. For perhaps twenty years, the pilots are the star performers. The system exists to serve them, to keep them airborne. They are a special breed. Then, in their early forties, they must abruptly step down to make room for younger pilots. Their glory days have ended.

Smith conducted in-depth interviews with twenty-two former players, many of them eminent hockey names: Dickie Moore, Glenn Hall, Ron Ellis, Henri Richard, Gary Dornhoefer, Jean Pronovost, Don Saleski, Ted Irvine. After the interviews, he placed them in groups, according to how they handled and survived the transition from a professional hockey career to what he calls "the real world." One group he called the "Smooth Transition Group," which, not surprisingly, contained many players from the pre-expansion days of the National Hockey League.

Typical of the "Smooth Transition Group" was Henri Richard, Maurice Richard's kid brother. Henri Richard played twenty seasons in the NHL, all of them with the Montreal Canadiens. He played on eleven teams that won the Stanley Cup. Richard told Smith he had absolutely no regrets leaving hockey. He said, "My transition only lasted one day." What helped was the long career with one team, the championships, and the fact that he had a business to go to the day he hung up his skates. In 1960, when he had been in the NHL five years, Richard bought a tavern in Montreal. "I was there every day when I played with Montreal," he told Smith. "When I was growing up, there were two things I wanted to do, play hockey and own a tavern. I knew I wouldn't be going far in school because of the hockey. I think I did the right thing and if I had to do it again, I'd do exactly the same thing."

Smith called another group "Rough Transition I," which includes players who had difficulty adjusting to life after hockey but eventually succeeded, forging satisfying careers. In this group are Jean Pronovost, Gary Dornhoefer and Ted Irvine. Pronovost played in the NHL for fourteen years, was an all-star, played for Team Canada twice and now works for Hockey Ministries International in Montreal, an evangelical Christian organization that works with athletes. Dornhoefer, who played most of his NHL career with the Philadelphia Flyers, helping them win Stanley Cups in 1974 and 1975, sells life insurance and works part-time in television for "Hockey Night in Canada." Dornhoefer was the only one who told Smith if he had to do it over again, he would not choose professional hockey. "Maybe I'd try the golf tour," he said. "You don't break legs doing that." Irvine started in the Boston Bruins organization, then played for the Los Angeles Kings, New York Rangers and St. Louis Blues. He told Smith it took him six years to adjust to life after hockey. He and his wife, Loretta, now own their own insurance and investment business in Winnipeg.

A group Smith calls "Rough Transition II" is for former players still struggling to adjust to life after hockey. One of them, Ron Ellis, actually left hockey twice, first in 1975, after playing for the Toronto Maple Leafs for eleven years, then permanently in 1981, after a four-year comeback. He told Smith that even at the height of his career, when he was playing well, he suffered severe bouts of depression. He said, "I would wonder if chasing this little black puck around was my purpose, if I was really doing what I was put on this earth to do."

The first time he quit he had just signed a new, four-year contract, following the most productive season of his NHL career when he played on a line with Darryl Sittler and Dave Williams. As he explains it, he became a born-again Christian that summer, attended training camp in September, then announced he was through with hockey because the fun was gone. For two years he managed a golf complex for a home-building firm, then, in 1977, when Canada was assembling a team of professionals to play in the World Cup in Vienna, he volunteered to play again. Ellis had been one of Team Canada's most effective pluggers in the dramatic 1972 series against the Soviet Union and he thought his international experience would be valuable.

After performing superbly in Vienna, Ellis returned to Canada and Jim Gregory, general manager of the Maple Leafs, asked if he would be interested in trying the NHL again. He told Smith, "I had a major decision to make, but I really felt God saying, 'I showed you, you can play hockey, play it for me.'" Ellis played four more years for the Maple Leafs and left hockey for good in 1981. He worked for a wholesale business, selling pens, then managed a tourist camp with his parents in the Muskokas. He taught physical education at a Christian school, tried the insurance business, then got into sporting goods. He told Smith, "It's hard to find your niche in life that can give you the same feelings you had as a player. You can break out of a slump with two or three goals one night. It's not like that in business or life."

Ellis's doctors told him that twice he came close to a complete nervous breakdown. Eight years after hockey, he thinks he is beginning to adjust to the real world.

For her thesis, Sally Gross interviewed active and former hockey players. The active players tended to be optimistic, and seldom concerned themselves with life after hockey. Gross was surprised that most of them regarded the fun, the friends and the lifestyle of professional hockey more important than money.

One told her that "working nine to five would drive me crazy." Another said, "I would miss the excitement of the game — the immediate rewards of your work. I enjoy the travel, the camaraderie, the youth and innocence of it all. I would be concerned replacing this." Another active player said, "Fun is a big part of the game. It makes you a better player. Hockey is a game — when you retire you grow up."

The former players told a different story. One of them told Gross, "What was really apparent to me when I quit was that, for the first time in my life, I had to manage my life. . . . I didn't have to do a lot of planning. They put the schedule in front of me with another year mapped out for me. When I quit, it was becoming quite apparent that my life was becoming unmanageable. I was on an emotional treadmill . . . running to try and keep up." Another former player said, "I guess sometimes bullshit baffles the brain and we swallow it hook, line and sinker. I think we get to think that we are damn near immortal and that it's never going to end for us."

Asked to identify aspects of hockey that might help them adjust to new careers after hockey, players mentioned "an ability to work as a team," "self-confidence," "handling pressure," "self-discipline," "humility," "patience," "perseverance," "competitiveness" and "an ability to work hard and make sacrifices." Aspects of a hockey career the players thought might hurt their transition to the real world included "the narrow focus of the game that restricts their knowledge of the outside world," "ego-boosting of fans," "day-to-day decisions by management," "the short work day" and "the clear, unambivalent hockey goals." One former player said, "When I played, basically there wasn't life after hockey. Not that I knew of anyway. I was like a race horse with blinders on, going through life believing only hockey existed."

Nearly all the players told Gross that what they valued more than anything else in hockey were their relationships with teammates. At first Gross thought perhaps hockey provided an enviable environment wherein players developed deep, personal friendships. After a few interviews, however, she thought differently. She came to regard the relationships not as deep and long-lasting friendships but as functional alliances for survival and success. Active and former players referred to the "chemistry" that creates a balance on a team, which cannot be upset if the team is to be successful. Most social activities are tribal rituals to promote team solidarity. Players who do not show up for beers after the game are judged to have violated a code.

"What is important is that, even on the informal, social level, the common ground of their relationships is focused on hockey. Several players said that they knew little about the lives of their teammates apart from hockey. They claimed that typically players do not like to reveal their personal side, especially if this means uncovering some weakness or flaw. As well, teammates are not comfortable with a player who is candid about his feelings."

Gross mentions the "distancing" that occurs when a player retires, or is traded. It is such a common reaction among professional athletes that few players think it is unusual. One of the former players said, "The twenty players on your team are very close . . . they live together for eight months of the year, they travel together . . . but the day you go to another organization, you're forgotten and replaced. If the guy was the comedian in the dressing-room someone else will take his spot, or if the guy was the clubhouse lawyer someone else will take his spot." Another former player told Gross it was not until three years after he retired that he realized the transient nature of team friendships.

About half of the players interviewed told Gross that during their playing days they prepared for a second career, either by working during the summer off-season or by taking courses. The others said that hockey required their full attention, that outside activities would distract them and might hurt their hockey careers. Most of the players who used the off-season for work or education were single. The married players preferred to spend their summers with their families since they saw so little of them during the season. One former player told Gross that because of his huge salary he would have felt guilty taking any time away from hockey.

Most of the players said they did not worry much about life after hockey when they were playing. Some of the active players expected that doors would be opened to them later because of their high-profile hockey careers, but most former players regarded the "door factor" as a myth. "There was a time when players were really national heroes," one of them told Gross. "The promotional factor is still there for the superstars, but the substrata is a lot larger now ... there aren't that many superstars."

Another former player said that after retirement from hockey, "the loss of feeling special underpinned all emotional adjustments." A former player who had his own business to go to when he left hockey still found retirement painful. He told Gross, "When the arena doors shut for the last time behind me, they sounded like the doors of a prison." Few of the players admitted they felt rejected by their former teams and teammates. Gross suspects they were being defensive, overemphasizing that they did not need to be socially accepted by former teammates, perhaps because it hurt too much to admit it.

"Most players indicated their perceptions had been fairly naïve," Gross says. "One player was surprised to discover how hard people work in the outside world, having himself been accustomed to a two-hour work day.... One player said that his hockey career, and the self-esteem it has provided him, has raised his personal expectations. Initially, he had felt that if hockey didn't work out he would take a labour job, but that now he wanted more."

Gross was surprised to find that few former players ever attend professional hockey games. Smith, who has more experience in the day-to-day realities of professional hockey, was not surprised. The burnout factor is stronger in hockey than most other team sports, notably baseball, football and basketball. The body contact and violence of hockey may be comparable to football, but the football seasons are not nearly as long or filled with so many games. Even in their early teens, serious hockey players often play a hundred games a season, with power-skating lessons on the side and extra sessions at summer hockey camps. Early in his book, Smith says many hockey programs are run by parents for parents, with children playing for their parents' wish fulfillment. It was not always so, and some of the biggest names in hockey — Jean Beliveau, Maurice Richard, Gordie Howe — never had to endure such a stiff dosage of organized hockey so early in their lives.

And there are other reasons. At a dinner table Smith illustrates the burnout by arranging the sugar bowl, ketchup bottle and salt and pepper shakers to form a square. Pointing to the accoutrements on the table, he says, "Inside there is the game." He makes swirling motions with his finger to indicate hockey players at work within the confines of the small square. Then he motions to just beyond the periphery of the square and says, "Outside are the press, the hype, the fans, the managers, the owners. The players see it as bullshit. They have no respect for it. They do not want to be part of it. When they're finished with hockey, they want to get right out of it."

The only exception Gross found were those who played for the Montreal Canadiens. Former Canadiens regularly attended games at the Forum, she said, because management provides them with a special viewing-room where they feel welcome and accepted.

The players who adjust best to life after hockey are those who had the most education and those who prepared for the end of their careers, usually by making the most of the summer off-seasons. Players drafted from college teams cope with alternative careers better than players drafted from the rough-and-tumble of Canadian junior hockey, where education is often neglected if not actively discouraged. Players who leave the game voluntarily adjust better than players who are dropped. Elite players do better after hockey than fringe players; they are treated with more respect during their careers, mostly they are spared the dispiriting trades and demotions to the minors and so they emerge from the game with a stronger sense of security and self-worth. Those who played in the National Hockey League before expansion in 1967 also adjusted better to life after hockey, probably because their salaries were meagre compared to the six-figure salaries of today — the average salary of an NHL player in 1987 was $155,000 — and because nearly all of them worked during the off-season.

The players who adjust least successfully to life after hockey are the modern, lavishly paid spear-carriers, the lunchbucket journeymen who make as much as neurosurgeons and are the mainstream of professional hockey. They are the ones on the second and third lines, the ones who rely more on emotion and intensity than skill, the ones who sacrifice everything for hockey. They are obsessive enough to make it, then to hang on for eight or ten or twelve years, the ones who play until they are told they can't play any more, the ones like Brian Spencer.

III

During the jury selection process, Brian sat at the defence table, sandwiched between his lawyers, Barry Weinstein to his left, Richard Greene to his right. The defence table was on the right side of the courtroom, across the room from the jury box, directly in front of Judge Fine's elevated desk. Chuck Burton and Robert Zaun, his paralegal assistant, sat at the table on the left side of the courtroom, closest to the jurors.

While the lawyers took their turns questioning the jurors, sometimes together, sometimes individually, Brian read scraps of papers and legal documents, daintily poured himself and his lawyers cups of water from the pewter pitcher on the table, and scribbled notes on a pad of yellow foolscap. He did his best to follow the advice of his lawyers as to how to sit, how to look at the jurors, how not to appear arrogant or smug or dangerous. He wore a light blue suit, a clean white shirt and a dark blue tie. The ensemble achieved a lighter, softer effect. He did not look at all like a man who could only be subdued by three detectives, two uniformed policemen, two attack dogs and a helicopter.

Brian tried to appear busy, but there was not much for him to do as the rest of his life was being decided. When the lawyers raised the issue of the death penalty, and when the jurors, every one of them, agreed that they could opt for it under the right circumstances, Brian thought of his months in the Palm Beach County Detention Center and what the inmates used to call the electric chair — "Old Smoky." There was the fear again. What would it be like on the morning of your own execution? What would be going through your mind? Would you be up to it? Would it matter?

When Weinstein rose to question the jurors, Brian looked across to the jury box and watched and listened. After three days, he was getting to know the prospective jurors as individuals with likes and dislikes and fears of their own. Most of them had been victims of crime — hold-ups, break-ins, assaults — and some had relatives who had been in jail. Nearly all of them had come to Florida from somewhere else, for their own reasons, as Brian had. Weinstein always ended his questioning by asking jurors if they had bumper stickers on their cars. He seemed mildly reluctant to ask, because it was not his question. It was his assistant, Richard Greene, who wanted to know; he believed anyone who went to the trouble of sticking a personal credo to the bumper of his car was the sort of person who wore his heart on his sleeve, who would stick by his beliefs. And so, as Weinstein finished questioning a large, oval-shaped man who had come to Florida from the Catskills and who worked in West Palm Beach for the Otis Elevator Company, he asked, "Do you have a bumper sticker on your car, sir?"

"Yes, I do," the man replied in a soft voice.

"And what does it say?"

"Elevator men do it up and down."

Brian liked the young man from the National Rifle Association, and the grim Second World War sergeant. And he liked the lumpy housewife who surprised everyone, including Judge Fine, by saying her hobby was drag racing.

On his notepad, Brian doodled and guessed the ages of the jurors, proud of being able to come within two years of anyone's age. He passed his guesses to Weinstein and Greene, trying to convince them a younger jury would be better for him. He did not want any "old biddies" who might be appalled by someone who owned guns or stayed out all night at places like the Banana Boat. It wasn't the oldness he detested, it was the biddiness. In the main, Brian liked old people. He preferred their company. In his playing days, when he used to flip souvenir pucks into the seats during the warm-up, or race the Zamboni to get a roar from the crowd, he was always the last player off the ice. He stood by the boards chatting up the fans, pulling off his chunky hockey gloves to sign autographs. The fans he enjoyed talking to most were the ones who remembered pot-bellied heaters, coal lamps and listening to Foster Hewitt on the radio.

Brian remembered old Hiram Loper, a pioneer rancher in Vanderhoof. Like Roy Spencer, he had come to British Columbia from Alberta and he was a man of independent mind. Brian used to call him "Uncle Hi." Before the trial, Irene Spencer sent Brian a photograph of Byron and Uncle Hi, taken in his room at the Jubilee Home in Prince George at a party to celebrate Hiram's one-hundredth birthday. She included a clipping of a story in the Prince George *Citizen*, which said Hiram still recited poetry and played the harmonica at square dances. He told the reporter from the *Citizen* that the greatest invention of all time was the steam engine because it "changed the face of the country." Television? "It will never do for people what the steam engine did," Hiram replied. As to why he never married, Uncle Hi said he never found the right girl and they all wanted too much money. Brian could not have said it better.

During the build-up to the trial, the past began to creep up on Brian. He often found himself thinking of Toronto, Long Island, Buffalo, Pittsburgh, even the scratchy bush-league towns where he ended his career — Binghamton, Springfield, Hershey. He recalled Fort St. James and the north central interior of British Columbia, where he had not spent an October day in more than two decades. One evening at Monica's, Brian watched a documentary on polar bears in the Canadian Arctic. He was fascinated by the snow and ice, the winds whistling off Hudson's Bay and the great, lumbering, white bears. This time the barren white expanse and the cold he said he hated seemed to be soothing, reassuring; the contrast to south Florida could not have been greater. At one point, he mused aloud, "Maybe I never should have left."

By mid-afternoon on the fourth day, the jury had been selected. Judge Fine adjourned the trial until eleven o'clock Friday morning, at which time the lawyers could present any motions. The trial would resume at two o'clock with opening statements by both sides, first Chuck Burton, then Barry Weinstein. If there was time, the first witness would be called to the stand.

In the evening, Shelly Spencer, Byron's wife, called Monica from her home in Maple Bay on Vancouver Island. Mrs. Spencer and Byron had left Victoria for Winnipeg, en route to Chicago and Florida early in the afternoon, Shelly told Monica, but there was a problem at the Winnipeg airport.

"What's that?" Monica asked.

"Byron's been refused entry into the United States."

"Oh, no."

As it turned out, Byron didn't have his witness's subpoena with him, and a computer check at the Winnipeg airport turned up an old marijuana conviction. Mrs. Spencer was allowed through, and she was on a plane headed to Chicago. Byron, still at Winnipeg, was becoming impatient and petulant. He threatened to chuck it all and fly back to British Columbia. He wasn't sure he wanted to go to West Palm Beach anyway.

Monica called Leon at his townhouse in Lake Worth. Leon was still at the Public Defenders Office at the Governmental Center. After hearing from Byron directly, Monica called Shelly back and asked about the subpoena. Shelly said she would courier it to Winnipeg.

"But Byron's thinking of flying back to your place," Monica told her. "He says he's going to wait at the airport in Winnipeg for two hours and if nothing's settled, he's going back."

"Where's Mrs. Spencer?" Shelly asked.

"She's in the air to Chicago."

Monica tried calling a CBC producer in Winnipeg, in case Byron had to stay there overnight. She couldn't reach him.

When Leon got home, he called Air Canada at the Winnipeg airport. He explained that Byron was needed in West Palm Beach for an important trial and the woman at the Air Canada desk promised she would page Byron. Leon then called United States Customs at the Winnipeg airport and got a recorded message. He called the RCMP to explain the situation and to ask for their assistance. The RCMP said their office at the airport was closed, but they'd send a car over and see what it was all about. Finally Leon called Shelly and asked about the subpoena. She said it was on its way to Winnipeg, adding that Byron had also forgotten his teeth.

"His teeth?" Leon said.

"His upper plate," Shelly explained. "Sometimes he just doesn't bother with it."

Monica called Shelly again and Shelly reported that Byron had taken a plane and was heading back to British Columbia. By midnight, Byron was in the air on his way to Vancouver, Mrs. Spencer was in the air on her way to Chicago, Byron's subpoena was in the air to United States Customs in Winnipeg and Byron's false teeth were on their way to Monica's apartment in West Palm Beach.

Shortly after midnight, the telephone rang again at Leon's townhouse. It was Mrs. Spencer, in her hotel room in Chicago. She sounded confused. "You just get a good night's sleep, dear," Leon said to her. "Everything's going to be all right, just leave the worrying to me. That's what I'm paid for."

CHAPTER FIVE

Friday:
Brian
and
Byron

I

The morning was overcast and cool, which in Florida can be a relief from the monotony of good weather, especially when you are not on vacation.

When Brian arrived at the courtyard at the Governmental Center, with his styrofoam cup of coffee and the morning paper, he was in good spirits. He felt rested and fresh, though the night before he had been out drinking with Monica's next-door neighbour, Sue Head, who often dropped in for a glass of wine and a cigarette, and an old friend named Rick.

Brian has many old friends, some from his early years in Florida, or his years with Diane, or his years with the Hulk, or the time he lived in the trailer in Loxahatchee. Old friends from saloons and eateries like the Drexel, the Banana Boat, Charley's, Barney's, and the Crab Pot. Old workmates from Fischbach & Moore, Hertz Rental Equipment, and Case Power. One week Rick, then Pete, then Dan, then Greg, then an old friend called Stormin' Norman. Some were lowlifers and roustabouts, barnacles attached to the underside of Brian's life, but there were others who were bank executives, company managers, policemen and lawyers. Brian remained steadfastly loyal to all his friends and they remained loyal to him. Brian possessed something they needed, but only occasionally, the way one might feel a need for a banana split.

Monica was not pleased Brian had been out drinking the night before the trial was to begin in earnest. Ever solicitous of Brian's moods — Brian said she was being a beagle — Monica decided not to tell him about Byron's adventures when he arrived home well after midnight. She thought it would upset him.

As it turned out, when Monica related the details in the morning, Brian thought it was hilarious, something out of the Keystone Kops. He was still chuckling about it as he waited for the morning session to begin. He had talked to Byron on the phone at Monica's and Byron told him the conclusion of the story. After he left Winnipeg, angry at not being allowed into the United States, he arrived late at night in Vancouver with only a few dollars in his pocket. He still had to find his way to Vancouver Island. He told a taxi driver at the airport about the day's events — trying to get to his brother's murder trial, the missing subpoena, his teeth — and the taxi driver said to Byron, "Hey, no problem." The driver had a private pilot's licence. He drove Byron to a nearby hangar, rented a plane, then flew him across the Strait of Georgia to Victoria. He didn't charge Byron for the trip.

Brian thought the whole episode was very Canadian.

II

Brian and Byron are not identical twins. Byron has red hair and is slighter, though sometimes their profiles look similar — the shape of the face, the mouth, the jaw. Their personalities are what set them apart; Byron is quieter, calmer, more thoughtful, less intense. He doesn't smile as easily as Brian. There are long pauses in his conversation, he speaks slowly and says "Gosh" a lot. In his speech and mannerisms, Byron is something of a rustic, with such favourite expressions as, "Close only counts in horseshoes and hand grenades." One afternoon driving by the airport in Victoria on his way to visit his mother, he remarked, "Well that's some how-do-you-do airport." It means the real thing, or something unexpectedly impressive, and it could apply to an airport, a hockey arena or a hamburger.

When they were growing up, they were very close. "We were never more than feet apart," Byron once said. One year when they were in their teens, they stayed away from home during a long stretch of winter, knocking about Vanderhoof. They had no place to stay, so they slept at the pulp mill, huddled for warmth by the mill burner. When the mill burner shut down at Christmas, they slept in parked cars. Byron remembers waking up one morning at about four, feeling the car going bumpety-bump along the street. He and Brian had been sleeping in the back seat and the car was being towed away. They opened the doors, jumped out and ran away. Other nights they slept in the hockey arena in Vanderhoof. They waited until everyone had left after a game, then hid in

145

the furnace room. During the night they broke into the concession booth and stole chocolate bars. They wandered the streets of Vanderhoof, tromping over the snow, snitching armloads of groceries from trucks. To this day, the name Vanderhoof brings back a visceral feeling of cold and loneliness. After Brian left home, after he left the reform school at Brannon Lake, the two brothers did not see much of each other. There were letters, the odd phone call, and Brian did return to the Fort in the summers early in his hockey career, but effectively the twins went their separate ways.

If the 1960s were Brian's testing time, his years of grim ambition, for Byron they were what they were for many young people his age, a blurry, surrealistic waltz through flowers and drugs and Lucy in the Sky with Diamonds. Even the Fort and the north central interior, with its brooding, Brigadoonish isolation, did not go untouched by the times that were spectacularly a-changing. There was good seasonal money in logging and, during his wildest, blurriest times, Byron figures he went through about $200,000, sometimes spending $2,000 a night on booze, drugs, travel and sex. On one occasion he was arrested in Mexico for trying to smuggle drugs out of the country and Brian had to go there to bail him out. Another time, at a wild how-do-you-do party at a house at the Fort, some guys took a few shots at Byron. He left, drove to his house, picked up his .303 rifle, returned to the party and started shooting up the house. He shot holes through the walls and windows, and that ended the harrassment. "They knew I'd do what I said, and the next guy would get it between the eyes," Byron said. Being a quiet, thoughtful fellow in Fort St. James is not like being a quiet, thoughtful fellow in, say, Toledo.

The police came, took Byron away and locked him in the jail overnight. They released him the next morning, but forbade him from owning any weapon for a period of two years. At the time, Byron had twelve rifles, two shotguns and two crossbows. They confiscated all the weapons but one, the .22-calibre rifle Roy Spencer had given Byron and Brian when they were boys. Byron hid the rifle from the police, and when they were gone he carefully greased it, wrapped it in burlap and buried it for three years.

It is the only rifle he owns now, and he keeps it with him at his house in Duncan, which overlooks Maple Bay, a picturesque, craggy inlet on the east coast of Vancouver Island. Byron lives there in a comfortable rented ranch bungalow with Shelly, and their two children, a son, Roy, and a daughter, Jamie.

Roy Spencer's death affected the Spencer family in different ways. For Brian, a young and determined but borderline hockey player, it meant sudden, unaccustomed celebrity, perhaps one of those answered prayers that becomes, in the end, a curse. Irene Spencer probably suffered the most, but in her quiet, self-effacing manner, she tried to keep up appearances. For a time she kept her job at the Hudson's Bay Company, but she did not socialize as much as she used to. After a few months she quit her job and lived alone at the house on the farm. She thinks she had a nervous breakdown. A year later, she moved to Whitehorse in the Yukon, stayed there two years, then moved to Cranbrook, a logging and mining town in the mountains of southeast British Columbia. Through a friend at a bridge club in Cranbrook, Irene met an engaging Englishman named Bill Morris and soon after they were married. She now calls herself Irene Spencer-Morris, and she and her new husband live in a townhouse in Sidney, just outside Victoria. Brian's arrest in Florida brought her new grief, which caused a nervous skin rash.

The night Roy was killed, Byron was playing for a team in Fort St. James called the Caledonia Blues. It was the elite team in town and one of the best in all of the north central interior. He got off work early that Saturday, because he was leaving on a two-day trip to play hockey in Burns Lake, a drive of about a hundred and fifty miles. As Byron waited for his ride, he talked with his father, who was working in the yard at the farm.

Byron remembered his father was greatly excited about Brian's game that night. He had made sure the generator was working, so they would be able to watch the game on television. Byron wished he could stay and watch the game with Roy, but the team needed him in Burns Lake for the game that night and for another one Sunday afternoon. Irene was preparing supper when Byron left.

Later that night, when Byron was on the ice, he noticed several Mounties at the players' bench. When he came off the ice, one of the Mounties asked if he was Byron Sepncer, and when Byron said he was the Mountie told him there was an important message at home and to call his mother as soon as possible. Byron said. "You bet," then jumped on the ice for another shift.

Byron had a hunch something might be wrong with his father. He was always in pain, and that winter he had been very sick. After the game, Byron went to the motel where the team was staying and phoned home. His mother told him about Roy at the television station. An hour later, Carl Miller, a friend of the family, arrived in Burns Lake in his Chrysler New Yorker and he took Byron home. Byron and his mother drove from Fort St. James over the snowy roads to Prince George, where Byron identified his father's body. His mother was not up to it. Alone with Roy, Byron wept and said his goodbyes.

"Everything had been going so well," he said. "I was working steadily, making good money for the first time. I was enjoying hockey and was actively involved with the community. Brian had made it to the NHL. Mom and Dad were happy, doing well, and they were proud of us. It was the best of times, and then the whole bloody world fell apart."

Byron remained in Fort St. James long after the rest of his family had gone. There was not much new to talk about in the small town, so Byron had the burden of answering the questions, over and over again — questions about Roy and the crazy stunt he pulled at the television station in Prince George, questions about Irene after she abruptly pulled out of Fort St. James and moved to Whitehorse, questions about Brian. The latter came in waves every time Brian was traded, and they kept coming long after he had left hockey and was living in Florida. "I'd tell a story to one person, then half an hour later I'd have to tell the same story to someone else," Byron said. "Nobody ever asked how I was doing, I guess maybe because they knew."

Byron met Shelly about the time his mother left for Whitehorse and they moved into the old family home. He worked as a logger, operating a skidder, a tractor-like wheeled vehicle designed to pull felled logs out of the forest. Shelly was eighteen when she arrived in Fort St. James in the early 1970s from Kirkland Lake, a mining town in northern Ontario. She had come to visit her sister, but she liked the place and decided to stay. She got a job as a bartender at the pub in the Fort St. James Hotel, which turned out to be an immersion course in the local folk ways. When she reported for work on her fist day she noticed a sign at the entrance to the pub that read, "All hunting knives and guns must be checked at the bar." At one time, the pub was known throughout British Columbia and much of western Canada as "The Zoo." Byron thinks the regulars feel they have a duty to uphold the pub's reputation, whether by deed or hyperbole, so it is hard to know what stories to believe.

At one time there was a thick partition between the white and Indian sections, sections which had been originally designated for "men" and "ladies and escorts." The wall eventually came down, but the whites and Indians continued to drink at opposite ends of the bar. Many of the loggers would go to the pub directly from work on Friday and not get home until Saturday morning. There were fights most nights, between whites and Indians, whites and whites, Indians and Indians, men and men, women and women, and men and women.

It was not that the pub was a dump, far from it. The manager of the pub, Larry Whitely, did a commendable job of furnishing, decorating and keeping the place clean, and he tried to maintain order if not peace. There were impressive stuffed animal heads on the walls. The food was excellent. There were even three pool tables, but, on nights when things got going, the cues and balls flew through the smoky air like shrapnel. One evening Byron was sitting at a table with a beer when he heard a *thuck* by his right ear as one of the ivory balls embedded itself in the wall behind him.

Shelly heard all the stories, apocryphal and otherwise, like the night the Indians carried a libidinous white man out to the parking lot where they thrashed him and cut off his testicles. During her first week at work, she watched an Indian man break a beer bottle and stab the jagged end into his wife's throat. They took the bleeding woman behind the bar, washed her off and patched her up, then she returned to her husband's table for the remainder of the evening. After that, Shelly was inclined to believe that some of the stories might be true. She was on duty the night Murray bit off the man's finger.

Then there was the hot summer afternoon a group of East Indian loggers came in, sat at a table somewhere in the DMZ between the Indians and whites, and ordered a round of beer. At first the East Indians seemed a little nervous, but after another round they began to relax. The Indians and whites regarded the newcomers with curiosity, with a certain bewildered detachment, until a spontaneous and rare alliance occurred and, as Shelly recalls, "all hell broke loose. The Indians and whites were bouncing the East Indians around like soccer balls."

Early in October 1981, Byron called Brian from Fort St. James to say he would like to come down to West Palm Beach for a visit. The nights were getting cold in the north central interior and Byron dreaded the approach of another winter. He was the last of the Spencer family still living in Fort St. James, and there were all those questions to answer. He and Shelly had split up, mainly because of his drinking, but there were other problems, too.

Three years earlier, his son Roy was injured in a freak accident while playing in the mud near the house. Roy was then four years old. A man building a sidewalk drove a backloader up Roy's back, the treads stopping just short of his head. Were it not for the soft mud, young Roy would have

Byron (left) and Brian (right) – Pee Wee trophy winners for Fort St. James in 1961.

Byron and Brian with their father, Roy, on the boat that Roy built.

Roy Spencer, 1966.

4 July, 1969.

Mr. Brian Spencer,
Box 67,
FORT ST. JAMES, B.C.

Dear Brian,

During the recent Amateur Draft Meetings in Montreal,
we acquired the exclusive rights to put you on our negotiating list
and we are prepared to negotiate a contract with you personally for
your professional services for the 1969-70 season and thereafter.

First, we must know if you have signed a CHA Contract
for the 1968-69 season, and do you consider yourself bound by it?
If not, why not?

If you do have a contract, and can obtain a release
or written consent to negotiate, we will proceed further.

We would appreciate hearing from you at your earliest
convenience, and upon doing so, we will make further arrangements.

Yours very truly,

Bob Davidson /sb

/sb   R.E. DAVIDSON,
                             Chief Scout.

Brian Spencer's draft pick letter from the Toronto Maple Leafs.

Brian Spencer's publicity photograph for the Toronto Maple Leafs.

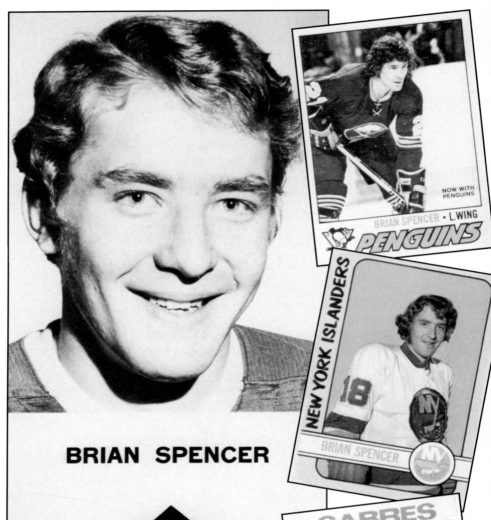

BRIAN SPENCER

1970-71

Erik Christensen, *The Globe and Mail*

Brian in training for
the Leafs, 1971.

Courtesy L. Antonacci

Brian and Janet on
their wedding day,
1976.

Brian and Diane, 1982.

Brian and John
Antonacci with
John's son J.P.,
playing ball hockey
in Toronto.

Brian and his 16 ton truck called "The Hulk," which he built himself.

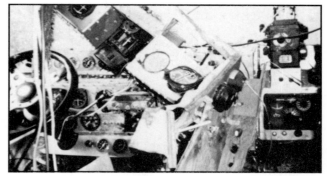

The vandalized inside of "The Hulk."

"The Hulk," after the sheriff and the looters had finished.

Monica, when she
and Brian worked at
Fischbach & Moore.

Brian and his mother,
before the trial
started.

been crushed to death; as it was, he suffered brain damage, with subsequent behavioural problems. At the age of thirty-two, Byron felt trapped by his responsibilities and his surroundings. His life wasn't going anywhere.

He had tried to keep in touch with Brian, but neither of them had ever been faithful correspondents. He knew about Brian's three daughters, knew that Brian had broken up with Linda, married again, had two sons, had left hockey and drifted down to Florida to start a new life. He thought they might have something to share. Byron considered leaving Fort St. James permanently to start over again in Florida with his twin brother. When he told Brian he would like to visit, Brian said, "By all means. You can stay with me and Diane in the trailer."

Byron moved in with Brian and Diane, out on Okeechobee Boulevard on the western edge of West Palm Beach, toward Loxahatchee. The trailer was on a sixteen-acre parcel of land owned by Harvey Sykes, an older man who was a friend of Brian. Brian still had the Hulk, but it was beginning to rot and rust. He had all sorts of tools and equipment strewn about the trailer, and he was working as a mechanic at Fischbach & Moore.

Byron found he had lots of time to himself because Brian was always working, even on Saturdays. At first Byron liked being in Florida. He enjoyed the warm weather, and initially he got along well with Diane. Byron thought she was "a hell of a nice woman." Diane spent more time with Byron than Brian did, and one day, feeling sorry for Byron being left alone in the trailer all day, she called up her younger sister and the three of them spent an afternoon at the beach. Many days Diane stayed around the trailer, but she was not what Byron considered a "domestic" person. She never did any cooking or laundry or housecleaning. The place was a mess.

She had other work to do, and at the oddest hours. She told Byron she had "interviews" and "job appointments" and "meetings" to attend. Byron often drove her to these appointments, which would take her all over Palm Beach

County and sometimes as far south as Fort Lauderdale and Miami. The appointments could be at any time of the day — morning, afternoon, evening. Sometimes she would not return to the trailer until dawn. She always looked terrific going to these appointments, with her long dark hair falling in waves to her shoulders. She wore expensive clothes and stiletto heels. Byron had no idea what Diane did on these appointments. "I'd park the car and she'd say she'd be an hour or half an hour and away she'd go."

Soon enough, Byron realized something was wrong, not with Diane's mysterious appointments, but with the effect she was having on Brian. They had been living together for about a year when Byron arrived, but he sensed Brian wanted her out of his life and could not ask her to leave. From the beginning, Brian tried to make it clear to Diane that they were sharing the trailer to reduce expenses, and that each was free to come and go as he or she pleased. He thought Diane understood this. Brian knew she was working as a prostitute, and that was fine with him. He regarded the arrangement as mainly platonic, with a little friendly sex from time to time.

Byron slept at one end of the trailer, Brian and Diane at the other. After Byron had been a guest for a few weeks, he would hear them arguing at night at the other end of the trailer. It got worse and worse.

"They'd be yelling, screaming. Brian's life was becoming so miserable and I could only take it for so long. He was almost a raving madman, a lunatic. She was driving him crazy. I talked to Diane about it and she said she was angry at Brian because he worked so much. She wanted him to treat her as a wife. I think she was really, truly, deeply in love with him, but he wasn't in love with her. That's what they fought and argued about all the time. She really believed that they were man and wife, but it wasn't like that with Brian. He'd have other girlfriends and she was jealous. She'd follow him around without him knowing. She was like a shadow he couldn't get away from."

One morning at the trailer, after another argumentative

night, Byron waited until Brian had left for work, then he confronted Diane and told her he did not like what was happening to his brother. Byron suggested she should "bow out quietly." Diane told Byron to mind his own business.

"Brian loves me," she said. "He just doesn't know it."

Soon after that session, Diane did move out. One day she called up her younger sister, they packed her belongings, and Diane left. She told Brian he would be sorry.

Byron took a job with a roofing company, working mainly with blacks in Riviera Beach. He got along fine with the blacks, drinking and playing pool with them after work. Byron was still thinking of staying with Brian in Florida permanently and Brian encouraged him. One day they drove out to Loxahatchee, several miles west of West Palm Beach, so Brian could show Byron a piece of land he wanted to buy. Loxahatchee, or Loxahatchee Groves as it is sometimes called, is a largely rural, swampy district, with horse ranches, trailer homes, wild turkeys, snakes, bobcats and otters. The roads are unpaved, the area is threatened regularly by floods, but most of the nearly four thousand residents are vehemently opposed to the sort of progress manifested by asphalted roads, shopping malls and luxury condos. They call themselves "Leave-it-aloners" and they sport T-shirts that read, "Loxahatchee: love it and leave it alone." The police keep a close watch on the district because of the district's many "stash houses," places where drugs are stored for future distribution. Low-flying planes have been known to swoop by, dropping mysterious packages. On one memorable afternoon several bales of marijuana fell out of the sky, broke open, and the contents wafted down on the heads of golfers at nearby Royal Palm Beach.

Brian and Byron planned to buy the property off F Road in Loxahatchee. They were going to build a house and a shop on it, and, as Byron said, "set up housekeeping." They could do most of the work themselves, clearing the land, building the house and the shop, equipping it with the tools and equipment they needed. Brian earned extra money building cedar decks, and Byron certainly knew how to take down trees and skin them. Brian had always dreamed of some day having his own workshop in a place where the sound of a power drill or a lathe would not disturb the neighbours. Tools were his ultimate luxury, and, though he loathed shopping for shirts or trousers or shoes, even food, if he passed a hardware shop on payday he would think nothing of spending one hundred dollars on a wrench the size of a baseball bat. Brian thought the Loxahatchee property would be a good place for his two boys to visit, perhaps even a good place to raise them.

After two months in Florida, however, Byron realized he could not live there. The weather was wonderful, he liked many of Brian's friends and the people he worked with at the roofing company, but he felt rootless and sensed a pervasive anomie about the place. So much surface sheen, so much emphasis on money, so much disenchantment. He had never before experienced such a flagrant, tawdry juxtaposition of rich and poor. The rich barricaded themselves in resort hotels and condo-castles, playing the British Raj in the land of the Big Mac. It was like the movie "Midnight Cowboy," in which the begrimed Ratso, dying and filthy poor, crawls on a Greyhound bus in New York absolutely convinced all would be well when he reached — Florida.

"I just wasn't built for that type of society," Byron said. "How the hell can you be happy in a sewer like that? All that lying and deception, the unemployment, and the crime — drugs, murder, rape. You see a man on one side of the street digging for food so his hunger pangs will go away, and ten feet away there's a man with so much money it's radiating from him. You can feel the wealth — like, it's glowing! So they hide behind concrete walls fifteen, twenty feet high, with guard dogs and steel cages. You see the money there, you see Palm Beach, and it's almost within your grasp. . . ."

Despite Byron's own drinking problem, he worried about Brian's habits. In Fort St. James, Brian had always been conscientious about his health, especially when he was serious about hockey. Even in the NHL, when the players gathered at a pub for the traditional post-game beerfest,

Brian often nursed a single beer all evening, knowing that he would feel terrible at the morning skate if he had a hangover. He used to become annoyed when someone smoked a cigarette near him.

Brian explained his drinking by saying it was part of the lifestyle of the hard-working, hard-living construction community. Most of his workmates stopped at a 7-Eleven on their way to work in the morning to buy cases of beer for the day. Also, working with tools and machines had always been an engrossing hobby when he was a hockey player, but when it was all he could do, he felt "misplaced" and "lower-classed." After years of people asking for his autograph, he felt looked down upon in Florida and he drank to fit in, and forget.

Byron became convinced Brian wasn't happy in Florida either. He liked most of Brian's friends, especially Dan Martinetti and Steve Dixon, but there were others who would pop up from time to time that Byron called "bad people." Brian had met most of them through Diane. Byron knew they were into drugs, as was Diane, and he thought some of them could be dangerous. They did not visit Brian at the trailer when Byron was there, but they would drop by the shop at Fischbach & Moore. Brian's loyalty to his friends was admirable, but sometimes it was simply the case that he couldn't say no. Byron thought Brian was heading for trouble.

Byron told him he didn't belong in Florida and urged him to come back to Canada. Brian would say that he hated the cold and he would clasp his arms as if the thought of it made him shiver. He would promise to think about it, but Byron knew that Brian was just putting him off. "He never could bullshit me," Byron said. He suspected Brian had become too "cityfied" ever to come home again.

"This whole Florida thing, Brian was running away," Byron said. "He was running from his past. He felt embarrassed by the divorces, by not being with his family, not being in the NHL. He felt like a failure, like he let everybody down, but it really wasn't like that. I told him he was a bloody hero back in Canada and he'd be welcomed with open arms. I told him he succeeded at something most people only dream about and if he'd come back with me I'd be beaming with pride because he's made it to the mountaintop."

After spending Christmas with Brian in West Palm Beach — they had a turkey dinner at a friend's house, then spent two hours at the beach because Byron wanted to tell his friends he went swimming on Christmas Day — Byron took a bus and headed home. He kept trying to convince Brian to come with him, but Brian said there was nothing for him up there. Byron did not like the way Brian looked. He saw something old and frightened in his eyes. Even at the bus depot, Byron tried one last time.

"How can I come back?" Brian asked.

Byron looked at him directly and said, "It's easy, you just go through the door of this bus with me right now."

"What about my things?"

"Forget them. Just make this first step, get on the bus and we're on our way."

"How *can* I do it?" Brian asked again.

"Just watch me, I'll show you," Byron told him, then he stepped up through the door of the bus.

Brian didn't move. "I'm sorry, Byron, I can't go."

Byron turned to him and said, "See you later. I love you."

The bus took four days to reach Los Angeles, where Byron bought a new shirt and a bottle of wine to celebrate New Year's. Then the bus headed north up the California coast, through Oregon and Washington to Vancouver, where Byron took another bus to Prince George, then another to Fort St. James. He arrived home on January 3, 1982. A month later, in the early hours of a Florida morning, someone shot and killed Michael Dalfo by the shell rock road in West Palm Beach.

In the summer of 1987, just before Brian's trial, Byron had not had a drink in more than five years, not since the morning shortly after he returned from Florida when he woke up with half a case of beer in his bedroom and asked himself, "What's this all about?" While he was in Florida he realized how much he missed Shelly and the children. He wanted to get on with his life. He wanted his family back.

He threw out the rest of the beer and stopped drinking that day. He had been told it would be difficult to forego booze in a place like Fort St. James, where lifelong friendships often are sustained by drink without the friends even knowing it. He would go to parties and hear stories and jokes that used to make him laugh, but sober they sounded silly and repetitious. It was difficult, and sad, and soon he knew he would have to leave. He and Shelly reconciled, Byron began to save money, but it was not until January, 1987, that he loaded his last belongings in a U-Haul and left the Fort to begin a new life on Vancouver Island. By early February 1987, Byron, Shelly and the children were settled in a comfortable home in Chemainus, a small town south of Nanaimo.

In the summer of that year, Byron and Shelly moved to the rented house in Duncan, mainly to be near a special school for Roy. His injury had resulted in ticks in his face and damaged tear ducts in one eye, which caused him to have to constantly rub the eye. Classmates made fun of the ticks in his face and his crooked smile. At the age of thirteen, Roy was still in grade five.

Byron knew that Brian not only would be welcomed back to Canada, but he could do well financially in Canada. And he would not have to go all the way back to Fort St. James, which he probably had outgrown. There were other parts of the country that were not as cold and isolated. Brian Spencer was a name that would still be recognized. He could coach at hockey schools, perhaps work with other former athletes trying to adjust to the real world.

There were ways to make money, which Byron had discovered when he did some freelance logging, selling timber from property he owned at Spencer's Ridge. Byron liked to explain how logging works, and he knew Brian would be good at it. First, he said, you go to a bush superintendent and haggle over the price of your logs.

"The price of logs goes up and down daily. You might get, say, $300 per one hundred board-feet of finished wood. Five thousand pounds of wood, six hundred and forty board-feet, is called a cunit. The bush superintendent comes out to see the trees, and we start haggling. I might ask for $75 a cunit, he might say $60, and we come to a price. Then I fall the trees, skin 'em and buck 'em. He'll give me the specifications, the lengths he needs. Then I'll deck 'em up and arrange for trucks. If I've got thirty loads, I'll hire three, four trucks. I'll need a power saw and a skidder. I can get a skidder during the seasonal layoffs, when they bring them out of the bush. They'll loan 'em to me and I'll just pay for the fuel. Each skidder can skid six, twelve trees, depending on the thickness.

"In seven days I felled, skidded, bucked and loaded enough wood to make $25,000. I used Roy Willick's loader, paid him with a credit of gravel. It costs $4 a cunit, $50 a load, so with thirty loads I owed Roy $1,500. The gravel comes to $2 a yard, so I owe Roy seven hundred and fifty yards of gravel. He might not need the gravel for a year or so. My only real expense was trucking. At $5 a cunit, $75 a load and thirty loads, that's about $2,200 — plus $1,000 fuel and miscellaneous. So for seven days, after expenses, I made about $20,000. Maybe a little more."

In January 1987, as Byron struggled to put his life in order, he heard that Brian had been arrested and charged with first-degree murder in West Palm Beach. From what he read in the newspapers, Byron realized Diane must have come back and Brian had taken her in again. He thought of Brian standing at the bus depot five years earlier in Florida. He kept thinking to himself, "If only he'd left that rathole. . . ." Byron was actually preparing to leave Fort St. James, making arrangements for the U-Haul, when the news of Brian's arrest made the local headlines. The only consolation was he would not have to answer those questions.

Before Brian's bail hearing in April, Byron got a job

operating heavy equipment in the mountains, building roads. The pay was good, the equivalent of $60,000 a year, and he had put in two ten-day shifts when he asked for five days off to attend the hearing. His boss said sure, your brother needs you, and we'll fly you back up to the job site as soon as you get back. When Byron returned, his job was gone. He couldn't do anything about it because he had only worked twenty days and he needed thirty days before he could take a complaint to the grievance board. An old friend from the Fort who lived in Courtenay confided to Byron one day that he had been hearing stories that these things must run in the family: first Roy Spencer at the television station, then Brian charged with murder down in Florida.

III

There was a tense atmosphere in Courtroom 315 when the afternoon session began sharply at two o'clock. After the long process of jury selection, the expectation was that matters were about to get very serious. There was no friendly bantering among the lawyers as Judge Fine entered and the bailiff ordered everyone to please stand. Both sides of the gallery were crowded with spectators and media. The Dalfo family and their friends occupied most of the front half of the left side, making their first appearance at the trial. Sue Head, Monica's neighbour, took a seat at the front of the right side of the gallery, directly behind Brian at the defence table. She felt faint from the tension. She turned to a friend and whispered, "I feel like throwing up."

After the jury was sworn in, Judge Fine gave them his instructions, then Chuck Burton stood and walked to the lectern in front of the jury. He wore a light grey suit, and he looked as much the fraternity president as ever, but he flashed only a subdued version of his charming smile. When he opened his mouth to speak his voice had a tight, constricted tone. He began, "The evidence will show that Michael Dalfo was brutally killed by this defendant in the early morning hours of February 4, 1982. . . ."

Brian sat at the defence table between Barry Weinstein and Richard Greene. He looked calm, a bit stone-faced.

Burton presented diagrams and photographs of the scene of the crime, and, using a wooden pointer, he tapped on them here and there to show the jurors where the body had been found, where it had been dragged, where the truck driver had been when he noticed the body, where there had been footprints of high-heeled shoes. Reading from notes he had written on sheets of yellow paper, Burton told the story of what happened that night, a story based entirely on what Diane had told the police on November 6, 1986, after she was granted immunity from prosecution.

Except for some minor details, to most of the spectators it all sounded like yesterday's news. There was the fourteen-year-old girl who lived in a trailer home near the isolated road where Dalfo was murdered — she was nineteen years old when the trial began — and Burton told the jurors she would testify that she had noticed footprints by the side of the road on her way to school in the morning. Burton described how Diane and Brian drove to Dalfo's townhouse, then to the isolated road where Diane heard Dalfo say something like, "If you touch me I'll call my lawyer." Then, after she ran down the road to PGA Boulevard, Diane said that Brian drove up in her Fiat and told her, "Now he can't call his lawyer."

A small detail in Burton's opening statement that was interesting to those who had followed the case was that, according to Diane, when they got back to the trailer on Skees Road Brian asked her for all her clothes. When she told him she had left her blue blazer on the road where they took Dalfo, Brian said they had to go back and get it. It was not clear from Burton's remarks if they went back together, or if Diane went alone. In her testimony to the police, Diane repeatedly said she was afraid of Dalfo — that was why she had wanted Brian to leave the Banana Boat and return home with her in the first place — and it was highly unlikely she would have been brave enough to return to the road alone if, as she told the police, she thought Brian had merely roughed up Dalfo, in which case he probably would have still been there, on the dirt road, waiting for her.

As for Diane's job with the escort service, Burton said it was true she earned one hundred dollars an hour, splitting the fee fifty-fifty with the agency, but she really didn't know she was expected to have sex with customers when she applied for the job. There were snickers among the spectators, but Burton went on to say that Diane intended to work for the escort agency for only four months, until she saved enough money to invest in a small restaurant on Okeechobee Boulevard.

Next, Burton used the pointer to tap on the photograph that showed where two spent .25-calibre shell casings were found. He showed where Dalfo's body had been dragged to a puddle in a clearing about forty yards from the shell rock road. He showed the jurors another photograph, this one of a dead Dalfo on a hospital table, with bullet holes, powder burns and pistol-whip bruises on his chin. He described Dalfo as being about five feet, nine inches tall and 160 pounds, and Diane as being only five feet, one inch and 120 pounds. In a mildly histrionic gesture, Burton lifted his right arm toward the ceiling, as if bracing it with his left hand, and, pretending to be a small, frightened woman, raised his voice to say Diane did not have the stature to reach up and pistol-whip Dalfo, or the strength to drag him forty yards to the muddy clearing.

Burton completed his opening statement in just under thirty minutes.

When Burton sat down, Barry Weinstein rose from the defence table, walked over to the lectern and again picked it up and moved it all the way to the railing behind the prosecution table. He rubbed a finger under his glasses, pinched the end of his nose, then raised his chin in a gesture of confidence, or defiance. He told the jurors, "As the evidence unfolds, you will hear about Diane Delena — not Brian Spencer. You will hear about Michael Dalfo — not Brian Spencer. You will hear about escort services — not Brian Spencer."

Weinstein wasted no time getting to the meaty stuff, which was Diane Delena and her job with Fantacee Island Escorts. "It was prostitution," he said, enunciating each of the four syllables as if he were snapping the stays of a satin bodice. "No ifs, ands or buts about that. Sex for money, lady of the evening — she was a prostitute."

Weinstein then went into the intricacies of the escort services, how they recruit women, what they pay them, how the individual agencies are controlled by an umbrella organization. Weinstein was touching on something new, or at least something that until then had not been reported on since Brian had been arrested in January. Little attention had been paid to the escort services, perhaps because they are so common in south Florida, so much a part of the social fabric, well below murder as an eyebrow-raiser. Until then, the motives discussed for Dalfo's murder had been personal and individual: jealousy, fear, spite, anger, the random fury of a washed-up hockey player for whom violence was a part of life, a gratuitous element in a rough game. No one, not even the police, had thought to connect Dalfo's death to the underworld of the sex trade and the violence of organized crime.

Leon Wright, sitting in the front row on the right side of the gallery, leaned forward and rested his forearms on the railing in front of him. Weinstein was using Leon's material. Leon had been studying the escort services for nine months and his investigation had taken him across the United States. All spring and summer and into the autumn he had been chasing down leads, following tentacles that reached out from a bank of telephones at a warehouse in West Palm Beach all the way to Texas, Nevada and Colorado. As a former homicide detective, he knew that even a single pimp with a single hooker uses certain "enforcement techniques" for protection or discipline. Prostitution cannot exist without them.

Weinstein continued, "The police did not investigate the escort services...."

Early on, Leon learned of an investigation called "Operation Greenback," which took place in 1982, coincidentally starting at about the time of Michael Dalfo's death. It was a combined operation, using undercover investigators from the Federal Bureau of Investigation, the Internal Revenue Service and the Drug Enforcement Administration.

They were investigating prostitution and money-laundering, which usually form a cozy symbiotic relationship in the bigger prostitution operations. Nearly all escort services are controlled by an underworld, criminal organization, but there is nothing illegal about an escort service. They are advertised regularly in newspapers and Yellow Pages and, though some might only offer pretty ladies as dinner companions for lonely gentlemen, most are fronts for prostitution and are used to launder money from criminal activities.

The result of Operation Greenback was the arrest of two people called Dan and Sally Phelps, both of whom were involved in running about a dozen escort services in south Florida, of which Fantacee Island Escorts was one. Dan and Sally Phelps — she was also called Ginger, Rachel, Linda and Ann, and among their colleagues they were known as "Doc and Ginger" — had been arrested in the summer of 1981 for bringing women from Colorado to Palm Beach County to work as prostitutes. The Operation Greenback investigators arrested the Phelpses in 1982 on a blue and white houseboat called the *Isis II*, moored at a marina at Hypoluxo, Florida. The raid on the *Isis II* netted itemized ledgers, paper shredders, index cards with nude photographs of the women who worked as escorts, plus a quantity of guns, some with the serial numbers chipped off. The Phelpses were convicted of conspiracy to launder money, but while awaiting an appeal in 1984, they jumped bail and have not been seen since.

Weinstein told the jurors he would call to the stand a crime scene expert, a police investigator who would testify that he found high-heeled shoe imprints in a muddy area off the shell rock where Diane said she had not been. Altogether, twenty-one soil samples were collected, twenty from the clearing where Dalfo's body was found. One of the twenty samples matched that found on Diane's shoes. Weinstein also told the jurors that not one police investigator, after more than five years of investigating, would be able to produce any physical evidence — not a blood stain, not a fingerprint, not a shoeprint, not a single strand of hair — linking Brian Spencer to the scene of the crime.

When Weinstein sat down, there was a moment of silence in the courtroom, the sort of expectant pause that in most other theatres precedes a standing ovation.

There was a brief recess, and in the corridor outside the courtroom, Brian walked down to a wooden bench where he lit a Marlboro. He was nervous about the large Dalfo clan gathered outside the courtroom. He had received several anonymous death threats, once just before the trial while he was having a drink at Tony Roma's Restaurant near Monica's. He worried that someone could be carrying a gun. He wondered if spectators should be screened by a metal detector. He mentioned this to Leon, who said he would check it out. Leon suggested Brian should not walk around the corridors too much by himself.

When court resumed, Burton called the FBI man from Washington to the stand. He listed his qualifications as an expert in "forensic mineralogy," then described the texture of the soil near the road where Dalfo's body was found. It was sandy soil, he said, made of silt, clay and rotted plant material. In March 1982, he had received the soil samples from the police in Palm Beach County, all in plastic 35-mm film containers. He examined each one, marking them "K-1," "K-2," "K-3," all the way to "K-20," the sample found closest to Dalfo's body, about thirty-six yards in from the shell rock road. The colours of the soil samples ranged from a light medium-grey near the road to a dark grey where Dalfo's body was found. The FBI man said the soil from the high-heeled shoes Diane was wearing that night matched the soil in the K-20 sample.

Chuck Burton asked the FBI man if he could say with a hundred percent accuracy that the soil from a woman's shoe was identical to soil found in a muddy field.

The FBI man answered, "Yes."

Irene Spencer had arrived that afternoon and made it to the courtroom in time to hear the testimony of the FBI man.

When court adjourned for the day, and for the Columbus Day long weekend, Brian and his friends decided to meet at the lounge at the Holiday Inn on PGA Boulevard, near Monica's townhouse. It was pouring rain. On the drive across the city, Brian was relaxed and looking forward to a three-day reprieve. He marvelled at Barry Weinstein's performance in the courtroom.

In the lobby of the Holiday Inn, Brian looked in the lounge and spotted his mother at the table, sitting with Monica and Sue. Irene wore her hair in a bun and she sipped a glass of tomato juice. Before he entered the lounge, Brian stopped abruptly at the doorway and said, "Oh, jeez, she doesn't know I'm smoking." He scrunched out his Marlboro in an ashtray, then walked in, bearhugged his mom and ordered two Budweisers.

CHAPTER SIX

The Long Weekend

I

It rained all night and was still raining when Leon Wright
woke up Saturday morning at his townhouse in Lake Worth.
Reports on the radio warned of a severe weather disturbance
to the southwest, something blowing in from the Yucatán
Peninsula. Leon's bedroom faces south, with a window at the
head of the bed that overlooks a small artificial lake. He
sleeps on a waterbed. All night the wind and rain lashed at
the window and in the dreamy, half-awake morning Leon felt
he was adrift on a soggy raft.

It was the start of the Columbus Day long weekend,
Thanksgiving Day weekend in Canada, but Saturday was
another working day for Leon. He had appointments all day
at the Public Defenders Office where he would be in-
terviewing more witnesses, an old friend of Brian from his
days at Fischbach & Moore, a bartender who used to work at
the Banana Boat. He had more leads to chase down — he was
trying to reach someone in Reno, Nevada — and at two
o'clock in the afternoon he was to meet Brian to prepare him
for prosecution questions in the event Weinstein decided to
put him on the stand.

Brian's lawyers intended to wait until after the prosecution had finished its case before deciding. There are
advantages and disadvantages in having a defendant testify.
He does not have to, of course, and Judge Fine had carefully
explained to the jurors that they must not be impressed
either way if the defendant chooses not to testify. But jurors
want the defendant to take the stand; they want to hear his

169

story, and a defendant who declines to testify — even one who is free on bail, unshackled, wearing nice clothes — comes across as someone with something to hide. Brian's lawyers were prepared for him to take the stand, and Brian himself wanted to do so; Leon and the lawyers would condition him for any white-hot cross-examination.

Brian being a former hockey player, and an irascible one at that, Chuck Burton dearly wanted him on the stand to show how unstrung hockey players can become in the heat of the game. He regarded Brian as a hockey goon, the type of player sent over the boards to do battle, to intimidate and to settle scores. Without a shot at Brian, Burton's case rested entirely on the testimony and credibility of Diane, a former prostitute. He had wanted to raise the fact that Brian owned guns, but Judge Fine disallowed that in the pre-trial motions because owning guns is not crime, and Brian had never been convicted of a felony. Burton had prepared a huge, coffee-table-sized blow-up of a fake driver's licence Brian had with him when he was arrested, one that used Brian's picture and the identification of a dead man. Burton expected it would make a dramatic impression on the jury, showing Brian as someone up to no good. Judge Fine had disallowed that, too. Burton knew the police had no physical evidence linking Brian to the crime scene, but if he could get him up there on the stand, just once; if he could goad him, rattle him — *wake up the Spin* — well, the jury might then have a different impression of this calm man with the blond curly locks.

Brian's lawyers and Leon understood the prosecution's tack. They knew Burton's most important witness was Diane, which meant they would have to attack her credibility. They knew Burton did not have much hard evidence to work with because the police investigation into Dalfo's murder had been shoddy. They expected Burton would try to portray Brian as a violent drifter, perhaps as a jealous lover, possibly bitter at the end of a glamorous career. They knew that Burton knew about Brian's convictions for drunk driving, his ten-day stay in jail in 1985, and that Brian owned a variety of rifles and handguns. They doubted Burton knew much about

Operation Greenback, and if he did, they did not expect him to make much of it.

Before he left for work, Leon called the woman who had said during jury selection that she remembered Diane from her neighbourhood in North Palm Beach. She was the lady in her sixties with the freshly-styled hair, the one in the pink pantsuit. She had told Judge Fine she could not believe anything Diane would say because of her "unsavoury reputation," and because she had this boyfriend named Douglas who was always in trouble with the law. Judge Fine had excused the woman from jury duty. Leon realized that the lawyers could not use what the lady had said during *voir dire*, not without risking a mistrial, but he thought if he could persuade her to testify independently she would make an effective defence witness. It was worth a try. He explained all this to her and asked more questions about Diane.

Leon enjoys the challenge of persuading people to say things to him that they would not say to anyone else. Once he managed to have the mother of a teenager who had killed someone admit to him that her son had been born out of wedlock. Her husband, a naval officer, had been away a long time, so the woman took a lover and became pregnant. Leon wanted to know about the boy's real father, because the lawyers were considering a defence of insanity and the boy might have inherited some berserk genes. It never came up in court, and the woman's husband never knew the boy wasn't his, still doesn't.

On the telephone in his kitchen, Leon reasoned patiently with the woman, but it was futile; she did not want to become involved. He gave her his office number and home number and asked her to call him if she changed her mind, and then, just before he hung up, Leon said softly, but with an understated power, "You've got to realize, ma'am, that a man's life is at stake."

She never returned his call.

As a former homicide detective, Leon has been involved in many investigations, sat in many courtrooms, and seen too many "solid" cases go down the toilet due to poor preparation or complacency. That was why he was so annoyed with Monica. She could have been an important witness for the defence, having once worked with Diane, but after being publicly perceived as Brian's girlfriend she would be worse than useless at the trial. "Buying Brian a new suit is nothing compared to how valuable she could have been," he said. "Even if she loves Brian, she could have waited six or eight months for him — because this man she says she loves is on trial for his life."

A case Leon will never forget involved a quiet, unassuming schoolteacher who was charged with first-degree murder for killing his wife. The man, whose name was Harris, did kill his wife, but it was not a killing that warranted a murder one charge. The man actually killed his son, too, another act in a bizarre play. Bizarre as it was, Leon likes to tell the story as a demonstration of the perils of overconfidence.

The son was a "mental case," a bad seed who had been causing his father emotional and physical grief for years. Harris managed some inexpensive townhouses not far from his house and one afternoon when he was inspecting an empty unit his son came by and they got into a violent fight, during which the man struck his son, who fell down, cracked his head and died. If he had called the police then, he could easily have made a case for self-defence. Instead, Harris buried his son under a sidewalk at the townhouse development. The son's disappearance caused no sensation because he had been known as a tumbleweed, taking off for months at a time.

Harris also had problems with his wife. Neighbours had seen her attempting to wash dishes in a clothes-dryer. She once chased a woman down the block with a knife. Harris cared for her for fifteen years, but he was so afraid of her that he slept in a separate bedroom, with a guard dog. During this time, Harris befriended a young deaf woman who moved into the neighbourhood, and even taught himself sign language. Over time they fell in love and had a baby.

One day Harris and his wife were out for a drive and he

stopped to inspect one of the townhouses. At the same time, the deaf woman and her daughter were driving through the neighbourhood. When she noticed Harris's car, she stopped and the little girl ran to the car, shouting, "Daddy! Daddy!" Harris's wife saw this, pulled out a knife she carried in her purse and chased after the deaf woman. Harris heard screams, rushed out and, while defending the deaf woman, knocked his wife to the ground. As happened to his son three years earlier, she cracked her head and died. Harris made the same mistake and later buried her, too.

He managed to convince the deaf woman that his wife was all right, but had gone to live elsewhere. When his other son asked about his mother, he said she had been put in a sanitorium. The son became suspicious, went to the police and they arrested Harris and charged him with first-degree murder. Leon worked on the case with Barry Weinstein, and when it came to trial, the prosecution offered a plea bargain of eight years. Harris had been in jail three years, which meant if he accepted the plea bargain, he might serve only another three years. But he refused the offer, saying he was innocent because his wife's death was an accident — no one ever found out about his son's death — and he believed in the American system of justice, confident the court would set him free. Even while the jury was deliberating, the state lawyer repeated the offer. This time Weinstein urged Harris to accept the plea. Again he refused. The jury found him guilty of first-degree murder and Harris was sentenced to life imprisonment, which meant twenty-five years without parole.

The case, of course, was entirely different from Brian's, but Leon worried that the same sort of complacency was setting in. Things had been going too smoothly. There was too much optimism, and that made him nervous.

Leon is continually confounded by people who regard the court process lightly, who do not take even life imprisonment or the death penalty seriously. Sometimes he prefers working on a weak case, because there is less chance of having your heart broken. Innocent people *are* convicted, and sometimes executed by the state. Leon was involved in at least one case where an innocent man went to the electric chair in Florida, and that fairly recently, in 1984. It was the case of James Adams, a black man executed for a murder that had happened more than ten years earlier in Fort Pierce, Florida. The case concerned racism more than anything else, but it did involve the execution of an innocent man.

Michael Radelet, a sociologist at the University of Florida in Gainesville, wrote a paper on the case as part of a project on "innocence research." Leon, who had joined the Public Defenders Office as various appeals were underway to save Adams from execution, helped Radelet with the research. Adams was one of fourteen children of a black family in rural Tennessee. When he was twenty-one, he and a brother were convicted of petty larceny for having stolen a pig, which the family ate. When Adams was twenty-six, he was convicted of rape and sentenced to a prison term of ninety-nine years. The victim was a white woman, who kept referring to Adams as a "nigger." The jury was entirely white, even though blacks represented fourteen percent of the population in that part of Tennessee; indeed, there was not a single black person among the five hundred people chosen for jury selection. There was also no physical evidence that Adams raped the woman. She said he did, and that was enough.

Adams turned out to be a model prisoner, and after he had served nine years the Board of Probation and Paroles recommended that his sentence be commuted to time served. Even the commissioner of the Tennessee Department of Correction wrote to Adams to praise Adams' attitude and the quality of his prison work and said, "all of us in the Department of Correction are most pleased to see men like yourself respond in such a splendid manner." However, the district attorney who had prosecuted Adams objected, which was enough to keep Adams behind bars. In prison, Adams had access to state-owned vehicles and, though a convicted rapist, he worked as a trustee at a nearby facility for teenage girls. When he learned he would not be released until the state prosecutor dropped his objections, Adams escaped by simply driving off in one of the prison trucks. Ten months later, in Florida, he was arrested for murder.

The victim was Edgar Brown, a sixty-one-year-old rancher and former deputy sheriff. On the morning of November 12, 1973, someone had entered Brown's home while he was away. When Brown returned, he was beaten with a poker. He died the next day.

Adams' car had been seen in Brown's driveway. A witness testified he definitely saw Adams driving the car, and another witness testified he thought he saw Adams driving the car. Adams said his car had been driven that morning by a friend, Vivian Nickerson, and another man, Kenneth Crowell. Adams said he was at Nickerson's home at the time of the murder. The only witness who actually saw someone leaving Brown's home at the time of the killing said the person was blacker than Adams and did not have a moustache. Adams' lawyers found three people who heard the witness, who positively identified Adams, say he was going to testify against Adams because "he's been going with my wife." A polygraph administered to this witness just before Adams' execution indicated his testimony at the trial in 1974 had been deceitful.

Vivian Nickerson said in a pre-trial deposition that Adams arrived at her home before the time of the murder, and that she had borrowed his car. At the trial, she changed her statement, saying Adams arrived at her home after the time of the murder. Nickerson, though only fifteen years old, was a large woman with a strikingly masculine appearance, and Radelet suggests she could have been the person seen leaving Brown's house. The witness testified he had heard a woman shout from inside, "In the name of God, don't do it!"

"But the most significant blow to the state's case against Adams concerns evidence that was not presented at trial," Radelet says in his paper. "En route to the hospital with Mr. Brown in an ambulance, Mrs. Brown found strands of hair clasped in his hand. This hair obviously came from the assailant. However, after it was given to the State Crime

Laboratory for comparison with samples of Adams' hair, it was determined that the hair was definitely *not* that of Adams."

The crime lab did not release its report until three days after the trial ended, and even then, when it could have been used to support a request for a new trial, the report was not given to Adams' lawyers. According to Radelet, "Adams was convicted because the state of Florida developed a very strong circumstantial case against him and because he was an easy target...." It was here that the Adams case was relevant to Brian's case, besides the fact that both involved a first-degree murder charge and the spectre of the death penalty. Brian may have been white, and free on bail, but he was an easy target, too. He was a former major-league athlete, one who had been known to be violent. He also faced some damning circumstantial evidence; he was living with the woman who had been physically linked to the scene of the crime.

Early in the investigation of the Adams case, Leon believed James Adams was guilty, but the more deeply he became involved, the more convinced he was that Adams was innocent. Leon had once believed in capital punishment as well, but when Adams died in the electric chair on May 10, 1984, he no longer supported it.

Leon dislikes most professional athletes. He was impressed by Gerry Hart, Brian's former teammate on the New York Islanders, and he admired the boxing skill of Muhammad Ali, whom he once met at a party in Philadelphia and found to be a quiet, shy man. Most former big-time athletes he regards as egocentric and immature, grown men wallowing in suspended adolescence.

He also does not like people who blame others for their misfortunes, which was how he had come to regard Brian, who constantly blamed other people — women mainly, especially his two former wives — for the bad things that happened to him. Leon liked Janet Spencer, Brian's second wife. He met her when she came to West Palm Beach with the two boys to attend Brian's bail hearing. What impressed him was her poise, the way she was bringing up the boys, how, despite a mountain of difficulties of her own, she had not turned them against their father. Leon suspected that Brian preferred women he could dominate, and that Janet probably was too strong for him.

He had found Brian more likeable when he first met him, when he was in jail. He looked better physically and seemed altogether a nicer person, personable, friendly, enthusiastic, generous and cooperative. There was a spark to him, a quick intelligence. And Brian kept himself busy. He helped other inmates write letters.

Leon wondered if Brian might be one of those people who function better when confined, figuratively or literally. He was a good student when he was in school; when he left, he drifted into bad company, bad times. He turned his life around in reform school, thrived on the discipline of training camp, and performed well in the regimens of professional hockey. But when his hockey career ended, he drifted again, and life turned sour. It is easy to know who you are and where you stand when your accomplishments and transgressions are tallied daily and compiled in columns of agate type. Jail offers a similar if sterner version of this, with its regulations, codes, schedules and uniforms.

When he was in jail Brian wrote a letter to *The Hockey News*, which brought sackloads of mail to the jail from all over North America. He received nearly three thousand letters, and he devoted himself to responding to each one. He autographed old hockey cards, shared reminiscences and told stories from his NHL days. Some of the letters went on for five and six handwritten pages.

His original letter appeared under a section called "Fan Forum," under the heading "Spencer Makes Plea." It read in full:

I skated off the ice for the last time professionally about 10 years ago. Maybe you remember me —
Spinner Spencer.

I'm writing you now from a Florida jail, waiting

trial on charges of murder. Believe me, jail is no place for a decent human soul. And believe me, while I've done a lot of things that didn't measure up, I didn't do this.

I know every accused person says the same. But I really didn't. I hope that God and the American justice system sees the truth and sets me free.

Meanwhile, I sit here with two passions, really two wishes that you, in your charity, might help fulfill.

First, I hope you find it in your heart to think a kindly thought and to say a prayer from and for my two lovely boys, aged nine and ten, that they come through this nightmare unscathed. And for sure, I hope you will say a prayer for their mother, a woman as rare as she is beautiful — who for the last five years now has had to endure and bravely struggle against a myriad of health problems.

Second, if you could please write me. You cannot know how devastating it is to be wrongfully locked in a cage day after day, or how depressing it is to continually be with only hardened criminals — angry, cold-eyed, violent men who have no sense of morality or dignity or shame.

Maybe the "glory days" are over, but not my memory of how incredibly uplifting the fans are, and what a joyous part of my life you were, you are, and you always will be.

If you do write, even a note, it will be the most wonderful gift, and I promise to write you in return.

Many thanks and God bless.

Brian (Spinner) Spencer

Brian's letters, like his moods, shift abruptly in style and content. Even his handwriting can change from one letter to the next, from a crude scrawl to an elegant, almost feminine script. There was much in *The Hockey News* letter that was

pure Brian ("I've done a lot of things that didn't measure up"),
but there was much that seemed stage-managed, prompted,
designed for maximum emotional impact ("a woman as rare
as she is beautiful"). Parts of the letter read as if someone on
Brian's Public-Defender team set out to create an impression,
a scenario, much as was done in arranging for his wife and
children to be at the bail hearing in April.

At first, Leon thought Brian might be someone who could
benefit from a serious life crisis, who would recognize and
seize the opportunity of a second chance and make
something of himself. He used to talk with Brian about
forming a speakers bureau, using former athletes from all the
major sports who would devote themselves to helping other
former athletes make the adjustment. Leon did not see it as a
charity; he thought it could be a big money-maker, and he
was willing to help manage the operation. He envisaged a
chain of spas and wooded retreats where broken-down jocks
could mend their souls and bodies. The athletes could raise
money by speaking at year-end banquets and awards
dinners. The public relations aspect alone would appeal to
large corporations, many of which already have lavish
recovery centres for their burned-out executives. And what
would delight a burned-out executive more than to share a
Nautilus or a sauna or a game of cribbage with Kareem
Abdul-Jabbar or Dave Winfield or Joe Montana or Bobby Orr
— or Brian Spencer? That was when Leon would say, "If
Brian played his cards right, he could be a rich man."

Leon believed Brian was innocent, based on the facts of
the case and Brian's demeanour. At their first session, he
asked Brian the ultimate question, "Did you do it?" It is never
an easy question. Family and friends rarely ask, because the
asking implies if not doubt, then something less than a
whole-hearted trust. Many lawyers do not like to ask,
because knowing the answer might diminish their enthusiasm and commitment. Leon had no qualms about asking
the question, having met and interviewed many murderers
during his years as a homicide detective. Brian said, "No."

When Leon arrived home late Saturday evening, there was a message from Paula Fairchild, one of the women who worked with Diane at Fantacee Island Escorts. The message was "Prostitutes know how to get information from hotels."

It related to an incident that had happened after Brian's bail hearing in April. Brian's mother and Byron had stayed at the Hyatt Hotel during the hearing. There was jubilation after Brian was temporarily set free and it was arranged that Brian, his family and friends and the lawyers would gather at the Crab Pot, a restaurant by the bridge to Singer Island, for a small celebration. Passing time before leaving for the restaurant, Byron and Brian's old friend from Toronto, John Antonacci, decided to get away from the reporters and photographers, so they went up to Byron's hotel room. As they were talking about the hearing and Brian's days with the Toronto Maple Leafs, the phone rang. It was Diane.

While Byron listened to her, frowning, Antonacci realized who was calling, and he whispered instructions in Byron's ear, coaching him on what to say, what not to say, what to ask her. As a policeman himself, a member of the RCMP, Antonacci thought Leon would be interested in this, so he encouraged Byron to keep Diane on the phone and to make notes. Then he left the room to find Leon, leaving Byron alone, struggling to cradle the receiver at his ear while he scratched his notes on scraps of hotel stationery.

When Leon arrived, he was furious. "I thought I told you not to have anything to do with that woman!" he shouted, shaking his fist in Byron's face. The incident caused a rift between Leon and Byron that continued up to the trial.

One of the conditions of Brian's release on bail was that he was to have no contact whatsoever with Diane before the trial. After the bail hearing, Leon had warned the family that Diane might try something sneaky, might try to make it appear that Brian was in communication with her. It could be that Diane, having lived with Brian, might know precisely what buttons to push to goad him into saying something threatening that could result in his bail being revoked. Leon had made it clear that if Brian said so much as a word to

Diane, he could be back in jail that day, a situation that would play right into the hands of the prosecution, who would love to have Brian back behind bars when the trial began.

In their telephone conversation, Diane had said she would like to talk to Brian, and would like to meet with Byron, but that was all Byron could remember. After Leon stormed in and shouted at him, Byron was so upset he tore up the notes and flushed them down the toilet. Early in August, Leon had called Byron at his home in Maple Bay and asked him to think back and try to remember what Diane had told him on the telephone that day. Still miffed four months later, Byron replied, "That's all fine and dandy, Leon, but under the circumstances I don't have much to say to you."

Even with the trial underway, Leon never stopped chasing down leads. He had called Paula, because he wanted to know how Diane knew that Brian's family was at the Hyatt, and how she knew exactly when to call to reach Byron. If it had been a ploy by the prosecution, a set-up, it could be useful information for the defence. Paula returned Leon's call to say that prostitutes know how to get information from hotels. Satisfied with her message, and knowing what she meant, Leon then slipped out to pick up an order of fried chicken, which he brought back to the townhouse and ate with his fingers, accompanied by a bottle of 1983 Rutherford Hill Merlot.

II

At noon on Sunday, Irene Spencer was alone in Monica's apartment, where she had slept on the couch in the living room Friday and Saturday night. There were signs of strain in her face, in her eyes, but for a woman in her mid-sixties she looked remarkably trim and fit, with the figure of a much younger woman. Monica had driven Brian to the Public Defenders Office for another session with Leon and his lawyers. Byron, who finally arrived Friday evening, still without his uppers, was across the road at Steve Dixon's apartment going through the stacks of Brian's letters.

After the session at the Holiday Inn on Friday, Brian had gone out with some friends and did not get back to Monica's until very late. He had been drinking and he entered the apartment noisily. Mrs. Spencer pretended to be asleep. She had given Brian a money order for $1,000 the evening before, telling him she hoped he would use it to visit her on Vancouver Island after the trial. In the morning, while Brian slept, his mother puttered around the apartment and found a snapshot of Brian taken the summer before at the ox-roast. She could tell by his pose that he had been drinking so heavily that day he could hardly stand up. Disappointed, and not wanting to unwittingly encourage such tendencies, she entered the bedroom as Brian slept and retrieved the money order from his shirt pocket.

When Byron returned, Irene went over to Steve's to look at Brian's letters. Steve was watching a football game on television, drinking Coors beer from a can, which he held in

an insulated holder. He showed Irene the letters, some piled
in bundles and in boxes on a couch by the window, others
stacked behind the couch. She gathered all the bundles and
boxes, arranged them in an enormous pile at the front
of the couch, then took a picture of them with Steve in the
foreground.

Then she sat down and began opening envelopes at
random. There was a letter from Dean Gelinas of Sudbury,
whose father had taken him to Maple Leaf Gardens on a
Saturday seventeen years earlier to watch a morning
practice.

> I was only 10 or 11 years old. So my dad brought me to
> the practice. I was in awe of the Gardens and
> everything. We went down to rinkside and a few of
> the players were skating around. Then you were
> skating around. My dad called out to see if you would
> come to talk to us. My dad knew it would give me a
> big thrill if one of the players came to talk to us or give
> us an autograph. So my dad called out to you and you
> came over to the side boards right away. I think my
> eyes popped out when you came over. An NHL player
> was going to talk to me! My dad asked a few
> questions about the game that night and you
> answered him so politely and professionally. You
> signed an autograph for me. Then my dad asked if
> you could get me a stick and you told him to come
> over to the other side of the boards near the Leaf
> dressing room. My dad and I trotted over to the other
> side and you gave me one of Paul Henderson's sticks.
> You also gave me a puck.
>
> I gotta say to you Brian that I remember how you
> took time to talk to me and my dad. We were there —
> two nobodys, my dad a really shy man and me a little
> kid, and you took time out to make my day and my
> dad's. I still feel Brian you made me a better person by
> taking time out to talk to us.

A letter from John Antonacci:

> Brian, out of something bad always comes something

*good. Maybe it's time for us to regroup. You belong
with Janet and your family. And you still are part of
the Antonacci family. Together we will get through
this. There is room for you and your family in our
home, when you get through this.*

*Your picture is on our fridge, and not a day goes
by without us thinking about you.*

A letter from the Berensons in Regina Beach,
Saskatchewan:

*It's hard for us to believe what's happened to you and
we want you to know that you're still one of the nicest
boys that we've known. We loved you for your
kindness, your thoughtfulness and the fact that you
appreciated any little thing we did for you. We still
prize the hockey stick you gave us and for the kind
words you wrote on it.*

*We're very sorry about what's happening to you
and want you to know that we're thinking of you and
are praying for your release and your future.*

A letter from Paul Henderson, a former Maple Leaf
teammate, now a committed Christian working for Athletes
in Action:

*First of all, I am sorry you are in this situation and
whether you are guilty or not makes no difference to
me how I feel toward you. I imagine you know that I
am a Christian and involved in the ministry. The
greatest news I have ever heard was that there is a
God that loves you and me in spite of everything we
have done. . . . The one good thing about your
circumstances is that you have the time to think
about what is really important. . . .*

A letter from Jason Spencer, when he was ten:

*Dear daddy,
How are you doing bub? Today I got your letter. I sit
here in my warm home when you read in a cold
lonely cell. Nothing to do, no one to talk to except*

*wait and live day by day. I can't wait until you get
out. Maybe we can bust whoever set you up and sue
his ugly ass for everything he's got. We can be a
family again. You'll be my father and I'll be your son.
I love you alot. You know that.*

After reading the letters and various newspaper and
magazine clippings, Irene reminisced about Roy and Fort St.
James and life at the farm. It always irritated her, and
saddened her, to read a story about Brian in which he
denigrated life in Fort St. James. Sometimes he referred to the
British Columbia interior as "the Ozarks of the North." In one
of the clippings she had read, Brian said, "Growing up in that
remote part of Canada left me socially unprepared for the big
city rich life I was thrown in."

"I don't think it was necessary for him to say that," Irene
said, walking back to Monica's apartment. "Any place is a
good place to grow up. You could be raised in Hamilton,
Ontario, and still not be prepared for the NHL. I don't know
how anyone can be prepared to be thrown into that
lifestyle."

It was hot and sunny, but the thick grass underfoot was
still wet from the rain. Men were playing touch football in the
field across from Monica's apartment. The latest weather
reports said a hurricane was forming in the Gulf of Mexico,
but early on Sunday afternoon there was only a soft,
welcome breeze.

"Brian's been surrounded with false glamour for many
years," Irene said. "He was brought up in a very strict,
hardworking family." Roy always was gentle and protective
of Irene, but when Brian and Byron were boys he was a
perfectionist and intolerant of misbehaviour. "I believe that
the boys were frightened of him and tried desperately to
please him at all times," she said. "This became increasingly
difficult as his illness progressed. I, too, was frightened —
frightened that in a fit of temper he might hurt the boys
physically — so I tried to keep them out of their father's way
as much as possible without making it too obvious. The
children didn't come home and play with other kids while
their parents did something else. We had to do everything

together, and it got to be a way of life. I actually think when the boys were growing up they appreciated that kind of life, but Brian always thought he was missing out on something — something somebody else had that he had heard about or read about, the bright lights. He wanted a taste of it."

Brian's arrest came as a brutal shock to his mother. She knew his marriage had ended and he had left Janet and the boys, but she thought he was adjusting well to life after hockey. He did not often call or write, but that was not unusual for Brian. She knew he was a superb mechanic, always happy when smeared in grease and clunking around with tools and equipment. All along she thought he was doing splendidly in Florida, working in a truck repair shop; then, late one night in January at her home in Cranbrook, British Columbia, she learned he had been arrested and charged with first-degree murder and kidnapping. She heard it on the late news on television.

"Brian doesn't seem to trust women. He certainly doesn't trust Linda, and he doesn't trust even Janet. He's been hurt, terribly hurt. Sometimes I think, secretly, he doesn't even trust me."

Irene Spencer was very fond of Janet. She was proud of how she was raising the two boys, Jason and Jarret. Brian brought her to Fort St. James one summer and Janet used to talk about washing the dinner dishes in a stream by the house on the farm. Mrs. Spencer called her "Jan," and Janet called Mrs. Spencer "Mom," and they continued to write to each other long after the marriage ended.

Brian met Janet soon after he was traded to the New York Islanders from the Maple Leafs at the start of the 1972-73 season. She was — it is no facile description — beautiful: tall and stylish, with long dark hair and cover-girl eyes. She was bright and articulate. She worked in group sales for the Islanders and Brian used any excuse to walk by her desk in the Islanders' offices. Brian's first season with the Islanders, then an expansion team, was one of his best ever. He played in 78 games, scored 14 goals and 24 assists, and was voted Most Popular Player by the booster club, but when Janet first met him she was not impressed. "I didn't want anything to do with an athlete," she said, "especially some chubby Canadian boy who played hockey."

Off the ice, Janet found Brian to be shy, boyish and unsophisticated. The Islanders' offices were located on Old Country Road on Long Island and when Brian first arrived he expected to find a dirt path. She liked his honesty and lack of pretension, and he was a persistent suitor. He wrote her love letters and sent roses to her desk, sometimes with poems. Janet thought he was an incurable romantic. "He had some winning ways," she said. "He could be very charming." Years later, Janet would say he was like the movie character Crocodile Dundee. After Brian was arrested in West Palm Beach, and long after their marriage had ended, she told a writer from *Newsday*, "Every woman should be as loved as I was."

Irene still does not know precisely when Brian and Janet were married. She found out about the marriage several years after the event, when Brian was playing for Buffalo. She is not sure when they broke up either; after Brian left Pittsburgh, and after two seasons in the minors, Irene received a letter from Janet telling her that the marriage was over. Until then, Irene assumed it was a successful union, having produced two wonderful boys. Janet told her she found Brian impossible to live with. Two years later, Brian sent his mother an Easter card from Florida; that was how Irene learned that Brian had left Long Island, leaving the boys with Janet. It reminded Irene of Roy Spencer's father, one day just taking off, abandoning his family in Red Lodge, Alberta. "It seems history was repeating itself," she said.

Irene saw Janet again at the bail hearing, then soon after she heard that Janet was very ill with cancer. She had had a double mastectomy, but the operation did not contain the disease. She had given up on surgery and radiation and was trying to fight it with a personal therapy of optimism, will power, vitamins and diet. As Brian's trial approached, Irene learned that Janet had taken a turn for the worse and might not last until Christmas.

By the time Irene returned to Monica's apartment, Brian and
Monica were back and with them were Rick Martin, Brian's
old roomie and closest friend when he played for the Buffalo
Sabres, and Martin's wife, Mikey. Martin puffed on a thick
cigar. He was born in Verdun, Quebec, and though he was
never as combative a player as Brian, he was enormously
strong, especially in the arms and shoulders. He has a
formidable handshake.

When he was a rookie with the Sabres in the 1971-72
season, Martin scored 44 goals, mostly with a quick, accurate
wrist shot. The shot seemed to surprise goaltenders, who,
since Bobby Hull entered the league in the 1950s, had become
accustomed to the booming slapshot. In the 1973-74 season,
when Brian was traded to the Sabres from the New York
Islanders at the end of the schedule, Martin scored 52 goals
and had established himself as one of the superstars of the
NHL. The late Punch Imlach, who coached the Sabres when
Martin first came up, called him "the greatest natural scorer
I've ever coached." As a member of the "French Connection"
line, with Gilbert Perreault and René Robert, Martin helped
to transform the Sabres into one of the best teams in the NHL
and a solid Stanley Cup contender.

When Floyd Smith took over as coach of the Sabres, he
put Brian on a line with Martin and Peter McNab. Martin
called Brian his "main man," and that year, 1974-75, was
probably Brian's most successful and satisfying season in the
NHL. He played in 73 games, scored 13 goals and 29 assists,
and the Sabres reached the Stanley Cup Finals against the
Philadelphia Flyers. More important, Brian loved Buffalo,
and with Rick Martin he established a friendship and rapport
he had never experienced in hockey. They were both tough,
engaging free spirits, probably incapable of rooming with
any of the other players. Only Martin could joke around by
dumping a pail of cold water on Brian in the dressing-room,
knowing how he hated the cold. And one night on the road,
when Martin kept pestering Brian, keeping him from
sleeping, Brian picked up Martin and slammed him to the
floor on his head. Martin lay there, unconscious, and all

Brian could think of was, "Oh no, I think I've killed one of our fifty-goal scorers." The next morning, at practice, Brian apologized to Martin, but Martin reacted as if nothing had happened. "He might not have remembered," Brian said. "He had finished a couple of bottles of wine."

They were friends away from the rink, too, and in chumming around with Martin, Brian learned to speak French. During their first summer together, Martin rebuilt an old Thunderbird, and Brian started work on what would emerge as the growling, belching Hulk.

Martin had visited Brian when he was in jail, and he had come to attend the trial. Another friend, John Long, would be arriving Monday, former Islander teammate Gerry Hart was expected Monday as well, and John Antonacci would be arriving from Toronto on Tuesday. Martin and Mikey had won a trip to Florida months earlier in a draw in Buffalo. They had saved the trip so it would coincide with Brian's trial.

Martin was his boisterous old self, cracking jokes, hoisting Budweisers. In Monica's living room, after Irene had arranged everyone for a group photograph, Martin explained a little bar bet that usually never fails to win him ten or twenty dollars. Whenever the conversation drifts to sports, and it usually does, Martin explains that eyesight is at least as important as strength and quickness, and to demonstrate this he asks the bartender to place a beer can — *Say that can of Bud over there* — on a shelf ten or fifteen feet away. With great attention to detail — *Could you turn the lights up a little, please* — Martin then squints at the can in the distance and slowly recites the tiny, four-line statement at the top of the label: "This is the famous Budweiser beer. We know of no other brand produced by any other brewer which costs so much to brew and age. Our exclusive Beechwood Aging. . . ."

Now that Budweiser was being produced in Canada, Martin was applying himself to memorizing the French version.

III

The weather warnings continued Monday, with bulletins every few minutes. Tropical Storm Floyd was heading toward Palm Beach County. Evacuation plans were being prepared. Temporary shelters were being designated in malls and community centers. A television weatherman explained that a storm becomes a hurricane when the winds reach seventy-five miles an hour, and off the west coast of south Florida, Floyd was already gusting to ninety-five. Sheets of hard rain swept in through the streets. Some of Leon's neighbours were installing plywood sheets over the windows of their townhouses.

After breakfast, Irene took Brian to a nearby mall and bought him some new shirts and a comfortable pair of brown shoes. She repeated her offer to Brian to visit her in British Columbia after the trial. She and Byron then packed their bags and drove across the city in her rented car to take rooms at the Hampton Inn, a hotel by the airport strip. She made plans to leave for home the following Saturday morning, whether there was a verdict or not.

It was another working day for Leon, more witnesses to prepare, more leads to chase down. He was having problems locating one out-of-state witness. He arrived home late in the afternoon, the wind and rain flailing at the windshield of his old yellow Plymouth with the "Jesus Saves" bumper sticker at the back. It is the "ghetto car" he uses to go to and from work, saving his sporty Toyota for weekends.

When Leon stepped in the door, leaving a trail of water on

the floor, he was agitated and pessimistic. He was thinking again how he did not like these "easy cases." While he was downtown, someone had told him they had seen Brian partying Saturday night at the Holiday Inn on PGA Boulevard. With stories and pictures of Brian in the newspapers every day, with the daily television reports, Brian was high-profile again, easily recognized at any of the night spots. Leon knew how small a town West Palm Beach could be. The jurors were unsequestered, free to roam the city, and Leon wondered what one of them would think if they saw Brian out having a swell time. And there were the death threats.

He wondered if Brian realized that had he used private lawyers, his defence would have been worth about $500,000, what with Leon's trips to Texas and Colorado, the cost of taking subpoenas and flying in witnesses, the consultations, the overtime. Weinstein and Greene, like Leon, also had worked on the case all weekend. Weinstein had gained back a lot of ground in court Friday with his strong opening remarks, but the lawyers were not taking any chances.

"It was a hit," Leon said, sitting on the couch in his living room that evening. "It was an execution. Someone picked up Dalfo at his home and brought him to that access road and executed him. It's not the style of a jealous man, an angry lover."

Guns had been seized on the *Isis II* houseboat when Dan and Sally Phelps had been arrested as part of Operation Greenback. One of the guns, a .22-calibre handgun, had the serial numbers filed off. Guns used in gangland executions usually have the serial numbers removed so they could not be traced. The weapon used to kill Dalfo had been a .25-calibre handgun. Leon had learned in the course of his investigation that someone connected with the escort service had purchased a .25-calibre handgun in Tampa before the Dalfo murder, and the numbers of that gun had also been removed.

Leon had found out that the federal undercover agents investigating the escort services and the money laundering operation had made an offer to buy the escort service. They wanted to see the money change hands, then follow it to the "laundry." It would have been important to the owners of the escort service that the operation appear to be running smoothly with a potential buyer on the scene, and then this customer, Michael Dalfo, starts causing trouble. Leon ran the scenario through his head.

"Late that night, after Diane had told the service about her problems, she drives back to Dalfo's with — who? Mr. X? They're just going to rough him up. They probably expected he'd be at his condo, inside, but when they arrive they find him standing outside. So they take him away, and he's loud, threatening to make trouble. So Mr. X does him in, and Diane's right there. He tells Diane not to talk."

What perplexed Leon was how people can so easily believe life and death dramas when they read about them in books or watch them on television or the movie screen, but find them hard to feature in real life. "Believe me, it's normal stuff," he said.

Leon had managed to track down a former employee of the escort service, a man who used to work for Dan and Sally Phelps and who had testified against them at their trial. The man was on a federal witness protection program, using an alias, and Leon had arranged for him to testify at Brian's trial. In the past week, however, Leon had lost touch with him. He could not locate him anywhere. That was what had been occupying so much of his time at the office all weekend.

But what if the prosecution, knowing the direction the defence was heading, decided to go along with them. Okay, so it's a hit, an execution, but who's to say Brian wasn't approached by someone in the escort service, offered some big money? Diane certainly was involved with the escort service, and he was living with her, and at that time in his life, with two ex-wives and five children. . . . What if Brian was Mr. X?

Leon let his head fall back on the couch and he stared up at the ceiling.

"Brian's innocent. I know he didn't do it. But the

prosecution just might try a stunt like that. It's been one of my concerns all along."

CHAPTER SEVEN

Tuesday: *The Burden of Proof*

I

Hurricane Floyd swept by Palm Beach County overnight and blew off into the Atlantic Ocean. The morning was warm, promising sunshine. There was a vague sense of disappointment among the locals; the juices were flowing, but the enemy didn't show.

Nothing sneaky about a hurricane; it will strike at High Noon, with a day's warning, so you can pour yourself a drink as it howls at the windows, pushes at the door and tries to crawl down the chimney. Easier to deal with a hurricane than the muggings, burglaries, assaults and other violence of urban life. In 1986, the Florida Department of Law Enforcement published a "crime clock" that showed a violent crime committed in the state every 4.3 minutes, a nonviolent crime every 37.6 seconds, a murder every 6.4 hours, a forcible rape every 1.4 hours, a robbery every 12.3 minutes, a motor vehicle theft every 7.5 minutes, an aggravated assault every 7.4 minutes, a burglary every 2 minutes, a larceny every minute. An FBI report described West Palm Beach, one of sixteen municipalities in Palm Beach County, as the most dangerous medium-sized city in the United States in 1986, with the highest rate of reported crimes in the nation. One in ten residents of West Palm Beach had been a crime victim in 1986. It was not the image the tourist brochures proclaimed, and tourism is to south Florida what casinos are to Las Vegas and Atlantic City, what logging is to Fort St. James.

When the FBI report arrived in July, acting Police Chief

Ron Albright tried to gather what roses he could among the thorns. He told the city commissioners of West Palm Beach that for the first six months of 1987, major crimes had decreased by two percent from the same period in 1986. And he said that between 1985 and 1986, arrests had increased to 12,025 from 10,315. It was a valiant effort, but to no avail. "I don't think we can PR this any more," Commissioner Helen Wilkes commented.

The findings of the report did not surprise Leon Wright. As he drives around West Palm Beach, nearly every major intersection reminds him of a case he has investigated for the Public Defenders Office, and all his cases involve capital crimes. He blames most of the serious crime on drugs, especially cocaine, and the migration to West Palm Beach of transients who come expecting the streets to be paved with gold. They do not even need a place to live. Many sleep in fields, on the beaches, or under bridges. One of Judge Fine's recent cases involved an incident of "bum-bashing," which has become something of a sport in West Palm Beach among restless toughs, many of them still in high school, who drive about looking for transients to bounce around.

Every week, *The Palm Beach Post* regularly carries a list of support groups available in Palm Beach County. On Mondays, Narcotics Anonymous meets at noon on North Dixie Highway. Another chapter meets in the evening at Lake Hospital in Lake Worth, after which Adult Children of Alcoholics meet in the hospital cafeteria. At the same time, at Humana Hospital in downtown West Palm Beach, there is a session of Emotions Anonymous, for "individuals seeking emotional stability. . . ." On Tuesdays, "parents of chemically dependent people" meet at the Lantana Recreation Building. Mothers Against Drunk Drivers meet every Tuesday evening at the Palm Beach County Criminal Justice Complex on Gun Club Road. The Impaired Nurses Support Group also meets every Tuesday, as does Stress Management for Kids. Tough Love meetings are held across the county on Wednesday evenings.

Despite all his experience as a cop in Philadelphia, Leon

has learned more about the ill effects of cocaine while he has worked the streets of West Palm Beach. There was the case of Emmett, charged with first-degree murder in the death of his wife's stepfather. Emmett was a hard-working, honest labourer — so honest that when he married a divorced mother of two children he used to turn over his entire pay to her, settling for a modest weekly allowance. One day after work a friend persuaded Emmett to try some cocaine. He did, but didn't think much of it. The friend persisted, and eventually Emmett developed a taste for the stuff. He was driving his wife's stepfather home after a Christmas dinner, and when he refused to loan Emmett twenty-five dollars to buy some crack, Emmett pulled a knife and stabbed him to death, then buried him by the railroad tracks. Leon blamed Emmett's startling metamorphosis on what he calls "cocaine psychosis," a condition that destroys the conscience so a person can't tell right from wrong.

Chuck Burton's last major case before the Brian Spencer trial also involved cocaine. That was in March 1987, when he prosecuted Ogden King, a thirty-two-year-old man from Virginia, in the murder of Elizabeth Curtis, his eighteen-year-old girlfriend. King and Curtis had been seeing each other for two years, and they were heavily into cocaine as well as bondage and group sex. Testimony at the trial revealed they used as much as an ounce of cocaine a day, which, at $100 a gram, was a $2,800 a day habit. A pathologist testified that at her death Curtis had 13.5 milligrams per litre of cocaine in her blood, 135 times the smallest amount known to cause death. That much cocaine produces an effect known as "cocaine bugs," a psychotic reaction during which a user experiences the sensation of bugs crawling under the skin.

Leon, like Byron Spencer, is appalled by the juxtaposition of rich and poor in Palm Beach County. West Palm Beach lies across the Intracoastal Waterway from Palm Beach, separated by three drawbridges. There were no murders and no rapes in Palm Beach in 1986, the year the FBI rated West Palm Beach the most dangerous mid-size city in the nation. There is an ordinance requiring non-residents who come to Palm Beach to work to be photographed and fingerprinted for special ID cards. There is another that prohibits men from jogging bare-chested.

Palm Beach was the result of Henry Morrison Flagler's dream to create a Riviera in America. He built the Royal Poinciana Hotel and the Palm Beach Inn, which was later renamed The Breakers. The sandspit is fourteen miles long, half a mile wide, and supports 8,664 homes. Garbage is collected five days a week. Ivan Lendl, the tennis star, once bought a forty-two-room mansion in Palm Beach for $4 million. He never lived in it. John Lennon and Yoko Ono bought an oceanfront home in Palm Beach for $725,000 in 1980, and Yoko sold it six years later for $3.3 million. At the time of Brian's trial, Lilly Pulitzer's Palm Beach palace was up for sale at $3.8 million. Palm Beach has 15,000 year-round residents, but the population increases to 45,000 at the height of The Season, which runs from about Christmas to Easter. Only twenty percent of Palm Beach homeowners qualify for Florida's "homestead exemption," a tax break for those whose Palm Beach dwellings are considered primary residences.

At the time of Brian's trial, the big news in Florida was the Jack Hagler Self-defense Act, a new, liberalized concealed-weapons law that permitted anyone not convicted of a felony to obtain a permit to carry a concealed weapon. As defined by the law, "weapons" included firearms, tear-gas guns, knives and billies. In addition to being felony free, the only other requirements were that applicants had to be finger-printed and take a firearms safety course. Within days of the new law being passed, 15,000 Floridians applied for the concealed weapon permits and authorities expected another 45,000 to apply when the news got around.

This led to a spate of self-help articles as to what constituted proper use of deadly force, including a pamphlet prepared by the Department of State and the Policy Studies Clinic of the Florida State University College of Law. The pamphlet explained that Florida law justifies the use of deadly force when "trying to protect yourself or another person from death or serious bodily harm," and, "trying to prevent a forcible felony, such as rape, robbery, burglary or kidnapping." It warned against improper uses of deadly force, providing this example: "Two neighbors got into a fight, and one of them tried to hit the other by swinging a garden hose. The neighbor who was being attacked with the hose shot the other in the chest. The court upheld his conviction for aggravated battery with a firearm, because an attack with a garden hose is not the kind of violent assault that justifies responding with deadly force."

The pamphlet explained that the first duty of someone who has been insulted, threatened or even physically attacked is to retreat, and it cited a recent court decision that said, "The use of deadly force against another human being is not countenanced by law even if that force is in response to conduct of human beings who act like animals."

The pamphlet used questions and answers to explain the appropriate uses of deadly force.

Q: What if someone is attacking me in my home?
A: The courts have created an exception to the duty to retreat called the "castle doctrine." Under the castle doctrine, you need not retreat from your own home to avoid using deadly force against an assailant. This only applies when you are inside your home.

Example: Two men were fighting in the common hallway between their apartments. One of them shot and killed the other. The Florida Supreme Court upheld the first degree murder conviction of the defendant, rejecting a claim of self-defense. The court said the defendant could have and should have retreated.

The defendant in the above example claimed that because he had one foot in the doorway of his apartment, he did not have to retreat. The court rejected this argument, saying the defendant should have gone inside and shut the door.

Q: When can I use deadly force in the defense of another person?
A: If you see someone who is being attacked, you can use deadly force to defend him if the circumstances would justify that person's use of deadly force in his own defense. In other words, you can "stand in the shoes" of the person being attacked.

According to the Jack Hagler Self-defense Act, concealed weapons must not be taken to football, baseball or basketball games. The pamphlet did not mention hockey games, but it advised Floridians: "You should never carry a gun into a situation where you might get angry."

II

When Brian arrived in the corridor outside Courtroom 315 Gerry Hart, his former teammate with the New York Islanders, was there to greet him. Hart stands about four inches shorter than Brian, but with his square build and wavy dark-blond hair, some thought he, and not Byron, was Brian's brother.

There were other similarities between Hart and Brian. Hart was born in Flin Flon, a small mining town in northern Manitoba, nearly as tough and as isolated as Fort St. James. Hart also never finished high school. He was a year older than Brian, and, though a defenceman, he played the same rugged, clumsy style of hockey, relying on hustle and intensity more than pure talent. He was a checker and a grinder. When Brian started out with the Toronto Maple Leafs, Hart played for the Detroit Red Wings, just down the highway. They both joined the expansion New York Islanders in 1972, and their NHL careers each lasted ten years.

There the similarities end, and Gerry Hart and Brian Spencer stand as foils to one another. From the time he started playing in the NHL, Hart prepared for his retirement from the game. He never felt secure. He knew that a career-ending injury could happen in any practice or game. In *Life After Hockey*, he told Michael Smith, "I learned to manage my money intelligently. My rule of thumb was: for every two dollars earned, save one and blow one. By following that principle I could be frugal and still have fun."

Hart learned early on how fickle success could be. He played well in his first year in the NHL, with Detroit, getting attention in the press, but near the end of the season he separated a shoulder. He tried to get back in the game before he was properly healed. His performance suffered, and he was sent down to the minors. When he returned to Detroit in the off-season, he felt like "a nobody." Friends did not return telephone calls, teammates were too busy to see him. "I was just suddenly another guy on the street," Hart said. "The doors that were once open were closed, and I discovered the reality of life."

When the Islanders won the Stanley Cup in 1981, Hart watched from the stands. After the game, he went to the Islanders dressing room to congratulate the players, but he felt odd, left out, and he didn't like it. He rarely goes to Islanders games any more, though he lives on Long Island. Hart arrived at Brian's trial as a successful businessman, involved in insurance and real estate development, living in a big home in Lloyd Harbor, driving a Mercedes, and happily married with two sons.

It was not the first time Hart had flown to West Palm Beach to be with Brian. He was one of the major character witnesses at the bail hearing in April, when he put up part of the $50,000 bond and flew in Janet and Brian's sons. When he was on the stand at the bail hearing, Hart told state attorney Fred Susaneck that if Brian were to be released on bail he could stay at Hart's winter home in Highland Beach, Florida.

"For how long?" Susaneck asked.

"Forever if he wants it," Hart replied.

Susaneck then asked Hart about Brian's temper.

"Would you please qualify that," Hart asked. "Because if you're talking in the context of a hockey player. . . ."

"I am talking in the context of a person," Susaneck interrupted. "Does Mr. Brian Spencer have a temper?"

"The only time I have ever seen an emotional display is in

the hockey game, when he is provoked — just like me," Hart said.

At this point, there was an outburst of cheers and applause, and Judge Fine ordered Brian's supporters to be removed from the courtroom. When court reconvened, Hart told Judge Fine he had not intended his answer to be construed as a smart remark. Judge Fine told Hart there was no need for him to apologize. When Susaneck resumed his questioning, he asked Hart to explain what an "enforcer" is in hockey. Weinstein objected that this was irrelevant. Judge Fine sustained the objection.

Weinstein and Greene arrived in the corridor Tuesday morning pushing a stack of bankers' boxes of evidence on a dolly. When court began, Hart, Rick and Mikey Martin, and John Long, Brian's friend from his Buffalo Sabres years, sat in the front row immediately behind the defence table. On the other side of the gallery, immediately behind the prosecution table, the family and friends of Michael Dalfo occupied the first six rows.

The first witnesses were routine ones, Albert Brihn, the Seacoast Utilities truck driver who discovered Dalfo's body, then the two paramedics who had responded to the "man down in wooded area" ambulance call early in the afternoon of February 4, 1982. Describing what he had found when he arrived, one of the paramedics said the body was lying "supine," the eyes were "contused," which made him believe the victim had been beaten, possibly with the barrel of a handgun.

When Chuck Burton showed him a photograph of Michael Dalfo lying in the shallow pool in the mud off the shell rock road, the paramedic studied it for several seconds, then said, "There was more blood than the photo shows." At that point, Dalfo's sister broke down in tears and had to be escorted from the courtroom. Weinstein had no questions for the first three witnesses; he was more interested in the fourth witness.

"The state calls Diane Fialco. . . ."

Many of the spectators were surprised that Diane was

being called so early; it was as if they expected the trial to follow a television or movie script, with the main characters appearing at a dramatic moment toward the end, when the plot was thickest. The lawyers knew, of course, and so did Monica, who entered quietly and took a seat at the back of the room as Diane walked up the aisle, through the gate, to sit in the witness stand to Judge Fine's right, next to the American flag. Monica knew all about Diane's appearance, and she did not want to miss her testimony, but she did not want Weinstein or Leon to notice her in court.

Brian's lawyers had speculated frequently on how Diane would be dressed for her appearance at the trial. Diane Delena-Fialco was Burton's key witness, truly his entire case, and it had been suggested that the prosecution would try to make her out to be a latter-day Mary Magdalene. She wore a loose-fitting pink jacket over a white blouse buttoned to the neck, with a pink skirt and white shoes, and in her ears were tiny pink globes. With her long, dark hair swept up in front, in a modified pompadour, the back strands falling to her shoulders, she looked less like a modern vision of Mary Magdalene, and more like Lily Tomlin playing an executive secretary. She seemed very nervous.

Diane was announced by her married name, and Burton, the first to question her, politely addressed her as "Mrs. Fialco." He asked her age, which was twenty-seven, and how long she had been married, which was three years. When he asked about the children, Richard Greene half stood at the defence table and said, "Objection. Can we approach the bench?"

"Sure," Judge Fine said.

It was only one of many objections from Greene, who kept bobbing up with objections all during jury selection and would keep bobbing up to the end of the trial, always with a pertinent point and an armload of case law to back him up. This time, the defence team merely wanted to remind the court that this was no motherhood issue. This time Judge Fine overruled him, allowing Diane to testify that she had two children, aged one and two.

When Burton asked Diane when she first met Brian, she said it was back in late 1980, when she was twenty-two. That was soon after Brian arrived in Florida, when he was working as a mechanic at Fischbach & Moore, where Diane's mother worked. "He fixed my car at my mom's house," Diane said.

Brian watched and listened, sitting between Weinstein and Greene at the defence table. He stopped scribbling on the sheet of foolscap in front of him. He sucked on a Rolaids tablet. Not once in her testimony, which would go on for nearly three hours, did Diane make eye contact with him.

Despite all his troubles with women, Brian seldom directed much venom towards Diane. He hardly talked about her at all, and when he did he was not nearly as scathing as he was towards Linda and Janet. It was because of Diane that he was on trial, and if he had not done what she had told the police he had done, and what she was about to tell the world he had done, her conduct was far worse than anything he had suffered at the hands of any human being. Perhaps there was just too much hate to be articulated, but for all of Brian's misogyny, justified or not, here was a woman who might actually be sending him to his death, and yet he seemed to regard her as an object of pity, something of a waif and a stray.

Probably it was more misogamy than misogyny, or a synthesis of the two, for there was no doubt when he railed against "them" he meant "women" or "wives." There was something about the institution of marriage and the effect it had on man-woman relationships that Brian found confining and stultifying. "The things they found attractive in you, now they want to take away," he said. "They want to change the exact reasons why you got together, and if they did they wouldn't want you."

Brian held a special, curious affection for the women who got away — Ingrid Hoff, the pretty classmate in Fort St. James; Sharon Brown, the classical pianist he met in his junior days in Saskatchewan. The ones he did not succeed with always were pretty, intelligent, talented, kind, generous and understanding. He romanticized them, idealized them, and, crude as he could be, he never discussed them in sexual terms. He also had a soft spot and a protective instinct for women with troubles, and for women who gave him pleasure and comfort, as long as they did not "crowbar" themselves into his life.

Brian knew Diane's mother at Fischbach & Moore, where he had a reputation as a mechanical wizard. Everyone at Fischbach & Moore knew Brian, and his popularity extended even to the executive offices. Middle managers and vice-presidents invited him to their homes, and he attended company picnics, sometimes in the rumbling Hulk. He told stories about hockey and growing up in northern Canada. He liked to be the centre of attention, and people remembered how intently he listened, how his personality could "capture" you.

Brian remembered clearly the day he fixed Diane's car. He told the story often to illustrate how women insinuate themselves into a man's life. He said, "She had a problem with her car and I fixed it and she started hanging around. She was one of those girls who were available, probably because she wasn't too desirable, or she'd have been taken by someone else. She was a juvenile delinquent. She was pretty spacey. Her parents kicked her out, so she started staying over a lot. You know, one day you find a dress, then a pair of shoes, then two pairs of shoes, then people start saying you're living together. That's how I met Diane — I fixed her car, and I was lonely."

Whatever Diane had done to him, and was doing to him by testifying against him at the trial, she had never crowbarred her way into Brian's life by getting pregnant, or by harping on the "niceties" and "rituals" of house and home. He never had to pay her alimony. Most of all, Diane did not try to take the wildness out of Brian, and never tried to change him into a wimp, which he believes wives feel duty-bound to do. Diane was as adventurous as Brian. When an escort-service client asked if she could bring along a man for a sexual foursome with him and his wife, Diane invited Brian to come with her to the appointment.

Chuck Burton asked Diane about her job at the escort service.

She told him that in the fall of 1981 she noticed an ad in the classified section of *The Palm Beach Post* for a "hostess job," which involved "dining, dancing and entertainment." She drove to an office on Northlake Boulevard to fill out an application, and she started working for the escort service shortly after Thanksgiving Day. She called herself Crystal. She was living with Brian at the trailer on Skees Road, but Brian had no objections. He told her it was her own affair.

"What type of people used the escort service?" Burton asked.

"Oh, all sorts," Diane answered. "Lawyers, doctors, judges. . . ." This prompted muffled laughter in the courtroom.

When asked about the arrangements at the trailer, Diane said she and Brian shared expenses fifty-fifty. And she said, "We were more friends than boyfriend and girlfriend, but it wasn't platonic."

Replying to Burton's questions, Diane described events on the night of February 3, 1982, going to Dalfo's apartment at about eleven o'clock, finding him wired on cocaine and drinking an orange liqueur, wearing only skimpy black briefs. She stayed about an hour, then left. In the courtroom, Diane's voice sounded taut, a nervous contralto, and you could hear her breathing into the courtroom microphone. "He kind of grabbed me by the arm when I was leaving. He offered me a cheque, but the agency doesn't accept cheques. He followed me outside."

She returned to the trailer, then took another call from the agency for an appointment at the Hyatt Hotel. On her way there, she stopped at the Banana Boat, where she saw Brian talking to another man and a woman. She told him about being at Dalfo's and said she was afraid he might have followed her. Brian said it was none of his business. Diane left, drove to the Hyatt and met her next client, with whom she stayed for about half an hour. On her way back to the trailer about two in the morning, she stopped at the Banana

Boat again, but Brian was not there. She drove home and watched television. When Brian called, she asked him to come home and he did.

Brian wanted to know what had happened at Dalfo's condominium apartment. After she told him, he demanded that she take him there. She drove over in her blue Fiat, with Brian sitting on the passenger side. When they arrived at the apartment, they saw Dalfo standing outside, still wearing only the black bikini briefs. Dalfo asked why she had returned and, according to Diane, Brian told him to get in the car. When he asked where they were going, Brian told him to shut up and told Diane to drive.

When Burton asked if Dalfo said anything, Greene objected, saying that would be "hearsay." There was a brief discussion at Judge Fine's desk, after which Burton repeated the question and Diane replied, "He said if we didn't take him back he was going to call his lawyer."

Diane drove to the isolated road off PGA Boulevard, where it was pitch dark. It was a shell rock road that had been recently graded and there were mounds of white, crushed rock along the side that looked like snowdrifts in the night. "I got out of the car and I was walking around, saying I want to go home," Diane testified. "I was walking all over, pacing, on the passenger side of the car. They got out. They were talking and arguing."

Burton asked if she saw any weapons.

"No, I didn't see any weapons. There was no light. It was just plain dark."

She said when Brian told her to take off, she ran down the road towards PGA Boulevard, then along the shoulder of PGA Boulevard. Minutes later, Brian drove up behind her, Diane got in the car, and Brian said, "He can't call his lawyer now."

Diane said she was wearing a blue and white dress, with a blue blazer and "wedge-type gold shoes, flat on the bottom." Over at the defence table, Weinstein scribbled a note on his pad.

When Burton asked Diane what she had said to Brian

when she heard later that Michael Dalfo had been shot and killed, she replied, "I don't recall." Burton actually meant to ask her what Brian had said, because earlier Diane had told the police Brian had remarked, "He deserved it."

Diane told Burton that originally she had lied to the police when she told them she did not return to Dalfo's that evening, and again when she told them she stayed with her customer at the Hyatt Hotel until four-thirty in the morning. She said Brian told her to say that because she needed an alibi. She lied because she was scared. "And I'm scared today, too," she said. No one in the courtroom doubted her.

At the end of his questioning, just before the noon hour recess, Burton walked closer to the witness stand and asked Diane, "Did you kill Michael Dalfo?"

She answered, "No."

"Did you participate in his murder?"

"Not at all."

Soon after she met Brian, back in 1980, Diane had witnessed his explosive anger firsthand. They were in her blue Fiat, heading north over the Skyway Bridge from Singer Island. Diane was driving. Suddenly there was loud, repeated honking behind them. Brian turned around and saw a van following close behind the Fiat, the driver leaning on his horn and giving them the finger. When Diane stopped at a light, Brian got out, walked back to the van, opened the door on the driver's side of the van and yelled, "What the hell's your problem?"

The driver, drunk and red-faced, started to get out of the van, but two women held him back. Brian slammed the door and walked back to the Fiat. He stood on the shoulder of the road for a moment, with the car door swung open. The driver of the van gunned the engine, twisted out of the line of traffic and headed directly at Brian, who jumped inside Diane's car as the van slammed into the door of the Fiat, tearing it off the hinges. The van skidded along the shoulder, then cut back into the traffic and headed north. Brian retrieved the door, threw it in the back seat and told Diane to give chase.

They caught up to the van at the next light. Brian jumped out and ran up to the van as the driver frantically rolled up his window. Brian pounded on the window, but it didn't break. He levelled a karate kick at the window, but still it wouldn't break. Brian stomped to the front of the van, reached up and ripped off the windshield wipers. The driver floored the accelerator and the van screeched forward, pinning Brian against the bumper of the car ahead. Then the driver of the van got out and he and Brian wrestled in the dust by the side of the road. During the fight, a plainclothes detective who had been in the line of cars, walked up shouting, "Hey! Hey!" When the detective flashed his badge, Brian immediately stopped fighting.

Brian told the story himself at lunch one day during the week of jury selection. He was in the dining room at a Howard Johnson's out on Okeechobee Boulevard, waiting for the soup of the day and a hot turkey sandwich. "How should I handle these things?" he asked, his voice breaking. "I mean, he almost snipped my legs off! Between the bumpers! The woman in the car ahead, she's complaining about her neck. That's how hard he hit my legs. They charged him with aggravated assault and leaving the scene of an accident. It should have been attempted murder as far as I'm concerned. I should have got half a million dollars. I couldn't walk for a week. My leg was swollen up as big as a small watermelon. I thought I might lose it."

The hot turkey sandwich arrived. Brian pushed it aside.

"And I wasn't charged. *He* was charged. It was the first time in my life I was the plaintiff."

This struck Brian as funny, and he laughed.

"So, the case goes to court. I'm a material witness for the prosecution — aggravated assault, leaving the scene of an accident. He's got this one-legged lawyer, and you know the first thing he starts into? I'm a hockey player. I'm a fighter. I'm aggressive!"

Brian was shouting and heads turned at other tables.

"He got a hundred-dollar fine! For leaving the scene of an accident. They dropped the criminal charge. On top of that, they said because I am a mechanic I can fix my own door! Isn't that something? He almost killed me, ran the door off the car — and they said I was a violent hockey player."

The waitress walked over and asked if there was something wrong with the hot turkey sandwich. Brian hadn't touched it.

"Oh, no," Brian said, looking up at her with a wide smile. "My stomach is just a little upset today."

In the corridor outside Courtroom 315, before court resumed at one-fifteen, Weinstein walked by the spectators sitting on the wooden benches, some of them puffing on last-minute cigarettes. Weinstein rattled a throat lozenge in his mouth and looked relaxed, optimistic, ready to go. On Friday afternoon, after the opening remarks, Brian began to think Weinstein might be doing a good job after all. He didn't have the style and charm of Burton, but he seemed well prepared and something of a terrier. Brian was beginning to regard Burton as one of those hockey players who give their best shot in the pre-game warm-ups.

As Diane entered the courtroom and walked up to the witness stand, she looked frail, a hurt puppydog expression on her face. She took her seat and Weinstein walked to his position in front of the jurors. Among the spectators the mood was *here it comes.* . . .

Weinstein began with general remarks on the escort-service business, then asked questions only slightly dripping with sarcasm. He established that Fantacee Island was one of several agencies, all controlled by the same people. He established that prostitution was involved ("I guess you could call it that," Diane said). He established that she charged $100 an hour, of which she could keep $50, that on some days in the height of the tourist season she made $1,000 a day. He established that she carried a beeper with her twenty-four hours a day. When he asked how many customers she had in a day, Diane's reply was vague, so

Weinstein tried to refresh her memory by asking, "More than one? More than two? More than three?"

Diane's husband, Les, watched from a seat at the rear of the gallery. When he had married Diane three years earlier, he knew nothing of her involvement with the escort agency. One of his brothers was listed as a possible witness for the defence, if the matter of character came up. Les Fialco was a trim, well-dressed, clean-cut young man — he could have passed as a Mormon missionary — and from time to time during Diane's testimony he dabbed at his eyes with one of his fingers. Brian knew Les. They were not close friends, but he liked him. Brian had attended the wedding.

Weinstein asked Diane if she had had sex with Dalfo when she was with him at his condominium apartment, and she said she wasn't sure. When Weinstein asked if she had sex with her next customer, the man at the Hyatt Hotel, she replied, "It's possible, probable, but I don't recall. It was a long time ago."

"Your memory of whether you had sex with Mr. Dalfo, or other customers, is sketchy, but it's not sketchy what happened with Mr. Spencer?" Weinstein asked.

Diane was starting to get into the spirit of things.

"I'll put it in perspective for Mr. Weinstein," Diane said, as if addressing Judge Fine. "It would be like him reciting every witness in every case he's ever had."

Weinstein walked to the witness stand and showed Diane the transcript of a deposition she made in Weinstein's office on September 18, 1987. After examining it, Diane said she did have sex with the client at the Hyatt Hotel.

On the night of the murder, Diane said, she had worn flat gold sandals, not high-heeled shoes. She said she ran down the road to PGA Boulevard, she heard no shots, she thought it was sometime between two and four in the morning, and they arrived back at the trailer on Skees Road between four and four-thirty. She said she heard about Dalfo's death two days later, when the police came to the trailer to question her.

Weinstein asked, "Brian never told you that he beat

Mr. Dalfo? Brian never told you that he shot Mr. Dalfo?"
Diane said Brian would not tell her any of the details,
"because he thought I wasn't strong enough to withstand the
questioning."

Weinstein demanded a yes or no.

"No," Diane said.

When it was Burton's turn again, he asked Diane if she
saw any gun that night. She said no. Burton then asked Diane
if Brian owned any guns, and Greene shot up from his chair to
object. He asked Judge Fine if they could approach the bench.
As the lawyers were getting up from their desks, Diane
started to say that Brian did own guns and she was told to
stop.

"But it wasn't overruled," she said.

After the conference with Judge Fine, Burton abandoned
his question on guns and asked Diane how being called as a
witness in the trial affected her marriage and Diane replied,
"Adversely."

"Is your husband in the courtroom?" Burton asked.

"Yes."

"*Objection!*" Greene shouted.

"Sustained."

At two-thirty, Judge Fine called for a recess, and Diane
left the courtroom with her husband, looking as frightened
and forlorn as when she had entered nearly three hours
earlier. It was the end of her day in court; she would not be
back again.

The first witness after the recess was Galen Leroy
Hassinger, a forty-one-year-old, silver-haired operations
manager of a television station in Fort Myers. Yes, he told
Burton, somewhat abashed, he had been at the Hyatt Hotel
on the evening of February 3, 1982. Yes, he had called
Fantacee Island Escorts "to engage the companionship of a
young woman." Yes, he thought the name Crystal sounded
familiar.

It was all very embarrassing for a middle-class businessman who had happened to feel adventurous on an out-
of-town business trip five years earlier. Police managed to

track him down with the help of Diane and Diane's mother. Detective Robert Halstedt, trying to build a "time frame" of the night of Dalfo's murder, questioned Diane on her comings and goings that evening. At first she said nothing of returning to Dalfo's with Brian, and she told Halstedt she had stayed at the Hyatt until four in the morning. Halstedt asked Diane to go to the Hyatt Hotel and find the room she went to that night, so Diane and her mother visited the hotel and wandered the corridors until Diane was sure she had found the room. Police then subpoenaed the hotel records and determined that Hassinger had been in the room.

Hassinger remembered that Diane had long dark hair and large breasts, and that she seemed distressed when she arrived. He thought she had been sniffing coke, as she was very talkative, telling him all about an upsetting experience with a previous client. He called her sometime after midnight, she arrived at one or one-thirty, and she left before two. He paid her $100 with his Mastercharge card.

When Burton mentioned that Diane originally told the police he had given her an extra $200 and she stayed until four in the morning, Hassinger responded, "No, I didn't have that much cash. That's why I used my Mastercharge. I was married then."

Richard Hanley, a starter and ranger at the PGA Golf Course, worked as a security guard at the entrance to Dalfo's condominium complex on the midnight-to-eight shift on the night Dalfo was killed. He knew Michael and his brother Christopher, but he did not remember seeing them that night. He was at his post at the gatehouse the entire shift, except for ten or fifteen minutes around two in the morning when a young couple arrived and needed directions to the cottage they had rented. Some time after he returned to the gatehouse, a woman drove up in a bronze Pinto and told Hanley she was supposed to see Dalfo, but he wasn't at his townhouse. He let her use the phone in the gatehouse to make a call.

Detective Halstedt, now a sergeant in charge of the intelligence division at the Palm Beach County Sheriff's

Office, had been a general assignment investigator in 1982 when the Dalfo case landed on his desk. He examined the crime scene, found the high-heel shoeprints along the side of the road off PGA Boulevard. The shoeprints were irregularly spaced, closer together near the spot where the .25-calibre shell casings were found, further apart towards PGA Boulevard, which indicated that whoever had been wearing the shoes had started to run.

Halstedt told the court that for months after Dalfo's body was found, all his leads kept bringing him back to one person, Diane Delena. In May 1982, he stopped Diane early in the morning while she was driving on Military Trail. He talked to her in his car for about twenty minutes, then she got into her car and he followed her to Dyer Boulevard, where Fischbach & Moore is located. "She drove straight to Brian Spencer," Halstedt said.

When it was Weinstein's turn, he was brief. He wanted to know about the shoeprints by the side of the road, and Halstedt repeated that they were high-heel shoeprints. "You could see the spike marks in the ground," he said. Weinstein picked up a plastic bag containing Diane's spike-heeled shoes and showed them to the detective, then he left the bag of shoes on the defence table, where the jurors could ponder them while he asked the rest of his questions. In all their investigations and searches, Weinstein wanted to know, did the detectives find any of Brian's fingerprints that would link him to the crime?

Halstedt replied, "No."

"Hair samples?"

"No."

"Blood?"

"No."

"Guns?"

"No."

"Did you find any physical evidence linking Mr. Spencer to the crime scene?" Weinstein asked.

"I did not," Halstedt said.

Weinstein established that the police at no time bothered

to investigate the escort services, did not check out Bill Workman's background, and never even looked for Dan and Sally Phelps. He asked if the detectives made any attempt to arrest Brian in the original investigation in 1982, and Halstedt said no. "Not even when Mr. Spencer once followed you to the police station and grabbed Diane and lifted her off the floor?"

"No, sir."

III

There comes a time in any murder trial when it is hard to resist the murder-mystery appeal, and *Florida v. Brian Spencer* had more than a few mysterious elements. The "whys" outnumbered the "whats" and "wheres" and "whens." Why would Brian want to kill Michael Dalfo? Anger? If anger, why so cold-bloodedly, and why with a .25-calibre handgun, a small gun that could have been designed for a woman's purse. If Brian had been angry enough to kill someone, surely he would have done it with his fists, which could be as lethal as any popgun pistol — and doubtless more satisfying. And if anger, why would he bother to drive across town to an isolated road? It would be like responding to a crosscheck on the ice by telling the offender to meet him after the game in the parking lot.

Jealousy? Everyone knew that the relationship between Brian and Diane was not an exclusive one, that they mostly shared the rent and were free to come and go. He never complained about her work for the escort agency, knowing it involved prostitution. When he had the time, he actually drove her to some of her appointments. Many knew Brian wanted her out of his life.

These were the questions Brian's friends and the reporters asked during the recesses and at lunch downstairs at the patio tables in the courtyard. Why would Diane think one of her customers would have followed her home when she lived in a trailer, in a bush neighbourhood? Why would she think Dalfo might have followed her when she heard him ordering more escort-service women? Why would Diane suddenly get the courage to return to the isolated road to pick up her blazer, when, according to her story, she thought Brian just roughed up Dalfo and left him there in the dark?

The security guard at Dalfo's condominium complex happened to leave his gatehouse only once in his midnight-to-eight shift, for ten or fifteen minutes at about two in the morning. Very convenient.

Weinstein made an issue of the high-heeled shoes, having determined that the shoeprints by the road where Dalfo was killed were high-heel shoeprints. Diane insisted that she wore flat sandals that night, and she had no reason to lie because she had already admitted that she was there. The FBI report proved conclusively that the mud from a pair of high-heeled shoes found among Diane's clothing at the trailer was the same mud found by the isolated road, and in the swampy clearing where Dalfo's body was found, but that only proved that the high-heeled shoes were there. Could Diane have loaned them to somebody, perhaps one of her colleagues at the escort service? Did someone break into the trailer and steal them? Or plant them in her closet after the fact? Could Diane have been set up? Could Diane and Brian have been set up? If Brian understood that to be the case could it explain his uncharacteristically soft attitude to Diane, a woman who was prepared to send him to the electric chair? And if they were set up, by whom? The heavies at the escort service? These were not people to trifle with. If that was the answer, could it explain Diane's silence — and perhaps Brian's silence as well — over the five years since the murder?

In August, two months before Brian's trial, Leon flew out to Colorado to visit the man who once worked for Dan and Sally Phelps at the escort service in West Palm Beach. The man's name was Harold Yearout, but under the federal witness protection program he and his wife lived under assumed names. Yearout, a former Tennessee policeman, had testified against Dan and Sally Phelps in the prostitution and money-laundering case investigated by the federal agents involved in Operation Greenback.

The arrangements for meeting Yearout were elaborate. Leon reached Yearout through his brother, and when he arrived in Colorado Springs Leon checked into a nondescript, one-storey motel. That was an important part of the arrangement, because Yearout wanted his meeting with Leon to take place at a table by the window where, with the curtains pulled open, a friend of his could keep watch on the scene from a truck parked outside.

In the session with Leon, Yearout talked about Dan and Sally Phelps and the escort agency. He remembered a troublesome client who was an "airhead," who smoked crack cocaine in a pipe and who physically and mentally abused the escorts he ordered. Yearout never met this client, but he had talked to him on the phone and once he and his wife, Mary, had driven by his townhouse, which he remembered as being at a golf course development near PGA Boulevard.

"The Phelpses were really hot over this guy," Yearout told Leon.

"So this guy was a nut?" Leon asked.

"Right."

"And he used the service a lot?"

"Right."

Yearout explained how the escort service handled troublesome customers, those who treated the girls badly or didn't pay up. First they would dig up all the information they could on the person for blackmail purposes and they would call him on the phone. If that didn't work they would use other "scare tactics." They had collectors who earned a percentage of any outstanding debts, such as $75 for a collected debt of $200. The collectors could be very persuasive.

Yearout told Leon that Dan Phelps once threatened him, saying, "I can have anything I want done to you. If I wanted to have you killed, I could have you killed, like I had this son-of-a-bitch killed one time." He remembered Sally Phelps carried a .25-calibre handgun, black with an ivory handle, in her purse. The serial numbers had been stripped off. Yearout's wife, Mary, was with Sally when she bought the gun in Tampa. She said she bought it from a bald-headed man they called "Kojak."

Leon asked Yearout if he ever heard of someone called Brian Spencer, "a jock, a professional hockey player." Yearout said he had, but it soon became obvious that the "Brian" or the "Spencer," or whoever, was "a coloured guy." As Leon persisted, Yearout became more convinced that the person he was thinking of was black. "I know black from white," he told Leon.

"Does the name Crystal ring a bell?" Leon asked.

Yearout was much clearer about that one.

"Yes, it does. She worked for the service. I think she and Sally had something going."

Later, Leon met with Yearout's wife, who once worked as a prostitute herself, starting when she was sixteen. She remembered Crystal as one of Sally's favourites and as someone who would do anything for anything. She also remembered how Dan and Sally Phelps were having a problem with a customer who was bothering the women and not paying his bills. "They hated him, absolutely hated him," she told Leon. "I didn't know why they serviced him, but apparently his money was good. I heard they were going to have him knocked."

Leon expected Yearout to be in West Palm Beach for the trial. He had been issued a subpoena to appear as a defence witness, to testify on how the escort service's enforcement operation worked. He did not show up and Leon could not find him anywhere in the country.

CHAPTER EIGHT

Wednesday: *Homeless*

I

Throughout 1987, and for some reason especially in Florida, one could hardly escape the music of Paul Simon's album *Graceland*. The African rhythms and grunts and clucks mixed with American-hip lyrics could have been a soundtrack for the languid climate of south Florida. On the car radio on the way to the courtroom on the morning of the seventh day of Brian's trial, Simon and Ladysmith Black Mambazo were singing:

> *Homeless, homeless*
> *Moonlight sleeping on a midnight lake . . .*

One by one, day by day, the cast was assembling. They were coming from all over the continent — from Long Island, Buffalo, Niagara Falls, Vancouver Island, Toronto. And they were coming not only from far away, but also from long ago. People who knew Brian well at one time were meeting and talking with people who knew Brian well at another time. They were like adventurers returning from a voyage to some terra incognita of an ancient map, but separately, individually, each one returning from a winter or a summer or a spring or an autumn. There were disparate revelations; an image was forming, and it was making Brian uneasy.

There was Gerry Hart, his teammate with the New York Islanders, Rick Martin from Brian's years with the Buffalo Sabres, and John Long, the insurance man, hockey fan and outdoorsman from upstate New York whom Brian regarded as "the closest thing to a Christ-figure I've ever known." And

Brian's mother, and Byron, of course, who after the strain of his efforts to be at Brian's side was growing restive at being forgotten in the shuffle by Leon and the lawyers, and hurt because he felt he was being ignored by Brian. John Antonacci, who once regarded Brian as an uncle and now worked in intelligence for the RCMP, had arrived the night before. Dave Keon, the captain of the Maple Leafs when Brian played in Toronto, would be in court Thursday.

Brian was beginning to feel crowded. He could play the role of Rick Martin's old roommate and buddy when he was with Rick Martin, and probably Rick Martin's old roommate and buddy and the colourful Buffalo Sabres left winger with Rick Martin and John Long, but as the party grew, the equation became more complicated and Brian found it harder and harder to know who he was supposed to be at any given moment. The more crowded it became, the less room there was to spin. With his mother in the circle, he could not speak of the north central interior as "the Ozarks of the North." With Byron, how could he complain about Linda crowbarring herself into his life without sounding foolish, when Byron objected to the marriage so much that he refused to be Brian's best man? And he dared not rail against Janet because she and Hart were still friends on Long Island.

All of them were offering Brian advice, opening their homes to him, telling him what he should do with his life after he was acquitted, but in private moments Brian was pessimistic about the outcome of the trial. He did not want to make any plans until the trial was behind him. As much as he loved his mother and twin brother, and was genuinely happy to see them, he could not comfortably socialize with them; he felt he had let them down, and they knew him too well. His soft-shoe routine worked with the rest of the gang, but it would not have worked with them. He was grateful for Gerry Hart's help at the bail hearing, and he welcomed him at his trial, but resentments were forming. Hart wanted Brian to return to Long Island, where there were lots of jobs and he could be near Janet and his two sons. At the lounge at the Holiday Inn after Tuesday's sessions, Brian complained Hart was always trying to control everything. He called him "Little Napoleon."

Brian was weary of always having to depend on someone's generosity, of always having to be grateful. He was thirty-eight years old, but for nearly twenty-five years, since he left home in his mid-teens, he had experienced prolonged periods of homelessness. There were brief exceptions, some satisfying, some not — during his marriages to Linda and Janet, when he lived in the Hulk, in the trailer on the land he owned in Loxahatchee — but for most of his life Brian had lived on someone else's goodwill or sufferance.

Being a perpetual guest affects a person's personality, forcing one to smooth rough edges, or to become a chameleon, either of which would have caused considerable tension and a terrible seething in someone as strong, free-spirited and honest as Brian, probably without his even knowing why. It would explain his rages, his moodiness, perhaps also his difficulty with intimacy, which was as much a problem in his marriages as any perceived treacheries and deceits. It was not that he shunned intimacy, just the opposite. He sought intimacy, yearned for it. God knows his bear-hugging affection for those he loved was genuine, but too often he chased intimacy the way a moth chases a flame; his vigorous sexuality was one of the more obvious manifestations of the quest. He found the genteel conventions of marriage artificial and stifling. That sort of intimacy suffocated the partners in the marriage, and marriage suffocated the affection, until there was nothing left. Marriage made something voluntary compulsory. Marriage changed people. Marriage betrayed him.

No doubt he would have been happier with a girl just like the girl who married dear old dad. Brian's father was as ornery and independent as a man can be, and yet Brian's mother loved him and never tried to change him. If Roy wanted to get out of bed and go night-hunting, fine; if he plopped a plate of beans over someone's head, that was just his way; if he wanted to build a hockey rink in the backyard and hook up the lights to a generator at the gravel pit, that was okay, too. Roy's friends probably could not stomach a weekend with him, but Irene stood by him for nearly forty years and honoured his memory after he died.

Brian's homelessness had begun soon after he left high school, when he was fifteen. There was the winter in Vanderhoof, when he and Byron had lived by their wits, foraging, stealing, walking the streets, sleeping by the mill burner, in the arena, in parked cars. Then there was reform school, after which arrangements were made for Brian to stay with Ed and Greta Godfrey, friends of the family in Kitimat. Brian quickly sensed a resentment towards him at the Godfreys, mainly from Greta, who contrasted his drive and ambition with her own two sons, who were quiet and phlegmatic. At hockey school in Nelson the summer before, Brian became friends with Rick Kennedy, a big, hardworking defenceman, so he left the Godfreys and moved in with Rick's family in Kitimat. Twenty years later, he remembered the Kennedys fondly. "They were a stable and religious family. I became part of the family, and after that — no problem. I was a dedicated athlete from that point on."

From Kitimat, Brian moved up to junior hockey, staying briefly with the Berensons in Regina, then with coaches and families in Calgary, Estevan and Swift Current. After that, the Toronto Maple Leafs' training camp in Peterborough, sharing a room at a downtown hotel; then down to Tulsa, sharing a hotel room, later an apartment, with teammate Bobby Liddington.

After his marriage to Linda, and during his first full year with the Leafs, he lived for a short time in a rented house in Scarborough. At the start of his second season with the Leafs, the year after his father was killed, Brian and Linda and their daughter Andrea moved across the city to the suburb of Islington, to a house on a street called The Wynd. Soon after moving to The Wynd, Linda returned to Tulsa with Andrea. "She was something I just didn't want to be around, but I didn't know how to get rid of," Brian said. "I should have gotten out of that marriage while there was still only one child. Every time she'd come around, every time I'd go to Tulsa to visit, she'd get pregnant."

Brian was living alone in the rented house on The Wynd when he met the Antonaccis, the Italian family in the neighbourhood. He got to know Greg and Will Antonacci, two brothers who were ardent hockey fans and who used to invite NHL players to their home. Greg and Will were fans of the Boston Bruins and John, Will's son, remembers being thrilled to see Ted Green of the Bruins at the dinner table one evening. That paled to insignificance, however, when young John discovered that one of his neighbours was Spinner Spencer of the Maple Leafs. John was thirteen when he met Brian, and they hit it off immediately. Brian brought John hockey sticks from Maple Leaf Gardens. He drove John and his girlfriend to the movies. He became Uncle Brian to John and "Quindici" to the Antonaccis.

It was a lonely time for Brian. It was the year after his father had been killed, Linda was gone, and he did not find much camaraderie or solace with the Maple Leafs. He regarded the Leafs as a team of twenty-two individuals, with no warmth or closeness — no sense of family. Brian liked Jim McKenny, the red-faced, good-timing defenceman who now works as a television broadcaster in Toronto, but he felt isolated from nearly all the other players. He regarded Will Antonacci — "Willy," he called him — as a father and a brother. What he treasured most about their friendship was that it was reciprocal, that each respected the other. Will had been going through some hard times himself and often he asked for Brian's opinion on delicate matters, which was a new experience for Brian. "I was missing something from the time I was fourteen, when I left home," Brian said. "I felt comfortable with the Antonaccis. They were a super family, just beautiful, and I was lost."

Brian rarely found a sense of family or home on the teams he played for. With the New York Islanders, he became a hit with the fans, and he made many friends off the ice, but he found no warmth or companionship on the team. The Islanders were an expansion team when he joined them in

1972, another ragtag group without spirit or harmony, another collection of individuals. He liked Bob Nystrom and later became friends with Gary Howatt, but during his brief stay with the Islanders Brian felt alienated. Denis Potvin, the brilliant rookie defenceman from Hull, joined the Islanders in 1973 and Brian was insulted and grieved when he heard that Potvin was telling other players Brian was not worth having on the team. Years later, when the Islanders became an NHL powerhouse and began winning Stanley Cups, they were a close-knit, cohesive team, but by then Brian was long gone.

The isolation and loneliness is always worse for the fringe player whose career can be ended not only by an injury, or a few bad games, but by a single bad shift on the ice. It has happened to Brian, and he has watched it happen to others. A player has a bad game, gets scored on twice in a shift, then sits out the next shift, then is relegated to the bench. Four or five games without playing, and he does not feel part of the team, part of the conversations. He begins to fade, and it is public, and it is humiliating.

The fringe player rarely feels secure enough to buy a home in the city where he is playing. His statistics are monitored more closely than the statistics of the superstars with their guaranteed, multi-year contracts. The brass would look like bunglers if they precipitously traded a player who might blossom later and strengthen a rival team. They are expensive investments, so they are watched and judged endlessly. "It was game to game, shift to shift," Brian said. "You never knew. After one damn game, somebody'd say, 'Hey, Spin — coach wants to see you.' You go to the room and there's your skates on the floor in a corner. You're told you've been traded, and sometimes you can't even go home and get your stuff. It's like being orphaned. When you're playing a road game, you might find out you're traded to the home team, so you go from one dressing-room to another, one hotel to another, one uniform to another. They should put Velcro on the crests."

Brian was happiest, and played his best hockey, with the

Buffalo Sabres. He arrived late in the 1972-73 season from the Islanders, then played three full seasons in Buffalo, where he became a crowd favourite dependably patrolling left wing, never timid in the corners. The Sabres were the first team he played for that felt like a family, and Buffalo was the first city in his professional career where he felt at home. Brian made lasting friendships with Sabres teammates Rick Martin, Rick Dudley, Jim Lorentz, Craig Ramsay, Jerry Korab and Jim Schoenfeld. He made friends away from the rink, too. Some of them visited him at the jail in West Palm Beach. Others sent him letters and money. Soon after his arrest, fans attending a Sabres game at the Memorial Auditorium in Buffalo hoisted a banner that proclaimed, "SPINNER DIDN'T DO IT."

In Buffalo, Brian had become involved in the community, promoting amateur sports, working for charities, visiting hospitals. One of Brian's biggest fans was a fifteen-year-old boy named Joey Gehen, who wanted some day to play in the NHL but was stricken with congenital heart disease, a disease that had taken his father three years earlier and his sister just a month earlier. When Brian felt down, he used to drive to Mercy Hospital in Lackawanna to spend time with the boy. It made Brian's own problems seem unimportant. On a bitterly cold afternoon in January 1976, when Joey Gehen was dying, Brian stayed two hours with him at his bedside. When he left the hospital, he discovered his car had been towed away. That's how it was with Brian — thrills and calamities, laughter and tears, ups and downs tumbling like clothes in a dryer. Nothing was ever predictable, and nothing ever went smoothly for very long.

In the spring of 1975, when Brian was playing the best hockey of his life, and the Buffalo Sabres were headed to the Stanley Cup finals, he got into a fistfight with a motorist in the Buffalo suburb of West Seneca and was sued for $186,000. It was settled out of court for $15,000. "I'm pulling my hair out," Brian said. "I'm still sending $3,400 a month to Linda in Tulsa, and I get this bill for $15,000. The Sabres had to front me the money."

After the 1976-77 season, the Sabres traded Brian to the Pittsburgh Penguins. If he'd had a choice of going to any team in the NHL, the Pittsburgh Penguins would have been last on his list. His first choice would have been the Boston Bruins, who have always been a lunchbucket, family-type team. Brian thought he would have been perfect for Boston and Boston would have been perfect for him. He thought if he had been traded to the Bruins his career would have lasted another three or four years. As it was, Brian and Janet found a home they liked in Pittsburgh, one Brian described as a "beautiful Hansel-and-Gretel cottage." The Penguins advanced him $15,000 to use as a down payment, they moved in, and Brian tried to make the best of it. As Brian expected, the Penguins turned out to be another loose assemblage of individuals, without much talent. Worse, they seemed to have no desire, no courage, and they were constantly being intimidated by other teams. In the 1977-78 season, Brian played in seventy-nine games with the Penguins, scoring nine goals, with eleven assists. He was only twenty-seven years old, but he was losing his enthusiasm for hockey, and much of it had to do with being in Pittsburgh.

Hockey was not as popular in Pittsburgh as it was in Buffalo, though it did have a local hockey tradition; the city had had an NHL team called the Pirates for five seasons in the 1920s, but in 1930 the team moved to Philadelphia, where it called itself the Quakers. When Brian arrived, baseball and football were the glamour sports in Pittsburgh. Some nights he drove to the Civic Arena for a game and would not be allowed in because the attendant didn't recognize him. He volunteered to attend sports banquets and promotional events in the city to promote ticket sales, but the Penguins' public relations department was so inept that many times the organizers of the events did not know Brian was coming and there was no seat at the table for him. Sometimes the organizers did not know there was a professional hockey team in Pittsburgh.

Things weren't going well at home, either. Brian had always wanted a home with a shop in it, where he could use his tools. He wanted a place where he could design, fabricate and invent machines. He had an enormous collection of tools and equipment — nuts, bolts, welding torches, every sort of widget and geegaw imaginable — and it had cost the Penguins $15,000 to hire a semi-trailer just to haul more than twenty tons of Brian's hardware from Buffalo. There was no room in the Hansel-and-Gretel cottage for a real shop, but Brian fashioned his own game room, with a pool table, a Franklin stove and antique tools he had collected over the years. He wanted a space that was his, with things he considered "identifying factors." He nailed a bearskin hide to one of the walls, then hung up some old Swede saws. When he left on an eleven-day trip with the Penguins, Janet had some girlfriends over for a party and she took down the bear hide, removed the saws and stashed Brian's other tools in closets and cupboards.

"She was embarrassed by the things she was supposed to be in love with me for," Brian said, his fury barely contained nearly ten years later. "She took me out of her life. That marriage was over when that bear hide came down."

Then came the interview with Bob Prince after the Penguins lost 9-0 to the Philadelphia Flyers, and the next morning, Brian was told he was being sent down to the Binghamton Dusters. He had to start home-hunting again, this time in the bush leagues.

Probably the home that satisfied Brian the most in all the years since he left Fort St. James wasn't a house at all, but the huge, grunting behemoth of a truck he called the Hulk. He started work on it in 1974 in Buffalo, when he and Rick Martin would spend most of the off-season summers tinkering with equipment and splashing around in oil and grease. It began as a Dodge van with diamond-shaped windows and it took about five years and nearly $40,000 to become the Hulk.

He found an old two and a half ton army truck in a junk-yard on Long Island and welded the van to the chassis. He later installed an airplane cockpit from a DC3 with more than two hundred functional gauges. With a radio in the cockpit, Brian could keep in touch with passing airplanes. He installed air-conditioning, carpeted sleeping quarters, a fridge and a stove, two-way radios, three television systems, cameras, video intercoms, video recording equipment, a compass from a tank, winches front and back, several engines, a full ten-wheel drive and much more — even a demilitarized .50-calibre machine gun, which he modified so it could be used as a camera for surveillance. It weighed sixteen and a half tons and was painted a dull camouflage green. At different times Brian called the Hulk "a mobile command base" and "a personal statement" and "a symbol of my reckless abandon." Beside the door on the driver's side, Brian had carefully lettered a small sign that said, "If you value your life as much as I value this truck don't fuck with it."

The only photographs that consistently show a happy, contented Brian are those taken when he is in or around or under the Hulk. He once drove it north to Toronto to show the Antonaccis, and he drove from Long Island to Florida in the Hulk. Off and on over a period of eight years, Brian lived in the Hulk for about two and a half years. In many ways the Hulk *was* Brian: clunky, strong, big, noisy, rebellious in its individuality, beautiful in its ugliness. "It never bored me," he said. "There was always something to do. It was the perfect friend. It was a home. It was a whole way of life. It was not comfortable but I was real happy with it. I'd go to bed in it with all this technology packed around me, all this Brian Spencer identification around me. I think when I built this thing, I was making a statement. Maybe that I don't like to be broken down and crippled. That I'm not timid, I can make it on my own. When I look at the drive train underneath, I see power and strength. I see me."

Brian considered the Hulk the best investment he ever made, the one thing nobody could take from him because they would not know what to do with it. In a Mother's Day card he sent to British Columbia in 1981, Brian enclosed a picture of the Hulk and scribbled a note inside the card detailing some of the features: "hydraulic outrigger system

... 16 tons, 61 mph ... air-conditioning ... demilitarized
.50-calibre machine gun. ..." Brian wrote to Irene, "Dad
would have loved this truck, Mother."

When Brian's hockey career ended, after he played thirty
games with the Hershey Bears in the 1979-80 season, he
trekked back to John Long's farm near Lewiston, New York,
not far from Niagara Falls and the Canadian border. Brian
kept many of his possessions, mainly tools, in a shed in a field
behind Long's house. Written in large letters on an outside
wall of the shed is "Heartbreak Hotel."

In the summer of 1980, Brian had decided to go to Florida,
alone, and he wanted to get rid of some of his things. The
perpetual guest likes to travel light. One of the items was a
large, expensive pool table he bought when he played in
Tulsa. Brian carried the pool table with him in all his moves,
to Toronto, Long Island, Buffalo and Pittsburgh. He did not
want to take it with him to Florida, so he agreed to sell it to
Rick Martin for $750. "It was a beautiful table," Brian
recalled. "It was worth at least $3,500, but I told Rick, 'Give
me $750 and it's yours.'" Brian also told Don Edwards, a
goaltender with the Sabres, that he could have his $500 set of
golf clubs for $20.

Brian was leaving on a Saturday for Long Island to say
goodbye to Janet and the boys, then he would head south for
a new life in Florida. Martin was supposed to come by
Saturday morning for the pool table. When Martin didn't
show, Brian hauled the table out of the shed. It had been
stored in sections, so Brian took the table out piece by piece
and assembled the wooden frame and legs and the heavy
slabs of slate in a field by the shed. With a chainsaw, he sliced
the frame into log-sized chunks, then sawed off the legs and
tossed them on a pile of firewood. Next, using a sledge-
hammer, he smashed the slate into rubble. When Edwards
failed to appear, Brian took the golf clubs from the shed and
broke them one by one over a manure spreader. "I felt
abused," Brian said. "They were getting these things for next
to nothing. Everyone thought I was crazy, but I was leaving
for Florida to change my life and all I was trying to say was,

'Look, guys, pay attention!' "

When Mrs. Spencer was in West Palm Beach for Brian's bail hearing, she and Byron and Darryl Sittler, once a captain of the Maple Leafs and a teammate of Brian, drove out to F Road in Loxahatchee to see the trailer where Brian had been living. The grass in the field by the trailer came to their shoulders, and there was a large swamp pond nearby where Brian used to bathe. The upright piano Brian played on nights when he was alone was still in the trailer — weeks later it was stolen — and some thirty feet from the trailer, beside an old bus, was the Hulk, or what was left of it, with New York licence plate 6339. It had been badly vandalized, pieces of equipment had been torn off, the windows were smashed, the carpeting ripped, and the cockpit was rusted and bent. It stood crippled and nearly hidden in the tall grass, baking in the sun.

Brian visited the trailer a few times during the summer, always reluctantly, as if it were a graveyard. On the floor of the trailer were twisted photographs, bubblegum cards, old shin guards, a red hockey glove, newspaper clippings, broken stereo speakers, a stiff and soiled Buffalo Sabres blazer and so much junk and litter he had to shuffle through it flat-footed. There were sleeping quarters at each end, separated by a bathroom where Brian had installed a shower and a men's urinal. The only living tenants were butterflies, lizards, the odd wayfaring bird and crowds of tiny red ants whose bites cause boil-like inflammations on the skin.

Most of the damage and thefts had occurred while Brian was in jail. He estimated that $10,000 worth of furniture, appliances and equipment had been stolen from the trailer alone, perhaps another $20,000 from the bus and the Hulk. Thieves had used an acetylene torch to cut through the back of the trailer to haul out the large pieces. Brian had bought the land in 1983 with a $15,000 down payment and monthly payments of $450. He had intended to build a redwood and cedar home on the property, with a separate workshop. Two years later, when Janet needed money for the boys in Long Island, Brian sold the land for $6,500. As he waited for his trial to begin, the new owner was after him to clear away the junk.

And on the way to court on Wednesday morning, Paul Simon and Ladysmith Black Mambazo were singing:

Strong wind destroy our home
Many dead, tonight it could be you
Strong wind, strong wind
Many dead, tonight it could be you

II

A clear reminder of the time elapsed since the murder of Michael Dalfo was the sight of Sandra Kennedy entering the courtroom to take the witness stand. She was nineteen years old, a tall, fair-haired woman, wearing red pants and a white blouse, living on her own in nearby Port St. Lucie. Early on the morning of February 4, 1982, the fourteen-year-old Sandra was walking along the shell rock road to catch the school bus on PGA Boulevard at six-forty-five. She lived with her family in a trailer home in a clearing at the north end of the road. It was still dark as she walked along the road, but there was enough morning light for her to notice a trail of shoeprints. They were on the right side of the road as she walked southward, and they looked like shoeprints made by "high-heeled wedge shoes." For a while Sandra tried to walk in them, but she gave up because they got to be too far apart.

"Did you hear anything the night before?" Chuck Burton asked her.

"No," Sandra said.

June Langley, the woman who answered the telephones for Fantacee Island Escorts and who was known as Liz on the job, was the next witness. She was an attractive woman, with blonde hair and a demure but engaging manner. She wore an off-white skirt and jacket, with a white blouse. She did not remove her tinted glasses when she sat in the witness stand.

She told the court she did not know prostitution was

involved when she took the job. She answered telephones for the escort service for fifteen months. The job paid only three dollars an hour, but it was an ideal position for her because she could work at home. In 1982, she was partially paralyzed and confined to a wheelchair. Her boss was a man named Bill Workman and she met him and his wife, Elaine, several times and found them to be "lovely people, really sweet." Most days things went smoothly at the escort agency, but Workman had told her that if ever there was any trouble she should call him immediately.

At the end of his questioning, as he was about to sit down and give way to Barry Weinstein, Burton casually tossed out a couple of questions he would later regret. He asked Langley if she ever considered the escort agency a "Mafia organization."

She answered, "Oh no, if you ever met Bill and Elaine you'd never think that."

"Did you ever think Bill and Elaine might kill somebody?"

"No, no, they were very sweet people."

When it Weinstein's turn he used Langley to establish the umbrella organization of the escort service, how a simple bank of thirteen telephones was all that was needed to run what appeared, in the Yellow Pages at least, to be thirteen different services. He asked about Workman, and he asked about Dan and Sally Phelps, all to establish how the real bosses "layered" themselves from the mundane activities of the escort services.

Langley met Dan and Sally Phelps only once, one night when they took her out to dinner. They owed her some back pay, and they wanted to thank her for the work she had done for the escort service. They never paid her the money they owed, but when they said goodbye they gave her a bottle of wine and a half a ham.

On the evening of February 3, 1982, the night Dalfo kept calling to order more women, Langley said she remembered he sounded normal the first time he called, but the second time he was angry and slurring his words. Later, when

Crystal called her from Dalfo's apartment, Langley heard
Dalfo shouting in the background. She told Weinstein, "The
first thing to come to my mind was how to get Bill there to
protect her."

Some of the jurors' gazes drifted from Langley in the
witness stand to Brian sitting across the courtroom at the
defence table.

"Any trouble, you were to call Bill or Elaine?" Weinstein
asked.

"Yes."

"And you called either Bill or Elaine that night?"

"Yes."

Paula Fairchild testified next, followed by her roommate,
Pamela Vineyard. Paula was thirty-two years old, hippy and
thick-legged. She wore a loose pink dress and her blonde hair
fell past her shoulders. She had long since left the escort
business and was in sales. She had worked briefly for
Fantacee Island Escorts, had gone on four dates, and had sex
on only one of them. When Langley called her on the evening
of February 3, 1982, Paula said she would do it as a favour,
but it would be her last date for the service. She had asked
Pamela to come with her because she was nervous. At the
time of the trial Pamela had a new job, visiting the elderly
and taking them shopping and to their doctors, but she
continued to work part-time as a call girl for an escort
service.

When the women arrived at Dalfo's condominium
apartment, he was waiting for them outside. She thought he
was acting strangely, jumping up and down and running
through the sprinklers on the lawn. Paula wanted to leave, so
she called Langley and told her she did not feel safe with
Dalfo. Langley told Paula to put Dalfo on the phone and she
would keep him talking so Paula and Pamela could get
away.

Sheila Andrews was the last date to visit Dalfo that night.
She appeared in court wearing a tight black skirt slit up the
back and a red blouse with puffed shoulders. By 1987 she was
working as a self-employed landscaper, but in 1982 she

worked as a call girl for Rainbow Dating Service in West Palm Beach. She got a call to visit Dalfo at two-thirty on the morning he was killed. She arrived at his apartment about three. He had told her there would be a security guard at a gatehouse at the entrance, but when Sheila arrived there was no one at the gatehouse, so she drove through and parked her car.

The door to Dalfo's apartment was open, but when she knocked on the door nobody responded. She heard a television set on, very loud, so she yelled, "Mike! Mike!" When no one came to the door, she left. On her way out she saw the security guard in the gatehouse. She asked if she could use his phone and she tried calling Dalfo, but there was no answer. She called her service, reported what had happened, then left about three-thirty.

Detective James Hamilton of the St. Lucie County Sheriff's Office, a crime scene specialist, testified that he arrived at the shell rock road at three-thirty on the afternoon of February 4, 1982. He saw policemen standing at the swampy area where the body was found and at first he thought that was the crime scene. Then he noticed drag marks, what looked like two grooves that could have been made by bare heels if a body had been dragged backwards by someone over the muddy ground, perhaps holding the body under the armpits. Detective Hamilton kept drifting away from the spot where the body was found, back to the edge of the shell rock road. He paced off the distance, measuring it as thirty-seven yards or about a hundred and eleven feet. By the side of the road he found scuffling marks, and further away three stains of human blood and two spent .25-calibre shell casings. They were about eighteen inches apart, which Hamilton said indicated two shots had been fired in rapid succession.

At this point, Burton stepped forward from the prosecution table, raised his arms in the air and gently clapped his cupped hands once, making a small *tock* sound in the courtroom. He asked Detective Hamilton if that was what a .25-calibre shot would have sounded like.

He answered, "Yes, about that loud."

Burton knew his case was weak, and he had been steadily losing ground as the trial progressed, but he scored some points with this dramatic gesture on the afternoon of the seventh day. The impression most people have of a gunshot murder is one of violence and noise, certainly noise enough for anyone in the vicinity to hear. But all along Diane had maintained she saw no gun and heard no shots. A gun small enough to be enclosed in a man's hand and a gunshot that goes *tock* instead of *bang!* might explain this, especially if the only witness had been running from the scene of the crime as fast as her high-heeled shoes — spiked or wedged — could carry her.

Detective Hamilton said the two shell casings were found about twenty-four feet from the shell rock road, in a spot toward where the body was found. High spike-heel shoeprints were also found beside the drag marks or grooves he thought were caused by someone's bare heels being dragged over the soft mud. The high-heel shoeprints followed the drag marks in a northeasternly direction, but only about halfway to where Dalfo's body was found.

Burton asked Detective Hamilton if he thought it was possible for someone five feet one or five feet two and weighing about a hundred and twenty pounds to drag someone five feet eight or five feet nine and a hundred and sixty pounds this way and that far. Before he could answer, Richard Greene barked an objection, arguing it was beyond the witness's expertise. Judge Fine sustained the objection.

After another session with the lawyers at the judge's desk — Brian always accompanied the lawyers to these discussions — Burton continued his line of questioning, asking Detective Hamilton if the high-heel shoeprints were where he would expect them to be for someone dragging a body backwards through the mud.

"No, sir," he replied. "They were off to the side . . . not where they should be for someone dragging a body."

Weinstein merely wanted it on the record that there were

high-heel shoeprints beside the drag marks, away from the shell rock road. Detective Hamilton said there were.

"Past the blood marks, past the casings?"

"Yes."

"The high-heel marks proceeded northeast?"

"Yes," Detective Hamilton said, qualifying his reply only to say that when he examined the marks the ground was very damp and he did his investigation in a driving rain.

Weinstein then concentrated on the police investigation of Dalfo's apartment. He asked Detective Hamilton about any fingerprints the police found in Dalfo's apartment. After checking his notes, he replied that many fingerprints were found after an investigation on February 5, 1982, and the fingerprints were processed several times, and they were all Michael Dalfo's fingerprints. Weinstein produced three photographs taken in Dalfo's apartment. The first showed a wooden cigar box containing cigarette papers, roach clips and a sifter, which Detective Hamilton confirmed were standard paraphernalia for marijuana use. The second photograph showed a small scale, mirrors and a razor, which Detective Hamilton confirmed were standard paraphernalia for cocaine or heroin use. The third photograph captured an overall view of Dalfo's living-room, showing a couch, a coffee table, a single chair and a bottle of brandy.

"Was there any evidence linking Mr. Spencer to that area?" Weinstein asked.

"No, sir," Detective Hamilton said.

At the break for lunch, Byron drove to Monica's apartment to see if his upper teeth had arrived. They hadn't. He was becoming increasingly restless, anxious to leave and return home. He and Leon had had another altercation during one of the witness-preparation sessions in the Public Defenders Office.

In these sessions, Leon and the lawyers try to simulate the interrogation that might take place in the courtroom to determine if the witnesses can handle themselves properly. Byron had been subpoenaed as a character witness, but Leon was never sure he would be needed because the issue of character might never arise. There were too many minuses on both sides. Burton's primary witness, Diane, had too many flaws, and Burton knew Weinstein had been digging up information about her that could be damaging if, as the lawyers say, "the door to character was opened." Similarly, it could be damaging if Brian's character came under scrutiny. There were his drunk-driving convictions, his hiding out before his arrest, his association with Diane, and his guns. There was also the risk of putting hockey itself on trial, with all the undercurrents of violence, mayhem, goons and enforcers. As to Byron being called to the stand, Leon was convinced that the jury would not be impressed by testimony from a defendant's twin brother. Still, ever cautious, Leon wanted Byron to be available. Byron sensed Leon's true feelings about his value to the defence efforts and felt all the more manipulated.

After the morning session, Brian sat for a moment on the wooden bench with his arm around his mother's shoulder. Leon and the lawyers bought two bags of sandwiches and brought them to Weinstein's office for a lunch-hour session before court resumed in the afternoon. Brian went with them, and when they arrived in the reception area of the Public Defenders Office on the ninth floor of the Governmental Building, Virginia, the receptionist, greeted them with her usual cheeriness. One of her favourite lines is, "When God made heaven and hell he put a little bit of heaven in Palm Beach County." This time, having met Brian and his mom earlier in the day, she said, "When I heard Brian say 'Mother,' I knew he was innocent."

In the afternoon, Detective William Springer took the stand. He was one of the policemen who had arrested Brian on the evening of January 18, 1987 on the parking lot at the Mount Vernon Motor Lodge. He explained that Brian and Diane were prime suspects in the Dalfo murder back in 1982, but within months the trail went cold and the investigation was put on a back burner. The investigation was reopened five years later because unsolved capital cases are reviewed regularly every five years. Detective Springer re-examined the entire Dalfo file in October 1986, and after reviewing the facts, the first person he wanted to contact was the woman who now called herself Diane Fialco.

The pathologist who examined Dalfo testified he observed the imprint of the barrel of a handgun on the left side of Dalfo's face. There were also scrapes and abrasions near the kidney area of Dalfo's body, consistent with a body being dragged for a distance. One of the .25-calibre bullets had entered the right side of Dalfo's head, beside his ear, and travelled "right to left, slightly upward, passing through the brain." The bullet exited through the left side of Dalfo's head, near his temple. The other bullet entered Dalfo's head to the right of his nose and did not exit. There were powder burns on the skin, which meant the end of the barrel of the gun had been pushed into Dalfo's head. The pathologist commented that a contact gunshot probably would have made less noise because of the muffling effect.

Weinstein asked only one question of the pathologist. "Did you find anything linking Brian Spencer to this death?"

"I found nothing that linked any individual to this death," the pathologist answered.

That was the end of the prosecution's case. At three o'clock, Judge Fine called a recess until Thursday morning. When the jury left the courtroom, the lawyers debated whether the charges of kidnapping and first-degree murder should be dropped. Greene, as expected, presented case after case of precedents involving similar charges. "There is insufficient evidence to prove that Mr. Spencer was the person involved with Mr. Dalfo," Greene argued. "There is all sorts of evidence someone else did this . . . and the state's own case raises the affirmative possibility that it may have been justified or in self-defence because their witnesses testified he was using cocaine, wired and acting crazy." As to the charge of first-degree murder, Greene said at the very least there was no evidence of premeditation.

Judge Fine said he would reserve his ruling until

Thursday morning on whether the charges should be dropped.

III

At a hotel bar down the street from the courthouse, Rick Martin and John Long discussed the day's evidence. Long had noticed that when Burton slapped his hand, making that *tock* sound, the juror who belonged to the National Rifle Association actually suppressed a laugh. Long, an avid outdoorsman and hunter, said, "If someone fired a .25-calibre handgun in that courtroom, it would have hurt your ears."

Martin, after telling a long joke about a Newfoundlander and a canoe, said the way Dalfo was dragged through the mud from the shell rock road was just the way a woman would drag an unconscious body. She would be struggling with the weight of the body, and she would be gripping him under the armpits. "A man as strong as Spinner would have just picked him up and carried him away."

Brian had another session with the lawyers when court recessed that afternoon, then he found his way home to Monica's alone. He did not feel like socializing. Long, Martin and Martin's wife Mikey ate dinner that evening at Tony Roma's, the rib restaurant down the road from Monica's apartment.

It took John Long nearly half an hour to tell a story about the time he and Brian decided on a whim to head north from Buffalo and drive all the way to Kirkland Lake, a hunting and fishing area in Ontario, about halfway between Buffalo and Hudson Bay. They drove with a case of beer between them on the front seat of Long's car. At a bar in Kirkland Lake, Long lost track of Brian, but he found an adventurous Canadian backwoods woman who invited him to her cabin, where they stayed for three days. Long returned to the bar late on a Sunday afternoon, full of remorse at having abandoned Brian the previous Friday night. As Long was framing a suitable apology, Brian walked in. Long expected the worst. Brian walked up to the bar and, before Long could utter a word, he said, "Jeez, I'm sorry, John, but I met this woman Friday and. . . ." Long waited three years before he told Brian his version.

Mikey Martin quietly listened to all the theories and second-guessing from the trial, the anecdotes of Brian's hockey days, the stories of his marriages, his magnetic appeal to women, and his astonishing sexual prowess. She had only one nagging question. "I'm curious," she said, coughing demurely at the table. "Just how big is his cock anyway?"

CHAPTER NINE

Thursday: *Presumption of Innocence*

I

Dave Keon stepped out of the elevator and quietly mingled with the crowd waiting in the corridor outside Courtroom 315. There were whispers of recognition and heads turned toward the trim, diminutive man in his late forties. He wore a conservative dark blue suit and, though there were wisps of grey in his closely cropped hair, he looked as fit as when he had played the game.

Even the Florida news people understood that someone important had arrived. All along they had not been much impressed by the sporting glamour of Gerry Hart or Rick Martin — or Brian Spencer, for that matter — but the name Dave Keon meant something to them. In Florida, where hockey players have about the same celebrity as South American soccer players, Keon at least was a Pele.

Keon lived in Palm Beach County. He worked as a real estate salesman and had an office on PGA Boulevard in Palm Beach Gardens. He and Brian had met a few times in Florida, but they were not close friends. Keon attended the bail hearing in April, prepared to be a character witness, but he was not called to testify. He invited Brian to his home for dinner one evening in August. Brian was excited at the prospect of chatting up his boyhood idol, but he left disappointed. He found Keon quiet, hard to talk to. During dinner, Brian felt he had to "crowbar" words out of his host's mouth. There were no plaques or trophies in the house, just one framed picture of Keon in a Maple Leaf uniform. And Dave Keon, Brian's captain when he played for the Maple

Leafs, was calling himself David Keon.

At his first training camp with the Leafs, Keon had been Brian's role model. Brian had watched how he ate his food, and what food he ate. He watched how he dressed, in what order he put on his equipment in the dressing-room, and he studied the personal drills Keon performed at practices. He listened to how he talked, how he laughed. One day at camp Jim McKenny, the Leaf defenceman, mentioned this to Keon, and Keon said, "Then he's really in trouble."

Despite having come from a similar background in the tough mining town of Rouyn-Noranda high up along the Quebec-Ontario border and being the same sort of tireless hustler, in every other way Keon was Brian's direct opposite. He broke in and starred in the competitive six-team NHL, played on four Maple Leaf teams that won the Stanley Cup, and was the spark plug that made those grinding, checking teams work. He won the Calder Trophy as rookie of the year in 1961, the Lady Byng Trophy in 1962 and 1963, and the Conn Smythe Trophy as Most Valuable Player in the thrilling 1967 Stanley Cup final. That was the year the Maple Leafs finished third in the standings, behind Montreal and Chicago, then went on to defeat first the Black Hawks, then the Canadiens, to win the last Stanley Cup awarded in Toronto.

For Toronto hockey fans, Keon is something of an icon, representing a style of hockey that has not been experienced at Maple Leaf Gardens for more than twenty years, and may never be seen there again. An astonishing statistic, and an indication of Keon's clean, graceful play, is that he did not get a major penalty until his fourteenth season in the NHL. Next to Keon, Brian was what Truman Capote once called "the talented untalented," too good ever to go home again, not good enough to walk with ease in the new place, doomed to a condition which caused "irritation with no resulting pearl."

At a place called Charley's Eating and Drinking Saloon, in a mall at Military Trail and PGA Boulevard, Keon appeared for lunch one day the previous August. He wore corduroy trousers and a dark blue, open-necked, short-sleeved shirt. It was two months before the trial, and he was concerned about Brian. "He's confident, but a little leery of the unknown," he said, sipping a club soda, waiting for his order of tomato and rice soup and tuna sandwich to arrive. "Probably all his life Brian's been able to do something about things, problems. Now he has to wait, go to trial, then wait for twelve people to make a decision. He finds that difficult. And they like to use the death penalty in this state."

Keon did not have to make the dramatic adjustments Brian did. When he arrived in Toronto from Rouyn-Noranda, he was sixteen years old, Toronto was as big and bright as it ever was for a young hockey player from the bush, but Keon eased in by playing for St. Michael's College Juniors. He was trained to be a Maple Leaf. His biggest transition was moving from a school of two hundred students in Rouyn-Noranda to a school of eight hundred students in Toronto. His junior hockey prepared him for the peculiar, big-city pressures of the NHL. He explained, "Kids who've been drafted and arrive in Toronto are in for total culture shock. Playing the game is the easy part. You go from being a private person to being an open book. Everything's reported — instantly, overnight. When you're a kid growing up in Noranda, or Fort St. James, you've got nobody covering you. They just report the scores at the end of the week. When you're playing Junior B in Toronto, you've got three newspapers covering you. In Junior A, you've got three newspapers covering you. When you make it to the NHL, you've got three newspapers covering you. It makes the transition easier."

For a player of his eminence, Keon's own hockey leave-taking was not much prettier than Brian's. In his last years as a Maple Leaf, Harold Ballard had taken over the team, and the glory days ended. There was dissension, feuds with the press, much small-mindedness, and the Leafs became a joke in the NHL. On one dispirited road trip to the west coast during the 1974-75 season, there were reports of heavy drinking among the Leafs, even on the airplanes. Dunc Wilson, a goaltender for the Leafs, was suspended for missing curfews and being late for the team bus. He was eventually put on waivers and taken by the New York Rangers for $30,000. On the same trip, Lawrence Martin of *The Globe and Mail*, reported that on the flight to Los Angeles Keon "lurched up and down the aisles and used the basest of four-letter words in conversations heard by many other passengers." The story went on:

> At one point, a middle-aged woman, sitting a few rows in front of Keon, obviously bothered by his language, asked: "Who is that man?"
>
> "That's Davey Keon, captain of the Toronto Maple Leafs," a man across the aisle answered. "Class guy, isn't he?"
>
> The following night, when the Leafs were beaten 8-0 by the Los Angeles Kings, Keon did not play effectively.

It was a brutal and sad way to treat a player like Keon who was on the downside of a brilliant hockey career. Martin, now the *Globe*'s correspondent in Moscow, defended the story, because he believed Leaf management had unfairly used Wilson as a scapegoat. He was probably right. After the 1974-75 season, Ballard told Keon he was not wanted, so Keon left the team for which he had played with such distinction for fifteen years and accepted an offer from the Minnesota Fighting Saints of the World Hockey Association.

He wished he had retired earlier. "It takes so much energy to practise, to travel, to play," he said. "If you don't have that energy, it doesn't matter how much ability you have. You just can't get it done."

Keon learned of Brian's arrest in January 1987 when he read about it in the Monday morning newspaper in West Palm Beach. He was not living in Florida in 1982, when Michael Dalfo was killed; he arrived in 1984 to see what it would be like to live in the sun twelve months of the year. He could not remember his immediate reaction to Brian's arrest, except to say it did not seem like Brian's style. "Everything that Brian has done had been a reaction — instantaneous reaction. He was aggressive. Playing hockey, get hit — *bang —*

a fight. A guy comes out, looks like he's going to hit you, so hit him first. That's the Brian Spencer I knew."

Another thing he thought about in the months after he read of Brian's arrest was, "If he did do it, why not just leave, hightail it back to Canada and go to the central interior? They'd never have found him. The fact that he didn't run, that he stayed in Florida from 1982 to 1987, is a good argument that he didn't do it."

II

When court resumed, it was obvious Chuck Burton had been doing his homework the night before. He brought to court some case law of his own to do battle with Richard Greene's boxes of precedents.

As to the kidnapping charge, he cited a recent case in Florida involving a woman who had been sexually assaulted after accepting a ride from a man who had stopped to offer her a lift. "The kidnapping charge was upheld, even though she got in the car voluntarily," Burton argued. As to the charge of first-degree murder, he cited another case that showed "a moment's reflection" can be enough to constitute premeditation, which constitutes first-degree murder.

Greene countered with his case law, digging into the bankers' boxes behind the defence table for mimeographed copies, armfuls of which he distributed at the front of the courtroom like a news vendor at a busy corner. When the arguing was done, Judge Fine ruled against Weinstein's motion for acquittal. He instructed the defence to call its first witness. Irene Spencer sat in the courtroom four rows behind her son. She'd hoped Judge Fine would end the trial that morning, without the jury having to deliberate on a verdict. She worried that the judge was sympathetic to the prosecution. She felt nauseous.

The first witness for the defence was Martin Malveso, a bartender. He wore brown pants and a short-sleeved yellow shirt and from behind a bushy brown beard his face looked world-weary and imperturbable. He had been working as a bartender in West Palm Beach for seventeen years. He had met Brian in 1981 and he liked him, though the friendship was never more than what he called "a bartender-customer relationship." Brian used to visit his bar three or four times a week and he always left a big tip. Malveso worked at the Banana Boat from 1980 until 1985. He was on duty the night Michael Dalfo was murdered.

Burton did not like Malveso. He had questioned him about that evening when he took a deposition from him before the trial. Each lawyer gets a crack at the other lawyer's witnesses, and when Burton interviewed Malveso under oath at the deposition hearing, Malveso said he had seen Brian at the Banana Boat throughout the evening, up until closing time at four-thirty in the morning. Burton knew that Malveso's testimony would provide an alibi for Brian, and he believed Malveso was lying.

In the courtroom, as he was being questioned by Weinstein, Malveso left the witness stand and walked to a lecturer's easel in front of the jury. There, using a thick, felt-tipped marker, he drew a diagram in red ink of the inside of the Banana Boat, showing the main bar, the dance area, the food stations. He remembered serving Brian a rum and Coke about one o'clock. He remembered Diane arriving, and he served her a glass of white wine. He remembered serving her again later that evening. He remembered Brian being at the oyster bar at about one-twenty or one-thirty. He remembered Brian talking to some people at the main bar at two or two-thirty. He remembered Brian back at the oyster bar between three-thirty and four. He remembered Brian at the main bar for last call at four-thirty.

When Weinstein asked how he was able to recall these details so well, Malveso replied that it was because it was a Wednesday evening, the first day of his work week, and he was breaking in a new bartender, and a new band had started that night.

"It sounds like it was your night to watch Brian Spencer?" Burton asked, his words fairly dripping with sarcasm.

"It sounds like it, but it wasn't," Malveso said.

Burton explained that the Banana Boat, now called Hooters, is at Okeechobee Boulevard and Military Trail, about three miles from Skees Road, where Brian and Diane shared a trailer, and two miles from the Florida Turnpike, which runs in a straight line nine miles north to PGA Boulevard. Burton estimated it would take three or four minutes to drive from the Banana Boat to the Turnpike, five or ten minutes to get from the Banana Boat to Skees Road. He did not estimate how long it would take to travel from the Banana Boat to PGA Boulevard and the shell rock road that runs off it. With sparse traffic, it would take about twenty minutes.

Burton asked Malveso if he remembered Brian being upset that evening.

"No, sir."

"Not angry?"

"No, sir."

"Not nervous?"

"No, sir."

Malveso said he first heard of Dalfo's death five days later, when Brian called him early Monday morning at his home. "The cops are trying to pin a bum rap on me," Brian told him, and then he asked Malveso if he remembered seeing him in the bar the previous Wednesday evening. Brian told Malveso detectives from the Palm Beach County Sheriff's Office would be getting in touch with him.

Weinstein asked Malveso if he ever spoke to Brian about the Dalfo case. Malveso said Brian came by once to thank him for being cooperative with the police, but they never discussed the case.

"Not in '82?" Weinstein asked.

"No."

" '83?"

"No."

" '84?"

"No."

" '85?"

"No."

" '86?"

"No."

" '87?"

"No."

When it was Burton's turn again, he asked if Malveso remembered seeing Brian at the Banana Boat the next night, Thursday, or Friday night, or the following Saturday night. Malveso said he did not remember seeing Brian on those nights.

"Do you remember where all your customers sit and eat oysters?" Burton asked.

"I don't know all my customers."

Burton spun on his heels and walked to his table with a look of disgust on his face. With his back to Malveso, he took a parting shot.

"You got a sudden memory jog?"

In a voice above a whisper, Malveso replied, "No, sir."

Next up were the agents involved in Operation Greenback, the federal investigation of prostitution, cocaine and money-laundering in south Florida that was set up in 1980. These were the men Leon tracked down, in locations across the United States.

The first was Michael Woodworth, a special agent with U.S. Customs who worked out of New York and Miami in the early 1980s and had since been posted in Laredo, Texas. Weinstein asked him if he knew Bill Workman, June Langley, Dan Phelps and Sally Phelps. Woodworth said yes, he knew all of them. The Phelpses had been convicted of transporting women across state lines for prostitution and money-laundering, technically violating the Bank Secrecy Act by not filing reports on transactions involving more than $5,000. Woodworth had no idea where the Phelpses were now, because while awaiting an appeal they had skipped bail and were now fugitives. He called the operation that controlled the thirteen escort services, among them Fantacee Island Escorts, "a major criminal enterprise."

Weinstein then asked Woodworth a thunderclap of a

question.

"Are you aware of anyone in the escort service connected with any murders?"

Before Woodworth could answer, Burton rose from his chair and objected, loudly. He asked to approach the bench. Weinstein continued, mentioning the names that had been given to Harold Yearout and his wife under the witness protection program.

Burton, standing at the prosecution table, called for a mistrial.

Angrily, but with a satisfying crunch of indignation, Weinstein shouted in his high-pitched voice, "Mr. Burton himself opened the door, when he asked Liz Langley if anyone from the escort service might kill someone."

He was referring to the two throwaway questions Burton had asked as Langley was about to leave the witness box the day before. One of them was, "Did you ever think Bill and Elaine might kill somebody?" To which Langley had replied, "No, no, they were very sweet people."

After much urgent whispering and gesticulating around Judge Fine, the tangle of lawyers unravelled and Weinstein strode again to the centre of the courtroom. Judge Fine had allowed him to re-ask the question, with the jury present. When he did, Woodworth's answer came as the echo to the thunderclap.

"Yes," he said.

Woodworth had heard that Dan Phelps once boasted he was going to have someone "hit." Later, Phelps had pointed to a story in a West Palm Beach newspaper about a murder somewhere up by the Florida Turnpike and said, "That was the guy."

The problem was that Woodworth only "had heard" that Phelps said this. He did not hear him say it himself. Woodworth probably heard it from Yearout, the man Leon interviewed in Colorado Springs. Judge Fine ruled Woodworth's remarks hearsay. He instructed the jury to disregard them.

Burton walked to the lecturer's easel, intending to use a

fresh page to draw a diagram of the organization of the escort services, but inadvertently he turned over the page which Weinstein had used during jury selection to emphasize the state's responsibility to prove Brian guilty. It was not the finest moment for the jurors to be reminded of:

Burden of proof
Presumption of innocence
Reasonable doubt

Burton quickly flipped back the page and on a fresh sheet he wrote:

Phelps
Workman
Telephone operator
Girls

He was trying to show that the operation of the escort services really was not all that elaborate. Woodworth repeated that it was far from a simple operation, and that he regarded it as "a criminal enterprise." Burton said if he — "little ol' me, not the Mafia" — stood on a street corner and sold cocaine he would be engaged in a criminal enterprise too. He asked if the escort service operation would have been a multi-billion-dollar organization. Woodworth said it was not that big.

According to Dennis Fagan, another U.S. Customs agent, two undercover members of Operation Greenback negotiated with the Phelpses to buy the thirteen escort services, which were essentially a bank of thirteen telephones and access to the girls. Operation Greenback was primarily interested in the money-laundering operation, which involved money from prostitution and cocaine. Fagan's role was bodyguard for the undercover agents. At the last meeting with the Phelpses before their arrest, the agents offered them $240,000 to buy the escort services, and they asked the Phelpses to launder another $250,000 in narcotics money. The Phelpses had hired a private pilot and were arranging to fly the money from a small airport south of West Palm Beach to the Bahamas when they were arrested in November 1982.

When Weinstein asked about any weapons confiscated from the Phelpses when they were arrested, Burton objected, and once again the lawyers trekked to Judge Fine's bench for a prolonged discussion. After much *sotto voce* haggling, barely out of earshot of the jury, Judge Fine called for a recess. He did not want to risk the jury overhearing the heated private discussion and he knew it was nearly time for lunch, so he instructed the jury to leave and return in the afternoon.

During the recess, Brian and Burton chatted amicably in the corridor. Brian lit a cigarette for Burton, and when the recess ended he opened the door to the courtroom and politely stepped aside to allow Burton to enter ahead of him. As they waited for Judge Fine, Weinstein and Burton traded pleasantries and joked about Greene's remarkable collection of case law. They were actually laughing with each other at the front of the courtroom when Judge Fine entered and the bailiff again ordered everyone to please stand.

With the jury out, Weinstein mentioned that four firearms were seized from the *Isis II*, the houseboat where the Phelpses were staying in Hypoluxo, a resort village about eight miles south of West Palm Beach. Three of the four firearms were declared legal, the fourth one, a .22-calibre handgun, was declared illegal because the serial numbers had been removed. Judge Fine wondered what the big deal was over the .22-calibre handgun. The serial numbers might have been filed, which would make it an illegal weapon, but it was not the same calibre as the gun that killed Dalfo. Weinstein said, "There was no reason to file the serial numbers unless it was used in criminal activities."

Burton did not want to be snookered again. He did not want the jury to listen to a discussion of the heavies of the escort service owning illegal handguns. He repeated what Judge Fine had said, that the illegal weapon seized from the *Isis II* was not a .25-calibre handgun, and he said the police never laid charges of possession of an illegal weapon. Almost plaintively, Burton complained that he was not allowed to mention that Brian owned three guns, one of which was a

Luger.

At lunch, Irene Spencer sat with Monica at one of the circular tables by the fountain in the outdoor courtyard at the Governmental Center. With them was Heather Bird, a reporter from *The Toronto Star*. There was a prickly tension at the table. Mrs. Spencer mused aloud, "I guess some people enjoy coming to court. For them it's entertainment — but not when it hits home." Monica sat with her back to Heather Bird, and Mrs. Spencer barely tolerated the reporter's presence. "I don't pay any attention to what I read in the newspapers," she said.

The first witness of the afternoon was Detective Al Bonanni, a true-life Miami Vice detective. He had been investigating prostitution, pornography and narcotics in Miami and environs for twelve years, since he was assigned in 1975 to the organized crime section of the Metro Dade Police Force. Operation Greenback needed his expertise when they were going after Dan and Sally Phelps in the early 1980s.

Bonanni had served two search warrants on the Phelpses, one for the *Isis II*, another for a warehouse complex they owned on Northlake Boulevard in West Palm Beach. At the warehouse, he found ledger sheets, with names of the women who worked as escorts opposite details of their physical attributes, likes and dislikes, and nude photographs. He also found paper shredders, used to destroy any pertinent information that could be used as evidence, and "bad lists" — names known to have been used by undercover policemen, and unsavoury customers known for kinky sexual proclivities, drug abuse or violence against the escorts. Bonanni called it "a very sophisticated organization, not fly-by-night."

Weinstein asked, "Do escort services usually have enforcement protection wings?"

"Yes," Bonanni said.

"Why?"

"A twofold purpose," Bonanni explained. "First, to

intimidate the girls. Second, to protect the girls, since they are reluctant to call the police as normal citizens would."

The jury was still out when the last witness for the defence took her place in the witness stand. Burton knew she was an important witness, one who could make Diane look bad, and Judge Fine agreed to hear what she had to say before the jury could weigh her words. She was Betty Lou Butler, a stylish redhead in her mid-forties. Butler's former husband, Lou Sennello, used to be vice-president and district manager at Fischbach & Moore on Dyer Boulevard in West Palm Beach. They divorced in 1985. Butler worked as an electrical estimator at Fischbach & Moore from 1980 to 1985, which is where she came to know Brian. It was where she also met Diane Delena, who used to hang around and attend company picnics and other social functions, because her mother worked there. Weinstein asked Butler about Diane's reputation for "truth and veracity."

"Very dishonest," she said.

Burton grimaced. The jury was absent, but they would be coming in shortly and if Judge Fine allowed Weinstein to re-ask the question he knew Butler's words would severely damage the credibility of Diane. Butler was an attractive, intelligent woman, an executive's wife, with no apparent axe to grind, no reason to attack Diane for lack of truth or veracity or anything else. In fact, Butler was a friend of Diane's mother.

Leon had tracked down Butler early in his investigation. She lived in Jupiter, a popular oceanside resort some ten miles up the coast from West Palm Beach. Brian was still locked up in the Palm Beach County Detention Center when Leon and Butler sat down in a room at the Public Defenders Office one morning the previous March. What she told Leon in her sworn deposition revealed a side of Brian only a few close friends knew.

Butler's son, Jimmy, had a serious problem with drugs. She had tried to find help from various agencies in Palm Beach County, and had enrolled Jimmy in different programs throughout the state, but nothing seemed to work, and his addiction to drugs worsened. Butler met Brian soon after he arrived in Florida, back in 1980 when he worked at Fischbach & Moore as a mechanic. She and her former husband often invited Brian to their home for dinner. She knew Jimmy admired Brian, probably because he had been a major-league athlete, so one day she asked Brian if he would try to help him. He did, spending much of his free time with the boy until his death when he was eighteen. Butler said Brian did more good for Jimmy than anyone else, and she told Leon, "Brian is one of the most giving people I have met."

Butler met Diane's mother, whose name was Marion, when they both were at Fischbach & Moore. They often exchanged stories of raising children. "Some of our children put us through things that are unbelievable," she told Leon. Butler had her own problems with Jimmy, but she felt sorry for Marion because Diane was causing her so much grief, hanging out with a tough crowd, always in trouble. She remembered the day Marion asked Brian if he could fix Diane's car, after which Diane spent much time at Fischbach & Moore, hanging out with Brian and the other mechanics.

Leon asked, "Who was the aggressor? Who was chasing whom?"

"Diane was the aggressor in every way," Butler said. "Wherever that man went, I don't care where it was, if he went to the men's washroom at Fischbach & Moore she would be standing outside the door waiting. I mean, the man couldn't move without her."

"Did you ever get the feeling Brian was trying to get away from her?"

"He told me time and time again that she's not very bright, that he just can't shake her, can't get rid of her. It was like she was a . . . a parasite."

Leon asked Butler if Brian ever talked to her about being involved with an escort service.

"Brian Spencer would never discuss anything like that with me due to respecting me. And I don't believe Brian Spencer would have anything to do with an escort business. I think the reason why Brian got involved with Diane is that she's an airhead, number one. She's physically appealing to men, she's young, and I think most men would — but I don't believe Brian would ever get involved with an escort service, ever. He doesn't have to."

"How do you feel about his truthfulness and veracity?" Leon asked.

"Brian has never, and I can swear to this, ever told me a lie. Brian's been in my husband's and my home. I've been very involved with Brian because of my son. I got to know Brian real well. Brian's probably one of the most unusual people I know. He can have greasy mechanic hands and he can play classical music on a piano."

Leon asked, "When you heard that Brian Spencer had been arrested and charged with murder, what was your reaction to that?"

"I couldn't believe it," Butler said, and she told Leon about how the police used to visit Fischbach & Moore back in 1982 in the months after Dalfo's murder, going to the warehouse, asking Brian questions. "I didn't believe it then and I definitely don't believe it now."

Leon asked, "Would you say Brian is the type of person that if a friend was in trouble he would try to help them and try to stay with them?"

"He'd be number one. He's the person you'd count on."

When the jury had assembled in the courtroom, Weinstein asked Butler the same question he had asked her earlier.

"What was Diane Delena's reputation for truth and veracity?"

Butler did not give the answer she gave when the jury was out. This time she said, "She's an habitual liar."

Burton objected, but Judge Fine overruled him. When it was his turn to ask questions, he seemed to have run out of steam. "How are you, Mrs. Butler?" he began. She nodded slightly and said she was fine. Burton asked if she ever had Diane Delena to her house for dinner. Butler said she never did. After a few more perfunctory questions, Burton turned and looked directly at Brian seated at the defence table, clad in his new blue suit, with his hair freshly styled. Almost as an afterthought, or as if he was thinking out loud, Burton asked, "He didn't look like he does now, did he?"

Greene barked an objection. Judge Fine sustained it. That was it. At two-forty on the afternoon of the eighth day of the trial, Weinstein rose from his chair and said, "The defence rests." Burton had no further questions.

When the jury was excused, Greene made another motion for acquittal on both counts, arguing that the state had not proved its case. Judge Fine immediately denied the motion. He said, "To me it's a jury decision."

Late that afternoon, at the lounge in the Holiday Inn on PGA Boulevard, which is about a mile and a half to the east of the shell rock road, Brian, Rick Martin and his wife Mikey, John Long, Monica and Betty Butler sat around two tables pushed together. They ordered drinks and sandwiches. Brian asked for two Budweisers. They discussed the day's events, told more jokes, and congratulated Butler on her performance in the witness stand. There was almost a festive mood, but when Brian finished his second Bud, he said he did not feel much like partying. He wanted to be alone.

CHAPTER TEN

Friday:
The
Verdict

I

Irene Spencer waited in the lobby of the Hampton Inn, a two-storey motel on Belvedere Boulevard, across from the Palm Beach International Airport. A neighbour of Monica's works at the airport and she had given Irene and Byron promotional coupons that entitled them to two free rooms at the motel for most of the week. Irene was alone, reading a newspaper at a small, glass-topped table in the lobby, sipping orange juice from a plastic cup and eating a buttered bran muffin, the motel's complimentary continental breakfast.

In two hours, Charles Burton and Barry Weinstein would deliver their closing arguments, and the jury would begin deliberating shortly after lunch. But Byron would not be there to hear the outcome of *Florida v. Brian Spencer*. Feeling useless and ignored, Byron had left West Palm Beach earlier that morning on a flight to Canada. He would not be in the courtroom to learn if his twin brother would be set free, or sentenced to twenty-five years in prison or to the electric chair. Irene was too nervous to drive downtown alone in her rented car, so I agreed to meet her at the motel and accompany her to the courthouse.

We walked to the parking lot, Irene's heels clicking on the pavement. At eight o'clock in the morning the air inside the parked car was baking hot. As we headed east on Belvedere Boulevard, Irene fiddled with the air-conditioning dials and soon a whoosh of cool air swept up into our faces from below the dashboard. All the way to Old Dixie Highway, a drive of about fifteen minutes in rush-hour traffic, Irene looked straight ahead out the window, immersed in her thoughts.

She wore a full green skirt and a tangerine-coloured blouse with short sleeves, a white collar, and girlish, puffed shoulders. Her tightly-curled blonde hair was shaped in a bun at the back, held with a clasp. She cradled her purse in her lap, white gloves draped over the clasp. She looked as if she might be heading out for a morning of bridge, which happens to be one of her passions. "There's a man in the park with a hole in the seat of his pants because he forgot to take out trump," I said, trying to lighten the mood as we rolled northward along Old Dixie Highway. She smiled, but spoke the dark thoughts that preoccupied her.

"Brian could have dropped by the motel last night," she said. "Byron felt badly hurt by Brian ignoring him." We drove on in silence, then she said, "Byron felt pushed out all week. He lost another job as a result of coming here for the trial."

Further north on Old Dixie Highway, approaching downtown, we passed the El Cid Bar, then turned at the Mount Vernon Lodge to head north up Olive Avenue. The names — Old Dixie, Olive Avenue, El Cid, Mount Vernon Lodge — rolled by like empty scenes behind the closing credits of a movie. Irene Spencer does not miss much. She knew that Brian had been drinking at the El Cid the night he was arrested, that later he stopped at the Mount Vernon Lodge, and that there the police and the dogs and the helicopter brought to an end what had been just another night of bar-hopping.

Irene mentioned a time she visited Janet and Brian when Brian played for the Buffalo Sabres. "He wasn't a drinker then. When he was with Janet, there used to be dust on the bottles." Silence, a few more blocks. "Janet left Brian, you know. She said it was impossible to live with him any more."

She recalled other times. When Brian was growing up in Fort St. James he had a paper route for a short time and one afternoon he found a dollar on the street about a quarter of a block from the nearest house. He picked up the dollar and ran to the house to ask if anyone there had lost the money. "He is extremely honest. I'm never happy when Brian is described as naïve and gullible. He always had friends when he was growing up, and he never had to buy them with pop or candy, never had to pick up the tab. Byron had the same number of friends, but only when he had money. Brian saved his money."

And despite his father's obsessive hockey ambitions for his sons, Brian had had other boyhood dreams. Late one afternoon, after school, he noticed a man crashing through the bushes at the edge of town. The man looked like he was running away, escaping, so Brian ran to the RCMP office to report what he had seen. Sure enough, Brian's description fit that of a man the Mounties were looking for, and thanks to Brian's tip they caught him. An RCMP sergeant dropped by the Spencer home that evening to commend Brian for his good work, calling him "a super sleuth." For a time Brian spoke of becoming a policeman when he grew up. Years later, when he was playing in the NHL, Brian would embellish the story, as he did so many others, by telling reporters he took part in a dangerous RCMP manhunt in the bush when he was only twelve years old. Who would know?

And Roy. Roy returned from the war weighing a solid one-hundred-and-eighty pounds. Besides working at the gravel pit, he did push-ups, chin-ups and sit-ups. He was proud of his body. Sometimes, for the snapshots Irene kept in the family albums, Roy posed without a shirt, tightening the muscles of his arms and his hard, packed chest. Murray Hill used to say Roy Spencer was built like a god. By the time of his death, however, his weight had dwindled to a sickly one-hundred-and-forty pounds. He had lost control of the boys, and Irene could not exert any discipline over them. When Brian was locked up overnight in Vanderhoof for stealing quarters from a laundromat, Roy appeared at the jail in the morning and looked in on Brian, then fifteen. Brian feared the worst, but all Roy could say was, "You've got some good reading material in there." It was one of those fragmentary but indelible moments when a son sees the mask of fatherhood slip enough to reveal a mere human.

Irene tried to stop Roy the night he drove off to the television station. She followed him into the yard after he stomped out of the house, imploring him to stop and think. "What about Brian?" she asked. She knew Roy would do whatever he set out to do, and she worried that somehow his behaviour would hurt Brian's hockey career. Without turning around, Roy shouted, "To hell with Brian!" And then he drove off to Prince George.

Roy carried survival gear in the trunk of his car, an ordinary precaution at that time of year in northern British Columbia, but Irene later discovered that the gear was much more elaborate than anything she had seen in the trunk before. He had been to Edmonton for a medical examination a few weeks earlier. He was very sick with uremic poisoning, and for years had been growing weaker. He returned from Edmonton with a portable breathing device called a Hand-E-Vent, which the doctor had prescribed for his bronchitis. Irene suspects he had been planning some sort of trip, and that the night he drove off in a rage to Prince George, for whatever reason, he had no intention of returning home.

We pulled into the parking lot across the street from the courthouse, but Irene did not want to leave the car right away. She was nervous, and she did not trust the system. She thought the prosecuting attorney might "hoodwink" the jury. The implications of Brian being found guilty had kept her awake at night. And she wanted to talk more about Brian and Roy and the family and Fort St. James. "There are things you should understand," she said, sitting in the rented car, holding her purse and her white gloves. "Many times I wished Brian were home, learning the gravel trade with Byron. I always thought that seventeen was too young for leaving home to play Junior A hockey. Brian was always a survivor, but it's a cruel, cold world. It's too late for me to correct the mistakes I made trying to raise the boys singlehanded and trying to protect a sick husband. I was too young, too scared to contradict Roy. He was always kind and protective of me. I couldn't think of hurting him."

For a while Irene sat looking out the window across at the courthouse where the bright morning light reflected off the white walls. Before she opened the door to get out, she said, "It's not easy for Brian and I to talk. He takes offence very easily. But I love him dearly." That was what she wanted me to understand.

II

At twelve minutes after ten, the jury entered Courtroom 315 and took their seats. Two minutes later, Chuck Burton, wearing a dark blue suit, rose from his seat at the prosecution table and walked to the lectern in front of the jury. Brian watched from the defence table. For the last day of his trial he wore a light tan sports jacket, dark brown pants, a white shirt and a yellow tie dotted with small crosses. Inside each lapel of Brian's jacket were strips of yellow tape on which were written, on the left side, "The Spin" and on the right, "Not Guilty." For the last day of the trial, an exercise in positive thinking.

Burton was allowed ninety minutes for his closing argument. He would go first, using part of the allotted time, then Weinstein would have his ninety minutes, then Burton would deliver the last of his remarks. The spectators' section was jammed, the Dalfo family and friends occupying most of the left side, Brian's friends, family, ex-teammates and the media filling nearly all of the right side. In a corner at the rear, Robert Decker of Coast Media Productions in California stood behind his video camera, which had been rolling since the moustachioed bailiff called the court to order. Decker had been videotaping the trial from the first day of jury selection to gather raw material for a television movie he intended to produce on Brian's life and hockey career. There were newspaper reporters and magazine correspondents from Toronto, Buffalo and New York, their presence a puzzle to the local media. The previous week, during jury selection, not one of the thirty-six potential jurors interviewed had ever heard of Brian Spencer. Christine Van Meter, the court reporter for *The Palm Beach Post*, mentioned in one of her stories that as far as south Florida was concerned, Brian Spencer might as well be a John Doe.

"This is not like television," Burton told the jury, standing at the lectern, reading from his notes on sheets of foolscap. "Everything doesn't get wrapped up in an hour."

Burton's first point concerned premeditation, the difference between first- and second-degree murder. Premeditation does not require weeks or days, not even hours or minutes, but only seconds. You decide to kill somebody and seconds later you do it; that's all you need for premeditation.

He admitted that many of the details of the case were vague, that the murder was committed more than five years ago, early on the morning of February 4, 1982, to the best of the experts' estimates "sometime between one and seven." Not even Diane Delena, now Mrs. Fialco, could say precisely when the killing happened, and she had been there on the shell rock road with Michael Dalfo. She had told the police so in a sworn statement, and she said it again in court before the jury. Burton said Diane obviously knew more about what happened that night, and he admitted that some of her testimony was unclear — she didn't know exactly when it happened, she didn't see a gun, she didn't hear any shots, and in her first statement to the police in 1982 she admitted she had lied when she said she was with a client at the Hyatt Hotel until four-thirty in the morning. She lied, Burton said, because the defendant told her to, because she needed an alibi, and because she was afraid of Brian Spencer.

Burton told the jury that a woman as small as Diane could not have pistol-whipped Dalfo and then dragged him forty yards from the road over the muddy field to the clearing where the body was found. "Common sense tells you that," Burton told the jury, and then he said, "If she helped whoever . . ." It was a little slip and Burton quickly corrected himself and began again, "If she helped the defendant. . . ."

A telling slip, one that the jury might not have noticed, but Brian's defence team, certainly Leon Wright, did. It was as if Burton finally had been swept up and caught by the scenario proposed by Brian's lawyers, or perhaps subconsciously he had come to accept that the murder had been done by some faceless, anonymous, hired killer — by "whoever." He might as well have said "by persons unknown."

Burton moved on to the matter of the shoes. So what if Diane could not remember the shoes she happened to be wearing of an evening more than five years ago? Burton looked at the jurors and, with a beseeching shrug, he said, "I remember wearing a tuxedo five years ago at my wedding, but I can't remember what shoes I was wearing." That won a few smiles from the jurors, but Burton no longer was playing the good-guy frat-president. There was an edge to his voice. He continued, "If she's such a liar, how come we can corroborate everything she's said?"

By this he meant that Diane's calls to the escort service had been corroborated by the woman who answered the telephone for Fantacee Island Escorts, that Diane's description of Dalfo's appearance and decorum had been corroborated by the other women who had been sent to his townhouse, that Brian had been at the Banana Boat when Diane dropped by on her way to visit poor Galen Leroy Hassinger at the Hyatt Hotel, that the police did find shoeprints where Diane said she had been running along the side of the shell rock road that night.

But — everything? What had *not* been corroborated was that Brian and Diane drove to Dalfo's townhouse that night in her Fiat, that Dalfo entered the car, that Brian and Dalfo engaged in a noisy argument, that Brian carried or ever owned a .25-calibre pistol, that Brian picked up Diane moments later on PGA Boulevard and told her, "Now he can't call his lawyer." What had *not* been demonstrated was that Brian had been anywhere within five miles of the scene of the crime at any time that evening. No fingerprints, no shoeprints, no blood, not a single strand of Brian's thick, ample, wavy hair. (In a restaurant in West Palm Beach one night Brian demonstrated a takeout in hockey by pushing me hard against the edge of the booth with his left shoulder, leaning his head into my right temple. At my hotel that evening I noticed dark-blond hairs on my shirt.)

Burton addressed the defence's contentions that something larger was involved. Operation Greenback? The customs agents? Dan and Sally Phelps? A bigtime criminal enterprise? "I mean, gimme a break," Burton said. "All the customs guys got was a three-year sentence for prostitution. There was no evidence that this agency had enforcers. The defence wants you to believe the agency put out a hit on this guy, this little Mike Dalfo who lives in a townhouse on PGA. They're not going to kill little Mike Dalfo. And they're not going to use a .25-calibre automatic." Burton described how, despite two gunshots in the head, Dalfo stayed alive all night and was still breathing early the next afternoon when Albert Brihn, the truck driver, found him on his back in the pool of water in the clearing. "This is not a big gun with a boom," not an enforcer's sort of weapon, Burton implied.

Leon watched from the front row, immediately behind the defence table, his forearms resting on the wooden ledge. He did not consider it unusual that a small automatic handgun had been used to kill Dalfo, since it is often the weapon of choice in these matters. It is easily concealed, easily discarded, and all the better that on a quiet night on an isolated road it does not go *boom!*

As to the suggestion that the murder was a gangland execution, carried out by some heavy from the escort service, Burton said it was "just ridiculous" to sugest that a hit man would bring along someone like Diane as a witness.

But what better way to lure Dalfo from his townhouse? Diane might have done what she said she did, returned to Dalfo's townhouse, invited him into her little Fiat — *Hey, Mike, I need a partner for an orgy* — then delivered him to "whoever" was waiting on the shell rock road.

Burton reminded the jurors of Martin Malveso, the bartender who claimed Brian had been at the Banana Boat all night, who even remembered when Brian was eating oysters.

"I mean, gimme a break," Burton repeated. "Malveso was Brian's buddy. Brian calls him up after the police questioned him and says, 'Hey, Marty, you remember I was in the Banana Boat?' And then he goes back later and says, 'Hey, Marty, thanks for what you done, pal.' Marty Malveso's a liar."

And then Burton portrayed Diane as a devoted wife and mother, married with two children, with a husband who knows nothing of her shady past. She agreed to testify under immunity, just like Oliver North did in the Iran-Contra hearings, but all this means is that she can't be prosecuted for what she says. She can be prosecuted if new evidence is uncovered. What does Diane have to gain by cooperating with the police? Her testimony is nothing less than a public confession of prostitution.

"Diane Fialco loses no matter which way this case turns out," Burton said.

As for the lack of evidence linking Brian Spencer to the crime scene, Burton said, "It's hard to get fingerprints out of the mud." And, "When he's dragging that body he's erasing his own shoeprints."

Betty Butler?

"Betty Butler's about as biased as a witness can get," Burton said. "She had the Spencer family over for dinner. She's been out with Brian alone."

Burton grasped at every straw he could find. He did not appear confident, nor did he look comfortable. He had been speaking for nearly forty minutes and at ten fifty-two he reached the last page of his notes at the lectern and found his best line.

"Sometimes," he said, "you have to go through a sinner to get to the devil."

Barry Weinstein leapt from his chair at the defence table and as he crossed the courtroom to the lectern in front of the jury he shouted, "Amazing! Simply amazing!" He picked up the lectern, walked it out of the way and plunked it down next to the prosecution table.

"Why would Brian Spencer murder Michael Dalfo? Why? For Diane Delena? She was a prostitute! She is a liar!"

Weinstein went at it like a mutt with a mouthful of pantcuff. If any of the spectators had been dozing off, they were awake now.

"Not one witness of the state connected Brian Spencer to the scene — only Diane Delena. There's nothing linking Brian Spencer to the crime — except Diane Delena. All the state has proved is that Diane Delena was there. Diane Delena knows more. . . ."

As he spoke, Weinstein held a clear plastic bag containing Diane's high-heeled shoes, the shoes with the mud, the mud from the field by the shell rock road. He lifted the bag in front of the jury, and then he walked over and dropped the bag on the edge of the prosecution table, about ten feet from the jury box. As Weinstein continued his closing argument many of the jurors rested their gaze on the bag of shoes with the spike heels. Burton himself stared at the bag as if it might speak to him.

Weinstein walked back and forth in front of the jury, then stopped and levelled an outstretched arm at the prosecution table. "They have not given you one piece of credible evidence." He turned back to the jury and continued in staccato bursts.

"Why would Brian Spencer do this?"

"What motive would he have to kill Michael Dalfo?"

"Where's the state coming from?"

"We know Diane was there. What we don't know is what else Diane knows."

He had spoken for only thirty-four of his allotted ninety minutes, but he was drawing to a close. He was slowing down, toning down. He plunged his left hand in the outside pocket of his suit jacket and, gesturing with the baby finger of his right hand, said in a soft but distinct voice, "Mr. Spencer's life is on the line." Then he spun around and walked all the way across the courtroom, straight to the defence table, where he stood behind Brian and placed both his hands on Brian's shoulders.

"Why ... why ... why ... why?"

With each "why" Weinstein pushed down hard on Brian's shoulders, rocking him forward. It was theatrical, but effective. The "whys" reverberated in the courtroom like the sound of crashing cymbals.

After forty-six minutes of speaking without a note, Weinstein ended his closing argument in a calm, controlled voice. "What will cry out plain and simple is that the state has not proved its case. There's nothing to it. Brian Spencer is not guilty. Brian Spencer is not guilty."

Weinstein sat down and quietly put his arm around Brian and pulled him to him. It was an intimate gesture, not intended for the jury or the spectators. Judge Fine called a fifteen-minute recess.

During the break, in the corridor outside the courtroom, even Brian, whom Burton was trying to send to the electric chair, felt solicitous toward the affable prosecuting attorney. He offered Burton a Marlboro, lit it for him, and as they waited for court to resume, Brian told Burton no matter what happened, he would bear him no grudge.

When it came time to conclude his closing argument, Burton went through the motions, repeating most of what he had said earlier. Little elfin Weinstein, who had appeared so tentative and twitchy at the start of the trial, now seemed a hard act to follow. But Burton tried.

"They say we didn't bring another witness. Unfortunately, Michael Dalfo's dead. . . ."

"I don't know why human beings murder human beings. . . ."

"What reason does she have to blame the defendant. . . ?"

"He brought Diane with him and that's his problem. . . ."

"Don't let him benefit because he didn't bring a crowd with him. . . ."

Burton said it was clear that Diane did not kill Dalfo, and

that nobody would use a .25-calibre pistol for a hit. As for Diane not seeing any gun, Burton argued — the non sequitur slipped right by him — that a .25-calibre pistol is easily concealed. As for Operation Greenback, all it resulted in was a sentence of three lousy years. "Blowing smoke, that's all it is," Burton said, and then he sat down. The closing arguments were over.

Judge Fine told the jurors they would commence their deliberations in the afternoon, that they would be sequestered until a verdict was reached, and that since there was no telling how long it would take, they should bring their toothbrushes in case they had to stay overnight. He said he would give them his instructions when they returned in the afternoon, then he ordered a recess for lunch.

Court resumed at ten minutes to two. Judge Fine read his instructions, then the bailiff distributed copies to the jurors. Judge Fine defined premeditation as "long enough to allow reflection." As to the matter of reasonable doubt, a concept with which jurors often have difficulty, Judge Fine told them they should find the defendant guilty if they have "an abiding conviction of guilt." Similarly, they should find the defendant not guilty if they have serious doubts he was at the scene of the crime. If the verdict is guilty of first-degree murder, there would be a hearing in two weeks to decide the penalty: life imprisonment, that is, twenty-five years with no parole; or death by electrocution.

At thirteen minutes after two, the bailiff led the jurors out of the courtroom and took them to the quiet conference room where they would determine the future of Brian Spencer.

Brian and his mother, Gerry Hart, Rick and Mikey Martin and John Long sat at a table in the deli of the Governmental Center to wait for the verdict. Brian wanted a cigarette, but he still could not smoke in front of Irene. He ordered a Budweiser. "If the jury comes back in a hurry, we don't have to worry," Long said. "We'll start to worry if it goes more than a few hours." Irene cradled her hands around a cup of coffee and looked out the window into the courtyard with the fountain, the potted trees and the office workers sitting at the circular tables under the metal umbrellas.

Weinstein and Greene decided to wait it out in Weinstein's office on the ninth floor of the Governmental Center. Leon visited the deli to pick up a bag of sandwiches and drinks for the defence team. He moved slowly. Two nights before, he had broken his right toe when he stubbed it on the stairs running to answer the telephone at his townhouse. The call was from Weinstein, who was upset at the way things had gone that day — he had learned that Harold Yearout would not be available as a witness — and wanted to hear Leon's thoughts on the case. Leon tried to calm Weinstein. "Just bring in your witnesses confidently," he said, hobbling on one foot. "You've got to give the jury a reason, and they'll walk the guy. They'll walk him."

To pass the time I visited Richard Jorandby, the Public Defender for Florida's Fifteenth Judicial Circuit. It is an elected office and Jorandby, a Republican, was serving his fourth four-year term. He has a spacious corner office on the ninth floor of the Governmental Center. The windows look out over a broad sweep of the Atlantic, over the yachts and mansions of Palm Beach.

Like most other Floridians, Jorandby came from some-where else, from the small town of Grafton, in North Dakota. Early in his law career he travelled extensively — Europe, India, China, the Soviet Union — and wrote travel stories for *The Palm Beach Post* under the byline Dick Jorandby. In 1975, during Jorandby's first term as Public Defender, he started a clothes bank so that all defendants could be properly dressed for their trials. In 1987, he was presiding over a staff of 115, with a state-funded budget of $3.8 million. Many of the lawyers working for the Public Defenders Office are young, fresh out of law school, putting in long, harried days for minimum, $20,000 incomes. The workload grows heavier every year, an increase which Jorandby attributes to drug-related crimes in south Florida. The number of trial cases handled by Jorandby's lawyers had risen from 7,438 in 1980 to more than 24,000 in 1986.

Jorandby is a trim, athletic man with a deep tan, black hair, a black moustache and very white teeth, a central-casting, riverboat-gambler face; all that was missing was the string tie. He had sat at the back of the courtroom to hear Weinstein's closing argument that morning. *Florida v. Brian Spencer* could be a big win for Weinstein, and for the public defender system, Jorandby said, but it could also be a big win for the prosecution. Controversy had been raging over the disproportionate number of blacks sent to the electric chair in Florida and the prosecution would love to redress matters by sending a prominent white defendant to a cell on death row.

The bailiff stood in the corridor outside Courtroom 315 holding a walkie-talkie. Brian had dreamt of the bailiff the night before. In the dream, Brian was sitting at the defence table in the courtroom, expecting the worst, and the judge asked the jury if they had reached a verdict. The foreman stood up and said yes, then the bailiff walked across the courtroom, took a sheet of paper from the foreman, walked over to the clerk of the court and the clerk stood up and read, "Guilty!" Then the big bailiff walked towards Brian carrying jingling handcuffs.

At fourteen minutes after three, the walkie-talkie crackled, the bailiff held it to his ear and heard someone say, "We've got a verdict."

At the deli in the courtyard, Irene got up from the table and said she would like to go for a walk. Brian, John Long, Gerry Hart and the Martins stayed behind, discussing the trial. Irene walked by the window, then headed south along a walkway between the parking lot and the courtroom building. She was barely out of sight around the corner when Long saw Dan Martinetti walking quickly across the courtyard toward the deli. Long beckoned him to join them, but Martinetti, waving both his arms wildly, signaled he wanted them to join him. Everyone at the table knew what he meant. Hart ran after Irene to tell her the verdict was in. Long left a twenty-dollar tip on the table.

When court convened, Judge Fine asked the foreman if

the jury had reached a verdict and he said yes. The bailiff took the sheet of paper from the foreman, then brought it to the clerk of the court at the table below Judge Fine's desk. Brian watched the bailiff walk across the courtroom, but it was not like the dream. This time Brian thought how odd it is that one's whole life can be determined by a sheet of paper, as it was that July afternoon when the Maple Leaf Gardens envelope had arrived at his home on the farm in Fort St. James.

On the first count, kidnapping, the clerk read the decision quickly and succinctly. "Not guilty." Cheers and handclaps in the courtroom. The bailiff turned around and scowled at the spectators to be quiet. The commotion had not quite died down when the clerk came to the second count, murder in the first degree. "Not guilty."

Reporters and photographers scrambled to the front of the courtroom. The Dalfo family and friends left quickly, heading directly for the elevator outside the courtroom. Monica had been watching from a bench at the rear of the courtroom and in the noise and confusion she remained seated, looking bewildered. Irene walked up the aisle, poking her way through the crowd, trying to hold on to her purse. When she reached Brian she lifted her arms and Brian pressed his mother to him with his huge, gnarled hands, then he buried his head in her shoulder and wept.

It had taken the jury only sixty-one minutes to reach a verdict. The quickest acquittal for murder one Weinstein could recall in Palm Beach County was three hours. "We were leaning toward innocent from the beginning," Howard Peller, the foreman of the jury, told a reporter. "Based on what we heard, there just wasn't enough evidence to find him guilty." The jury required two votes to reach the verdict. A juror who did not want to be identified said he was the only one who thought Brian was guilty in the first vote. "I changed my vote because I had to agree with everyone else that there wasn't enough proof," he said.

On the way out of the courtroom, the reporters encircled

Brian in the aisle and, above the noisy hubbub, shouted the usual questions: What do you think? What are you going to do now? How's it feel to be you? Just like the old times in the locker room, and Brian responded in kind, spooning out the platitudes they wanted. "I know more better people than bad people. . . ." "I thought of friends I've made, the miles I've travelled. . . ." "I wish everybody a happy life. Michael Dalfo hasn't got a chance. He's dead, and that's a sad thing."

At an impromptu victory party in the Public Defenders Office late in the afternoon, Brian took a call from "As It Happens," The Canadian Broadcasting Corporation's national radio show that is broadcast live every evening across Canada. It was an opportunity for Brian to talk to the entire country. Host Michael Enright asked Brian how he reacted to the verdict. "I had my heart in my mouth," he said.

Gerry Hart brought a case of champagne to the party. The public defender lawyers, and Jorandby himself, even the cleaning man, gathered in a small lobby by shelves of law books and statutes to celebrate the victory with plastic goblets of Moet et Chandon. Barry Weinstein rushed around bestowing Brian Spencer bearhugs on everyone he encountered and bellowing tough, manly expressions like, "Forget that shit!" In a toast to Brian, Hart proposed, "Tomorrow is the first day of the rest of your life," to which Brian responded, "Maybe something good can come out of something bad." The party carried on across the city at a restaurant called The Olive Tree in North Palm Beach. Brian, his mother, Monica, Brian's friends, Leon and the lawyers occupied two long tables pushed together in the middle of the restaurant. Late in the evening, after a rousing song by the singing waiters, a man dining with his wife at another table leaned across and asked what the party was for.

"That young man in the long curly hair over there, he's just been acquitted of first-degree murder," someone told him.

"Well, isn't that nice," the man said.

III

There was a meeting in a room at the Holiday Inn on Singer Island Saturday afternoon to discuss what to do with Brian now that he was a free man. Gerry Hart, Rick Martin and John Long considered where he would be able to find work, where he would fit in best, where he might start over again. Brian listened, warmed by their concern, laughing at the jokes, but he felt patronized and mildly resentful at being treated like some errant boy scout. He had not made plans for after the trial, because he did not want to raise false expectations for himself or anyone else, least of all his family. In the end, Brian agreed to fly to Buffalo and spend some time at John Long's cabin in the woods where he could relax, recover from the stress of the trial and consider his future.

Hart headed back to Long Island, Rick and Mikey Martin returned to Buffalo. On Sunday evening, Brian, Monica, Long and I ate dinner at a Denny's Restaurant across from the Palm Beach International Airport. Monica was suffering from exhaustion and a pinched nerve in her neck, which had been bothering her all week. Long would be flying to Baltimore Monday for a business meeting, but he would be in Buffalo to meet Brian when he arrived there on Tuesday.

Brian told yet more hockey stories. There was the slapshot that had soared over the net, into the stands and right up between the knees of a large woman seated twenty rows back from the glass. "With my luck, it's a wonder she didn't get pregnant," Brian cracked, and we all laughed.

And then Brian told an extraordinary story, one that

Monica and John Long had perhaps heard before; they reacted as if it was nothing new. Brian said that when he was playing in Pittsburgh, he suspected Janet was having an affair. He had taped some of her telephone conversations. What especially angered Brian was that the man he thought she was seeing was someone he called "the Donald Trump of Pittsburgh, some guy with a $100,000 private box at the arena." He imagined them in the private box during a Penguins game, when he was down below on the ice. One day, Brian told the man he wanted to talk with him at the Igloo Club at Pittsburgh's Civic Arena. Before the meeting, Brian strapped on a .38-calibre handgun under his sports jacket. "I told him I knew what was going on, and he said, 'Oh no, she loves you, Brian.' I thought of drilling him through the head, but I didn't. I just wanted to see his face turn white."

On Monday, Brian and I drove out to the Palm Beach County Detention Center on Gun Club Road. Brian was in good spirits; he felt rested and ready to start his new life. It was hot, in the high 80s, with the sun directly overhead. As we walked from the parking lot to the entrance of the detention centre, Brian stopped on the lawn in front of the building and pointed up to the top floor of the tall, cream-coloured building, to a line of narrow windows in the west wing. They were the windows of Holding Cell 6A, where he had stayed three months while waiting for his bail hearing.

West Wing 6A was another of Brian's temporary shelters, another home where for a time he was a guest, making adjustments. He was the only white man in a cell with eighteen blacks, some of whom had been waiting for trial for more than a year. They resented any preferential treatment for Brian, such as lengthy visits by family, friends or reporters, and they resented Brian's mail, which arrived in batches of hundreds of letters every Monday.

Violence and intimidation were normal at this institution. One day Brian had to visit the centre's doctor to have his ears checked, and as he was returning to the holding cell he encountered a small, frail, white teenager who was being escorted to his third holding cell. He had been beaten, actually bounced around the cells and stomped on, his canteen had been stolen, and he had been in the jail for only half an hour. Brian always joined the end of the food line, because he knew he would be shunted back by the others. The taunt always was the same: "What you gonna do 'bout it, white man?" Brian made a stand once, the morning in the showers when one of them walked up and smoothed his hand down his back. Brian snapped around and shouted, "Get your fucking hands off me!" He squared off to fight, but the man backed away and left him alone.

Despite the isolation and ugliness, Brian adapted well to jail. Old teammates and friends dropped by to visit. Brian busied himself writing letters to those who had responded to his appeal in *The Hockey News*. That was when Leon met him, and Leon thought Brian never looked better than when he was in the detention centre. He listened attentively, took advice well. There was an elderly black man who had been in the same holding cell for eighteen months, during which time he had not received a single letter. Brian let the man open some of his fan mail, which he did eagerly and with much flourish. Brian became friendly with the commander of the detention centre, a man named Major Bud Kerr. He wanted to visit Kerr to thank him for his help while he was in jail.

Brian entered the building and walked up to a cubicle in the small, tiled lobby. He could not see through the mirrored, one-way glass of the cubicle and he had to speak into a microphone to ask if he could see Major Kerr. A voice asked who wanted to know.

"Brian Spencer," Brian said.

The voice asked for identification, then a flap opened and a metal tray slid out. Brian opened his wallet, pulled out a slip of identification, deposited it in the tray and the tray slid back inside the cubicle. A few moments later, the flap opened and the tray slid out again, this time with a clip-on visitor's badge. Then the disembodied voice asked, "Howarya doin', Brian?"

We waited at a large metal door, which slowly rumbled open, allowing us inside a chamber where we faced a thick glass door. "I never thought I'd be trying this hard to get back in," Brian said, as a buzzer signaled that the glass door was unlocked. We walked along narrow corridors with framed pictures of officials gracing the cream-coloured walls. Some of the guards passing by recognized Brian and stopped to shake his hand. Finally we came to an open door and entereᴅ a large room with a long table in the middle. Standing at the end of the table was a tall, sinewy, uniformed man in his early fifties. Major Bud Kerr bore a striking resemblance to photographs I had seen of Roy Spencer.

"I just wanted to thank you for what you did for me when I was in here," Brian began.

"Aw, hell, Brian, forget it," Kerr said. "That was a bullshit rap."

They talked for about fifteen minutes. Kerr said that in his seventeen years as commander, he's met only a handful of inmates he'd liked, and Brian was one of them. "I like athletes," he told Brian. "I used to be a jockstrap myself — baseball, in Georgia."

Later, Brian dropped by the Governmental Center to see Weinstein, Greene and Leon. Weinstein told him that Diane had called that morning to thank him for not being too hard on her in court. At the deli in the courtyard, Brian met Ed O'Hara, also a public defender lawyer, who brought with him a printout of Brian's driving offences. There were two pages, single-spaced — speeding, drunk driving, an accident Brian could not even remember. Brian's driver's licence had been suspended until 1990 and he hoped O'Hara might be able to do something about it. "Oh, I don't know, Brian," O'Hara muttered, his eyes going down the entries on the printout. "Murder's one thing, but these traffic boys, that's another matter."

Monica drove Brian to the airport Tuesday morning and he arrived in Buffalo early in the afternoon. He stayed with John Long for a while. They drove to Long's cottage, hunted pheasant. Brian had a few beers the first day he arrived, but stayed off the sauce for the rest of his visit.

Late in October, a friend of Janet's called to say that Janet had taken a sudden turn for the worse. Brian flew to New York, where Gerry Hart met him and took him to Long Island. Brian stayed with Janet, Jason and Jarrett. Hart arranged a job for Brian at a rock quarry, but because he did not have a driver's licence his job at the site was standing in the snow directing truck traffic, which he hated. He also worked part-time at a neighbourhood bar as a bouncer, mainly checking identification at the door. Hart had engaged an agent for Brian, and the agent lined up a ghost writer who was prepared to do an as-told-to book on Brian's life and career. Brian cooperated for a time, but only perfunctorily, and the book project was dropped.

Soon there were arguments with Janet's relatives, shouting matches with Janet. Janet hung on, having good days and bad days, but by mid-November Brian could take no more. He enjoyed his time with the boys, but the tension in the household was unbearable. With no goodbyes, he packed his belongings, took a cab to the airport, and boarded a plane for Palm Beach. On arrival he telephoned Monica at her office in the Governmental Center. He asked her to come and get him. She left her desk at once, picked him up in her white Renault and took him home.

On the flight from West Palm Beach to Toronto the Wednesday after the trial ended, I rooted in my bag for my notebook and pulled out the Sunday edition of *The Palm Beach Post*. There was a story on the trial, headlined "Ex-hockey pro's trial bizarre." A photograph of Brian caught him standing in the corridor outside the courtroom, staring out a window. The story began, "As murder trials go, it was an odd one." It was a standard retrospective newspaper story, with the details of the murder and the trial rehashed, the only puzzle being why so many people from far away were interested in Brian Spencer.

Before the trial began, I had thought hockey itself might be on trial, but apart from a few questions on the game during jury selection, mainly to determine if any of the jurors were familiar with the case, Brian might as well have been a pipefitter or a bank clerk. There was no mention of hockey violence or hockey goons, or fear and intimidation, or what happens to a major-league athlete when his career is over. There was nothing about Roy Spencer's tragic death, or what it was like growing up in a part of North America still rooted in the nineteenth century. A novelist attending the trial in hopes of gaining an insight into the human condition would have come out dry.

My mind drifted back to the first time I met Brian late in the summer of 1971. I had concluded then, after three weeks researching a magazine article, that he was one of the most complicated young men I had ever encountered. He was propelled by rage and ambition, but he had an intelligent, searching, introspective side. Back then he had told me, "I'm not a cool guy, not a real on-the-ball type of guy. I like to laugh and joke, but I can't tell a joke. It's just not in me. I'm too serious."

He is a shy man, distrustful of strangers, uncomfortable in ordinary social situations. Most often, Brian's words can't keep up with his brain, which produces the rage that can smoulder in petulance until it explodes. He reminds me of the story of two bums lounging on a bench listening to Mozart through a church window. One turns to the other and says, "Wasn't he lucky to be able to write that music?" "Lucky?" the other bum asks, to which the first bum replies, "Yes, wouldn't it be terrible to go through life with that *inside* your head?"

As a boy Brian had shown an interest, and some promise, in music and art. At the age of ten, with no tutoring, he could plunk out tunes on a piano and strum chords on a guitar. He could draw, not as well as Murray Hill, but with an instinct for shape and perspective. Years later, courting Janet, he even tried poetry, but all these attempts at expression never went beyond a rudimentary level and produced more frustration than satisfaction. He channelled his effort and considerable energy into hockey, where he could express himself very well indeed. If he could not communicate as fully as he would have liked in music, or art or words, he could certainly do so with his body, with his fists and his sexuality.

Hockey served Brian well, probably kept him out of serious trouble at an earlier age. He was headed that way as a young man, hanging around with a tough crowd, bored and restless, eventually sentenced to a term in reform school. When he began to play hockey seriously, at the summer camp in Nelson, in junior hockey on the prairies, in the NHL for ten years, he functioned well and except for a few skirmishes with cashiers, parking-lot attendants and other motorists, kept his nose clean. When hockey ended, he drifted down to Florida where the restraints were loosened and soon he was in trouble again: drinking, fighting, drunk driving, living the vagabond's life, charged with first-degree murder. "I'm hot and cold," he would say. "One day I'm ecstatic about things, the next day the depression is on. It's a great way to be in a sport like hockey, you go a thousand miles an hour. But when you don't have that outlet and try to implement into regular civilian society, it's difficult." Brian's use of "implement" instead of "integrate" was typical — headed in the right direction, but slightly off, wide of the goal.

Brian came along in hockey at exactly the right time for a tough, hardworking, borderline player — two years after the NHL expanded from six teams to fourteen teams, the birth of the rival World Hockey Association, followed by another NHL expansion to twenty-one teams. For the next ten years there was big-time work for pluggers. It might explain the bitterness Brian displayed toward hockey wives who did not "earn" the right to be part of the major-league whirl, and in some subconscious, inchoate way there might also have been guilt at the overnight celebrity he achieved because of his father's death. Perhaps adhering to some Dostoevskian code of justice Brian felt he deserved to be punished for something.

Did he kill Michael Dalfo?, I am asked all the time, and I

will be asked again, as will Brian. Seventeen years after I first met him, and following a year of commuting to Florida to try to know him better and to attend the trial, I find it difficult to answer the question — as Judge Fine put it on the last day — with an abiding conviction. None of Brian's teammates, family or friends can claim to know him intimately, or even to have kept in touch with him consistently over the years. Brian says he didn't do it, the jury found him not guilty, and a good case can be made that he was set up as a convenient scapegoat.

The times I'm tempted to think the worst, I remember Brian's exuberance and love of life, the good companion and friend that he was at the ox-roast picnic the summer before the trial. There he performed a song he had composed about a buddy called Shorty who unwittingly picked up a transvestite in a bar. Strumming a guitar, accompanied by John Long playing a Jew's harp, and with much hooting and yipeeing in the background, Brian sang:

> *Some folks like to stay at home*
> *And like to lay around*
> *And decent ladies never roam*
> *When Shorty comes to town.*
>
> *Spin's laugh was heard 'round the world*
> *and way up in the skyyyy*
> *For Shorty's lovely blonde-haired girl*
> *Turned out to be a guyyyy.*

What I'm left with are the lasting contradictions, never far below the surface. Seventeen years later, he remained as much a mystery as ever, probably more so.

In March 1988, Brian flew to Toronto to spend a week with John Antonacci. He went skiing with Jim McKenny, his old teammate with the Maple Leafs. He watched a Maple Leaf workout one morning at the Gardens. Defenceman Borje Salming skated over to the boards to say hello. Harold Ballard came by and told Brian to make himself at home. He

gave him tickets for a game that evening between the Leafs
and the Minnesota North Stars. The next day, Brian's picture
appeared on the front of the sports section of *The Toronto
Sun*, under a headline that read, "Spinner's back to say
thanks." In the story, Brian said, "This is where I was born as
a hockey player. It's like coming home."

Brian and John took their skates and sticks to an outdoor
rink in a field near John's home in the west end. Brian had
skated a few times at an indoor rink in Fort Lauderdale — you
don't forget — and soon he was gliding across the lines, blond
hair flying, boinking the puck off the pipes. It was a mild,
late-winter day, with the smell of earth under the snow.

John took a break and sat with some young boys on the
bench who were pulling on their skates. He had told Brian he
was going to have some fun with them. "Know who that guy
is?" John asked them. They shook their heads. He asked if
they had ever heard of Brian Spencer. They shook their heads
again.

"Spinner Spencer?" John tried.

"Didn't he play in the NHL?" one of the boys asked.

"Oh yeah, he's been there."

To the mountain top, Byron would say. And down
again.

EPILOGUE

Three
Months
Later

On Thursday, June 2, 1988, just before midnight on a dark, deserted street in Riviera Beach, Florida, Brian Spencer was shot and killed.

The news trickled in over the summer. Shortly before seven o'clock on that Thursday evening, Brian was watching the news on television in the apartment he shared with Monica in Palm Beach Gardens when he heard a loud knock on the door. Brian hated answering telephones and doors — there were the death threats, which continued after his acquittal — so he shouted for Monica, who was brushing her teeth in the bathroom. Before Monica could get to the hallway, Greg Cook, an old friend Brian had not seen for months, opened the door and walked in with a can of beer in his hand. He shouted, "Spinner!" Monica shushed him to be quiet.

Greg asked Brian if he would come with him to fix a friend's car — something about a voltage regulator — and of course Brian said he would. Brian could fix anything, and he could hardly ever say no. As Brian pulled on his work clothes, Greg told Monica not to worry, he'd take good care of Brian. Before they left, Brian told Monica he'd be back in half an hour, a little joke, then he hugged her goodbye and he and Greg left the apartment and drove off in Greg's 1984 Ford Ranger, a small, grey and silver pick-up truck.

They ended up drinking beer at Hooters, formerly the Banana Boat, at Okeechobee Boulevard and Military Trail. From there they headed south and dropped by the

Catamaran, a bar by the jai alai fronton in West Palm Beach. After that, they visited Singer Island, the resort district of Riviera Beach, and on their way back to Palm Beach Gardens, they drove through a tough, seedy part of Riviera Beach on Avenue E, a predominantly black district just north of West Palm Beach.

Greg's story is that at about eleven-thirty that night he stopped to buy $10 worth of crack, then, as he and Brian were heading home, he pulled over to the side of Avenue E. It was an odd place to stop, but Greg told the police that there was a 7-Eleven store ahead and Brian wanted to see if he had enough cigarettes to last the night. They were in the 2200 block of Avenue E, an uninhabited stretch of Riviera Beach, near the old city hall, with a school on one side and a darkened parking lot on the other. As they were stopped by the side of the road, a white, two-door, 1977 Buick LeSabre pulled up in front of them. A tall, slim, black man got out, approached the driver's side of the truck wielding a long-barrelled, large-calibre hand-gun, put the gun to Greg's head and said, "This is a robbery. Give me your money." Greg reached into his pants pocket, pulled out $3 and handed the money through the window of the truck. When the gunman turned to Brian and asked for money, according to Greg, Brian refused. He shrugged and said he didn't have any money. Without hesitating, the man reached across Greg and pulled the trigger, sending the bullet through Brian's left shoulder and into his heart. Fire from the gun scorched both of Greg's forearms.

Greg floored the accelerator, jerking the truck ahead, sideswiping the left side of the Buick. The truck spun off the shoulder and down the street. Expecting more shots, Greg made a sharp righthand turn at the next intersection. He felt Brian bump against him.

"You all right?" Greg shouted.

"Yeah, I'm okay," Brian replied, and then Greg heard a gurgling sound and Brian's head slumped into his right shoulder.

Greg drove a few blocks to a fire station near Blue Heron

Road, where paramedics examined Brian, then rushed him to St. Mary's Hospital, two miles south down Old Dixie Highway. Brian was pronounced dead on arrival at twelve minutes after midnight.

The police questioned Greg throughout the night, and they impounded his truck so that the ballistics experts could examine it, investigating such details as the possible trajectory of the bullet and anything else that might support, or contradict, Greg's version of the incident. It was just after dawn when Greg and two Riviera Beach detectives drove across town to Palm Beach Gardens and the apartment complex near Military Trail and PGA Boulevard. The grass was still wet with dew as the three men walked from the parking lot to the covered entrance, then up a flight of stairs in the shade to the second floor. Monica was awake when they knocked on the door.

"Are you Monica Jarboe?" one of the detectives asked.

When Monica said yes, the detective asked if Brian Spencer lived there, and when she said yes to that he told her, "Well, I'm sorry to have to tell you that Brian's dead."

Monica backed up and shut the door. She had a tight, stabbing feeling in her throat. The next thing she remembered was sitting at the dining-room table with the detectives and Greg. When she first saw Greg and the detectives, she thought Brian might be in trouble. She thought he might even have been arrested for some stupid thing, maybe one of those parking-lot fights. With Brian, she would have believed a lot of things, but she could not believe he was dead.

Brian had been trying to turn his life around. Slowly, to be sure, but he was making progress. He had not had a drink since before his trip to Toronto in March, not even a cold Bud. After the trial in October, he lost his job at Case Power when the shop was unionized, and he still didn't have a Florida driver's license. But he worked at odd jobs, filling in here and there repairing heavy equipment, working at his specialty of diesel mechanics, occasionally taking on freelance mechanical work on weekends. He had been trying to get himself in shape physically, too. He and Monica played tennis some evenings at the lighted courts across the street from the apartment. He was actually working on a suntan. Two Saturdays before, Brian took Monica to the beach near Jupiter, ten miles north up the Atlantic coast. He hardly ever went to the beach, maybe half a dozen times in his eight years in Florida. He liked to go on long bicycle rides around Palm Beach Gardens on Monica's ten-speed, which he discovered in the storage room of their apartment after the trial in October. Unable to drive, he enjoyed the freedom the bicycle gave him. Late on that Thursday afternoon when Monica arrived home from work and parked in the lot outside the apartment, Brian pedalled up to her car and, shirtless, his eyes squeezed shut, he stuck out his arm stiffly and offered her a white wild flower. He could be playful in that way, so she accepted the flower, pretending to be a princess, and then she embraced him and sighed, "My hero!"

They had been spending a lot of time in the apartment, talking and watching television, making plans. They were preparing to move to a larger apartment in the same complex, one that would be more private, backing onto a wooded area. During the day when Monica worked at the Governmental Center in downtown West Palm Beach, Brian stayed home and packed their belongings in cardboard boxes and stacked them in the dining-room for the move.

Monica had paid his way to Boston in May so he could visit some old hockey friends and watch the Bruins and Edmonton Oilers in the Stanley Cup Final. Brian promised to pay her back later in June when he expected to receive $5,000 from Robert Decker, a young film producer in California who wanted to make a television movie of Brian's life. The screenwriters strike in Hollywood had delayed the project, but actor Richard Dean Anderson, star of the television series "MacGyver," told Decker he wanted to play Brian in the movie. Anderson had been a hockey player in his teens. Decker told Brian he would make a minimum of $25,000 from the movie, and if it was a success he could make considerably more.

The manuscript for this book on Brian had been

completed and Brian was looking forward to travelling across Canada in the fall to talk on radio and television about his life in and out of hockey. He was good at that sort of thing, and he loved the attention. He didn't want his story sugar-coated or trivialized. For a time this book was to be titled *Spinner*, but Brian preferred *Gross Misconduct*, which came out of a conversation we had back in March, 1987. Brian called me from the Palm Beach County Detention Center and said, "Boy, I'm up on a real gross misconduct this time." He used to say he did not want to be portrayed as another of those poor Canadian boys who used department-store catalogues for shin guards. He had read too many "bullshit jock biographies."

Brian wanted to take Monica with him so he could show her Canada, especially the north central interior and Fort St. James. He hoped they would be able to make the trip in September because the scenery is so spectacular at that time of year, and the tour could be a birthday present for them, with his birthday falling on the third of the month and hers on the eleventh.

In the apartment, Brian always sat on the "Spin couch," Monica on the "Beagle couch." He had his own names for everything, creating a language Monica called "Spindub." He liked watching nature shows on TV, best of all with a bucket of fried chicken beside him. It wasn't until the winter of his thirty-eighth year that Brian developed a craving for Popsicles. He saved the Popsicle sticks to make sculptures for Monica, and if she ever threw out any of the sticks he would root through the trash to retrieve them. Three weeks before the shooting on Avenue E in Riviera Beach, they were watching television and Brian turned to Monica, who was sewing on the Beagle couch, and he asked her, "Do you think we're becoming Ozzie and Harriet?"

When Greg and the detectives left, Monica waited most of an hour before making the phone calls. It would be the middle of the night in British Columbia. She needed to compose herself to find the courage and the words.

She called Byron at his home on Vancouver Island, waking him at four o'clock in the morning. She called the Antonaccis in Toronto, and John Antonacci called John Long in Niagara Falls, New York, and Long called Brian's old teammate Rick Martin, who was in Montreal attending a wedding. Byron called Janet on Long Island where she lived with Jason and Jarret. She sounded weak. The cancer had reached her throat and she could speak only for brief periods and in whispers. Janet was hanging on, living one day at a time. No one called Linda, Brian's long-ago first wife. Linda read about Brian's murder in a newspaper in Tulsa on Friday, then she told Andrea, Nicole and Kristen what had happened to their father.

After talking to Monica, Byron called the police in Riviera Beach to confirm his brother's death. He waited for a long time, sitting in the dark of his living-room, which overlooks the Strait of Georgia. He considered flying to Florida to see Brian one last time. At first light, he called his mother in Sidney. He knew she liked to get up early, at six o'clock, and she always went downstairs to the kitchen of her townhouse and listened to the radio as she made breakfast. Byron did not want her to hear about Brian on the newscast.

By the end of the day, Irene Spencer decided she wanted Brian to be cremated in Florida and his ashes brought back home to Fort St. James for a memorial service the following Thursday in the hockey arena. She wanted Brian's ashes to be buried beside his father.

The story received front-page treatment in Florida, of course, and quickly spread across North America, featured most prominently in the cities where Brian lived and played his wild, exuberant hockey — Toronto, New York, Buffalo, Pittsburgh. Gerry Hart, Brian's old friend and teammate who had helped so much at the bail hearing and later at the trial, heard of Brian's death on Sunday, when he returned to his home in Long Island from vacation. He told Pat Calabria of *Newsday*, "He was an individual who marched to a different tune than the rest of us. . . . Brian was a decent human being and was more generous of himself than he should have been. . . ."

Red Berenson, who recognized Brian's ability at the hockey school in Nelson in the late 1960s, remembered Brian as "a raw player, a raw person, but he was so full of enthusiasm. He was just like a piece of dynamite, not in the sense that he could explode, but that he was so alive." In Niagara Falls, New York, John Long, who was as close to Brian as anyone, said, "He was a stray puppy. When he met somebody who seemed to attract him or who paid attention to him, his tail would start wagging."

Leon Wright, the investigator at the Public Defenders Office, wasted no words when he heard of the killing. "Brian was assassinated," he said. "It was coming. It was coming." Leon immediately called Barry Weinstein, who had moved to Colorado to practice law, and they remembered the morning in Weinstein's office after the trial when they both advised Brian to leave West Palm Beach and never return.

More ominously, Byron told a reporter who called him from Florida that he had had a premonition of Brian's death when he visited West Palm Beach for the trial in October. Byron said he met two of Brian's old friends at Monica's apartment one afternoon, and he didn't like them. He thought they were "wired," and he refused to shake their hands. He and Brian had an argument about it, and Byron warned his twin bother, "You're going to die with those guys one day." In the story headlined, "Twin Foretells Spencer's Death," Byron is quoted as saying, "I've been waiting for that phone call every day, and it finally came."

Monica arrived at the airport in Toronto late on the morning of Wednesday, June 8. She wore a long pink dress and as she cleared customs she pushed a baggage cart ahead of her. The hardest part was having to explain to the customs officials the small, square cardboard box in the basket near the handle of the cart, the package stamped "FRAGILE HANDLE WITH CARE." She had to show them a letter that entitled her to take the ashes across the border, and Brian's death certificate. An entry at the bottom of the death certificate marked "Usual occupation" read "Hockey player."

John Long and John Antonacci greeted her, waiting outside the glassed-in customs area in the crowded concourse. Long had brought along a friend, Gene Warner, a reporter with *The Buffalo News* who knew Brian and had covered the trial in October. He had spoken with the police in Riviera Beach that morning and learned that the toxicology tests showed a blood alcohol level in Brian's body of between 0.15 and 0.20 per cent, enough to be considered legally intoxicated in Florida. Tests for cocaine in his urine were negative.

They drove to the Antonacci home in the west end of Toronto where Loretta Antonacci had prepared a table of salads and coldcuts in the dining room. Monica changed into a blouse and slacks. She had another flight to catch later in the day, one that would take her to Vancouver, where she would board another plane for Prince George. There she would meet Byron for the ninety-mile drive to Fort St. James.

In the dining room, they were telling Spin stories. John Long told of the time, when Brian played for the Sabres, when he and Rick Martin and Brian had gone on a hunting and fishing trip in Kirkland Lake. They were at a bar one evening and there was an amateur talent contest at which all the contestants were judged by the applause of the audience. There was a backwoodsman who played a mean guitar and he had won the contest several years in a row, but Martin decided to challenge him, so he got on the stage and sang his best song. He did such a rousing rendition of "Lucille" that when the whistling and stomping and shouting died down he had been declared the winner — until Long persuaded Brian to get on stage.

"What for?" Brian asked his friend.

"The stomach roll," Long said.

Martin then led Brian, barechested, on a leash to the stage, where Brian astounded the crowd by rolling his stomach muscles, undulating his abdominal wall up and down and down and up, as if had swallowed a bowling ball. More whistles, stomps and shouts, and then Brian jumped from the stage and landed on the floor on his knuckles, then jumped back up to the stage, landing on his knuckles again. And for an encore, Brian jumped off and back on to the stage again, this time landing on the knuckles of his *toes*. The crowd went wild. Brian was declared the winner.

The story made Monica laugh, and she said, "Brian could do anything with his toes. He could turn the pages of a book. He could light a cigarette. He could open a beer bottle. I think he could drive a car with his toes."

And the time at Long's farm when Brian volunteered to repair a lawn mower, a huge, snarling machine with a rotary blade known as a Bush Hog. After a few minutes, Brian came in the house with blood on his jeans, and Long asked what happened. "Just a cut," Brian said, but when Long checked he saw an open, bloody gash down the back of Brian's calf. He told Brian he was taking him to the hospital and Brian asked if he could go upstairs to clean up first. Long waited nearly half an hour, then Brian came down and said he wouldn't have to go to the hospital after all. He pulled up his pant leg to show Long twenty-seven stitches he had applied with a needle and thread in the bathtub. He asked if there was any whiskey in the house and when Long produced a bottle of Canadian Club, Brian unscrewed the top and splashed the entire contents down his leg.

There were stories of when Brian first came to Oklahoma, when he would capture the odd stray cat and skin it to keep his trapline edge, and to provide soft foot-warmers. Squirrels, raccoons, beaver, cats, it made no big difference. Monica hoped that Brian would not be remembered as a violent person, as a goon, as so many of the newspaper articles were saying. The Brian she knew and wanted to remember could be very soft. He sent her cards, as he did the previous Christmas, in which he wrote, "I'll always be difficult to capture — my soul, my spirit. I may be primal, I don't know, but don't ever say I don't notice every little thing you do. Your concern, your strength. Please don't." He dotted the "i" in Spin with a tiny heart.

Byron and Shelly and Byron's friend, Deeper Gainer, met
Monica at the airport in Prince George. They drove in
Deeper's truck to Fort St. James, stopping once by the side of
the highway so that Monica could watch two moose foraging
in a clearing. After a few minutes, Deeper blasted the horn
and the moose crashed into the woods.

It was dark and raining when they reached Fort St. James.
Irene Spencer, her husband, Bill, and many of the Spencers'
old friends in town gathered at the big log home of Betty
Muren and Ted Ewer for coffee, tea and sandwiches.

At the hockey arena the next afternoon, a small table had
been set up on the concrete floor, directly in front of the
penalty box. Chairs were arranged in rows in a wide
semi-circle around the table, on which was the marble urn
containing Brian's ashes. As the people walked in, their heels
making hollow, clicking sounds in the arena, they heard a
crackly version of Willie Nelson singing "Angel Flying Too
Close to the Ground," one of Brian's favourite songs. Nearly
two hundred people showed up, many of them choosing to sit
on the grandstand benches on the opposite side of the arena.
Many of them were Indians who knew Roy Spencer as the
man who worked at the gravel pit at Spencer's Ridge, and
who once had a job delivering groceries to the reserve.

Murray and Bonnie Hill were there, Murray in his
cleanest jeans and a new, open-necked plaid shirt. Floyd
Kennedy, another childhood friend of Brian's, drove in from
Telkwa, west of Vanderhoof, for the service. Ingrid was
there. And Linda, who had come all the way from Tulsa,
bringing with her Andrea, Nicole and Kristen because she
wanted them to see where Brian grew up and to know the
good side of him. They stayed with Joyce Helwig, who had
been a classmate of Brian's, and her husband Johnny.

Rev. Doug Coubrough, a United Church of Canada
minister from Vanderhoof, led Monica by the arm to the
table, where she lit a candle beside the urn. To the minister's
right there was a sign that said, "HOME," to his left a sign that

said, "VISITORS." Mr. Coubrough began the eulogy by saying, "Thank you, oh Lord, for the life of Brian." Later he quoted Matthew: "Consider the lilies of the field, how they grow; they neither toil nor spin; yet I tell you, even Solomon in all his glory was not arrayed like one of these...." A few mourners picked up on the "spin" part.

At the end, Sharon Buck, a handsome woman in her early forties, walked to the front with her guitar to sing a song Brian enjoyed when he was in grade school. She is the daughter of Earl Buck, the two-fisted cowboy Roy Spencer once battled on the road into town, and for the service she wore slacks, a dark tweed jacket, with a rancher's string tie at her neck. She sang in a strong, sinewy, country and western twang, and her voice filled the arena. The song had a childlike innocence, which made it all the more powerful and moving. Women fumbled in their purses for Kleenex, and the men stared down at their boots.

I see a candlelight down in the little green valley

Where morning glory vines are twining around the door....

Monica couldn't sleep the Thursday night when Brian left with Greg. Late in the evening she left her apartment and walked to the grassy field on the other side of the street. It was warm, breezy. The song in her head that night was a song by a group named U2, called "With Or Without You." Early one morning in March, 1987, Brian called her from the Palm Beach County Detention Center and she heard the song being played loudly in the background. The jail always was noisy. As he was talking, Monica interrupted him to say, "Brian, that's your song." She meant the lines, "And you give, and you give, and you give yourself away...." It was just before midnight when she walked across the road to her apartment and the shot rang out in the dark on Avenue E.

As the summer wore on, more details filtered in. Irene Spencer wrote a letter to Gerry Hart in Long Island to apologize on Brian's behalf for their falling out in the months after the trial. Hart wanted to take Jason and Jarret on a Canadian holiday, to his hometown of Flin Flon in northern Manitoba, then further west to British Columbia where they could visit Irene and stay with Byron and Shelly. Janet thought it was a good idea, and she was grateful, but she wanted to stay with the boys as long as she could.

The police in Riviera Beach found the 1977 white Buick LeSabre, which had been stolen. It turned up after an anonymous caller called a local Crimestoppers program. They arrested Leon Daniels, a twenty-four-year-old black drifter in Florida who called himself Lump. Daniels turned himself in, and the police were looking for another man named Larry Willie Johnson, who had served time at the Lantana Correctional Institute in Florida after pleading guilty to attempted first degree murder in 1985. They believed Johnson was the gunman. The police said whoever killed Brian later sold the gun for $40 and used the money to buy cocaine. Later in June, Daniels appeared in a courtroom in West Palm Beach for his arraignment with Richard Greene, the tall, blond lawyer who was part of Brian's defense team in October. Greene asked that the Public Defenders Office be withdrawn from the case and that a private lawyer be appointed to defend Daniels at public expense.

Leon Wight came to believe that the killing probably was a random robbery and murder, a stupid, senseless and tragic mistake, but he will always have some doubts. Leon believed that the gunman had no intention of killing anyone, but he panicked. Brian would have resented the intrusion, probably he would have been annoyed, and he would have been concerned for his friend beside him in the cab of the truck. Brian would not have been an easy victim. He might have read the fear in the gunman's eyes.